Praise for the incomparable bestsellers of

JUDITH McNAUGHT

"One of the finest writers of popular fiction"*

NIGHT WHISPERS

"Never miss a McNaught! *Night Whispers* heads like the *Titanic* toward its iceberg of a climax—with shocking revelations. . . . Judith McNaught has written her most stunning work of fiction to date. Sexy, smart, and page-turning, this is a must-read."

—Barnesandnoble.com*

"Fiery passion, taut suspense, and unforgettable characters. . . . McNaught has truly outdone herself with *Night Whispers*. It is a testimony to her impressive talent. . . . Equal parts romance and suspense, this is a must-read for mystery and romance fans alike."

—*Rendezvous*

REMEMBER WHEN

"An enchanting novel. . . . Judith McNaught is a treasure."
—*The Literary Times*

UNTIL YOU

"*Until You* is a laughing, loving book, a page-turner and a delight."

—*The Advocate* (Baton Rouge, LA)

WHITNEY, MY LOVE

"The ultimate love story, one you can dream about forever."
—*Romantic Times*

Books by Judith McNaught

Whitney, My Love
Double Standards
Tender Triumph
Once and Always
Something Wonderful
A Kingdom of Dreams
Almost Heaven
Paradise
Perfect
Until You
Remember When
Night Whispers

Published by POCKET BOOKS

JUDITH McNAUGHT

ONCE AND ALWAYS

POCKET BOOKS

New York   London   Toronto   Sydney   Singapore

An *Original* Publication of POCKET BOOKS

 POCKET BOOKS, a division of Simon & Schuster, Inc.
1230 Avenue of the Americas, New York, NY 10020

ISBN: 0-7434-6710-8

First Pocket Books printing January 1987

10 9 8 7 6 5 4 3 2 1

POCKET and colophon are registered trademarks of Simon & Schuster, Inc.

For information regarding special discounts for bulk purchases, please contact Simon & Schuster Special Sales at 1-800-456-6798 or business@simonandschuster.com

Cover design and illustration by Melody Cassen
Photo credits: A. Woolfitt/PictureQuest, Tommy Flynn/Photonica

Printed in the U.S.A.

To my father, who always made me feel
that he was proud of me
and
To my mother, who helped me do
the things that made him proud
What a team you are!

ONCE AND ALWAYS

Chapter One

ENGLAND
1815

"OH, THERE YOU ARE, JASON," THE RAVEN-HAIRED beauty said to her husband's reflection in the mirror above her dressing table. Her gaze slid warily over his tall, rugged frame as he came toward her; then she returned her attention to the open jewel cases spread out before her. A nervous tremor shook her hand and her smile was overly bright as she removed a spectacular diamond choker from a case and held it out to him. "Help me fasten this, will you?"

Her husband's face tightened with distaste as he looked at the necklaces of glittering rubies and magnificent emeralds already spread across her swelling breasts above the daring bodice of her gown. "Isn't your display of flesh and jewels a little vulgar for a woman who hopes to masquerade as a grand lady?"

"What would *you* know about vulgarity?" Melissa Fielding retorted contemptuously. "This gown is the height of fashion." Haughtily she added, "Baron Lacroix likes it very well. He specifically asked me to wear it to the ball tonight."

"No doubt he doesn't want to be troubled with too many fasteners when he takes it off you," her husband returned sarcastically.

1

"Exactly. He's French—and terribly impetuous."

"Unfortunately, he's also penniless."

"He thinks I'm beautiful," Melissa taunted, her voice beginning to shake with pent-up loathing.

"He's right." Jason Fielding's sardonic gaze swept over her lovely face with its alabaster skin, slightly tilted green eyes, and full red lips, then dropped to her voluptuous breasts trembling invitingly above the plunging neckline of her scarlet velvet gown. "You are a beautiful, amoral, greedy . . . bitch."

Turning on his heel, he started from the room, then stopped. His icy voice was edged with implacable authority. "Before you leave, go in and say good night to our son. Jamie is too little to understand what a bitch you are, and he misses you when you're gone. I'm leaving for Scotland within the hour."

"Jamie!" she hissed wrathfully. "He's all you care about—" Without bothering to deny it, her husband walked toward the door, and Melissa's anger ignited. "When you come back from Scotland, I won't be here!" she threatened.

"Good," he said without stopping.

"You bastard!" she spat, her voice shaking with suppressed rage. "I'm going to tell the world who you really are, and then I'm going to leave you. I'll never come back. Never!"

With his hand on the door handle, Jason turned, his features a hard, contemptuous mask. "You'll come back," he sneered. "You'll come back, just as soon as you run out of money."

The door closed behind him and Melissa's exquisite face filled with triumph. "I'll never come back, Jason," she said aloud to the empty room, "because I'll never run out of money. You'll send me whatever I want. . . ."

"Good evening, my lord," the butler said in an odd, tense whisper.

"Happy Christmas, Northrup," Jason answered automatically as he stamped the snow off his boots and handed his wet cloak to the servant. That last scene with Melissa, two weeks earlier, sprang to his mind, but he pushed the memory

2

away. "The weather cost me an extra day of travel. Has my son already gone to bed?"

The butler froze.

"Jason—"A heavyset, middle-aged man with the tanned, weathered face of a seasoned seaman stood in the doorway of the salon off the marble entrance foyer, motioning to Jason to join him.

"What are you doing here, Mike?" Jason asked, watching with puzzlement as the older man carefully closed the salon door.

"Jason," Mike Farrell said tautly, "Melissa is gone. She and Lacroix sailed for Barbados right after you left for Scotland." He paused, waiting for some reaction, but there was none. He drew a long, ragged breath. "They took Jamie with them."

Savage fury ignited in Jason's eyes, turning them into furnaces of rage. "I'll kill her for this!" he said, already starting toward the door. "I'll find her, and I'll kill her—"

"It's too late for that." Mike's ragged voice stopped Jason in mid-stride. "Melissa is already dead. Their ship went down in a storm three days after it left England." He tore his gaze from the awful agony already twisting Jason's features and added tonelessly, "There were no survivors."

Wordlessly, Jason strode to the side table and picked up a crystal decanter of whiskey. He poured some into a glass and tossed it down, then refilled it, staring blindly straight ahead.

"She left you these." Mike Farrell held out two letters with broken seals. When Jason made no move to take them, Mike explained gently, "I've already read them. One is a ransom letter, addressed to you, which Melissa left in your bedchamber. She intended to ransom Jamie back to you. The second letter was meant to expose you, and she gave it to a footman with instructions to deliver it to the *Times* after she left. However, when Flossie Wilson discovered that Jamie was missing, she immediately questioned the servants about Melissa's actions the night before, and the footman gave the letter to her instead of taking it to the *Times* as he was about to do. Flossie couldn't reach you to tell you Melissa had taken Jamie, so she sent for me and gave me the letters. Jason," Mike said hoarsely, "I know how much you loved the boy. I'm sorry. I'm so damned sorry. . . ."

Jason's tortured gaze slowly lifted to the gilt-framed portrait hanging above the mantel. In agonized silence he stared at the painting of his son, a sturdy little boy with a cherubic smile on his face and a wooden soldier clutched lovingly in his fist.

The glass Jason was holding shattered in his clenched hand. But he did not cry. Jason Fielding's childhood had long ago robbed him of all his tears.

PORTAGE, NEW YORK
1815

Snow crunched beneath her small, booted feet as Victoria Seaton turned off the lane and pushed open the white wooden gate that opened into the front yard of the modest little house where she had been born. Her cheeks were rosy and her eyes bright as she stopped to glance at the starlit sky, studying it with the unspoiled delight of a fifteen-year-old at Christmas. Smiling, she hummed the last bars of one of the Christmas carols she'd been singing all evening with the rest of the carolers, then turned and went up the walk toward the darkened house.

Hoping not to awaken her parents or her younger sister, she opened the front door softly and slipped inside. She took off her cloak, hanging it on a peg beside the door, then turned around and stopped in surprise. Moonlight poured through the window at the top of the stairway, illuminating her parents, who were standing just outside her mother's bedroom. "No, Patrick!" Her mother was struggling in her father's tight embrace. "I can't! I just can't!"

"Don't deny me, Katherine," Patrick Seaton said, his voice raw with pleading. "For God's sake, don't—"

"You promised!" Katherine burst out, trying frantically to pull free of his arms. He bent his head and kissed her, but she twisted her face away, her words jerking out like a sob.

"You promised me on the day Dorothy was born that you wouldn't ask me to again. You gave me your word!"

Victoria, standing in stunned, bewildered horror, dimly realized that she had never seen her parents touch one another before—not in teasing, nor kindness—but she had no idea what it was her father was pleading with her mother not to deny him.

Patrick let go of his wife, his hands falling to his sides. "I'm sorry," he said stonily. She fled into her room and closed the door, but instead of going to his own room, Patrick Seaton turned around and headed down the narrow stairs, passing within inches of Victoria when he reached the bottom.

Victoria flattened herself against the wall, feeling as if the security and peace of her world had been somehow threatened by what she had seen. Afraid that he would notice her if she tried to move toward the stairs, would know she had witnessed the humiliatingly intimate scene, she watched as he sat down on the sofa and stared into the dying embers of the fire. A bottle of liquor that had been on the kitchen shelf for years stood now on the table in front of him, beside a half-filled glass. When he leaned forward and reached for the glass, Victoria turned and cautiously placed her foot on the first step.

"I know you're there, Victoria," he said tonelessly, without looking behind him. "There's little point in our pretending you didn't witness what just took place between your mother and me. Why don't you come over here and sit by the fire? I'm not the brute you must think me."

Sympathy tightened Victoria's throat and she quickly went to sit beside him. "I don't think you're a brute, Papa. I could never think that."

He took a long swallow of the liquor in his glass. "Don't blame your mother either," he warned, his words slightly slurred as if he had been drinking since long before she arrived.

With the liquor impairing his judgment, he glanced at Victoria's stricken face and assumed she had surmised more from the scene she'd witnessed than she actually had. Putting a comforting arm around her shoulders, he tried to ease her distress, but what he told her increased it a hundredfold: "It isn't your mother's fault and it isn't mine. She can't love me, and I can't stop loving her. It's as simple as that."

Victoria plunged abruptly from the secure haven of childhood into cold, terrifying, adult reality. Her mouth dropped open and she stared at him while the world seemed to fall apart around her. She shook her head, trying to deny the horrible thing he had said. Of course her mother loved her wonderful father!

"Love can't be forced into existence," Patrick Seaton said, confirming the awful truth as he stared bitterly into his glass. "It won't come simply because you will it to happen. If it did, your mother would love me. She believed she would learn to love me when we were wed. I believed it, too. We *wanted* to believe it. Later, I tried to convince myself that it didn't matter whether she loved me or not. I told myself that marriage could still be good without it."

The next words ripped from his chest with an anguish that seared Victoria's heart: "I was a fool! Loving someone who doesn't love you is hell! Don't ever let anyone convince you that you can be happy with someone who doesn't love you."

"I—I won't," Victoria whispered, blinking back her tears.

"And don't ever love anyone more than he loves you, Tory. Don't let yourself do it."

"I—I won't," Victoria whispered again. "I promise." Unable to contain the pity and love exploding inside her, Victoria looked at him with tears spilling from her eyes and laid her small hand against his handsome cheek. "When I marry, Papa," she choked, "I shall choose someone *exactly* like you."

He smiled tenderly at that, but made no reply. Instead he said, "It hasn't all been bad, you know. Your mother and I have Dorothy and you to love, and that is a love we share."

Dawn had barely touched the sky when Victoria slipped out of the house, having spent a sleepless night staring at the ceiling above her bed. Clad in a red cloak and a dark blue woolen riding skirt, she led her Indian pony out of the barn and swung effortlessly onto his back.

A mile away, she came to the creek that ran alongside the main road leading to the village, and dismounted. She walked gingerly down the slippery, snow-covered bank and sat down on a flat boulder. With her elbows propped on her knees and her chin cupped in her palms, she stared at the gray water flowing slowly between the frozen chunks of ice near the bank.

The sky turned yellow and then pink while she sat there, trying to recover the joy she always felt in this place whenever she watched the dawning of a new day.

A rabbit scurried out from the trees beside her; behind her a horse blew softly and footsteps moved stealthily down the steep bank. A slight smile touched Victoria's lips a split second before a snowball whizzed past her right shoulder, and she leaned neatly to the left. "Your aim is off, Andrew," she called without turning.

A pair of shiny brown top boots appeared at her side. "You're up early this morning," Andrew said, grinning at the petite, youthful beauty seated upon the rock. Red hair shot with sparkling gold was pulled back from Victoria's forehead and secured with a tortoiseshell comb at the crown, then left to spill over her shoulders like a rippling waterfall. Her eyes were the deep, vivid blue of pansies, heavily lashed and slightly tilted at the corners. Her nose was small and perfect, her cheeks delicately boned and blooming with health, and at the center of her small chin there was a tiny but intriguing cleft.

The promise of beauty was already molded into every line and feature of Victoria's face, but it was obvious to any onlooker that her beauty was destined to be more exotic than fragile, more vivid than pristine, just as it was obvious that there was stubbornness in her small chin and laughter in her sparkling eyes. This morning, however, her eyes lacked their customary luster.

Victoria leaned down and scooped up a pile of snow with her mittened hands. Automatically Andrew ducked, but instead of launching the snowball at him, as she would normally have done, she threw it into the creek. "What's wrong, bright-eyes," he teased. "Afraid you'll miss?"

"Of course not," Victoria said with a morose little sigh. "Move over and let me sit down."

Victoria did so, and he studied her sad expression with mild concern. "What has you looking so grim?"

Victoria was truly tempted to confide in him. At twenty, Andrew was five years her senior and wise beyond his age. He was the only child of the village's wealthiest resident, a widow of seemingly delicate health who clung possessively to her only son at the same time that she relinquished to him all responsibility for the running of their huge mansion and the 1,000 acres of farmland surrounding it.

Putting his gloved finger beneath her chin, Andrew tipped her face up to his. "Tell me," he said gently.

This second request was more than her heartsick emotions could withstand. Andrew was her friend. In the years they had known each other, he had taught her to fish, to swim, to shoot a pistol, and to cheat at cards—this last he claimed to be necessary so she would know if *she* was being cheated. Victoria had rewarded his efforts by learning to outswim, outshoot, and outcheat him. They were friends, and she knew she could confide almost anything to him. She could not, however, bring herself to discuss her parents' marriage with him. Instead she brought up the other thing worrying her—her father's warning.

"Andrew," she said hesitantly, "how can you tell if someone loves you? Truly loves you, I mean?"

"Who are you worried about loving you?"

"The man I marry."

Had she been a little older, a little more worldly, she would have been able to interpret the tenderness that flared in Andrew's golden brown eyes before he swiftly looked away. "You'll be loved by the man you marry," he promised. "You can take my word for it."

"But he must love me at least as much as I love him."

"He will."

"Perhaps, but how will I *know* if he does?"

Andrew cast a sharp, searching look at her exquisite features. "Has some local boy been pestering your papa for your hand?" he demanded almost angrily.

"Of course not!" she snorted. "I'm only fifteen, and Papa is very firm that I must wait until I'm eighteen, so I'll know my own mind."

He looked at her stubborn little chin and chuckled. "If 'knowing your own mind' is all Dr. Seaton is concerned about, he could let you wed tomorrow. You've known your own mind since you were ten years old."

"You're right," she admitted with cheerful candor. After a minute of comfortable silence, she asked idly, "Andrew, do you ever wonder who you'll marry?"

"No," he said with an odd little smile as he stared out across the creek.

"Why not?"

"I already know who she is."

Startled by this amazing revelation, Victoria snapped her head around. "You do? Truly? Tell me! Is it someone I know?"

When he remained silent, Victoria shot him a thoughtful, sidewise look and began deliberately packing snow into a hard ball.

"Are you planning to try to dump that thing down my back?" he said, watching her with wary amusement.

"Certainly not," she said, her eyes twinkling. "I was thinking more in the line of a wager. If I can come closer to that rock atop the farthest boulder over there, then you must tell me who she is."

"And if I come closer than you do?" Andrew challenged.

"Then you may name your own forfeit," she said magnanimously.

"I made a dire error when I taught you to gamble," he chuckled, but he was not proof against her daring smile.

Andrew missed the far-off target by scant inches. Victoria stared at it in deep concentration; then she let fly, hitting it dead-on with enough force to send the rock tumbling off the boulder along with the snowball.

"I also made a dire error when I taught you to throw snowballs."

"I always knew how to do that," she reminded him audaciously, plunking her hands on her slim hips. "Now, who do you wish to marry?"

Shoving his hands into his pockets, Andrew grinned down at her enchanting face. "Who do *you* think I wish to marry, blue eyes?"

"I don't know," she said seriously, "but I hope she is very special, because you are."

9

"She's special," he assured her with gentle gravity. "So special that I even thought about her when I was away at school during the winters. In fact, I'm glad to be home so I can see her more often."

"She sounds quite nice," Victoria allowed primly, feeling suddenly and unaccountably angry at the unoffending female.

"I'd say she's closer to 'wonderful' than 'quite nice.' She's sweet and spirited, beautiful and unaffected, gentle and stubborn. Everyone who knows her comes to love her."

"Well then, for heaven's sake, why don't you marry her and have done with it!" Victoria said grimly.

His lips twitched, and in a rare gesture of intimacy, Andrew reached out and laid his hand against her heavy, silken hair. "Because," he whispered tenderly, "she's still too young. You see, her father wants her to wait until she's eighteen, so she'll know her own mind."

Victoria's enormous blue eyes widened as she searched his handsome face. "Do you mean me?" she whispered.

"You," he confirmed with smiling solemnity. "Only you."

Victoria's world, threatened by what she had seen and heard last night, suddenly seemed safe again, secure and warm. "Thank you, Andrew," she said, suddenly shy. Then, in one of her lightning-quick transformations from girl to charming, gently bred young woman, she added softly, "How lovely it will be to marry my dearest friend."

"I shouldn't have mentioned it to you without first speaking with your father, and I can't do that for three more years."

"He likes you immensely," Victoria assured him. "He won't object in the least when the time comes. How could he, when you are both so much alike?"

Victoria mounted her horse a little while later feeling quite gay and cheerful, but her spirits plummeted as soon as she opened the back door of the house and stepped into the cozy room that served the dual purpose of kitchen and family gathering place.

Her mother was bending over the hearth, busy with the waffle iron, her hair pulled back in a tidy chignon, her plain dress clean and pressed. Hanging from nails beside and above the fireplace was an orderly assortment of sifters, dippers, graters, chopping knives, and funnels. Everything was neat and clean and pleasant, just like her mother. Her father was already seated at the table, drinking a cup of coffee.

Looking at them, Victoria felt self-conscious, sick at heart, and thoroughly angry with her mother for denying her wonderful father the love he wanted and needed.

Since Victoria's sunrise outings were fairly common, neither of her parents showed any surprise at her entrance. They both looked up at her, smiled, and said good morning. Victoria returned her father's greeting and she smiled at her younger sister, Dorothy, but she could scarcely look at her mother. Instead, she went to the shelves and began to set the table with a full complement of flatware and dishes—a formality that her English mother firmly insisted was "necessary for civilized dining."

Victoria moved back and forth between the shelves and the table, feeling ill at ease and sick to her stomach, but when she took her place at the table, the hostility she felt for her mother slowly began to give way to pity. She watched as Katherine Seaton tried in a half dozen ways to make amends to her husband, chatting cheerfully with him as she hovered solicitously at his elbow, filling his cup with steaming coffee, handing him the pitcher of cream, offering him more of her freshly baked rolls in between trips to the hearth, where she was preparing his favorite breakfast of waffles.

Victoria ate her meal in bewildered, helpless silence, her thoughts twisting and turning as she sought for some way to console her father for his loveless marriage.

The solution came to her the instant he stood up and announced his intention of riding over to the Jackson farm to see how little Annie's broken arm was mending. Victoria jumped to her feet. "I'll go with you, Papa. I've been meaning to ask you if you could teach me how to help you—in your work, I mean." Both her parents looked at her in surprise, for Victoria had never before shown the slightest interest in the healing arts. In fact, until then, she had been a pretty, carefree child whose chief interests were in gay amusements and an occasional mischievous prank. Despite their surprise, neither parent voiced an objection.

Victoria and her father had always been close. From that

day forward, they became inseparable. She accompanied him nearly everywhere he went and, although he flatly refused to permit her to assist him in his treatment of his male patients, he was more then happy to have her help at any other time.

Neither of them ever mentioned the sad things they had discussed on that fateful Christmas night. Instead they filled their time together with cozy conversations and lighthearted banter, for despite the sorrow in his heart, Patrick Seaton was a man who appreciated the value of laughter.

Victoria had already inherited her mother's startling beauty and her father's humor and courage. Now she learned compassion and idealism from him as well. As a little girl, she had easily won over the villagers with her beauty and bright, irresistible smile. They had liked her as a charming, carefree girl; they adored her as she matured into a spirited young lady who worried about their ailments and teased away their sullens.

Chapter Two

〜〜〜〜〜

"VICTORIA, ARE YOU ABSOLUTELY CERTAIN YOUR mother never mentioned either the Duke of Atherton or the Duchess of Claremont to you?"

Victoria tore her thoughts from aching memories of her parents' funeral and looked at the elderly, white-haired physician seated across from her at the kitchen table. As her father's oldest friend, Dr. Morrison had taken on the responsibility of seeing the girls settled, as well as of trying to care for Dr. Seaton's patients until the new physician arrived. "All Dorothy or I ever knew was that Mama was estranged from her family in England. She never spoke of them."

"Is it possible your father had relatives in Ireland?"

"Papa grew up in an orphans' home there. He had no relatives." She stood up restlessly. "May I fix you some coffee, Dr. Morrison?"

"Stop fussing over me and go sit outside in the sunshine with Dorothy," Dr. Morrison chided gently. "You're pale as a ghost."

"Is there anything you need, before I go?" Victoria persisted.

"I need to be a few years younger," he replied with a grim

13

smile as he sharpened a quill. "I'm too old to carry the burden of your father's patients. I belong back in Philadelphia with a hot brick beneath my feet and a good book on my lap. How I'm to carry on here for four more months until the new physician arrives, I can't imagine."

"I'm sorry," Victoria said sincerely. "I know it's been terrible for you."

"It's been a great deal worse for you and Dorothy," the kindly old doctor said. "Now, run along outside and get some of this fine winter sunshine. It's rare to see a day this warm in January. While you sit in the sun, I'll write these letters to your relatives."

A week had passed since Dr. Morrison had come to visit the Seatons, only to be summoned to the scene of the accident where the carriage bearing Patrick Seaton and his wife had plunged down a riverbank, overturning. Patrick Seaton had been killed instantly. Katherine had regained consciousness only long enough to try to answer Dr. Morrison's desperate inquiry about her relatives in England. In a feeble whisper, she had said, ". . . Grandmother . . . Duchess of Claremont."

And then, just before she died, she had whispered another name—Charles. Frantically Dr. Morrison had begged her for his complete name, and Katherine's dazed eyes had opened briefly. "Fielding," she had breathed. ". . . Duke . . . of . . . Atherton."

"Is he a relative?" he demanded urgently.

After a long pause, she'd nodded feebly. "Cousin—"

To Dr. Morrison now fell the difficult task of locating and contacting these heretofore unknown relatives to inquire whether either of them would be willing to offer Victoria and Dorothy a home—a task that was made even more difficult because, as far as Dr. Morrison could ascertain, neither the Duke of Atherton nor the Duchess of Claremont had any idea the girls existed.

With a determined look upon his brow, Dr. Morrison dipped the quill in the inkwell, wrote the date at the top of the first letter, and hesitated, his brow furrowed in thought. "How does one properly address a duchess?" he asked the empty room. After considerable contemplation, he arrived at a decision and began writing.

Dear Madam Duchess,

It is my unpleasant task to advise you of the tragic death of your granddaughter, Katherine Seaton, and to further advise you that Mrs. Seaton's two daughters, Victoria and Dorothy, are now temporarily in my care. However, I am an old man, and a bachelor besides. Therefore, Madam Duchess, I cannot properly continue to care for two orphaned young ladies.

Before she died, Mrs. Seaton mentioned only two names—yours and that of Charles Fielding. I am, therefore, writing to you and to Sir Fielding in the hope that one or both of you will welcome Mrs. Seaton's daughters into your home. I must tell you that the girls have nowhere else to go. They are sadly short of funds and in dire need of a suitable home.

Dr. Morrison leaned back in his chair and scrutinized the letter while a frown of concern slowly formed on his forehead. If the duchess was unaware of the girls' existence, he could already foresee the old lady's possible unwillingness to house them without first knowing something about them. Trying to think how best to describe them, he turned his head and gazed out the window at the girls.

Dorothy was seated upon the swing, her slim shoulders drooping with despair. Victoria was determinedly applying herself to her sketching in an effort to hold her grief at bay.

Dr. Morrison decided to describe Dorothy first, for she was the easiest.

Dorothy is a pretty girl, with light yellow hair and blue eyes. She is sweet-dispositioned, well-mannered, and charming. At seventeen, she is nearly of an age to marry, but has shown no particular inclination to settle her affections on any one young gentleman in the district. . . .

Dr. Morrison paused and thoughtfully stroked his chin. In truth, many young gentlemen in the district were utterly smitten with Dorothy. And who could blame them? She was pretty and gay and sweet. She was angelic, Dr. Morrison decided, pleased that he had hit upon exactly the right word to describe her.

But when he turned his attention to Victoria, his bushy white brows drew together in bafflement, for although Victoria was his personal favorite, she was far harder to describe. Her hair was not golden like Dorothy's, nor was it truly red; rather, it was a vivid combination of both. Dorothy was a pretty thing, a charming, demure young lady who turned all the local boys' heads. She was perfect material for a wife: sweet, gentle, soft-spoken, and biddable. In short, she was the sort of female who would never contradict or disobey her husband.

Victoria, on the other hand, had spent a great deal of time with her father and, at eighteen, she possessed a lively wit, an active mind, and a startling tendency to think for herself.

Dorothy would think as her husband told her to think and do what he told her to do, but Victoria would think for herself and very likely do as *she* thought best.

Dorothy was angelic, Dr. Morrison decided, but Victoria was . . . not.

Squinting through his spectacles at Victoria, who was resolutely sketching yet another picture of the vine-covered garden wall, he stared at her patrician profile, trying to think of the words to describe her. Brave, he decided, knowing she was sketching because she was trying to stay busy rather than dwell on her grief. And compassionate, he thought, recalling her efforts to console and cheer her father's sick patients.

Dr. Morrison shook his head in frustration. As an old man, he enjoyed her intelligence and her sense of humor; he admired her courage, spirit, and compassion. But if he emphasized those qualities to her English relatives, they would surely envision her as an independent, bookish, unmarriageable female whom they would have on their hands forever. There was still the possibility that when Andrew Bainbridge returned from Europe in several months, he would formally request Victoria's hand, but Dr. Morrison wasn't certain. Victoria's father and Andrew's mother had agreed that, before the young couple became betrothed, their feelings for one another should be tested during this six-month period while Andrew took an abbreviated version of the Grand Tour.

Victoria's affection for Andrew had remained strong and constant, Dr. Morrison knew, but Andrew's feelings for her were apparently wavering. According to what Mrs. Bainbridge had confided to Dr. Morrison yesterday, Andrew seemed to be developing a strong attraction to his second cousin, whose family he was currently visiting in Switzerland.

Dr. Morrison sighed unhappily as he continued to gaze at the two girls, who were dressed in plain black gowns, one with shining golden hair, the other's gleaming pale copper. Despite the somberness of their attire, they made a very fetching picture, he thought fondly. A picture! Seized by inspiration, Dr. Morrison decided to solve the whole problem of describing the girls to their English relatives by simply enclosing a miniature of them in each letter.

That decision made, he finished his first letter by asking the duchess to confer with the Duke of Atherton, who was receiving an identical letter, and to advise what they wished him to do in the matter of the girls' care. Dr. Morrison wrote the same letter to the Duke of Atherton; then he composed a short note to his solicitor in New York, instructing that worthy gentleman to have a reliable person in London locate the duke and the duchess and deliver the letters to them. With a brief prayer that either the duke or the duchess would reimburse him for his expenditures, Dr. Morrison stood up and stretched.

Outside in the garden, Dorothy nudged the ground with the toe of her slipper, sending the swing twisting listlessly from side to side. "I still cannot quite believe it," she said, her soft voice filled with a mixture of despair and excitement. "Mama was the granddaughter of a duchess! What does that make us, Tory? Do we have titles?"

Victoria sent her a wry glance. "Yes," she said. "We are 'Poor Relations.' "

It was the truth, for although Patrick Seaton had been loved and valued by the grateful country folk whose ills he had treated for many years, his patients had rarely been able to pay him with coin, and he had never pressed them to do so. They repaid him instead with whatever goods and services they were able to provide—with livestock, fish, and fowl for his table, with repairs to his carriage and to his home, with freshly baked loaves of bread and baskets of juicy, handpicked berries. As a result, the Seaton family had never wanted for food, but money was ever in short supply, as evidenced by the oft-mended, hand-dyed gowns Dorothy and Victoria were both wearing. Even the house they lived in had been provided by the villagers, just as they provided one for Reverend Milby, the minister. The houses were loaned to the occupants in return for their medical and pastoral services.

Dorothy ignored Victoria's sensible summation of their status and continued dreamily, "Our cousin is a duke, and our great-grandmother is a duchess! I still cannot quite believe it, can you?"

"I always thought Mama was something of a mystery," Victoria replied, blinking back the tears of loneliness and despair that misted her blue eyes. "Now the mystery is solved."

"What mystery?"

Victoria hesitated, her sketching pencil hovering above her tablet. "I only meant that Mama was different from every other female I have ever known."

"I suppose she was," Dorothy agreed, and lapsed into silence.

Victoria stared at the sketch that lay in her lap while the delicate lines and curves of the meandering roses she'd been drawing from her memory of last summer blurred before her moist eyes. The mystery was solved. *Now* she understood a great many things that had puzzled and troubled her. Now she understood why her mother had never mingled comfortably with the other women of the village, why she had always spoken in the cultured tones of an English gentlewoman and stubbornly insisted that, at least in her presence, Victoria and Dorothy do the same. Her heritage explained her mother's insistence that they learn to read and speak French in addition to English. It explained her fastidiousness. It partially explained the strange, haunted expression that crossed her features on those rare occasions when she mentioned England.

Perhaps it even explained her strange reserve with her own husband, whom she treated with gentle courtesy, but nothing more. Yet she had, on the surface, been an exemplary wife. She had never scolded her husband, never complained about her shabby-genteel existence, and never quarreled with him. Victoria had long ago forgiven her mother for not loving her father. Now that she realized her mother must have been reared in incredible luxury, she was also inclined to admire her uncomplaining fortitude.

Dr. Morrison walked into the garden and beamed an encouraging smile at both girls. "I've finished my letters and I shall send them off tomorrow. With luck, we should have your relatives' replies in three months' time, perhaps less." He smiled at both girls, pleased at the part he was trying to play in reuniting them with their noble English relatives.

"What do you think they'll do when they receive your letters, Dr. Morrison?" Dorothy asked.

Dr. Morrison patted her head and squinted into the sunshine, drawing upon his imagination. "They'll be surprised, I suppose, but they won't let it show—the English upper classes don't like to display emotion, I'm told, and they're sticklers for formality. Once they've read the letters, they'll probably send polite notes to each other, and then one of them will call upon the other to discuss your futures. A butler will carry in tea—"

He smiled as he envisioned the delightful scenario in all its detail. In his mind he pictured two genteel English aristocrats—wealthy, kindly people—who would meet in an elegant drawing room to partake of tea from a silver tray before they discussed the future of their heretofore unknown—but cherished—young relatives. Since the Duke of Atherton and the Duchess of Claremont were distantly related through Katherine they would, of course, be friends, allies. . . .

Chapter Three

"HER GRACE, THE DOWAGER DUCHESS OF CLARE-
mont," the butler intoned majestically from the doorway of
the drawing room where Charles Fielding, Duke of Atherton, was seated. The butler stepped aside and an imposing
old woman marched in, trailed by her harassed-looking
solicitor. Charles Fielding looked at her, his piercing hazel
eyes alive with hatred.

"Don't bother to rise, Atherton," the duchess snapped
sarcastically, glaring at him when he remained deliberately
and insolently seated.

Perfectly still, he continued to regard her in icy silence. In
his mid fifties, Charles Fielding was still an attractive man,
with thick, silver-streaked hair and hazel eyes, but illness
had taken its toll on him. He was too thin for his tall frame
and his face was deeply etched with lines of strain and
fatigue.

Unable to provoke a response from him, the duchess
rounded on the butler. "This room is too hot!" she snapped,
rapping her jeweled-handled cane upon the floor. "Draw the
draperies and let in some air."

"Leave them!" Charles barked, his voice seething with the loathing that the mere sight of her evoked in him.

The duchess turned a withering look in his direction. "I have not come here to suffocate," she stated ominously.

"Then get out."

Her thin body stiffened into a rigid line of furious resentment. "I have not come here to suffocate," she repeated through tightly clenched teeth. "I have come here to inform you of my decision regarding Katherine's girls."

"Do it," Charles snapped, "and *then* get out!"

Her eyes narrowed to furious slits and the air seemed to crackle with her hostility, but instead of leaving, she slowly lowered herself into a chair. Despite her advanced years, the duchess sat as regally erect as a queen, a purple turban perched upon her white head in place of a crown, a cane in her hand instead of a scepter.

Charles watched her with wary surprise, for he had been certain she'd insisted upon this meeting only so she could have the satisfaction of telling him to his face that the disposition of Katherine's children was none of his business. He had not expected her to sit down as if she had something more to say.

"You have seen the girls' miniature," she stated.

His gaze dropped to the miniature in his hand and his long fingers tightened convulsively, protectively around it. Naked pain darkened his eyes as he stared at Victoria. She was the image of her mother—the image of his beautiful, beloved Katherine.

"Victoria is the image of her mother," her grace snapped suddenly.

Charles lifted his gaze to hers and his face instantly hardened. "I am aware of that."

"Good. Then you will understand why I will not have that girl in my house. I'll take the other one." Standing up as if her business had been concluded, she glanced at her solicitor. "See that Dr. Morrison receives a bank draft to cover his expenses, and another draft to cover ship passage for the younger girl."

"Yes, your grace," her solicitor said, bowing. "Will there be anything more?"

"There will be a great deal *more,*" she snapped, her voice strained and tight. "I shall have to launch the girl into society, I shall have to provide a dowry for her. I shall have to find her a husband, I—"

"What about Victoria?" Charles interrupted fiercely. "What do you plan to do about the older girl?"

The duchess glowered at him. "I've already told you—that one reminds me of her mother, and I won't have her in my house. If you want her, you can take her. You wanted her mother rather badly, as I recall. And Katherine obviously wanted you—even when she was dying, she still spoke your name. You can shelter Katherine's image instead. It will serve you right to have to look at the chit."

Charles's mind was still reeling with joyous disbelief when the old duchess added arrogantly, "Marry her off to anyone you please—anyone *except* that nephew of yours. Twenty-two years ago, I wouldn't countenance an alliance between your family and mine, and I still forbid it. I—" As if something had just occurred to her, she broke off abruptly, her eyes beginning to gleam with malignant triumph. "I shall marry Dorothy to Winston's son!" she announced gleefully. "I wanted Katherine to marry the father, and she refused because of you. I'll marry Dorothy to the son—I'll have that alliance with the Winstons after all!" A slow, spiteful smile spread across her wrinkled face, and she laughed at Charles's pinched expression. "After all these years, I'm still going to pull off the most splendid match in a decade!" With that, she swept out of the room, followed by her solicitor.

Charles stared after her, his emotions veering between bitterness, hatred, and joy. That vicious old bitch had just inadvertently given him the one thing he wanted more than life itself—she had given him Victoria, Katherine's child. Katherine's image. A happiness that was almost past bearing surged through Charles, followed almost immediately by boiling wrath. That devious, heartless, conniving old woman was going to have an alliance with the Winstons—exactly as she had always wanted. She had been willing to sacrifice Katherine's happiness to have that meaningless alliance, and now she was going to succeed.

The rage Charles felt because she, too, was gaining what

she had always wanted nearly eclipsed his own joy at getting Victoria. And then suddenly a thought occurred to him. With narrowed eyes, he contemplated it, mulled it over, studied it. And slowly he began to smile. "Dobson," he said eagerly to his butler. "Bring me quill and parchment. I want to write out a betrothal announcement. See that it is delivered to the *Times* at once."

"Yes, your grace."

Charles looked up at the old servant, his eyes burning with feverish jubilation. "She was wrong, Dobson," he announced. "That old bitch was wrong!"

"Wrong, your grace?"

"Yes, wrong! She's not going to pull off the most splendid match in a decade. *I* am!"

It was a ritual. Each morning at approximately 9 o'clock, Northrup the butler opened the massive front door of the Marquess of Wakefield's palatial country mansion and was handed a copy of the *Times* by a footman who had brought it from London.

After closing the door, Northrup crossed the marble foyer and handed the newspaper to another footman stationed at the bottom of the grand staircase. "His lordship's copy of the *Times*," he intoned.

This footman carried the paper down the hall and into the dining room where Jason Fielding, Marquess of Wakefield, was customarily finishing his morning meal and reading his mail. "Your copy of the *Times*, my lord," the footman murmured diffidently as he placed it beside the marquess's coffee cup and then removed his plate. Wordlessly, the marquess picked up the paper and opened it.

All of this was performed with the perfectly orchestrated and faultlessly executed precision of a minuet, for Lord Fielding was an exacting master who demanded that his estates and townhouses run as smoothly as well-oiled machines.

His servants were in awe of him, regarding him as a cold, frighteningly unapproachable deity whom they strove desperately to please.

The eager London beauties whom Jason took to balls, operas, plays—and bed—felt much the same way about him,

23

for he treated most of them with little more genuine warmth than he did his servants. Nevertheless, the ladies eyed him with unveiled longing wherever he went, for despite his cynical attitude, there was an unmistakable aura of virility about Jason that made feminine hearts flutter.

His thick hair was coal black, his piercing eyes the green of India jade, his lips firm and sensually molded. Tough, rugged strength was carved into every feature of his sun-bronzed face, from his straight dark brows to the arrogant jut of his chin and jaw. Even his physical build was overpoweringly masculine, for he was six feet two inches tall, with wide shoulders, narrow hips, and firmly muscled legs and thighs. Whether he was riding a horse or dancing at a ball, Jason Fielding stood out among his fellow men like a magnificent jungle cat surrounded by harmless, domesticated kittens.

As Lady Wilson-Smyth once laughingly remarked, Jason Fielding was as dangerously attractive as sin—and undoubtedly just as wicked.

That opinion was shared by many, for anyone who looked into those cynical green eyes of his could tell there wasn't an innocent or naive fiber left in his lithe, muscular body. Despite that—or more accurately, *because* of it—the ladies were drawn to him like pretty moths to a scorching flame, eager to experience the heat of his ardor or bask in the dazzling warmth of one of his rare, lazy smiles. Sophisticated, married flirts schemed to occupy his bed; younger ladies of marriageable age dreamed of being the one to thaw his icy heart and bring him to his knees.

Some of the more sensible members of the *ton* remarked that Lord Fielding had good reason to be cynical where women were concerned. Everyone knew that his wife's behavior when she first came to London four years ago had been scandalous. From the moment she arrived in town, the beautiful Marchioness of Wakefield had indulged in one widely publicized love affair after another. She had repeatedly cuckolded her husband; everyone knew it—including Jason Fielding, who apparently didn't care. . . .

The footman paused beside Lord Fielding's chair, an ornate sterling coffeepot in his hand. "Would you care for more coffee, my lord?"

His lordship shook his head and turned to the next page of the *Times*. The footman bowed and retreated. He had not expected Lord Fielding to answer him aloud, for the master rarely deigned to speak to any of his servants. He did not know most of their names, or anything about them, nor did he care. But at least he was not given to ranting and raving, as many of the nobility were. When displeased, the Marquess merely turned the chilling blast of his green gaze on the offender and froze him. Never, not even under the most extreme provocation, did Lord Fielding raise his voice.

Which was why the amazed footman nearly dropped his silver coffeepot when Jason Fielding slammed his hand down on the table with a crash that made the dishes dance and thundered, *"That son of a bitch!"* Leaping to his feet, he stared at the open newspaper, his face a mask of fury and disbelief. "That conniving, scheming— He's the only one who would dare!" With a murderous glance at the thunderstruck footman, he stalked out of the room, grabbed his cloak from his butler, stormed out of the house, and headed straight for the stables.

Northrup closed the front door behind him and rushed down the hall, his black coattails flapping. "What happened to his lordship?" he demanded, bursting into the dining room.

The footman was standing beside Lord Fielding's recently vacated chair, staring raptly at the open newspaper, the forgotten coffeepot still suspended from one hand. "I think it was somethin' he read in the *Times*," he breathed, pointing to the announcement of the engagement of Jason Fielding, Marquess of Wakefield, to Miss Victoria Seaton. "I didn't know his lordship was plannin' to wed," the footman added.

"One wonders if his lordship knew it either," Northrup mused, gaping in astonishment at the newspaper. Suddenly realizing that he had so forgotten himself as to gossip with an underling, Northrup swept the paper from the table and closed it smartly. "Lord Fielding's affairs are no concern of yours, O'Malley. Remember that if you wish to stay on here."

Two hours later, Jason's carriage came to a bone-jarring stop in front of the Duke of Atherton's London residence. A groom ran forward and Jason tossed the reins to him, bounded out of the carriage, and strode purposefully up the front steps to the house.

"Good day, my lord," Dobson intoned as he opened the front door and stepped aside. "His grace is expecting you."

"I'll bet he damned well is!" Jason bit out scathingly. "Where is he?"

"In the drawing room, my lord."

Jason stalked past him and down the hall, his long, quick strides eloquent of his turbulent wrath as he flung open the drawing room door and headed straight toward the dignified, gray-haired man seated before the fire. Without preamble, he snapped, "You, I presume, are responsible for that outrageous announcement in the *Times?*"

Charles boldly returned his stare. "I am."

"Then you will have to issue another one to rescind it."

"No," Charles stated implacably. "The young woman is coming to England and you are going to marry her. Among other things, I want a grandson from you, and I want to hold him in my arms before I depart this world."

"If you want a grandson," Jason snarled, "all you have to do is locate some of your other by-blows. I'm sure you'll discover they've sired you *dozens* of grandsons by now."

Charles flinched at that, but his voice merely lowered ominously. "I want a *legitimate* grandson to present to the world as my heir."

"A legitimate grandson," Jason repeated with freezing sarcasm. "You want me, your illegitimate son, to sire you a *legitimate* grandson. Tell me something: with everyone else believing I'm your nephew, how do you intend to claim my son as your grandchild?"

"I would claim him as my great-nephew, but *I* would know he's my grandson, and that's all that matters." Undaunted by his son's soaring fury, Charles finished implacably, "I want an heir from you, Jason."

A pulse drummed in Jason's temple as he fought to control his wrath. Bending low, he braced his hands on the arms of Charles's chair, his face only inches away from the older man's. Very slowly and very distinctly, he enunciated, "I have told you before, and I'm telling you for the last time, that I will never remarry. Do you understand me? *I will never remarry!"*

"Why?" Charles snapped. "You aren't entirely a woman-hater. It's common knowledge that you've had mistresses and that you treat them well. In fact, they all seem to tumble into love with you. The ladies obviously like being in your bed, and you obviously like having them there—"

"Shut up!" Jason exploded.

A spasm of pain contorted Charles's face and he raised his hand to his chest, his long fingers clutching his shirt. Then he carefully returned his hand to his lap.

Jason's eyes narrowed, but despite his suspicion that Charles was merely feigning the pain, he forced himself to remain silent as his father continued. "The young lady I've chosen to be your wife should arrive here in about three months. I will have a carriage waiting at the dock so that she may proceed directly to Wakefield Park. For the sake of propriety, I will join the two of you there and remain with you until the nuptials have been performed. I knew her mother long ago, and I've seen a likeness of Victoria—you won't be disappointed." He held out the miniature. "Come now, Jason," he said, his voice turning soft, persuasive, "aren't you the slightest bit curious about her?"

Charles's attempt at cajolery hardened Jason's features into a mask of granite. "You're wasting your time. I won't do it."

"You'll do it," Charles promised, resorting to threats in his desperation. "Because if you don't, I'll disinherit you. You've already spent half a million pounds of your money restoring my estates, estates that will never belong to you unless you marry Victoria Seaton."

Jason reacted to the threat with withering contempt. "Your precious estates can burn to the ground for all I care. My son is dead—I no longer have any use for legacies."

Charles saw the pain that flashed across Jason's eyes at the mention of his little boy, and his tone softened with shared sorrow. "I'll admit that I acted precipitously in announcing your betrothal, Jason, but I had my reasons. Perhaps I can't force you to marry Victoria, but at least don't set your mind against her. I promise you that you'll find no fault with her. Here, I have a miniature of her and you can see for yourself how beautiful . . ." Charles's voice trailed off as Jason turned on his heel and stalked from the room, slamming the door behind him with a deafening crash.

Charles glowered at the closed door. "You'll marry her, Jason," he warned his absent son. "You'll do it if I have to hold a gun to your head."

He glanced up a few minutes later as Dobson came in carrying a silver tray laden with a bottle of champagne and two glasses. "I took the liberty of selecting something appropriate for the occasion," the old servant confided happily, putting the tray on the table near Charles.

"In that case you should have selected hemlock," Charles said wryly. "Jason has already left."

The butler's face fell. "Already left? But I didn't have an opportunity to felicitate his lordship on his forthcoming nuptials."

"Which is fortunate indeed," Charles said with a grim chuckle. "I fear he'd have loosened your teeth."

When the butler left, Charles picked up the bottle of champagne, opened it, and poured some into a glass. With a determined smile, he lifted his glass in a solitary toast: "To your forthcoming marriage, Jason."

"I'll just be a few minutes, Mr. Borowski," Victoria said, jumping down from the farmer's wagon that was loaded with Dorothy's and her belongings.

"Take yer time," he said, puffing on his pipe and smiling. "Me an' yer sister won't leave without you."

"Do hurry, Tory," Dorothy pleaded. "The ship won't wait for us."

"We got plenty o' time," Mr. Borowski told her. "I'll get you to the city and yer ship afore nightfall, and that's a promise."

Victoria hurried up the steps of Andrew's imposing house, which overlooked the village from a hilltop, and knocked on the heavy oaken door. "Good morning, Mrs. Tilden," she said to the plump housekeeper. "May I see Mrs. Bainbridge for a moment? I want to tell her good-bye and give her a letter to send on to Andrew, so he'll know where to write to me in England."

28

"I'll tell her you're here, Victoria," the kindly house-keeper replied with an unencouraging expression, "but I doubt she'll see you. You know how she is when she's having one of her sick spells."

Victoria nodded sagely. She knew all about Mrs. Bain-bridge's "sick spells." According to Victoria's father, Andrew's mother was a chronic complainer who invented ailments to avoid doing anything she didn't wish to do, and to manipulate and control Andrew. Patrick Seaton had told Mrs. Bainbridge that to her face several years ago, in front of Victoria, and the woman had never forgiven either of them for it.

Victoria knew that Mrs. Bainbridge was a fraud, and so did Andrew. For that reason, her palpitations, dizzy spells, and tingling limbs had little effect on either of them—a fact that, Victoria knew, further antagonized her against her son's choice of a wife.

The housekeeper returned with a grim look on her face. "I'm sorry, Victoria, Mrs. Bainbridge says she isn't well enough to see you. I'll take your letter to Mr. Andrew and give it to her to send on to him. She wants me to summon Dr. Morrison," she added in tones of disgust. "She says she has a ringing in her ears."

"Dr. Morrison sympathizes with her ailments, instead of telling her to get out of bed and do something useful with her life," Victoria summarized with a resigned smile, handing over the letter. She wished it wasn't so costly to send mail to Europe, so she could post her letters herself, instead of having Mrs. Bainbridge include them in her own letters to Andrew. "I think Mrs. Bainbridge likes Dr. Morrison's attitude better than she liked my father's."

"If you ask me," Mrs. Tilden said huffily, "she liked your papa a sight too much. It was almost more than a body could stand, watchin' her dress herself up before she sent for him in the middle of the night and—not," she broke off and corrected herself quickly, "that your papa, dear man that he was, ever played along with her scheme."

When Victoria left, Mrs. Tilden brought the letter up-stairs. "Mrs. Bainbridge," she said, approaching the wid-ow's bed, "here is Victoria's letter for Mr. Andrew."

"Give it to me," Mrs. Bainbridge snapped in a surprisingly strong voice for an invalid, "and then send for Dr. Morrison at once. I feel quite dizzy. When is the new doctor supposed to arrive?"

"Within a week," Mrs. Tilden replied, handing the letter to her.

When she left, Mrs. Bainbridge patted her gray hair into place beneath her lace cap and glanced with a grimace of distaste at the letter lying beside her on the satin coverlet. "Andrew won't marry that country mouse," she said contemptuously to her maid. "She's nothing! He's written me twice that his cousin Madeline in Switzerland is a lovely girl. I've told Victoria that, but the foolish baggage won't pay it any heed."

"Do you think he'll bring Miss Madeline home as his wife, then?" her maid asked, helping to plump the pillows behind Mrs. Bainbridge's back.

Mrs. Bainbridge's thin face pinched with anger. "Don't be a fool! Andrew has no time for a wife. I've told him that. This place is more than enough to keep him busy, and his duty is to it, and to me." She picked up Victoria's letter with two fingers as if it were contaminated and passed it to her maid. "You know what to do with this," she said coldly.

"I didn't know there were this many people, or this much noise, in the entire world," Dorothy burst out as she stood on a dock in New York's bustling harbor.

Stevedores with trunks slung on their shoulders swarmed up and down the gangplanks of dozens of ships; winches creaked overhead as heavily loaded cargo nets were lifted off the wooden pier and carried over the sides of the vessels. Shouted orders from ships' officers blended with bursts of raucous laughter from sailors and lewd invitations called out by garishly garbed ladies waiting on the docks for disembarking seamen.

"It's exciting," Victoria said, watching the two trunks that held all their worldly possessions being carried on board the *Gull* by a pair of burly stevedores.

Dorothy nodded agreement, but her face clouded. "It is, but I keep remembering that at the end of our voyage, we'll be separated, and it is all our great-grandmother's fault. What can she be thinking of to refuse you her home?"

"I don't know, but you mustn't dwell on it," Victoria said with an encouraging smile. "Think only of nice things. Look at the East River. Close your eyes and smell the salty air."

Dorothy closed her eyes and inhaled deeply, but she wrinkled her nose. "All I smell is dead fish. Tory, if our great-grandmother knew more about you, I *know* she would want you to come to her. She can't be so cruel and unfeeling as to keep us apart. I shall tell her all about you and make her change her mind."

"You mustn't say or do anything to alienate her," Victoria warned gently. "For the time being, you and I are entirely dependent upon our relatives."

"I won't alienate her if I can help it," Dorothy promised, "but I shall make it ever so clear, in tiny ways, that she ought to send for you at once." Victoria smiled but remained silent, and after a moment, Dorothy sighed. "There is one small consolation in being hauled off to England—Mr. Wilheim said that, with more practice and hard work, I might be able to become a concert pianist. He said that in London there will be excellent instructors to teach and guide me. I shall ask, no, *insist,* that our great-grandmother permit me to pursue a musical career," Dorothy finished, displaying the determined streak that few people suspected existed behind her sweet, complaisant facade.

Victoria forebore to point out the obstacles that leapt to her mind as she considered Dorothy's decision. With the wisdom of her additional year and a half of age, she said simply, "Don't 'insist' too strongly, love."

"I shall be discreet," Dorothy agreed.

Chapter Four

"Miss Dorothy Seaton?" the gentleman in-quired politely, stepping aside as three burly English seamen with heavy sacks slung over their shoulders elbowed past him and strode off down the dock.

"I am she," Dorothy said, her voice trembling with fright and excitement as she gazed at the impeccably dressed, white-haired man.

"I have been instructed by her grace, the Duchess of Claremont, to escort you to her home. Where are your trunks?"

"Right there," Dorothy said. "There's only one."

He glanced over his shoulder and two liveried men climbed off the back of a shiny black coach with a gold crest on the door and hurried forward. "In that case, we can be on our way," the man said as her trunk was lifted up and loaded atop the coach.

"But what about my sister?" Dorothy said, her hand clasping Victoria's in a stranglehold of eager terror.

"I'm certain that the party meeting your sister will be here directly. Your ship arrived four days ahead of schedule."

"Don't worry about me," Victoria said with a bright confidence she didn't quite feel. "I'm certain the duke's carriage will be here any minute. In the meantime, Captain Gardiner will let me stay on board. Run along now."

Dorothy enfolded her sister in a tight hug. "Tory, I'll contrive some way to persuade our grandmother to invite you to stay with us, you'll see. I'm scared. Don't forget to write. Write every day!"

Victoria stayed where she was, watching Dorothy climb daintily into the luxurious vehicle with the gold crest on the door. The stairs were put up, the coachman snapped his whip, and the four horses bounded off as Dorothy waved good-bye from the window.

Jostled by sailors leaving the ship in eager search of "foine ale and tarts," Victoria stood on the dock, her gaze clinging to the departing coach. She had never felt so utterly alone in her life.

She spent the next two days in bored solitude in her cabin, the tedium interrupted only by her short walks on deck and her meals with Captain Gardiner, a charming, fatherly man who seemed to greatly enjoy her company. Victoria had spent a considerable amount of time with him over the past weeks, and they had shared dozens of meals during the long voyage. He knew her reasons for coming to England, and she regarded him as a newly made friend.

When by the morning of the third day no coach had arrived to convey Victoria to Wakefield Park, Captain Gardiner took matters into his own hands and hired one. "We were early getting into port, which is a rare occurrence," he explained. "Your cousin may not think to send someone for you for days yet. I have business to conduct in London and I cannot leave you on board unprotected. In the time it would take to notify your cousin of your arrival, you can be there yourself."

For long hours, Victoria studied the English countryside decked out in all its magical spring splendor. Pink and yellow flowers bloomed in profusion across hedgerows that marched up and down the hills and valleys. Despite the jostling and jarring she received every time the coach wheels passed over a rut or bump, her spirits rose with every passing mile. The coachman rapped on the door above her and his ruddy face appeared. "We're 'bout two miles away, ma'am, so if you'd like to—"

Everything seemed to happen at once. The wheel hit a deep rut, the coach jerked crazily to the side, the coachman's head disappeared, and Victoria was flung to the floor in a sprawling heap. A moment later, the door was jerked open and the coachman helped her out. "You hurt?" he demanded.

Victoria shook her head, but before she could utter a word, he rounded on two men dressed in farmers' work clothes who were sheepishly clutching their caps in their hands. "Ye bloody fools! What d'ye mean pullin' out in the road like that! Look what ye've done, me axle's broken—" The rest of what he said was laced with stout curses.

Delicately turning her back on the loud altercation, Victoria shook her skirts, trying unsuccessfully to rid them of the dust and grime they'd acquired from the floor of the coach. The coachman crawled under his coach to inspect his broken axle, and one of the farmers shuffled over to Victoria, twisting his battered cap in his hands. "Jack 'n' me, we're awful sorry, ma'am," he said. "We'll take you on ter Wakefield Park—that is, if you don't mind us puttin' yer trunk in back with them piglets?"

Grateful not to have to walk the two miles, Victoria readily agreed. She paid the coachman with the traveling money Charles Fielding had sent her and climbed onto the bench between the two burly farmers. Riding in a farm cart, although less prestigious than a coach, was scarcely any bumpier and far more comfortable. Fresh breezes cooled her face and her view of the lavish countryside was unrestricted.

With her usual unaffected friendliness, Victoria soon succeeded in engaging both men in a conversation about farming, a topic about which she knew a little and was perfectly happy to learn more. Evidently, English farmers were violently opposed to the implementation of machines for use in farming. "Put us all out of work, they will," one of the farmers told her at the end of his impassioned condemnation of "them infernal things."

Victoria scarcely heard that, because their wagon had turned onto a paved drive and passed between two imposing iron gates that opened onto a broad, seemingly endless stretch of gently rolling, manicured parkland punctuated with towering trees. The park stretched in both directions as far as the eye could see, bisected here and there by a stream that meandered about, its banks covered with flowers of pink and blue and white. "It's a fairyland," Victoria breathed aloud, her stunned, admiring gaze roving across the carefully tended banks of the picturesque stream and the sweeping landscape. "It must take dozens of gardeners to care for a place this size."

"That it do," Jack said. "His lordship's got forty of 'em, countin' the ones what takes care of the *real* gardens—the gardens at the house, I mean." They had been plodding along the paved drive for fifteen minutes when the cart rounded a bend and Jack pointed proudly. "There it is— Wakefield Park. I heert it has a hunnert and sixty rooms."

Victoria gasped, her mind reeling, her empty stomach clenching into a tense knot. Stretched out before her in all its magnificent splendor was a three-story house that altogether surpassed her wildest imaginings. Built of mellow brick with huge forward wings and steep rooftops dotted with chimneys, it loomed before her—a palace with graceful terraced steps leading up to the front door and sunlight glistening against hundreds of panes of mullioned glass.

They drew to a stop before the house and Victoria tore her gaze away long enough for one of the farmers to help her down from the wagon seat. "Thank you, you've been very kind," she said, and started slowly up the steps. Apprehension turned her feet to lead and her knees to water. Behind her, the farmers went to the back of the wagon to remove her bulky trunk, but as they let down the back gate, two squealing piglets hurtled out of the wagon into empty air, hit the ground with a thud, and streaked off across the lawns.

Victoria turned at the sound of the farmers' shouts and giggled nervously as the red-faced men ran after the speedy little porkers.

Ahead of her, the door of the mansion was flung open and a stiff-faced man dressed in green and gold livery cast an outraged glance over the farmers, the piglets, and the dusty, disheveled female approaching him. "Deliveries," he told Victoria in a loud, ominous voice, "are made in the *rear*."

Raising his arm, he pointed imperiously toward the drive that ran alongside the house.

Victoria opened her mouth to explain she wasn't making a delivery, but her attention was diverted by a little piglet, which had changed direction and was headed straight toward her, pursued by a panting farmer.

"Get that cart, those swine, and your person out of here!" the man in the livery boomed.

Tears of helpless mirth sprang to Victoria's eyes as she bent down and scooped the escaped piglet into her arms. Laughing, she tried to explain. "Sir, you don't under—"

Northrup ignored her and glanced over his shoulder at the footman behind him. "Get rid of the lot of them! Throw them off—"

"What the hell is going on here?" demanded a man of about thirty with coal black hair, stalking onto the front steps.

The butler pointed a finger at Victoria's face, his eyebrows levitating with ire. "That woman is—"

"Victoria Seaton," Victoria put in hastily, trying to stifle her mirth as tension, exhaustion, and hunger began pushing her perilously close to nervous hysteria. She saw the look of unconcealed shock on the black-haired man's face when he heard her name, and her alarm erupted into hilarity.

With uncontrollable laughter bubbling up inside her, she turned and dumped the squirming piglet into the flushed farmer's arms, then lifted her dusty skirts and tried to curtsy. "I fear there's been a mistake," she said on a suffocated giggle. "I've come to—"

The tall man's icy voice checked her in mid-curtsy. "Your mistake was in coming here in the first place, Miss Seaton. However, it's too close to dark to send you back to wherever you came from." He caught her by the arm and pulled her rudely forward.

Victoria sobered instantly; the situation no longer seemed riotously funny, but terrifyingly macabre. Timidly, she stepped through the doorway into a three-story marble entrance hall that was larger than her entire home in New York. On either side of the foyer, twin branches of a great, curving staircase swept upward to the next two floors, and a great domed skylight bathed the area in mellow sunlight from high above. She tipped her head back, gazing at the domed glass ceiling three stories above. Tears filled her eyes and the skylight revolved in a dizzy whirl as exhausted anguish overcame her. She had traveled thousands of miles across a stormy sea and rutted roads, expecting to be greeted by a kindly gentleman. Instead she was going to be sent back, away from Dorothy— The skylight whirled before her eyes in a kaleidoscope of brilliant blurring colors.

"She's going to swoon," the butler predicted.

"Oh, for God's sake!" the dark-haired man exploded, and swept her into his arms. The world was already coming back into focus for Victoria as he started up the right-hand branch of the broad marble staircase.

"Put me down," she demanded hoarsely, wriggling in embarrassment. "I'm perfectly—"

"Hold still!" he commanded. On the landing, he turned right, stalked into a room, and headed straight for a huge bed surrounded by blue and silver silk draperies suspended from a high, carved wood frame and gathered back at the corners with silver velvet ropes. Without a word, he dumped her unceremoniously onto the blue silk coverlet and shoved her shoulders back down when she tried to sit up.

The butler rushed into the room, his coattails flapping behind him. "Here, my lord—hartshorn," he panted.

My lord snatched the bottle from his hand and rammed it toward Victoria's nostrils.

"Don't!" Victoria cried, trying to twist her head away from the terrible amoniac odor, but his hand persistently followed her face. In sheer desperation, she grasped his wrist, trying to hold it away while he continued to force it toward her. "What are you trying to do," she burst out, "feed it to me?"

"What a delightful idea," he replied grimly, but the pressure on her restraining hand relaxed and he moved the bottle a few inches away from her nose. Exhausted and humiliated, Victoria turned her head aside, closed her eyes, and swallowed audibly as she fought back the tears congealing in her throat. She swallowed again.

"I sincerely hope," he drawled nastily, "that you are not considering getting sick on this bed, because I'm warning you that *you* will be the one to clean it up."

Victoria Elizabeth Seaton—the product of eighteen years of careful upbringing that had, until now, produced a sweet-tempered, charming young lady—slowly turned her head on the pillow and regarded him with scathing animosity. "Are you Charles Fielding?"

"No."

"In that case, kindly get off this bed or allow me to do so!"

His brows snapped together as he stared down at the rebellious waif who was glaring at him with murder in her brilliant blue eyes. Her hair spilled over the pillows like liquid golden flame, curling riotously at her temples and framing a face that looked as if it had been sculpted in porcelain by a master. Her eyelashes were incredibly long, her lips as pink and soft as—

Abruptly, the man lunged to his feet and stalked out of the room, followed by the butler. The door closed behind them, leaving Victoria in a deafening silence.

Slowly she sat up and put her legs over the side of the bed, then eased herself to her feet, afraid the dizziness would return. Numb despair made her feel cold all over, but her legs were steady as she gazed about her. On her left, light blue draperies heavily embellished with silver threads were pulled back, framing an entire wall of mullioned windows; at the far end of the room, a pair of blue-and-silver-striped settees were placed at right angles to an ornate fireplace. The phrase "decadent splendor" drifted through her mind as she dusted off her skirts, cast one more look about the room, and then gingerly sat back down on the blue silk coverlet.

An awful lump of desolation swelled in her throat as she folded her hands in her lap and tried to think what to do next. Evidently she was to be sent back to New York like unwanted baggage. Why then had her cousin the duke brought her here in the first place? Where was he? *Who* was he?

She couldn't go to Dorothy and her great-grandmother, because the duchess had written Dr. Morrison a note that made it clear that Dorothy, and Dorothy alone, was welcome in her home. Victoria frowned, her smooth brow furrowing in confusion. Since the black-haired man had been the one to carry her upstairs, perhaps *he* was the servant and the stout, white-haired man who'd opened the door was the duke. At first glance, she'd assumed he was a ranking servant—like Mrs. Tilden, the housekeeper who always greeted callers at Andrew's house.

Someone knocked at the door of the room, and Victoria guiltily jumped off the bed and carefully smoothed the coverlet before calling, "Come in."

A maid in a starched black dress, white apron, and white cap entered, a silver tray in her hands. Six more maids in identical black uniforms marched in like marionettes, carrying buckets of steaming water. Behind them came two footmen in gold-braid-trimmed green uniforms, carrying her trunk.

The first maid put the tray on the table between the settees, while the other maids disappeared into an adjoining room and the footmen deposited the trunk at the end of the bed. A minute later, they all trooped right back out again in single file, reminding Victoria of animated wooden soldiers. The remaining maid turned to Victoria, who was standing self-consciously beside the bed. "Here's a bite for you to eat, miss," she said; her plain face was carefully expressionless, but her voice was shyly pleasant.

Victoria went over to the settee and sat down, the sight of the buttered toast and hot chocolate making her mouth water.

"His lordship said you were to have a bath," the maid said, and started toward the adjoining room. Victoria paused, the cup of chocolate partway to her lips. "His lordship?" she repeated. "Would that be the . . . gentleman . . . I saw at the front door? A stout man with white hair?"

"Good heavens, no!" the maid replied, regarding Victoria with a strange look. "That would be Mr. Northrup, the butler, miss."

Victoria's relief was short-lived as the maid hesitantly added, "His lordship is a tall man, with black curly hair."

"And *he* said I should have a bath?" Victoria asked, bristling.

The maid nodded, coloring.

"Well, I do need one," Victoria conceded reluctantly. She ate the toast and finished the chocolate, then wandered into the adjoining room where the maid was pouring perfumed bath salts into the steaming water. Slowly removing her travel-stained gown, Victoria thought of the short note

39

Charles Fielding had sent her, inviting her to come to England. He had seemed so anxious to have her here. *"Come at once, my dear,"* he had written. *"You are more than welcome here—you are eagerly awaited."* Perhaps she wasn't to be sent away after all. Perhaps "his lordship" had mistaken the matter.

The maid helped her wash her hair, then held up a fluffy cloth for Victoria and helped her out of the tub. "I've put away your clothes, mum, and turned down the bed, in case you'd like a nap."

Victoria smiled at her and asked her name.

"My name?" the maid repeated, as if stunned that Victoria should care to ask. "Why, it's—it's Ruth."

"Thank you very much, Ruth," Victoria said, "for putting away my clothes, I mean."

A deep flush of pleasure colored the maid's freckled face as she bobbed a quick curtsy and started for the door. "Supper is at eight," Ruth informed her. "His lordship rarely keeps country hours at Wakefield."

"Ruth," Victoria said awkwardly as the maid started to leave, "are there two . . . ah . . . 'lordships' here? That is, I was wondering about Charles Fielding—"

"Oh, you're referrin' to his grace!" Ruth glanced over her shoulder as if she was fearful of being overheard before she confided, "He hasn't arrived yet, but we're expectin' him sometime tonight. I heard his lordship tell Northrup to send word to his grace that you've arrived."

"What is his—ah—grace like?" Victoria asked, feeling foolish using these odd titles.

Ruth looked as if she was about to describe him; then she changed her mind. "I'm sorry, miss, but his lordship doesn't permit his servants to gossip. Nor are we allowed to be familiar-like with guests." She curtsied and scurried out in a rustle of starched black skirts.

Victoria was startled by the knowledge that two human beings were not permitted to converse together in this house, simply because one was a servant and the other a guest, but considering her brief acquaintance with "his lordship," she could fully imagine him issuing such an inhuman edict.

Victoria took her nightdress from the wardrobe, pulled it

over her head, and climbed into bed, sliding between the sheets. Luxurious silk caressed the bare skin of her arms and face as she uttered a weary prayer that Charles Fielding would prove to be a warmer, kindlier man than his other lordship. Her long dark lashes fluttered down, lying like curly fans against her cheeks, and she fell asleep.

Chapter Five

SUNLIGHT STREAMED IN THROUGH THE OPEN WIN-
dows and a breeze glided through the room, softly caressing
Victoria's face. Somewhere below, a horse's hooves clattered on a paved drive, and two birds landed simultaneously
on her windowsill, embarking on a noisy quarrel over territo-
rial rights. Their irate chirping slowly penetrated Victoria's
slumber, stirring her from happy dreams of home.

Still half-asleep, she rolled over onto her stomach, bur-
rowing her face into the pillow. Instead of the slightly rough
fabric that covered her pillow at home and smelled of
sunshine and soap, her cheek encountered smooth silk.
Dimly aware that she was not in her own bed with her
mother downstairs making breakfast, Victoria squeezed her
eyes closed, trying to recapture her tranquil dreams, but it
was already too late. Reluctantly, she turned her head and
opened her eyes.

In the bright light of midmorning, she stared at the silver
and blue draperies that surrounded her bed like a silken
cocoon, and her mind abruptly cleared. She was at Wakefield Park. She had slept straight through the night.

Shoving her tousled hair out of her eyes, she pulled herself up into a sitting position and leaned back against the pillows.

"Good morning, miss," Ruth said, standing at the opposite side of the bed.

Victoria stifled a scream of shock.

"I didn't mean to startle you," the little maid apologized hastily, "but his grace is downstairs and he said to ask if you would join him for breakfast."

Vastly encouraged by the news that her cousin the duke actually wished to see her, Victoria flung back the covers.

"I've pressed your gowns for you," Ruth said, opening the armoire. "Which one would you like to wear?"

Victoria chose the best of the five—a soft black muslin with a low, square neckline, embellished with tiny white roses she'd carefully embroidered on the full sleeves and hem during the long voyage. Refusing Ruth's offer to help her dress, Victoria pulled the gown on over her petticoats and tied the wide black sash about her slim waist.

While Ruth made the bed and tidied the spotless room, Victoria slid into the chair at the dressing table and brushed her hair. "I'm ready," she told Ruth as she stood up, her eyes alight with hopeful anticipation and her cheeks blooming with healthy color. "Could you tell me where to find . . . ah . . . his grace?"

Victoria's feet sank into the thick red carpet as Ruth led her down the curving marble staircase and across the foyer to where two footmen were standing guard beside a pair of richly carved mahogany doors. Before she had time to draw a steadying breath, the footmen swept the doors open with a soundless flourish, and Victoria found herself stepping into a room perhaps ninety feet in length, dominated by a long mahogany table centered beneath three gigantic chandeliers dripping with crystal. She thought the room was empty at first, as her gaze moved over the high-backed gold velvet chairs that marched along both sides of the endless table. And then she heard the rustle of paper coming from the chair at the near end of the table. Unable to see the occupant, she walked slowly around to the side and stopped. "Good morning," she said softly.

Charles's head snapped around and he stared at her, his

face draining of color. "Almighty God!" he breathed, and slowly came to his feet, his gaze clinging to the exotic young beauty standing before him. He saw Katherine, exactly as she had looked so many years ago. How well, and how lovingly, he remembered that incredibly beautiful, fine-boned face with its gracefully winged eyebrows and long, thick lashes framing eyes the color of huge iridescent sapphires. He recognized that soft, smiling mouth, the elegant little nose, that tiny, enchanting dimple in her stubborn chin, and the glorious mass of red-gold hair that tumbled over her shoulders in riotous abandon.

Putting his left hand on the back of the chair to steady himself, he extended his shaking right hand to her. "Katherine—" he whispered.

Uncertainly, Victoria put her hand in his outstretched palm, and his long fingers closed tightly around hers. "Katherine," he whispered again hoarsely, and Victoria saw the sparkle of tears in his eyes.

"My mother's name was Katherine," she said gently.

His grip on her hand tightened almost painfully. "Yes," he whispered. He cleared his throat and his voice became more normal. "Yes, of course," he said, and shook his head as if to clear it. He was surprisingly tall, Victoria noticed, and very thin, with hazel eyes that studied her features in minute detail. "So," he said briskly, "you are Katherine's daughter."

Victoria nodded, not quite certain how to take him. "My name is Victoria."

An odd tenderness glowed in his eyes. "Mine is Charles *Victor* Fielding."

"I—I see," she mumbled.

"No," he said. "You don't see." He smiled, a gentle smile that took decades off his age. "You don't see at all." And then, without warning, he enfolded her in a tight embrace. "Welcome home, child," he said in an emotion-choked voice as he patted her back and hugged her close. "Welcome." And Victoria felt oddly as if she might truly be home.

He let her go with a sheepish smile and pulled out a chair for her. "You must be starved. O'Malley!" he said to the footman who was stationed at a sideboard laden with covered silver dishes. "We're both famished."

"Yes, your grace," the footman said, turning aside and beginning to fill two plates.

"I apologize most sincerely for not having a coach waiting for you when you arrived," Charles said. "I never dreamed you would arrive early—the packets from America are routinely late, I was told. Now, then, did you have a pleasant voyage?" he asked her as the footman placed a plate filled with eggs, potatoes, kidneys, ham, and crusty French rolls before her.

Victoria glanced at the array of ornate gold flatware on either side of her plate and breathed a prayer of gratitude to her mother for teaching Dorothy and her the proper uses for each piece. "Yes, a very pleasant voyage," she answered with a smile, then added with awkward shyness,"—your grace."

"Good heavens," Charles said, chuckling, "I hardly think we need stand on such ceremony. If we do, then I shall have to call you Countess Langston or Lady Victoria. I shan't like that a bit, you know—I'd much prefer 'Uncle Charles' for myself and 'Victoria' for you. What do you say?"

Victoria found herself responding to his warmth with an affection that was already taking root deep in her heart. "I'd like that very much. I'm sure I'd never remember to answer to Countess Langston—whoever that is—and Lady Victoria doesn't sound at all like me either."

Charles gave her an odd look as he placed his napkin on his lap. "But you are both of those people. Your mother was the only child of the Earl and Countess of Langston. They died when she was a young girl, but their title was of Scottish origin and it passed to her. You are her eldest child; therefore the title is now yours."

Victoria's blue eyes twinkled with amusement. "And what am I to do with it?"

"Do what we all do," he said, and chuckled. "Flaunt it." He paused while O'Malley deftly slid a plate in front of him. "Actually, I think there's a small estate in Scotland that might go with the title. Perhaps not. What did your mother tell you?"

"Nothing. Mama never spoke of England or her life here. Dorothy and I always assumed she was . . . well, an ordinary person."

"There was nothing 'ordinary' about your mama," he said softly. Victoria heard the thread of emotion in his voice and wondered about it, but when she started to question him about her mother's life in England, he shook his head and said lightly, "Someday I shall tell you all about . . . everything. But not yet. For now, let's get to know each other."

An hour passed with unbelievable swiftness as Victoria answered Charles's pleasantly worded questions. By the time breakfast was over, she realized, he had smoothly gleaned from her an exact picture of her life, right up to the time of her arrival at his door with an armful of squealing piglet. She'd told him about the villagers at home, about her father, and about Andrew. For some reason, hearing about the last two seemed to severely dampen his spirits, yet those were the two people he seemed to be most interested in. About her mother, he carefully avoided inquiring.

"I confess I'm confused about the matter of your betrothal to this fellow Andrew Bainbridge," he said when she was finished, his forehead etched with a deep frown. "The letter I received from your friend Dr. Morrison made no mention of it. Quite the opposite—he said you and your sister were alone in the world. Did your father give his blessing to this betrothal?"

"Yes and no," Victoria said, wondering why he looked so distressed about it. "You see, Andrew and I have known each other forever, but Papa always insisted that I must be eighteen before I became formally betrothed. He felt it was too serious a commitment for a younger female to make."

"Very wise of him," Charles agreed. "However, you became eighteen before your father passed away, and yet you still are not formally betrothed to Bainbridge, is that correct?"

"Well, yes."

"Because your father still withheld his consent?"

"Not exactly. Shortly before my birthday, Mrs. Bainbridge—Andrew's widowed mama—proposed to my father that Andrew should take a shortened version of the Grand Tour to test our commitment to each other, and to give him

46

what she called a 'last fling.' Andrew thought the idea was nonsensical, but my papa was fully in agreement with Mrs. Bainbridge.''

"It sounds to me as if your father was extremely reluctant to have you marry the young man. After all, you've known each other for years, so there was no real need to test your commitment to each other. That sounds very much like an excuse, not a reason. For that matter, it seems to me that Andrew's mother is also opposed to the match."

The duke sounded as if he were firmly setting his mind against Andrew, which left Victoria no choice but to explain the whole, embarrassing truth. "Papa had no reservations about Andrew making me an excellent husband. He had serious reservations about my life with my future mother-in-law, however. She is a widow, you see, and very attached to Andrew. Besides that, she is prone to all sorts of illnesses that make her somewhat ill-tempered.''

"Ah," said the duke in an understanding way. "And how serious are these illnesses of hers?"

Victoria's cheeks warmed. "According to what my father told her on one occasion when I was present, her illnesses are feigned. When she was very young, she did have a certain weakness of the heart, but Papa said that getting out of bed would help her far more than staying in it and wallowing in self-pity. They—they didn't like each other very well, you see.''

"Yes, and I can understand why!" The duke chuckled. "Your papa was entirely right to throw obstructions in the way of your marriage, my dear. Your life would have been very unhappy.''

"It won't be unhappy at all," Victoria said firmly, determined to marry Andrew with or without the duke's approval. "Andrew realizes that his mother uses her illnesses to try to manipulate him, and he doesn't let it stop him from doing what he wishes to do. He only agreed to go on this tour because my father insisted he should.''

"Have you received many letters from him?"

"Only one, but you see, Andrew left for Europe only a fortnight before my parents' accident three months ago, and it takes almost that long to get letters to and from Europe. I wrote to him, telling him what happened, and I wrote to him

47

again, just before I sailed for England, to give him my direction here. I expect he's on his way home right now, thinking he is coming to my rescue. I wanted to stay in New York and wait for him to return, which would have been much simpler for everyone, but Dr. Morrison wouldn't hear of it. He was convinced for some reason that Andrew's feelings would not withstand the test of time. No doubt Mrs. Bainbridge told him something like that, which is the sort of thing she would do, I suppose."

Victoria sighed and glanced out the windows. "She would much prefer Andrew to marry someone of more importance than the daughter of a penniless physician."

"Or better yet, that he marry no one at all and remain tied to her bedside?" the duke ventured, his brows raised. "A widow who feigns illnesses sounds like a very possessive, domineering sort to me."

Victoria couldn't deny it, so rather than condemn her future mother-in-law, she remained charitably silent on that subject. "Some of the families in the village offered to let me remain with them until Andrew returned, but that solution wasn't a very good one. Among other things, if Andrew returned and found me staying with them, well, he would have been furious."

"With you?" his grace asked, frowning in annoyance at poor Andrew.

"No, with his mother, for not insisting that I stay with her instead."

"Oh," he said, but even though her explanation completely vindicated Andrew of any possible blame, Charles seemed somewhat depressed by it. "The man sounds like a countrified paragon of virtue," he muttered.

"You will like him very much," Victoria predicted, smiling. "He will come here to bring me home, you'll see."

Charles patted her hand. "Let's forget about Andrew and be glad you're here in England. Now, tell me how you like it thus far. . . ."

Victoria told him she liked what she had seen very much, and Charles responded by describing the life he had planned for her here. To begin with, he wanted her to have a new wardrobe and a trained lady's maid to assist her. Victoria was about to refuse when she caught sight of the dark, forbidding figure striding toward the table with the silent sureness of a dangerous savage, his buckskin breeches molding his muscular legs and thighs, his white shirt open at his tanned throat. This morning, he seemed even taller than she'd thought yesterday, lean and superbly fit. His thick black hair was slightly curly, his nose straight, his stern mouth finely chiseled. In fact, if it weren't for the arrogant authority stamped in his rugged jawline and the cynicism in his cold green eyes, Victoria would have thought him almost breathtakingly handsome.

"Jason!" Charles said heartily. "Allow me to properly present you to Victoria. Jason is my nephew," he added to Victoria.

Nephew! She'd hoped he might only be a visitor, but he was a relative who probably lived with Charles, she realized now. The knowledge made Victoria feel slightly ill at the same time that her pride forced her to lift her chin and calmly meet Jason's ruthless stare. Acknowledging the brief introduction with a curt nod, he seated himself across from her and looked at O'Malley. "Is it too much to hope that there is any food left?"

The footman quailed visibly. "I—no, my lord. There isn't. That is, there's enough to eat, but it may not be quite warm enough. I'll go down to the kitchens at once and have cook fix something fresh and hot." He rushed out.

"Jason," Charles said, "I've just been suggesting to Victoria that she ought to have a suitable lady's maid and a wardrobe more appropriate to—"

"No," Jason said flatly.

Victoria's urge to flee promptly overpowered every other instinct. "If you'll excuse me, Uncle Charles," she said, "I—I have some things to do."

Charles shot her a grateful, apologetic look and politely stood up as she arose, but his obnoxious nephew merely lounged back in his chair, observing her retreat with bored distaste.

"None of this is Victoria's fault," Charles began as the footmen started to close the doors behind Victoria. "You must understand that."

"Really?" Jason drawled sarcastically. "And does that whining little beggar understand that this is my house and I don't want her here?"

The doors closed behind her, but Victoria had already heard enough. *A beggar! A whining beggar!* Humiliation washed over her in sickening waves as she fled blindly down the hall. Apparently, Charles had invited her here without his nephew's consent.

Victoria's face was pale but set as she walked into her room and opened her trunk.

Back in the dining room, Charles was pleading with the hardened cynic across from him. "Jason, you don't understand—"

"You brought her to England," Jason snapped. "Since you want her here so badly, take her to London to live with you."

"I can't do that!" Charles argued vehemently. "She's not ready to face the *ton* yet. There's much to be done before she can make her debut in London. Among other things, we'll need an older woman to stay with her as a chaperone for the sake of appearances."

Jason nodded impatiently at the footman who was hovering at his elbow with the silver coffeepot, waiting for permission to pour, and when he had finished dismissed him from the room. Then he turned to Charles and said harshly, "I want her out of here tomorrow—is that clear? Take her to London or send her home, but get her out! I'm not going to spend a cent on her. If you want to give her a London season, then you'll have to find some other way to pay for it."

Charles wearily rubbed his temples. "Jason, I know you aren't as heartless and unfeeling as you sound right now. At least let me tell you about her."

Leaning back in his chair, Jason regarded him with icy boredom while Charles plowed doggedly ahead. "Her parents were killed a few months ago in an accident. In one tragic day Victoria lost her mother, her father, her home, her security—everything." When Jason remained silent and unmoved, Charles ran out of patience. "Dammit! Have you forgotten how you felt when you lost Jamie? Victoria has lost all three of the people she loved, including the young man she was halfway betrothed to. She's foolish enough to believe the fellow will come running to her rescue in the next few weeks, but his mother's against the match. You mark my words, he'll yield to his mama's wishes now that Victoria is an ocean away. Her sister is now the ward of the Duchess of Claremont, so even her sister's companionship is denied Victoria now. Think how she feels, Jason! You're not unacquainted with death and loss—or have you forgotten the pain?"

Charles's words hit home with enough force to make Jason wince. Charles saw it and he pressed his advantage. "She's as innocent and lost as a child, Jason. She has no one left in the world except me—and you, whether you like it or not. Think of her as you would think of Jamie in these same circumstances. But Victoria has courage, and pride. For instance, even though she laughed about it, I could tell that her reception here yesterday humiliated her terribly. If she thinks she isn't wanted, she'll find some way to leave here. And if that happens," Charles finished tautly, "I'll never forgive you. I swear I won't!"

Jason abruptly pushed his chair back and stood up, his expression closed and hard. "By any chance, is she another one of your by-blows?"

Charles's face whitened. "Good God, no!" When Jason still looked skeptical, Charles added desperately, "Think what you're saying! Would I have announced your betrothal to her, if she were my daughter?"

Instead of pacifying Jason, that assurance merely called to mind the betrothal that had so enraged him. "If your little angel is so damned innocent and so courageous, why did she agree to barter her body for marriage to me?"

"Oh, that!" Charles waved his hand in dismissal. "I made that announcement without her knowledge; she knows nothing of it. Call it overenthusiasm on my part," he said smoothly. "I assure you, she has no wish to marry you." Jason's glacial expression began to thaw and Charles hastened to heap on more reassurance. "I doubt Victoria would have you, even if you wanted her. You're much too cynical and hard and jaded for a gently bred, idealistic girl like her. She admired her father and she told me openly that she wanted to marry a man like him—a sensitive, gentle, idealistic man. Why, you're nothing like that," he continued, so carried away with near-victory that he didn't realize his speech bordered on insult. "I daresay if Victoria knew she was supposedly betrothed to you, she'd swoon dead away! She'd take her own life before—"

"I think I have the picture," Jason interrupted mildly.

"Good," Charles said with a swift smile. "Then may I suggest we keep that little betrothal announcement a secret from her? I'll think of some way to rescind it without causing embarrassment to either of you, but we can't do it immediately." When Jason's eyes narrowed on his smile, Charles quickly sobered. "She is a child, Jason—a brave, proud girl who is trying to make the best of things in a cruel world she isn't equipped to face. If we revoke the betrothal too soon after her arrival here, she'll be a laughingstock in London. They'll say you took one look at her and cried off."

A vision of dark-lashed, glowing blue eyes and a face too beautiful to be real drifted through Jason's mind. He remembered the entrancing smile that had touched her soft lips a few minutes ago, before she became aware of his presence in the dining room. In retrospect, she did seem rather like a vulnerable child.

"Go talk to her, please," Charles implored.

"I'll talk to her," Jason agreed shortly.

"But will you make her feel welcome?"

"That depends on how she behaves when I find her."

In her room, Victoria snatched another armload of clothes from the armoire while Jason Fielding's words hammered painfully in her brain. *Whining little BEGGAR . . . I don't want her here. . . . Whining little BEGGAR . . .* She hadn't found a new home at all, she thought hysterically. Fate had merely been playing a vicious joke on her. She stuffed the clothes into her trunk. Standing up again she turned toward the armoire and let out a gasp of fright. "You!" she choked, glaring at the tall, forbidding figure lounging just inside the doorway, his arms crossed over his chest. Angry with herself for letting him see her fright, she put her chin up, absolutely determined not to let him intimidate her again. "Someone should have taught you to knock before you enter a room."

"Knock?" he repeated with dry mockery. "When the

door is already open?" He shifted his attention to her open trunk and raised his eyebrows. "Are you leaving?"

"Obviously," Victoria replied.

"Why?"

"Why?" she burst out in disbelief. "Because I am *not* a whining little beggar, and for your information, I *hate* being a burden to anyone."

Instead of looking guilty because she'd overheard his cutting remarks, he looked slightly amused. "Didn't anyone ever teach *you* not to eavesdrop?"

"I was not eavesdropping," Victoria retorted. "You were assassinating my character in a voice that could be heard all the way to London."

"Where are you planning to go?" he asked, ignoring her criticism.

"That's none of your business."

"Humor me!" he snapped, his manner suddenly turning cold and commanding.

Victoria shot him a mutinous, measuring look. Leaning in the doorway, he looked dangerous and invincible. His shoulders were wide, his chest deep, and his white shirt-sleeves were rolled up, displaying darkly tanned, very muscular forearms whose strength she had already experienced when he carried her upstairs yesterday. She also knew he had a vile temper, and judging from the ominous look in his hard jade eyes, he was even now considering shaking the answer out of her. Rather than give him that satisfaction, Victoria said frigidly, "I have a little money. I'll find a place to live in the village."

"Really?" he drawled sarcastically. "Just out of curiosity, when your 'little money' runs out, how will you live?"

"I'll work!" Victoria informed him, trying to shatter his infuriating composure.

His dark brows shot up in sardonic amusement. "What a novel idea—a woman who actually wants to work. Tell me, what sort of work can you do?" His question snapped out like a whip. "Can you push a plow?"

"No—"

"Can you drive a nail?"

"No."

"Can you milk a cow?"

53

"No!"

"Then you're useless to yourself and to anyone else, aren't you?" he pointed out mercilessly.

"I most certainly am not!" she denied with angry pride. "I can do all sorts of things, I can sew and cook and—"

"And set all the villagers gossiping about what monsters the Fieldings are for turning you out? Forget it," he said arrogantly. "I won't permit it."

"I do not remember *asking* for your permission," Victoria retorted defiantly.

Caught off guard, Jason stared hard at her. Grown men rarely dared to challenge him, yet here was this slip of a girl doing exactly that. If his annoyance hadn't matched his surprise, he would have chucked her under the chin and grinned at her courage. Suppressing the unprecedented urge to gentle his words, he said curtly, "If you're so eager to earn your keep, which I doubt, you can do it here."

"I'm very sorry," the defiant young beauty announced coolly, "but that won't do."

"Why not?"

"Because I simply cannot imagine myself bowing and scraping and quaking with fear each time you pass, like the rest of your servants are expected to do. Why, that poor man with the sore tooth nearly collapsed this morning when you—"

"Who?" Jason demanded, his ire momentarily replaced by stupefaction.

"Mr. O'Malley."

"Who the hell is Mr. O'Malley?" he bit out, controlling his temper with a supreme effort.

Victoria rolled her eyes in disgust. "You don't even know his name, do you? Mr. O'Malley is the footman who went for your breakfast, and his jaw is so swollen—"

Jason turned on his heel. "Charles wants you to stay here, and that's the end of it." In the doorway, he stopped and turned, his threatening gaze pinning her to the spot. "If you're thinking of leaving despite my orders, I'd advise you not to do it. You'll put me to the trouble of coming after you, and you won't like what happens when I find you, believe me."

"I am not frightened of you or your threats," Victoria lied proudly, rapidly trying to sort through her alternatives. She didn't want to hurt Charles by leaving, but neither would her pride permit her to be a "beggar" in Jason's home. Ignoring the ominous glitter in his green eyes, she said, "I'll stay, but I intend to work for my food and lodging here."

"Fine," Jason snapped, feeling as if she was somehow emerging the victor in this conflict. He turned to leave, but her businesslike voice stopped him.

"May I ask what my wages will be?"

Jason sucked in a furious breath. "Are you *trying* to irritate me?"

"Not at all. I merely wish to know what my wages will be, so I can plan for the day when I . . ." Her voice trailed off as Jason rudely stalked out.

Uncle Charles sent up word asking her to join him for lunch, which turned out to be a very enjoyable meal, since Jason wasn't present. However, the rest of the afternoon dragged and, in a fit of restlessness, Victoria decided to stroll outside. The butler saw her coming downstairs and swept open the front door for her. Trying to show him she harbored no ill will about yesterday, Victoria smiled at him. "Thank you very much, ah—?"

"Northrup," he provided, his manner polite, his expression carefully blank.

"Northrup?" Victoria repeated, hoping to draw him into conversation. "Is that your given name or your surname?"

His gaze slid to hers, then away. "Er—my surname, miss."

"I see," she continued politely. "And how long have you worked here?"

Northrup clasped his hands behind his back and rocked forward on the balls of his feet, looking solemn. "For nine generations, my family has been born and has died in service to the Fieldings, miss. I expect to carry on that proud tradition."

"Oh," Victoria said, carefully suppressing a chuckle at his profound pride in holding a job that seemed to entail nothing more important than opening and closing doors for people.

As if he read her thoughts, he added stiffly, "If you have

any problems with the staff, miss, bring them to me. As head of the household, I will endeavor to see that they are rectified immediately."

"I'm certain I won't need to do that. Everyone here is very efficient," Victoria said kindly. Too efficient, she thought as she wandered into the sunshine.

She walked across the front lawns, then shifted direction and went around the side of the house, intending to visit the stables to see the horses. With a half-formed idea of using apples to befriend them, Victoria went round to the back and asked directions to the kitchen.

The gigantic kitchen was filled with frantically busy people who were rolling out dough on wooden tables, stirring kettles, and chopping vegetables. In the center of the bedlam, an enormously fat man in a spotless white apron the size of a tablecloth stood like a frenzied monarch, waving a long-handled spoon and shouting instructions in French and English. "Excuse me," Victoria said to the woman at the nearest table. "May I have two apples and two carrots if you can spare them?"

The woman glanced uncertainly at the man in the white apron, who was glowering at Victoria; then she disappeared into another room adjoining the kitchen, returning a minute later with the apples and carrots. "Thank you, ah—?" Victoria said.

"Mrs. Northrup, miss," the woman said uneasily.

"How nice," Victoria replied with a sweet smile. "I've already met your husband, the butler, but he didn't tell me you worked here, also."

"Mr. Northrup is my brother-in-law," she corrected.

"Oh, I see," Victoria said, sensing the woman's reluctance to talk in front of the moody fat man, who seemed to be in charge. "Well, good day, Mrs. Northrup."

A flagstone path bordered by woods on the right led to the stables. Victoria walked along, admiring the splended vista of rolling, clipped lawns and lavish gardens on her left, when a sudden movement a few yards away on her right made her stop short and stare. At the perimeter of the woods, a huge gray animal was foraging about in what appeared to be a small compost pile. The animal caught her scent and raised its head, its feral gaze locking with hers, and Victoria's blood froze. *Wolf!* her mind screamed.

Paralyzed with terror, she stood rooted to the spot, afraid to move or make a sound, while her benumbed brain registered haphazard facts about the terrifying beast. The wolf's heavy gray coat was mangy-looking and thick, but not thick enough to hide its protruding ribs; it had terribly large jaws; its eyes were fierce. . . . Judging from the animal's grotesque gauntness, it appeared to be nearly starved to death. Which meant it would attack and eat anything it could catch—including herself. Victoria took a tiny, cautious step backward toward the safety of the house.

The animal snarled, its upper lip curling back, baring a set of huge white fangs to her view. Victoria reacted automatically, hurling her apples and carrots to him in a desperate effort to distract him from his obvious intention of eating *her.* Instead of pouncing on the missiles she'd thrown at him, as she expected him to, the animal jerked away from its garden feast and bolted into the woods with its tail between its legs. Victoria spun on her heel and raced into the house via the nearest back door, then ran to a window and peeked out at the woods. The wolf was standing just inside the perimeter of the trees, hungrily staring at the compost pile.

"Is something wrong, miss?" a footman asked, coming up behind her on his way toward the kitchen.

"I saw an animal," Victoria said breathlessly. "I think it was a—" She watched as the gray beast trotted stealthily back to the garden and gobbled the apples and carrots; then it ran back into the woods, its bushy tail still between its legs. The animal was frightened! she realized. And starved. "Do you have any dogs around here?" she asked, suddenly wondering if she'd been about to make a mistake that would make her appear exceedingly foolish.

"Yes, miss—several of 'em."

"Are any of them big, thin, and black and gray in color?"

"That'd be his lordship's old dog, Willie," he said. "He's always around here, beggin' fer somethin' to eat. He ain't mean, if that's worryin' you. Did you see him?"

"Yes," Victoria said, growing angry as she remembered how the starved creature had been gobbling spoiled vegetables from the compost pile as if they were beefsteaks. "And he's nearly starved. Someone ought to feed the poor thing."

"Willie always acts like he's starved," the footman replied with complete indifference. "His lordship says if he eats any more, he'll be too fat to walk."

"If he eats any less, he'll be too weak to live," Victoria retorted angrily. She could perfectly imagine that heartless man starving his own dog. How pathetic the animal looked with his ribs sticking out like that—how gruesome! She went back to the kitchen and requested another apple, some carrots, and a plate of table scraps.

Despite her sympathy, Victoria had to fight down her fear of the animal as she neared the compost pile and spotted him watching her from his hiding place just inside the woods. It was a dog, not a wolf, she could see that now. Remembering the footman's assurance that the dog wasn't vicious, Victoria walked as close to him as she dared and held out the plate of scraps. "Here, Willie," she said softly. "I've brought you some good food." Timidly, she took another step forward. Willie laid his ears back and bared his ivory fangs at her, and Victoria lost her courage. She put the plate down and fled toward the stables.

She dined with Charles that night, and since Jason was again absent, the meal was delightful; but when it was over and Charles retired, she again found herself with time on her hands. Other than her trip to the stables and her adventure with Willie, she had done nothing today except wander aimlessly around with nothing to do. Tomorrow, she decided happily, she would go to work. She was used to being busy and she desperately needed something more to fill her empty hours. She hadn't mentioned to Charles her intention of earning her keep, but she was certain that when he found out, he would be relieved that she was carrying her own weight and sparing him future tongue-lashings from his ill-tempered nephew.

She went up to her room and spent the rest of the evening trying to write a cheerful, optimistic letter to Dorothy.

Chapter Six

VICTORIA AWOKE EARLY THE NEXT MORNING TO THE sound of birds chirping in the tree outside her open windows. Rolling over onto her back, she gazed at a bright blue sky filled with huge, puffy white clouds, the sort of sky that positively beckoned her outdoors.

Washing and dressing hurriedly, she went downstairs to the kitchens to get food for Willie. Jason Fielding had sarcastically asked if she could push a plow or drive a nail or milk a cow. She couldn't do the first two, but she had often seen cows milked at home and it didn't look particularly difficult. Besides, after six weeks of confinement on the ship, any sort of physical activity was appealing.

She was about to leave the kitchen with a plate of scraps when a thought struck her. Ignoring the outraged stare of the man in the white apron, who Charles had told her last night was the chef and who was watching her as if she were a madwoman invading his pot-bedecked kingdom, she turned to Mrs. Northrup. "Mrs. Northrup, is there anything I could do—to help here in the kitchen, I mean?"

Mrs. Northrup's hand flew to her throat. "No, of course not."

Victoria sighed. "In that case, could you tell me where I will find the cows?"

"The cows?" Mrs. Northrup gasped. "What—whatever for?"

"To milk them," Victoria said.

The woman paled but said nothing, and after a puzzled moment, Victoria shrugged and decided to find them herself. She headed out the back door to search for Willie. Mrs. Northrup wiped the flour off her hands and headed straight for the front door to find Mr. Northrup.

As Victoria neared the compost pile, her eyes nervously scanned the woods for a sign of the dog. Willie—what an odd name for such a large, ferocious-looking animal, she thought. And then she saw him, lurking just inside the perimeter of the trees, watching her. The short hairs on the back of her neck stood up, but she carried the bowl of scraps as close to the woods as she dared. "Here, Willie," she coaxed softly. "I've brought your breakfast. Come get it."

The huge beast's eyes flickered to the plate in her hand, but he stayed where he was, watchful, alert.

"Won't you come a little closer?" Victoria continued, determined to befriend Jason Fielding's dog, since she could never befriend the man.

The dog was no more cooperative than his master. He refused to be coaxed and kept his threatening gaze focused on her. With a sigh, Victoria put the plate down and walked away.

A gardener directed her to where the cows were kept, and Victoria walked into the spotless barn, her nose tickled by the scent of sweet-smelling hay. She paused uncertainly as a dozen cows looked up, regarding her with huge, liquid brown eyes as she walked along the row of stalls. She stopped at one with a stool and bucket hanging on the wall, thinking that this cow would surely be the most likely prospect for milking. "Good morning," she said to the cow, patting its smooth face reassuringly while she tried to bolster her courage. Now that the moment was at hand, Victoria wasn't at all certain she remembered exactly how one went about milking a cow.

Stalling for time, she strolled around the cow and plucked a few pieces of straw from its tail, then reluctantly took down the stool and placed the bucket in position beneath the animal's pendulous udder. She sat down and slowly rolled up the sleeves of her gown, then arranged her skirts about her. Unaware of the man who had just stalked into the barn, she stroked the animal's flank and drew a long, hesitant breath. "I may as well be perfectly honest with you," she confessed to the cow. "The truth is—I haven't actually done this before."

Her rueful admission stopped Jason in mid-stride at the entrance to the stall, and his eyes warmed with fascinated amusement as he gazed at her. Seated upon the milking stool with her skirts spread about her as carefully as if she were seated upon a throne, Miss Victoria Seaton presented a very fetching picture. Her head was bent slightly as she concentrated on the task before her, providing him with a delightful view of her patrician profile with its elegant cheekbones and delicate little nose. Sunlight from the window above glinted in her hair, turning it into a shimmering red-gold waterfall that tumbled over her shoulders. Long curly eyelashes cast shadows on her smooth cheeks as she caught her lower lip between her teeth and reached down to move the bucket an inch forward.

The action drew Jason's gaze to the thrusting fullness of her breasts as they pushed invitingly against the bodice of her black gown, but her next words made his shoulders shake with laughter. "This," she told the cow in a revolted voice as she stretched her hands forward, "is going to be as embarrassing for me as it is for you."

Victoria touched the cow's fleshy teats and jerked her hands away with a loud "Ugh!" Then she tried again. She squeezed twice, quickly, then she leaned back and gazed hopefully at the bucket. No milk dropped into it. "Please, please, don't make this difficult," she implored the cow.

Twice more she repeated the same process, and still nothing happened. Frustration made her yank too hard the next time, which brought the cow's head swinging around as it glared reproachfully at her. "I'm doing my part," Victoria said, glaring right back, "the least you could do is yours!"

Behind her, a laughing masculine voice warned, "You'll curdle her milk if you glower at her like that."

Victoria jumped and whirled around on the stool, sending her coppery hair spilling over her left shoulder. "You!" she burst out, flushing in mortification at the scene he had obviously witnessed. "Why must you always creep up on people without a sound? The least you could do is—"

"Knock?" he suggested, his eyes glinting with laughter. With slow deliberation, he lifted his hand and rapped his knuckles twice upon the wooden beam. "Do you always talk to animals?" he asked conversationally.

Victoria was in no mood to be mocked, and she could see by the gleam in his eyes he was doing exactly that. With as much dignity as she could muster, she stood up, smoothed her skirts, and tried to walk past him.

His hand shot out and caught her arm in a firm but painless grip. "Aren't you going to finish milking?"

"You've already seen that I can't."

"Why not?"

Victoria put her chin up and looked him right in the eye. "Because I don't know how."

One dark brow lifted over an amused green eye. "Do you want to learn?"

"No," Victoria said, angry and humiliated. "Now, if you'll remove your hand from my arm—" She jerked her arm free without waiting for him to acquiesce. "—I'll try to find some other way to earn my keep here."

She felt his narrowed gaze on her as she walked away, but her thoughts soon shifted to Willie as she neared the house. She saw the dog, lurking just inside the woods, watching her. A chill skittered down her spine, but she ignored it. She had just been intimidated by a cow, and she adamantly refused to be cowed by a dog.

Jason watched her walk away, then shrugged off the memory of an angelic-looking milkmaid with sunlight in her hair and went back to the work he'd abandoned when Northrup rushed into his study to inform him that Miss Seaton had gone to milk the cows.

Sitting down at his desk, he glanced at his secretary. "Where were we, Benjamin?"

"You were dictating a letter to your man in Delhi, my lord."

Having failed to milk the cow, Victoria sought out the

gardener who had directed her to the barn. She went up to the bald man, who seemed to be in charge of the others, and asked if she could help plant the bulbs they were putting in the huge circular flower beds in the front courtyard.

"Stick to your duties at the barn and get out of our way, woman!" the bald gardener roared.

Victoria gave up. Without bothering to explain that she had no duties at the barn, she went in the opposite direction toward the back of the house to seek the only kind of work she was actually qualified to do—she went to the kitchen.

The head gardener watched her, threw down his trowel, and went to find Northrup.

Unobserved, Victoria stood just inside the kitchen, where eight servants were busily preparing what appeared to be a luncheon of stew complemented with fresh seasoned vegetables, flaky, newly baked bread, and a half dozen side dishes. Disheartened by her last two attempts to make herself useful, Victoria watched until she was absolutely certain she could actually handle this task; then she approached the volatile French chef. "I would like to help," she said firmly.

"Non!" he screamed, evidently believing her to be a servant in her plain black dress. "Out! Out! Get out. Go attend your duties."

Victoria was heartily sick of being treated like a useless idiot. Very politely, but very firmly, she said, "I can be of help here, and it is obvious from the way everyone is rushing about that you can use an extra pair of hands."

The chef looked ready to explode. "You are not trained," he thundered. "Get out! When André needs help, he will ask for it and *he* will do zee training!"

"There is nothing the least bit complicated about making a stew, monsieur," Victoria pointed out, exasperated. Ignoring his purpling complexion at her casual dismissal of the complexity of his culinary skills, she continued in a bright, reasonable tone, "All one has to do is cut up vegetables on this table here—" She tapped the table beside her. "—and toss them into that kettle there." She pointed to the one hanging above the fire.

An odd, strangled sound emerged from the apoplectic man before he tore off his apron. "In five minutes," he said as he stormed out of the kitchen, "I will have you thrown out of zis house!"

In the crackling silence he left behind, Victoria looked around at the remaining servants, who were staring at her in frozen horror, their eyes mirroring everything from sympathy to amusement. "Goodness, girl," a kindly, middle-aged woman said as she wiped flour from her hands onto her apron, "what possessed you to stir him up? He'll have you thrown out on your ear for this."

Except for the little maid named Ruth who looked after Victoria's room, this was the first friendly voice Victoria had heard from any of the servants in the entire house. Unfortunately, she was so miserable at having created trouble when she only wished to help that the woman's sympathy nearly reduced her to tears.

"Not that you weren't right," the woman continued, with a gentle pat on Victoria's arm, "about it bein' that simple to make a stew. Any one of us could carry on without André, but his lordship demands the best—and André is the best chef in the country. You may as well go and pack your things, for it's certain-sure you'll be turned off the place within the hour."

Victoria could scarcely trust her voice enough to reassure the woman on that head. "I'm a guest here, not a servant—I thought Mrs. Northrup would have told you that."

The woman's mouth dropped open. "No, miss, she did not. The staff isn't permitted to gossip, and Mrs. Northrup would be the last to do it, her bein' related by marriage to Mr. Northrup, the butler. I knew we had a guest stayin' at the house, but I—" Her eyes darted to Victoria's shabby-genteel black dress and the girl flushed. "May I fix you somethin' to eat?"

Victoria's shoulders drooped with frustrated despair. "No, but I'd—I'd like to make something to ease Mr. O'Malley's swollen jaw. It's a poultice, made of simple ingredients, but it might lessen the pain of his infected tooth."

The woman, who said her name was Mrs. Craddock, showed Victoria where to find the ingredients she asked for and Victoria went to work, fully expecting "his lordship" to come stalking into the kitchen and publicly humiliate her at any moment.

Jason had just started to dictate the same letter he'd been dictating when he learned Victoria had gone out to the barn to milk a cow, when Northrup again tapped on the door of his study.

"Yes," Jason snapped impatiently, when the butler was before him. "What is it now?"

The butler cleared his throat. "It's Miss Seaton again, my lord. She . . . er . . . that is, she attempted to assist the head gardener with his planting of the flower beds. He mistook her for a servant, and now he wonders, since I informed him she is not a servant, if you are displeased with his work and sent her there to—"

Jason's low voice vibrated with annoyance. "Tell the gardener to get back to work, then tell Miss Seaton to stay out of his way. And you," he added darkly, "stay out of mine. I have work to do." Jason turned to his thin, bespectacled secretary and snapped, "Now, where were we, Benjamin?"

"The letter to your man in Delhi, my lord."

Jason had dictated only two lines when there was a commotion outside his door and the cook barged in, followed by Northrup, who was trying to outrun him and block his path. "Either she goes, or I go!" Monsieur André boomed, marching up to Jason's desk. "I do not permit that red-haired wench in my kitchen!"

With deadly calm, Jason laid down his quill and turned his glittering green gaze on the chef's glaring face. "What did you say to me?"

"I said I do not permit—"

"Get out," Jason said in a silky-soft voice.

The cook's round face paled. *"Oui,"* he said hastily, as he began backing away, "I will return to the kitch—"

"Out of my *house,*" Jason clarified ruthlessly, "and off my property. Now!" Surging to his feet, Jason brushed past the perspiring chef and headed for the kitchens.

Everyone in the kitchens jumped and spun around at the sound of his incensed voice. "Can any of you cook?" he demanded, and Victoria assumed that the chef had resigned because of her. Horrified, she started to step forward, but Jason's ominous gaze impaled her, threatening her with dire consequences if she dared to volunteer. He looked around at the others in angry disgust. "Do you mean to tell me none of you can cook?"

Mrs. Craddock hesitated, then stepped forward. "I can, my lord."

Jason nodded curtly. "Good. You're in charge. In future, please dispense with those nauseatingly rich French sauces I've been forced to eat." He turned the icy blast of his gaze on Victoria. "You," he ordered ominously, "stay *out* of the barn and leave the gardening to the gardeners and the cooking to the cooks!"

He left, and the servants turned to Victoria, looking at her with a mixture of shock and shy gratitude. Too ashamed of the trouble she'd caused to meet their eyes, Victoria bent her head and began mixing the poultice for Mr. O'Malley.

"Let's go to work," Mrs. Craddock said to the others in a brisk, smiling voice. "We have yet to prove to his lordship that we can manage very well without having our ears boxed and our knuckles rapped by André."

Victoria's head snapped up, her shocked gaze flying to Mrs. Craddock.

"He is an evil-tempered tyrant," the woman confirmed. "And we are deeply grateful to be rid of him."

With the exception of the day her parents died, Victoria couldn't remember a worse day than this one. She picked up the bowl containing the mixture her father had taught her to make to ease the pain of an afflicted tooth and walked out.

Failing to find O'Malley, she went searching for Northrup, who was just emerging from a book-lined room. Beyond the partially open doors, she glimpsed Jason seated at his desk with a letter in his hand, talking to a bespectacled gentleman who was sitting across from him.

"Mr. Northrup," she said in a suffocated voice as she handed him the bowl, "would you be kind enough to give this to Mr. O'Malley? Tell him to apply it to his tooth and gum several times a day. It will help take away the pain and swelling."

Distracted yet again by the sound of voices outside his study, Jason slapped the paper he was reading onto the desk and stalked to the door of his study, jerking it open. Unaware of Victoria, who had started up the staircase, he demanded of Northrup, *"Now* what the hell has she done?"

"She—she made this for O'Malley's tooth, my lord," Northrup said in a queer, strained voice as he raised his puzzled gaze to the dejected figure climbing the stairs.

Jason followed his gaze and his eyes narrowed on the slender, curvaceous form garbed in mourning black. "Victoria," he called.

Victoria turned, braced for a tongue-lashing, but he spoke in a calm, clipped voice that nevertheless rang with implacable authority. "Do not wear black anymore. I dislike it."

"I'm very sorry my clothes offend you," she replied with quiet dignity, "but I am in mourning for my parents."

Jason's brows snapped together, but he held his tongue until Victoria was out of hearing. Then he told Northrup, "Send someone to London to get her some decent clothes, and get rid of those black rags."

When Charles came down for lunch, a subdued Victoria slid into the chair on his left. "Good heavens, child, what's amiss? You're as pale as a ghost."

Victoria confessed her follies of the morning and Charles listened, his lips trembling with amusement. "Excellent, excellent!" he said when she was finished and, to her amazement, started to chuckle. "Go ahead and disrupt Jason's life, my dear. That is *exactly* what he needs. On the surface he may appear cold and hard, but that is only a shell—a thick one, I'll admit, but the right woman could get past that and discover the gentleness inside him. When she does bring out that gentleness, Jason will make her a very happy woman. Among other things, he is an extremely generous man. . . ." He raised his brows, letting the sentence hang, and Victoria stirred uneasily beneath his intent gaze, wondering if Charles could possibly be harboring the hope that she was that woman.

Not for a moment did she believe there was any gentleness inside Jason Fielding and, moreover, she wanted as little to do with him as possible. Rather than tell that to Uncle Charles, she tactfully changed the subject. "I should receive word from Andrew in the next few weeks."

"Ah, yes—Andrew," he said, his eyes darkening.

67

Chapter Seven

CHARLES TOOK HER FOR A CARRIAGE RIDE TO THE neighboring village the next day, and although the outing filled her with nostalgic homesickness for her former home, she enjoyed herself immensely. Flowers bloomed everywhere—in flower boxes and gardens where loving care was lavished upon them, and wild on the hills and in the meadows, tended only by mother nature. The village with its neat cottages and cobbled streets was utterly charming and Victoria fell in love with it.

Each time they emerged from one of the little shops along the street, the villagers who saw them stopped and stared and doffed their hats. They called Charles "your grace," and although Victoria could tell that he was usually at a loss for their names, he treated them with unaffected pleasantness, regardless of their station in life.

By the time they returned to Wakefield Park that afternoon, Victoria felt much more optimistic about her new life and was hoping for the opportunity to know the villagers better.

To avoid causing any more trouble for herself, she limited the rest of her day's activities to reading in her own room and two more forays to the compost pile, where she tried unsuccessfully to coax Willie to come closer to her for his food.

She lay down before supper and fell asleep, lulled by the notion that further dissension between herself and Jason Fielding could be avoided if she simply stayed out of his way, as she had thus far today.

She was wrong. When she awakened, Ruth was placing an armful of pastel frocks in the armoire. "Those aren't mine, Ruth," Victoria said sleepily, frowning in the candlelight as she climbed out of bed.

"Yes, miss, they are!" Ruth said enthusiastically. "His lordship sent to London for them."

"Please inform him that I won't wear them," Victoria said with firm politeness.

Ruth's hand flew to her throat. "Oh, no, miss, I couldn't do that. Really I couldn't!"

"Well, I can!" Victoria said, already heading to the other armoire in search of her own clothes.

"They're gone," Ruth said miserably. "I—I carried them out. His lordship's orders—"

"I understand," Victoria said gently, but within her she felt a temper she didn't know she possessed come to a simmering boil.

The little maid wrung her hands, her pale eyes hopeful. "Miss, his lordship said I may have the position of your personal maid, if I'm able to do it properly."

"I don't need a maid, Ruth."

The girl's shoulders sagged. "It would be so much nicer than what I do now. . . ."

Victoria wasn't proof against that pleading expression on her face. "Very well, then," she sighed, trying to force a smile to her lips. "What does a 'personal maid' do?"

"Well, I help you dress and make certain-sure your gowns are always clean and pressed. And I fix your hair, too. May I? Fix your hair, I mean? You have such beautiful hair, and my ma always said I have a way with hair—makin' it look pretty, I mean."

Victoria agreed, not because she cared for having her hair styled, but because she needed time to calm herself before she confronted Jason Fielding. An hour later, dressed in a flowing peach silk gown with wide, full sleeves that were trimmed with horizontal strips of peach satin ribbon, Victoria silently surveyed herself in the mirror. Her heavy copper hair had been twisted into burnished curls at the crown and entwined with peach satin ribbons, her high cheekbones were tinted with rich, angry color, and her brilliant sapphire eyes were sparkling with resentment and shame.

She had never seen, never imagined, a gown as glorious as the one she wore, with its low-cut, tightly fitted bodice that forced her breasts high and exposed a daring expanse of flesh. And she had never taken less pleasure in her appearance than she did now, when she was being forced to display a frivolous disregard for her dead parents.

"Oh, miss," Ruth said, clasping her hands in satisfied delight, "you're so beautiful, his lordship won't believe his eyes when he sees you."

Ruth's prediction was true, but Victoria was too furious to derive the slightest gratification from Jason's stunned expression when she walked into the dining room.

"Good evening, Uncle Charles," she said, pressing her cheek to his as Jason came to his feet. Rebelliously she turned and faced him, standing in resentful silence while his gaze slid boldly over her, from the top of her shining red-gold curls to the swelling flesh exposed above her bodice and right down to the toes of the dainty satin slippers he had provided. Victoria was somewhat accustomed to the admiring glances of gentlemen, but there was nothing gentlemanly about Jason's insolent, lazy perusal of her body. "Are you quite finished?" she asked tersely.

His unhurried gaze lifted to her eyes and a wry smile quirked his stern lips when he heard the antagonism in her voice. He reached forward and Victoria took a quick, automatic step backward, before she realized he simply intended to pull out her chair.

"Have I made another social blunder—like failing to knock?" he inquired in a low, amused voice, his lips offensively close to her cheek as she took her seat. "Is it not the custom in America for a gentleman to seat a lady?"

Victoria jerked her head away. "Are you seating me, or trying to eat my ear?"

His lips twitched. "I may do that," he replied, "if the new

cook provides us with a poor meal." He glanced at Charles as he returned to his own seat. "I dismissed the fat Frenchman," he explained.

Victoria felt a momentary pang of guilt for her part in the affair, but she was so angry at Jason's peremptory disposal of her gowns that not even guilt could take the edge off her anger. Intending to have the matter out with him in private, *after* dinner, she directed all her conversation to Charles; but as the meal continued, she became uncomfortably aware that Jason Fielding was studying her across the brace of candles in the center of the table.

Jason lifted his wineglass to his lips, watching her. She was furious with him, he knew, for having those shabby black gowns taken away, and she was dying to loose a tirade at his head—he could see it in those flashing eyes of hers.

What a proud, spirited beauty she was, he thought impartially. She had seemed a pretty little thing before, but he hadn't expected her to blossom into a full-fledged beauty tonight, simply by shedding those unflattering black gowns. Perhaps he hated the dismal mourning color so much that it had tainted his view of her. Either way, he had no doubt Victoria Seaton had led the boys back home a merry chase. No doubt she would dazzle the boys in England, too. Dazzle the boys *and* men, he corrected himself.

And therein lay his problem: despite her lush, alluring curves and that intoxicating face, he was rapidly becoming convinced she was an inexperienced innocent, exactly as Charles had claimed. An inexperienced innocent who had landed on his doorstep, and for whom he was now unwillingly responsible. The image of himself as her protector— the fierce guardian of a young maiden's virtue—was so ludicrous that he nearly laughed aloud, yet that was the role he was going to be forced to play. Everyone who knew him would surely find it as preposterous as he did, considering his notorious reputation with women.

O'Malley poured more wine into his glass, and Jason drank it while trying to decide the most expedient way to get her safely off his hands. The more he considered it, the more convinced he became that he ought to provide her with the London season that Charles was so anxious that she have.

With Victoria's lush beauty, it would be easy enough to launch her successfully into society. And with the added attraction of a small dowry, provided by himself, it would be equally easy to get her safely wed to some suitable London fop. On the other hand, if she really believed her Andrew would come for her, she might insist upon waiting for months, even years, before accepting another man, and that possibility did not suit Jason at all.

In line with his half-formed plan, he waited until there was a break in the talk and said to her in a deceptively casual tone, "Charles tells me that you are practically betrothed to . . . er . . . Anson? Albert?"

Victoria's head snapped around. "Andrew," she said.

"What is he like?" Jason prodded.

A fond smile drifted across Victoria's features as she thought about that. "He is gentle, handsome, intelligent, kind, considerate—"

"I think I have the general idea," Jason interrupted dryly. "Take my advice and forget about him."

Suppressing the urge to throw something at him, Victoria said, "Why?"

"He isn't the man for you. In four days, you've turned my household upside down. What possible sport could you have with a staid country bumpkin who will want to lead a peaceful, organized life? You'd be wise to forget him and make the most of your opportunities here."

"In the first place—" Victoria burst out, but Jason interrupted her, deliberately sowing seeds of discontent. "Of course, there's every chance that if *you* don't forget about Albert, Albert will probably forget about *you*. Isn't the saying 'out of sight, out of mind'?"

Holding onto her temper with a superhuman effort, Victoria clamped her teeth together and said nothing.

"What, no argument?" Jason prodded, admiring the way anger turned her eyes to a smoky midnight blue.

Victoria lifted her chin. "In my country, Mr. Fielding, it is considered ill-bred to argue at the table."

Her veiled reprimand filled him with amusement. "How very inconvenient for you," he remarked softly.

Charles leaned back in his chair, a tender smile curving his lips as he watched his son spar with the young beauty who reminded him so much of her mother. They were perfect for each other, he decided. Victoria wasn't in awe of Jason. Her spirit and warmth would gentle him, and once gentled, he would become the sort of husband young girls dream of having. They would make each other happy, she would give Jason a son.

Filled with contentment and joy, Charles imagined the grandson they would give him once they were married. After all these years of emptiness and despair, he and Katherine were actually going to have grandchildren together. True, Jason and Victoria were not getting along so well right now, but that was to be expected. Jason was a hard, experienced, embittered man, with good reason. But Victoria had Katherine's courage, her gentleness, her fire. And Katherine had changed his own life. She had taught him the meaning of love. And loss. His mind drifted back over the events of the past that had led up to this momentous evening. . . .

By the time he was twenty-two, Charles already had a well-deserved reputation as a libertine, gambler, and rake-hell. He had no responsibilities, no restrictions, and absolutely no prospects, for his older brother had already inherited the ducal title and everything that went with it—everything excluding money, that is. Money was ever in short supply, because for 400 years, the Fielding men had all exhibited a strong proclivity toward all manner of expensive vices. In fact, Charles was no worse than his father, or his father's father before him. Charles's younger brother was the only Fielding ever to show a desire to fight the devil's temptations, but he did it with typical Fielding excess by deciding to become a missionary and go off to India.

At approximately that same time, Charles's French mistress announced she was pregnant. When Charles offered her money, not matrimony, she wept and ranted at him, but to no avail. Finally she left him in a rage. A week after Jason was born, she returned to Charles's lodgings, unceremoniously dumped their child into his arms, and disappeared. Charles had no desire to be saddled with a baby, yet he could not bring himself to simply abandon the boy to an orphans' home. In a moment of sheer inspiration, he hit upon the idea of giving Jason to his younger brother and his ugly wife, who were about to leave for India "to convert the heathens."

Without any hesitation, he gave the baby to these two God-fearing, childless, religious zealots—along with nearly every cent he had, to be used for Jason's care—and washed his hands of the whole problem.

Until then he had managed to support himself well enough at the gaming tables, but capricious luck, which had always been with him, eventually deserted him. By the time he was thirty-two, Charles was compelled to face the fact that he could no longer maintain a reasonably genteel standard of living, as befitted a man of his birth, with the proceeds of his gambling alone. His problem was common to the impecunious younger sons of great noble houses, and Charles solved it in the time-honored way: he decided to exchange his illustrious family name for a fat dowry. With careless indifference, he proposed marriage to the daughter of a wealthy merchant, a young lady of great wealth, some beauty, and little intelligence.

The young lady and her father eagerly accepted his suit, and Charles's older brother, the duke, even agreed to give a party to celebrate the forthcoming nuptials.

It was on that auspicious occasion that Charles again encountered his very distant cousin, Katherine Langston, the eighteen-year-old granddaughter of the Duchess of Claremont. When last he had seen her, he had been paying a rare visit to his brother at Wakefield and Katherine had been a child of ten, staying for the holidays at a neighboring estate. For an entire fortnight she had followed him nearly everywhere he went, gazing at him with open adoration in her big blue eyes. He had thought her an uncommonly pretty little moppet then, with an enchanting smile and more spirit than females twice her age, as she took fences beside him astride her mare and charmed him into flying kites with her.

Now she had grown into a young woman of breathtaking beauty, and Charles could scarcely tear his eyes from her. With an outward appearance of bored impassivity, he studied her stunning figure, her flawless features, and her glorious red-gold hair as she stood off to the side of the crowded room, looking serene and ethereal. Then he strolled over to her with a glass of Madeira in one hand and casually draped his other arm across the mantel, boldly and openly admiring her beauty. He expected her to voice a token objection to his forwardness, but Katherine did not voice any objection at all. She did not blush beneath his frank appraisal, nor did she turn away from it. She simply tipped her head to the side as if she was waiting for him to finish. "Hello, Katherine," he said finally.

"Hello, Charles," she answered, her soft voice calm, unruffled.

"Are you finding the party as insufferably dull as I am, my dear?" he asked, surprised at her composure.

Instead of stammering some inanity about it being a delightful party, Katherine had raised her disconcertingly direct blue gaze to his and quietly replied, "It is a fitting prelude to a marriage that is to be undertaken for cold, monetary reasons, and no other."

Her blunt candor amazed him, but not nearly as much as the strange, accusing look that darkened her blue eyes before she turned and started to walk away. Without thinking, Charles reached out to stop her from leaving. The touch of her bare arm beneath his hand sent a tingling jolt through his entire nervous system, a jolt that Katherine must also have felt because her whole body stiffened. Instead of drawing her toward him, Charles guided her forward, out onto the balcony. In the moonlight he turned to her and, because her accusation had stung, his voice was hard. "It's presumptuous of you to assume money is my only reason for marrying Amelia. People have other reasons for marrying."

Again those disconcerting blue eyes of hers gazed into his. "Not people like us," she contradicted calmly. "We marry to increase our family's wealth, power, or social position. In your case, you are marrying to increase your wealth."

Charles was, of course, trading his aristocratic lineage to gain money, and although it was a commonly accepted practice, she made him feel less of a man for doing so. "And what about you?" he taunted. "Will you not marry for one of those reasons?"

"No," she replied softly. "I will not. I will marry because I love someone, and am loved in return. I will not settle for a marriage like my parents had. I want more from life than that and I have more to give."

The softly spoken words had been filled with such quiet conviction that Charles had simply stared at her before he finally said, "Your lady grandmother will not be pleased if you marry for love and not position, my dear. Gossip has it that she wants an alliance with the Winstons and she means for you to secure it for her."

Katherine smiled for the first time, a slow, enchanting smile that illuminated her face and turned Charles's bones to water. "My grandmother and I," she said lightly, "have long been at outs over this matter, but I am as determined as she to have my way."

She looked so beautiful, so fresh and unspoiled, that the armor of cynicism that had surrounded Charles for thirty years began to melt, leaving him suddenly lonely and empty. Without realizing what he was doing, he lifted his hand and reverently traced her smooth cheek with his fingertips. "I hope the man you love is worthy of you," he said tenderly.

For an endless moment, Katherine had searched his features as if she could see beyond his face, into his tired, disillusioned soul. "I think," she whispered softly, "that it will be more a question of whether *I* can be worthy of *him*. You see, he needs me rather badly, although he is only just now coming to realize it."

After a moment her meaning slammed into him, and Charles heard himself groan her name with the sudden feverish longing of a man who has just found what he has unconsciously been searching for his entire life—a woman who could love him for himself, for the man he could be, the man he wanted to be. And Katherine had no other reason to want him or love him; her bloodline was as aristocratic as his own, her connections far better, her wealth vastly superior.

Charles gazed at her, trying to deny the feelings that were coursing through him. This was insane, he told himself. He scarcely knew her. He was no young fool who believed that grown men and women tumbled into love with one another at first glance. He had not even believed in love at all until that moment. But he believed in it now, for he wanted this beautiful, intelligent, idealistic girl to love him and only him. For once in his life, he had found something rare and fine and unspoiled, and he was determined to keep this girl that way—to marry her and cherish her, to protect her from the cynicism that seemed to erode everyone in their social class.

The prospect of eventually breaking his betrothal to Amelia did not trouble his conscience, for he harbored no illusions as to her reasons for agreeing to marry him. She was attracted to him, he knew, but she was marrying him because her father wanted to be allied with the nobility.

For two blissful, magnificent weeks, Katherine and he had managed to keep their growing love a secret; two weeks of stolen moments alone, of quiet walks through the countryside, of shared laughter and dreams of the future.

At the end of that time, Charles could no longer put off the required meeting with the Dowager Duchess of Claremont. He wanted to marry Katherine.

He was prepared for the duchess to object, for although his family was an old and noble one, he was an untitled younger son. Still, such marriages took place often enough, and he had expected her to put up a token argument and then capitulate because Katherine wanted this union as badly as he. He had *not* expected her to be almost demented with wrath, or to call him a "dissolute opportunist" and a "corrupt, lecherous degenerate." He hadn't expected her to rail about his ancestors' and his own promiscuous behavior, or to call his forebears "irresponsible madmen, one and all."

But most of all, he had not expected her to swear that if Katherine married him, she would disown her and cut her off without a cent. Such things simply weren't done. But when he left the house that day, Charles knew the woman would do exactly as she threatened. He returned to his lodgings and spent the night in alternate states of rage and despair. By morning, he knew that he could not—would not—marry Katherine, for although he was willing to try to earn an honest living, with his own two hands if need be, he could not bear to see his proud, beautiful Katherine brought low because of him. He would not cause her to be cut off from her family and publicly shunned by society.

Even if he thought he could make up to her for the disgrace she would endure, he knew he could never let her become a common house-drudge. She was young and idealistic and in love with him, but she was also accustomed to beautiful gowns and servants to do her every bidding. If he had to work for a living he could not possibly give her those things. Katherine had never washed a dish, or scrubbed a floor, or pressed a shirt, and he would not see her reduced to doing these things because she had been foolish enough to love him.

When he was finally able to arrange a brief, clandestine meeting with her the following day, Charles told her of his decision. Katherine argued that the luxuries of life meant nothing to her; she pleaded with him to take her to America, where it was said any man could make a decent living if he was only willing to work for it.

Unable to endure her tears or his own anguish, Charles had gruffly told her that her ideas were foolish, that she could never survive a life in America. She had looked at him as if *he* was afraid to work for a living, and then she had brokenly accused him of wanting her dowry, not her— exactly as her grandmother had told her he did.

To Charles, who was unselfishly sacrificing his own happiness for her, her accusation had cut like a knife. "Believe that if you wish," he had snapped, forcing himself to turn away from her before he lost his resolve and eloped with her that very day. He started for the door, but he could not bear to have her think he had only wanted her money. "Katherine," he said, pausing without turning. "I beg you not to believe that of me."

"I don't," she whispered brokenly. Neither did she believe he would put an end to their hopeless, tormented longing for each other by marrying Amelia the following week. But that was exactly what Charles did. It was the first entirely unselfish act of his life.

Katherine attended his wedding with her grandmother, and for as long as he lived, Charles would never forget the look of betrayal in Katherine's eyes when he finished pledging his life to another woman.

Two months later, she married an Irish physician and left with him for America. She did it, Charles knew, because she was furious with her grandmother and because she could not bear to remain in England near Charles and his new wife. And she did it to prove to him, in the only way she knew how, that her love for him could have survived anything— including a life in America.

That same year, Charles's older brother was killed in a

stupid drunken duel and Charles inherited the dukedom. He did not inherit a great deal of money with the title, but it would have been enough to keep Katherine in modest luxury. But Katherine was gone; he had not believed that her love was strong enough to withstand a few discomforts. Charles didn't care about the money he inherited; Charles didn't care about anything anymore.

Not long afterward, Charles's missionary brother died in India, and sixteen years later, Charles's wife Amelia died.

The night of Amelia's funeral, Charles got thoroughly blindly inebriated, as he often did in those days, but on that particular night, as he sat in the gloomy solitude of his house, a new thought occurred to him: someday soon he, too, was going to die. And when he did, the ducal holdings would pass out of the hands of the Fieldings forever. Because Charles had no heir.

For sixteen years, Charles had lived in an odd, empty limbo, but on that fateful night as he contemplated his meaningless life, something began to grow within him. At first it was only a vague restlessness, then it became disgust; it grew into resentment, and then slowly, very slowly, it built into fury. He had lost Katherine; he had lost sixteen years of his life. He had endured a vapid wife, a loveless marriage, and now he was going to die without an heir. For the first time in 400 years, the ducal title was in danger of passing entirely out of the Fielding family, and Charles was suddenly determined not to throw it away, as he had thrown away the rest of his life.

True, the Fieldings had not been a particularly honorable or worthy family, but, by God, the title belonged to them and Charles was determined to keep it there.

In order to do that he needed an heir, which meant he would have to marry again. After all his youthful sexual exploits, the thought of climbing atop a woman now and fathering an heir seemed more tiresome than exciting. He thought wryly of all the pretty wenches he had bedded long ago—of the beautiful French ballerina who had been his mistress and had presented him with a bastard. . . .

Joy brought him surging to his feet. He didn't need to marry again, because he already had an heir! He had Jason. Charles wasn't certain if the laws of succession would allow the ducal title to pass to a bastard son, but it made no difference to him. Jason was a Fielding, and those very few people who had known of Jason's existence in India believed he was the very legitimate son of Charles's younger brother. Besides, old King Charles had bestowed a dukedom on three of his bastards, and now he, Charles Fielding, Duke of Atherton, was about to follow suit.

The next day, Charles hired investigators to make inquiries, but it was two long years before one of the investigators finally sent a report to Charles with specific information. No trace could be found of Charles's sister-in-law, but Jason had been discovered in Delhi, where he had apparently amassed a fortune in the shipping and trading business. The report began with Jason's current direction; it ended with all the information the investigator had discovered about Jason's past.

Charles's proud exultation at Jason's financial successes promptly dissolved into horror and then sick fury as he read of his sister-in-law's depraved abuse of the innocent child he had handed into her care. When he was finished, he vomited.

More determined now than ever to make Jason his rightful heir, Charles sent him a letter, asking him to return to England so that he could formally acknowledge him as such.

When Jason didn't reply, Charles, with a determination that had long been dormant in his character, set off for Delhi himself. Filled with inexpressible remorse and absolute resolve, he went to Jason's magnificent home. In their first meeting, he saw firsthand what the investigator's report had already told him: Jason had married and fathered a son and was living like a king. He also made it very clear that he wanted nothing to do with Charles, or with the legacy Charles was trying to offer him. In the ensuing months, while Charles stubbornly remained in India, he slowly succeeded in convincing his cold, reticent son that he had never condoned or imagined the unspeakable abuses Jason had suffered as a child. But he could not convince him to return to England as his heir.

Jason's beautiful wife, Melissa, was enthralled with the idea of going to London as the Marchioness of Wakefield, but neither her tantrums nor Charles's pleadings had the slightest effect on Jason. Jason didn't give a damn for titles, nor did he possess an ounce of sympathy for the Fieldings' impending loss of a duchy.

Charles had nearly given up when he hit upon the perfect argument. One night, while he was watching Jason play with his little son, it dawned on him there was one person Jason would do anything for: Jamie. Jason positively doted on the little boy. And so Charles immediately changed his tack. Instead of trying to convince Jason of the benefits to be had for himself by returning to England, he pointed out that by refusing to permit Charles to make him his heir, Jason was denying little Jamie his birthright. The title, and all that went with it, would eventually be Jamie's.

It worked.

Jason appointed a competent man to handle his business in Delhi and moved his family to England. With every intention of building a "kingdom" for his little boy, Jason voluntarily spent enormous sums of money restoring the rundown Atherton estates to a splendor far beyond any they had ever possessed.

While Jason was busily supervising the restoration work, Melissa rushed off to London to take her rightful place in society as the new Marchioness of Wakefield. Within a year, gossip about her amorous affairs was raging through London like wildfire. A few months later, she and the child were dead. . . .

Charles shook himself from his sad reverie and glanced up as the covers were being removed from the table. "Shall we depart from custom tonight?" he suggested to Victoria. "Instead of the men remaining at the table for port and cigars, would you object if we had them with you in the drawing room? I'm loathe to give up your company."

Victoria was unaware of the custom, but in any case she was perfectly happy to break it and said so. When she was about to enter the rose and gold drawing room, however, Charles drew her back and said in a low voice, "I notice you've put off mourning early, my dear. If that was your decision, I applaud it—your mother hated black; she told me that when she was a little girl and was forced to wear it for her own parents." Charles's penetrating gaze held hers. "Was it your decision, Victoria?"

"No," Victoria admitted. "Mr. Fielding had my clothes removed and replaced with these today."

He nodded sagely. "Jason has an aversion to symbols of mourning, and judging from the dagger-glances you threw his way at supper, you aren't happy about what he's done. You should tell him so," he said. "Don't let him intimidate you, child; he can't abide cowards."

"But I don't want to upset you," Victoria said worriedly. "You said your heart isn't strong."

"Don't worry about me," he said, chuckling. "My heart is a little weak, but not so weak it can't take some excitement. In fact, it would probably do me a world of good. Life was incredibly dull before you arrived."

When Jason was seated and enjoying his port and cigar, Victoria tried several times to do as Charles had bidden her, but each time she looked at Jason and tried to bring up the matter of her clothing, her courage deserted her. He had dressed for dinner tonight in beautifully tailored charcoal gray trousers and matching coat, with a dark blue waistcoat and a pearl gray silk shirt. Despite his elegant attire and the casual way he had stretched his long legs out in front of him and crossed them at the ankles, he seemed to radiate barely leashed, ruthless power. There was something primitive and dangerous about him, and she had the uneasy feeling that his elegant clothing and indolent stance were nothing but disguises meant to lull the unwary into believing he was civilized, when he wasn't civilized at all.

He shifted slightly and Victoria stole another glance at him. His dark head was tilted back, his thin cigar clamped between his even white teeth, his hands resting on the arms of his wing chair, his tanned features cast into shadow. A chill crept up her spine as she wondered what dark secrets lay hidden in his past. Surely there must be many to have made him so cynical and unapproachable. He looked like the sort of man who had seen and done all sorts of terrible, forbidden things—things that had hardened him and made him cold. Yet he was handsome—wickedly, dangerously handsome with his panther-black hair, green eyes, and superb build. Victoria couldn't deny that, and if she weren't half-afraid of him most of the time, she would have liked to talk to him. How tempting it would be to try to befriend him—as tempting as sin, she admitted to herself—as foolish as trying to befriend the devil. And probably just as dangerous.

Victoria drew a careful breath, preparing to politely but firmly insist that her mourning clothes be returned, just as Northrup appeared and announced the arrival of Lady Kirby and Miss Kirby.

Victoria saw Jason stiffen and shoot a sardonic glance at Charles, who responded with a bewildered shrug and turned to Northrup. "Send them away—" he began, but he was too late.

"No need to announce us, Northrup," said a firm voice, and a stout woman sailed into the salon, trailed by puce satin skirts, heavy perfume, and a lovely brunette about Victoria's age. "Charles!" Lady Kirby said, beaming at him. "I heard you were in the village today with a young lady named Miss Seaton, and naturally I had to see her for myself."

Scarcely taking time to draw a breath, she turned to Victoria and said brightly, "You must be Miss Seaton." She paused, her narrowed eyes scrutinizing every feature on Victoria's face in a way that gave Victoria the feeling she was looking for flaws. She found one. "What an intriguing dent in your chin, my dear. However did it happen? An accident?"

"Of birth," Victoria averred, smiling, much too fascinated by the peculiar woman to be offended. In fact, she was beginning to wonder if England was filled with intriguing, ill-mannered, blunt people whose eccentricities were either encouraged or overlooked because of their titles and excessive wealth.

"How sad," said Lady Kirby. "Does it bother you—or hurt?"

Victoria's lips trembled with laughter. "Only when I look in the mirror, ma'am," she replied.

Dissatisfied, Lady Kirby swung away and confronted Jason, who had arisen and was standing at the fireplace, his elbow propped on the mantel. "So, Wakefield," she said, "from the looks of things here, the announcement in the paper would seem to be correct. I'll tell you the truth—I never believed it. Well, was it?"

Jason lifted his brows. "Was it what?"

Charles's voice boomed out, drowning Lady Kirby's words. "Northrup, bring the ladies some refreshment!" Everyone sat down, Miss Kirby taking the chair beside Jason, while Charles swiftly embarked on an animated discussion of the weather. Lady Kirby listened impatiently until Charles ran out of monologue; then she turned abruptly to Jason and said pointedly, "Wakefield, is your engagement on or off?"

Jason raised his glass to his lips, his eyes cold. "Off."

Victoria saw the varying reactions to that one word on the faces around her. Lady Kirby looked satisfied, her daughter looked delighted, Charles looked miserable, and Jason's face was inscrutable. Victoria's sympathetic heart instantly went out to him. No wonder Jason seemed so grim and callous—the woman he loved must have broken their engagement. It struck her as odd, however, when the Kirby ladies turned to her as if they expected her to say something.

Victoria smiled blankly, and Lady Kirby took up the conversational gauntlet. "Well, Charles, in that case, I gather you mean to bring out poor Miss Seaton during the season?"

"I intend to see that *Countess Langston* takes her rightful place in society," he corrected coolly.

"Countess Langst—" Lady Kirby gasped.

Charles inclined his head. "Victoria is Katherine Langston's oldest child. Unless I mistake the rules of succession, she is now heir to her mother's Scottish title."

"Even so," Lady Kirby said stiffly, "you'll not have an easy time making a suitable match for her." She turned to Victoria, oozing feigned sympathy. "Your mama created quite a scandalbroth when she ran off with that Irish laborer."

Indignation on her mother's behalf shot white-hot sparks through Victoria's entire body. "My mother *married* an Irish *physician*," she corrected.

"Without her grandmother's permission," Lady Kirby countered. "Gently bred girls do not marry against their families' wishes in this country." The obvious implication that Katherine was not gently bred made Victoria so angry she dug her fingernails into her palms.

"Oh, well, society eventually forgets these things," Lady Kirby continued generously. "In the meantime, you will have much to learn before you can be presented. You will have to learn the proper forms of address for each peer, his wife and children, and of course there's the etiquette involved in paying calls and the more complicated problems of learning seating arrangements. That alone takes months to master—whom you may seat next to whom at table, I mean. Colonials are ignorant of such things, but we English place the greatest importance on these matters of propriety."

"Perhaps that explains why we always defeat you in war," Victoria suggested sweetly, goaded into defending her family and her country.

Lady Kirby's eyes narrowed. "I meant no offense. However, you shall have to curb your tongue if you hope to make a suitable match as well as live down your mother's reputation."

Victoria stood up and said with quiet dignity, "I will find it very hard to live *up* to my mother's reputation. My mother was the gentlest, kindest woman who ever lived. Now, if you'll excuse me, I have some letters to write."

Victoria shut the door behind her and went down the hall to the library, a gigantic room with Persian carpets scattered across the polished wood floors and bookshelves lining the long walls. Too angry and upset to actually sit down at one of the desks and write a letter to Dorothy or Andrew, she wandered over to the shelves of books, looking for something to soothe her spirits. Bypassing the tomes on history, mythology, and commerce, she came to a poetry section. Her gaze wandered distractedly over the authors, some of whom she had already read—Milton, Shelley, Keats, Byron. Without any real interest in reading, she haphazardly chose a slender volume simply because it was protruding several inches beyond the others on the shelf and carried it over to the nearest grouping of comfortable chairs.

She turned up the oil lamp on the table and settled down in the chair, forcing herself to open the book. A sheet of pink, perfumed notepaper slid out and drifted to the floor. Victoria automatically picked it up and started to put it back, but the first words of the torrid little note, which was written in French, leapt out at her:

Darling Jason,
    I miss you so. I wait impatiently, counting the hours
until you will come to me. . . .

Victoria told herself that reading another person's letter
was ill-bred, unforgivable, and completely beneath her dignity, but the idea of a woman waiting impatiently for Jason
Fielding to come to her was so incredible that Victoria
couldn't bridle her amazed curiosity. For her part, she
would be more inclined to wait impatiently for him to go
away! She was so engrossed in her discovery that she didn't
hear Jason and Miss Kirby coming down the hall as she
continued to read:

    I am sending you these lovely poems in the hope you
    will read them and think of me, of the tender nights we
    have shared in each other's arms. . . .

"Victoria!" Jason called irritably.
Victoria leapt to her feet in guilty nervousness, dropped
the book of poetry, snatched it up, and sat back down.
Trying to look absorbed in her reading, she opened the book
and stared blindly at it, completely unaware that it was
upside down.
"Why didn't you answer me?" Jason demanded as he
strolled into the library with the lovely Miss Kirby clinging
to his arm. "Johanna wanted to tell you good-bye and to
offer her suggestions if you need to buy anything in the
village."
After Lady Kirby's unprovoked attack, Victoria couldn't
help wondering if Miss Kirby was now implying that Victoria couldn't be trusted to choose her own purchases. "I'm
sorry, I didn't hear you call," she said, trying to compose
her features so she'd look neither angry nor guilty. "As you
can see, I've been reading, and I was quite engrossed." She
closed the book and laid it on the table, then forced herself to
gaze calmly at the pair. The look of revolted disgust on
Jason's face made her step back in alarm. "Is—is something
wrong?" she asked, fearfully certain that he somehow remembered that the note was in the book and suspected her
of reading it.

"Yes," he snapped, and turned to Miss Kirby, who was staring at Victoria with an expression similar to his. "Johanna, can you recommend a tutor from the village who can teach her to read?"

"Teach me to read?" Victoria gasped, flinching from the scornful pity on the brunette's beautiful face. "Don't be silly, I don't need a tutor—I know perfectly well how to read."

Ignoring her, Jason looked at Miss Kirby. "Can you name a tutor who would come here and teach her?"

"Yes, I believe so, my lord. Mr. Watkins, the vicar, might do it."

With the long-suffering look of one who has already been forced to tolerate too many insults and will not endure yet another one, Victoria said very firmly, "Oh, really, this is absurd. I do not need a tutor. I *know* how to read."

Jason's manner turned to ice. "Don't lie to me ever again," he warned. "I despise liars—particularly lying women. You can't read a word and you damned well know it!"

"I do not believe this!" Victoria said, oblivious to Miss Kirby's horrified gasp. "I can read, I tell you!"

Pushed past endurance by what he perceived as her flagrant attempt to deceive him, Jason took three long strides to the table, grabbed the book, and thrust it into her hands. "Then read it!"

Angry and humiliated at being treated this way, particularly in front of Miss Kirby, who was making no attempt to hide her enjoyment of Victoria's plight, Victoria snatched open the cover of the little book and saw the perfumed note.

"Go ahead," he mocked. "Let's hear you read."

Deliberating, Victoria slanted a speculative, sideways glance at him. "Are you absolutely certain you want me to read this aloud?"

"Aloud," Jason said curtly.

"In front of Miss Kirby?" she questioned innocently.

"Either read it or admit you can't," he snapped.

"Very well," Victoria said. Swallowing the laughter bubbling in her throat, she read dramatically: "Darling Jason, I miss you so. I wait impatiently, counting the hours until you will come to me. I am sending you these lovely poems in the

87

hope you will read them and think of me, of the tender nights we have shared in each other's ar—"

Jason jerked the book out of her hands. Raising her eyebrows, Victoria looked him right in the eye and blandly reminded him, "That note was written in French—I translated it as I read."

She turned to Miss Kirby and said brightly, "There was more, of course. But I *don't* think this is the sort of reading material one ought to leave lying around when there are gently bred young ladies about. Do you?" Before either of them could reply, Victoria turned and walked out of the room, her head high.

Lady Kirby was waiting in the hall, ready to leave. Victoria bid both women a cool good-bye, then started up the stairs, hoping to escape Jason's inevitable wrath, which she was certain he intended to unleash upon her the moment the ladies left. However, Lady Kirby's parting remark caused an explosion in Victoria's mind that obliterated everything else. "Don't feel badly about Lord Fielding's defection, my dear," she called as Northrup helped them into their cloaks. "Few people actually believed the betrothal announcement in the paper. Everyone was certain that once you had actually arrived here, he'd find some way to cry off. The rogue has made it plain to everyone that he won't marry anyone—"

Charles pushed her out the door under the guise of escorting her to her carriage, and Victoria halted and swung around on the stairway. Like a beautiful, outraged goddess she stood trembling with wrath, staring down at Jason. "Am I to understand," she enunciated furiously, "that the engagement you said was 'off' was *our* engagement?"

Jason's only answer was a tightening of his jaw, but his silence was a tacit admission, and she glared at him with blue sparks shooting from her eyes, heedless of the servants who were staring at her in paralyzed horror. "How dare you!" she hissed. "How dare you let anyone think I would consider marrying you. I wouldn't marry you if you were—"

"I don't recall *asking* you to marry me," Jason interrupted sarcastically. "However, it's reassuring to know that if I ever took leave of my senses and *did* ask you, you'd have the consideration to turn me down."

Perilously close to tears because she was losing her composure but could not shake his, Victoria passed a look of scathing scorn over him. "You are a cold, callous, arrogant, unfeeling monster, without respect or feeling for anyone—even the dead! No woman in her right mind would want you! You're a—" Her voice broke and she turned and ran up the stairs.

Jason watched her from the foyer, where two footmen and the butler stood riveted to the floor, waiting in frozen dread for the moment when the master would unleash his fury on this chit of a girl who had just done the unforgivable. After a long moment, Jason shoved his hands in his pockets. He looked round at the stricken butler and lifted his brows. "I believe I have just received what is commonly called 'a crushing setdown,' Northrup."

Northrup swallowed audibly but said nothing until Jason had strolled up the stairs; then he rounded on the footmen. "Attend to your duties, and see that you don't gossip about this with anyone." He strode away.

O'Malley gaped at the other footman. "She fixed me a poultice and it cured me sore tooth," he breathed in awe. "Mayhap she fixed his lordship something to cure his temper, while she was at it." Without waiting for a reply he headed straight to the kitchen to inform Mrs. Craddock and the kitchen staff of the amazing incident he had just witnessed. With Monsieur André gone—thanks to the young lady from America—the kitchen had become a pleasant place to pass an occasional moment when Northrup's eagle eye was focused on someone else.

Within an hour the well-trained, perfectly regimented household staff had all paused just long enough to listen in disbelief to the tale of the drama that had occurred on the staircase. Within another half hour, the story of his lordship's unprecedented lapse from icy dignity to warm humanity in the face of extreme provocation had spread from the house to the stables and the gamekeepers' cottages.

Upstairs, Victoria's hands shook with pent-up anguish as she pulled the pins from her hair and stripped off the peach gown. Still fighting her tears, she hung it in the wardrobe, pulled on a nightdress, and climbed into bed. Homesickness washed over her in drowning waves. She wanted to leave here, to put an ocean between herself and people like Jason Fielding and Lady Kirby. Her mother had probably left England for the same reason. Her mother . . . Her beautiful, gentle mother, she thought on a choked sob. Lady Kirby wasn't fit to touch the hem of Katherine Seaton's skirts!

Memories of her former happy life crowded in around Victoria until the bedroom at Wakefield was filled with them. She remembered the day she had picked a bouquet of wild flowers for her mother and soiled her dress in the process. *"Look, Mama, aren't they the prettiest things you've ever seen?"* she had said. *"I picked them for you—but I soiled my dress."*

"They're very pretty," her mother had agreed, hugging her and ignoring the soiled dress. *"But you are the prettiest thing I've ever seen."*

She remembered when she was seven years old and sick from a fever that had brought her near death. Night after night, her mother had sat at her bedside, sponging her face and arms while Victoria drifted between wakefulness and delirium. On the fifth night, she had awakened in her mother's arms, her own face wet from the tears running down her mother's cheeks. Katherine was rocking her back and forth, weeping and whispering the same disjointed plea again and again: *"Please don't let my little girl die. She's so little and she's afraid of the dark. Please, God . . ."*

In the plush, silken cocoon of her bed at Wakefield, Victoria turned her face into the pillow, her body shaking with wrenching sobs. "Oh, Mama," she wept brokenly. "Oh, Mama, I miss you so. . . ."

Jason paused outside her bedroom and raised his hand to knock, then checked himself at the sound of her harsh weeping, his forehead furrowed into a frown. She would probably feel better if she cried everything out of her system, he thought. On the other hand, if she continued crying like that, she would surely make herself ill. After a few seconds' uncertainty he went to his own room, poured some brandy into a glass and returned to hers.

He knocked—as she had arrogantly instructed him to do earlier—but when she didn't answer, he opened the door and went inside. He stood at her bedside, watching her shoulders shake with the spasms of wrenching grief that tore from her.

He had seen women cry before, but their tears were always dainty and deliberate, intended to bend a man's will. Victoria had stood on that stairway hurtling verbal spears at him like an enraged warrior, then had retreated to her own room to weep in pathetic secret.

Jason put his hand on her shoulder. "Victoria—"

Victoria rolled over onto her back and jerked up onto her elbows, her eyes the deep blue of wet velvet, her thick sooty lashes sparkling with tears. "Get out of here!" she demanded in a hoarse whisper. "Get out this very minute, before someone sees you!"

Jason looked at the tempestuous, blue-eyed beauty before him, her cheeks flushed with anger, her titian hair tumbling riotously over her shoulders. In her prim, high-collared white nightdress, she had the innocent appeal of a bewildered, heartbroken child; yet there was defiance in the set of her chin and angry pride blazing in her eyes, warning him not to underestimate her. He remembered her daring impertinence in the library when she deliberately read that note aloud and then made no effort to hide her satisfaction at disconcerting him. Melissa had been the only woman who ever dared defy him, but she did it behind his back. Victoria Seaton did it right to his face, and he almost admired her for it.

When he made no move to leave, Victoria irritably dashed the tears from her cheeks, tugged the bedcovers up to her chin, and began inching backward until she was sitting up against the pillows. "Do you realize what people would say if they knew you were in here?" she hissed. "Have you no principles?"

"None whatsoever," he admitted impenitently. "I prefer practicality to principles." Ignoring Victoria's glower, he sat down on the bed and said, "Here, drink this."

He held a glass of amber liquid close enough to her face for Victoria to smell the strong spirits. "No," she said, shaking her head. "Absolutely not."

"Drink it," he said calmly, "or I'll pour it down your throat."

"You wouldn't!"

"Yes, Victoria, I would. Now drink it down like a good girl. It will make you feel better."

Victoria could see there was no point in arguing and she was too exhausted to put up a physical fight. She took a resentful sip of the vile amber liquid and tried to thrust it back into his hand. "I feel much better," she lied.

A spark of amusement lit his eyes, but his voice was implacable. "Drink the rest."

"*Then* will you go away?" she said, capitulating ungraciously. He nodded. Trying to get it over with as if it were bad-tasting medicine, she took two quick swallows; then she doubled over choking as the liquid seared a fiery path all the way down to the pit of her stomach. "It's awful," she gasped, falling back against the pillows.

For several minutes Jason remained silent, giving the brandy time to spread its comforting warmth through her. Then he said calmly, "In the first place, Charles announced our engagement in the newspaper, not I. Secondly, you have no more desire to be betrothed to me than I do to you. Isn't that correct?"

"Absolutely," Victoria averred.

"Then why are you crying because we *aren't* betrothed?"

Victoria gave him a look of haughty disdain. "I was not doing anything of the sort."

"You weren't?" Amused, Jason looked at the tears still clinging to her curly lashes and handed her a snowy white handkerchief. "Then why is your nose red, your cheeks puffy, your face pale, and—"

A self-conscious giggle, induced by the brandy, welled up inside Victoria, and she dabbed at her nose. "It's very ungentlemanly of you to remark on that."

A lazy smile transformed his harsh features. "Surely I haven't done anything to give you the impression that I'm a gentleman!"

It was the exaggerated dismay in his voice that brought a reluctant smile to her lips. "Nothing whatsoever," she assured him. Taking another sip of the brandy, she leaned back against the pillows. "I wasn't crying over that ridiculous engagement—that only made me angry."

"Then why were you crying?"

Rolling the glass between her palms, she studied the swirling liquid. "I was crying for my mother. Lady Kirby said I would have to live down her reputation, and it made me so furious I couldn't think what to say." She shot a quick glance at him beneath her lashes, and because he seemed to be genuinely concerned and approachable for once, she continued haltingly, "My mother was kind and gentle and sweet. I began remembering just how wonderful she was, and it made me cry. You see, ever since my parents died, I have these—peculiar spells where I feel perfectly fine one moment and then suddenly, I start to miss them terribly, and it makes me cry."

"It's natural to cry for people you love," he said, so gently that she could hardly believe it was him speaking.

Strangely comforted now by his presence and his deep, resonant voice, Victoria shook her head. "I cry for myself," she confessed guiltily. "I cry from self-pity because I've lost them. I never realized I was so cowardly."

"I've seen brave men cry, Victoria," he said quietly.

Victoria studied his hard, sculpted features. Even with the softening effect of candleglow on his face, he looked supremely invulnerable. It was impossible to imagine him with tears in his eyes. With her normal reserve greatly diminished by the brandy, Victoria tipped her head to the side and asked softly, "Have you ever cried?"

Before her disappointed gaze, his expression became aloof. "No."

"Not even when you were a little boy?" she persisted, trying to lighten his mood by teasing him.

"Not even then," he said shortly.

Abruptly he made a move to stand up, but Victoria impulsively laid her hand on his sleeve. His gaze narrowed on her long fingers resting on his arm, then lifted to her wide, searching eyes. "Mr. Fielding," she began, awkwardly trying to maintain their short truce and to strengthen it if possible. "I know you don't like having me here, but I won't be staying long—only until Andrew comes for me."

"Stay as long as you like," he said with a shrug, his expression cool.

"Thank you," Victoria said, her lovely face mirroring her bewilderment at his abrupt changes of mood. "But what I wanted to say was that I would like it very much if you and I could be on, well, friendlier terms."

"What sort of 'friendlier terms' did you have in mind, my

lady?" Mellowed by the brandy, Victoria missed the sarcasm in his voice. "Well, if you don't put too fine a point on it, we're distant cousins." She paused, her eyes searching his enigmatic face for some sign of warmth. "I haven't any relations left, except Uncle Charles and you. Do you suppose we could treat each other like cousins?"

He looked stunned by her proposal, then amused. "I suppose we could do that."

"Thank you."

"Get some sleep now."

She nodded and snuggled down under the covers. "Oh, I forgot to apologize—for the things I've said to you when I'm angry, that is."

His lips twitched. "Do you regret any of them?"

Victoria lifted her brows, eyeing him with a sleepy, impertinent smile. "You've deserved every word."

"You're right," he admitted, grinning. "But don't press your luck."

Suppressing the urge to reach out and tousle her heavy hair, Jason went back to his own room and poured a brandy for himself, then sat down and propped his feet up on the table in front of his chair. Wryly, he wondered why Victoria Seaton should bring out this odd streak of protectiveness in him. He had intended to send her straight back to America when she arrived—and that was *before* she had disrupted his household. Perhaps it was because she was so lost and vulnerable—and so young and dainty—that she made him feel paternal. Or perhaps it was her candor that threw him off balance. Or those eyes of hers that seemed to search his face as if she were looking for his soul. She had no flirtatious wiles; she didn't need any, he thought wryly—those eyes could seduce a saint.

Chapter Eight

"I CAN'T TELL YOU HOW SORRY I AM ABOUT LAST night," Charles told her at breakfast the next morning, his face lined with worry and contrition. "I was wrong to announce your betrothal to Jason, but I had so hoped the two of you might suit. As for Lady Kirby, she is an old hag, and her daughter's been dangling after Jason for two years, which is why they both came galloping over here to have a look at you."

"There's no need to explain all that again, Uncle Charles," Victoria said kindly. "No harm was done."

"Perhaps not, but in addition to all her other unpleasant qualities, Kirby is the worst of gossips. Now that she knows you're here, she'll make certain everyone else does, which means we'll soon be deluged with visitors eager to have a look at you. That, in turn, means a suitable chaperone will have to be present so that no one can cast aspersions on you for living with two men." He glanced up as Jason walked in, and Victoria tensed, praying that their truce of last night would hold up in the light of day.

"Jason, I was just explaining to Victoria the need for a chaperone. I've sent for Flossie Wilson," he added, referring to his maiden aunt, who had once helped care for little Jamie. "She's a complete peagoose, but she's my only female relative, and the only acceptable chaperone for Victoria that I know of. Despite her lack of sense, Flossie does know how to go about in society."

"Fine," Jason said absently, coming to stand beside Victoria's chair. He looked down at her, his expression unfathomable. "I trust you're suffering no ill effects from your foray into deprivation last night with the brandy?"

"None at all," she said brightly. "Actually, I rather liked it, once I became accustomed to it."

A lazy smile slowly dawned across his tanned face and Victoria's heart skipped a beat. Jason Fielding had a smile that could melt a glacier! "Beware of liking it overmuch—" he said, and teasingly added, "—cousin."

Lost in hopeful plans to make Jason her friend, Victoria paid no further attention to what the men were discussing until Jason spoke directly to her. "Did you hear me, Victoria?"

Victoria looked up blankly. "I'm sorry, I wasn't listening."

"On Friday, I'm expecting a visit from a neighbor who has just returned from France," Jason repeated. "If he brings his wife, I'd like to introduce you to her." Victoria's momentary flash of pleasure at his ostensibly friendly overture was doused by his blunt explanation for it. "The Countess of Collingwood is an excellent example of how you ought to conduct yourself in society. You would be wise to observe her behavior and emulate her."

Victoria flushed, feeling like an ill-behaved child who has just been told she ought to follow someone else's example. Moreover, she had already met four English aristocrats—Charles, Jason, Lady Kirby, and Miss Johanna Kirby. With the exception of Charles, she found them all very difficult to deal with, and she did not relish the prospect of meeting two more. Nevertheless, she stifled her ire and set aside her dread. "Thank you," she said politely. "I'll look forward to meeting them both."

Victoria spent the next four days pleasantly occupied with writing letters or in Charles's company. In the afternoon of the fifth day, she went down to the kitchens for another plate of scraps for Willie.

"That animal is going to be fat enough to ride if you continue feeding him this way," Mrs. Craddock warned her good-naturedly.

"He has a long way to go before that," Victoria said, returning her smile. "May I have that large bone over there, too—or are you planning to use it for soup?"

Mrs. Craddock assured her she was not, and gave the huge bone to Victoria. Thanking her, Victoria started to leave, then remembered something and turned back. "Last night, Mr. Field—I mean, his lordship," she corrected herself, watching the servants freeze at the mere mention of Jason, "said the roast duck was the best he has ever tasted. I'm not certain he remembered to mention it to you," Victoria explained, knowing perfectly well that Jason would probably never bother to do so, "but I thought you would like to know."

Mrs. Craddock's plump cheeks reddened with pleasure. "Thank you, my lady," she replied politely.

Victoria dismissed the title with a smile and a wave, then vanished out the door.

"Now, there is a *true* lady," Mrs. Craddock said to the others when Victoria left. "She is gentle and kind and not at all like those insipid misses you find in London, or the high-and-mighty ones his lordship has brought here from time to time. O'Malley says she's a countess. He heard his grace say so the other night to Lady Kirby."

Victoria carried the food out to the spot where she had been bringing Willie his meals for the last nine days. Instead of hanging back in the safety of the trees for several minutes, as he usually did, he trotted out a few steps when he saw her. "Here," she said, laughing softly, "look what I've brought for you."

Victoria's heart began to pound with victory as the huge silver and black dog came nearly to within her reach—much closer than ever before. "If you'll let me pet you, Willie," she continued, inching closer to him and holding out the bowl, "I'll bring you another delicious bone tonight after supper."

He stopped short, watching her with a mixture of fear and mistrust. "I know you want this," she continued, taking another tiny step toward him, "and I want to be your friend. You probably think this food is a bribe," she continued, slowly bending down and putting the bowl between them. "And you're quite right. I'm as lonely as you are, you see, but you and I could be great friends. I've never had a dog, did you know that?"

His glittering eyes shifted greedily to the food and then back to her. After a moment he moved closer to the bowl, but his eyes never left her, not even when he bent his head and began wolfing down his meal. Victoria continued talking softly to him as he ate, hoping to reassure him. "I can't imagine what Mr. Fielding was thinking of when he chose your name—you don't look at all like a Willie. I'd have named you Wolf, or Emperor—something as fierce-sounding as you look."

As soon as he finished, the dog started to retreat, but Victoria quickly held out her left hand, showing him the huge bone she held. "You must take it from my hand if you want it," she warned. He eyed the bone for only a moment before his huge jaws clamped down on it, tugging it from her hand. She expected him to race into the woods with it, but to her delight, after a tense, wary pause, he flopped down near her feet and began chewing it to splinters. Suddenly Victoria felt as if the heavens were smiling down on her. No longer did she feel unwanted and unwelcome at Wakefield—both Fielding men were now her friends, and soon she would have Willie as a companion, too. She knelt down and stroked his huge head. "You need a good brushing," she said, watching his sharp ivory fangs gnaw on the bone. "I wish Dorothy could see you," she continued wistfully. "She loves animals and she has a way with them. Why, she'd have you doing tricks for her in no time at all." The thought made Victoria smile, and then it made her ache with loneliness.

It was midafternoon of the following day when Northrup came to impart the intelligence that Lord Collingwood had arrived and that Lord Fielding desired her to come to his study.

Victoria glanced apprehensively in the mirror above her

dressing table and then sat down to pin her hair into a neat chignon, preparing to meet a stout, coldly proud aristocrat of Lady Kirby's age.

"Her coach broke down on the way here and two farmers took her up with them," Jason was telling Robert Collingwood, a dry smile on his face. "In the course of removing her trunk from the cart, two of the piglets escaped, and Victoria caught one of them just as Northrup opened the door. He saw the piglet in her arms and mistook her for a peasant girl, so he told her to go round the back to make her delivery. When Victoria balked at that, he ordered a footman to evict her from the property," Jason finished, handing Robert Collingwood a glass of claret.

"Good God," said the earl, laughing. "What a reception!" Lifting his glass in a toast, he said, "To your happiness and your bride's continued patience."

Jason frowned at him.

Trying to clarify what he saw was a confusing toast, Robert explained, "Since she didn't turn around and take the first ship back to America, I can only assume Miss Seaton has a great deal of patience—a most desirable trait in a bride."

"The betrothal announcement in the *Times* was Charles's doing," Jason said flatly. "Victoria is a distant cousin of his. When he learned she was without family, and was coming here to him, he decided I ought to marry her."

"Without first consulting you?" Robert said incredulously.

"I learned I was betrothed in exactly the same way everyone else learned it—by reading the *Times*."

The earl's warm brown eyes lit with amused sympathy. "I imagine you were surprised."

"Infuriated," Jason corrected. "Since we're on that subject, I was hoping your wife would accompany you today so Victoria could meet her. Caroline is only a few years older than Victoria and I think they could become friends. To be frank, Victoria is going to need a friend here. Evidently there was some scandal in the *ton* when her mother married an Irish physician, and old Lady Kirby is obviously planning to

stir up the pot again. In addition, Victoria's great-grandmother is the Duchess of Claremont, and she apparently
isn't going to acknowledge the girl. Victoria is a countess in
her own right, but that alone won't gain her real acceptance
in society. She'll have Charles's support behind her, of
course, and that will help. No one will dare give her the cut
direct."

"She'll have the weight of your influence behind her too,
and that is considerable," Collingwood pointed out.

"Not," Jason disagreed dryly, "when it comes to trying to
establish a young woman's reputation as a virtuous innocent."

"True." Robert chuckled.

"In any event, Victoria has met only the Kirby women as
samples of the English aristocracy. I thought your wife
might give her a better impression. In fact, I suggested she
view Caroline as a good example of acceptable manners and
behavior—"

Robert Collingwood threw back his head and burst out
laughing. "Did you indeed? Then you'd better hope Lady
Victoria doesn't follow your advice. Caroline's manners are
exquisite—exquisite enough to fool even you, I gather, into
believing she's a model of propriety—but I'm constantly
bailing her out of scrapes. I've never known a more willful
young woman in my life," he finished, but his words were
threaded with tenderness.

"In that case, Victoria and Caroline should get on fa-
mously," Jason said dryly.

"You're taking quite an interest in her," Robert said,
eyeing him closely.

"Only as a reluctant guardian."

Outside the study door, Victoria straightened the skirts of
her apple green muslin gown, knocked softly and then went
in. Jason was seated behind his desk in a high-backed,
leather-upholstered chair, talking to a man in his early
thirties. When they saw her, both men stopped talking and
arose in precise, if accidental, unison—a simple movement
that seemed to emphasize the similarities between them.
Like Jason, the earl was tall and handsome and athletically
built, but his hair was sandy and his eyes were a warm

brown. He had that same aura of calm authority Jason had, but he was less frightening. Humor lurked in his eyes and his smile was friendly rather than sardonic. Still, he did not look like a man one would wish to have as an enemy.

"Forgive me for staring," Victoria said softly when Jason had finished making the introductions. "But when I first saw you standing together, I thought I saw a similarity between you."

"I'm certain you meant that as a compliment, my lady," Robert Collingwood said, grinning.

"No," Jason joked, "she didn't."

Victoria thought frantically for some suitable reply and could find none, but she was spared further embarrassment by the earl, who shot an indignant look at Jason and said, "What possible answer can Miss Seaton make to that?"

Victoria didn't hear Jason's reply because her attention was diverted by another occupant of the room—an adorable little boy of about three who was standing beside the earl, staring at her in mute fascination, a forgotten sailboat clutched in his sturdy arms. With his curly, sandy hair and brown eyes, he was a miniature replica of his father, right down to the identical tan riding breeches, brown leather boots, and tan jacket he was wearing. Utterly captivated, Victoria smiled at him. "I don't believe anyone has introduced us . . ." she hinted.

"Forgive me," the earl said with smiling gravity. "Lady Victoria, permit me to make known to you my son, John."

The little boy put his boat down on the chair behind him and executed a solemn, adorable bow. Victoria responded by sinking into a deep curtsy, which startled a childish giggle from him. Then he pointed a chubby finger at her hair and glanced at his father. "Red?" he uttered with childish delight.

"Yes," Robert agreed.

The child beamed. "Pretty," he whispered, which wrung a laugh from his father.

"John, you are entirely too young to try your hand at charming the ladies," said Collingwood.

"Oh, but I'm not a lady," Victoria said, her heart going

out to the enchanting little boy. Jauntily she told him, "*I* am a sailor!" He looked so dubious that Victoria added, "Oh, but I am—and a prodigiously good one, too. My friend Andrew and I used to build boats and sail them all the time with the rest of the children—although our boats weren't nearly as grand as yours. Shall we take yours down to the creek?"

He nodded and Victoria looked to his father for permission. "I'll take excellent care of him," she promised. "And the ship, of course."

When the earl consented, John put his hand in Victoria's and they trooped out of the study.

"She obviously likes children," Robert observed as the two adventurers left.

"She's scarcely more than a child herself," Jason said dismissively.

The earl turned his head and glanced at the alluring young woman walking through the foyer. Returning his gaze to Jason's, he lifted his brows in amused contradiction, but he said nothing.

Victoria spent the better part of an hour sitting on a blanket on the bank of the creek that carved a picturesque path through the sweeping front lawns. Sun bathed her face and warmed her limbs as she sat beside John inventing stories about pirates and storms that supposedly plagued her ship during the crossing from America. John listened, enraptured, clutching the long length of fishing line Victoria had got from Northrup and attached to the ship. When he grew bored with the tame sailing afforded his small vessel here in the shallows, she took the line from him and they walked along, Victoria guiding the vessel downstream to where the creek became very deep and raced beneath a wide, graceful stone bridge, its waters churned by a fallen tree. "Here," she said, handing him the fishing line again. "Don't let go, or we'll run aground on that snarled tree down there."

"I won't," he promised, smiling as his three-masted ship bobbed and dipped in the swirling water.

Victoria wandered down the steep bank and was happily gathering a bouquet of the pink, blue, and white wild flowers that carpeted the incline when John shrieked and went bounding awkwardly after the line that had obviously pulled free of his grasp. "Stay there!" she called urgently, and ran to him.

Trying manfully not to cry, he pointed to the little ship, which was now gliding straight into the limbs of the fallen tree beneath the bridge. "It's gone," he whispered chokily as two tears welled in his brown eyes. "Uncle George made it for me. He'll be sad."

Victoria bit her lip, hesitating. Although the water was obviously deep and running fast here, she and Andrew had both rescued their own ships from the far more perilous river where they had always sailed them. She raised her head and scanned the steep bank, making certain they were downhill, well out of sight of the house and everyone in it; then she made her decision.

"It's not gone, it's just run aground on a reef," she said lightly, hugging him. "I'll get it." She was already stripping off her sandals, stockings, and the new green muslin gown Jason had provided for her. "Sit here," she said, "and I'll get it."

Clad only in her chemise and light petticoat, Victoria waded into the creek until the bottom fell away beneath her feet, then struck out with long, expert strokes for the far end of the tree. Beneath the bridge the water was icy and deep as it tumbled and churned around the branches, but she had no trouble locating the little craft. She had considerable trouble, however, freeing the strong fishing line from the branches. She dove under twice, to the delighted glee of little John, who had apparently never seen anyone swim or dive before. Despite the cold water and her sodden petticoats, the swim was invigorating, and Victoria reveled in the freedom of it. "I'll get the ship loose this time," she called to John, waving. Watching to make certain the child wasn't going to try to come in after her, she yelled, "Stay right there, I don't need any help."

He nodded obediently and Victoria dove under, tracing the line with her cold fingers beneath the tree, feeling for the place where it had wrapped itself around a submerged limb, working her way toward the opposite end.

"Northrup said he saw them walking toward the bridge

about—" Jason stopped abruptly as the word "help" drifted to them.

Both men broke into a run, racing at an angle across the lawn toward the distant bridge. Sliding and skidding, they scrambled down the steep, flower-covered bank toward John. Robert Collingwood caught his son by the shoulders, his voice rough with alarm. "Where is she?"

"Under the bridge," the little boy replied, grinning. "Under the tree, getting Uncle George's boat for me."

"Oh, Christ! That little fool—" Jason gasped, already stripping off his jacket and running toward the water. Suddenly a laughing, red-haired mermaid broke the surface in a high, showy arc. "I have it, John!" she called, her streaming hair covering her eyes.

"Good!" yelled John, clapping.

Jason skidded to a stop, his mindless terror giving way to black fury as he watched her blithely swimming toward the bank with long, graceful strokes, the little sailboat trailing far behind in her wake. With his booted feet planted wide apart and a thunderous expression on his face, he waited impatiently for his prey to swim into reach.

Robert Collingwood sent a sympathetic look at his furious friend and took his son's hand. "Come with me to the house, John," he ordered firmly. "I believe Lord Fielding has something he wishes to say to Miss Victoria."

"Thank you?" the little boy predicted.

"No," he said wryly. "Not 'thank you.' "

Victoria waded backward out of the water, reeling in the little boat as she walked, talking to an absent John. "See, I told you I could rescue the—" Her back collided with an immovable object at the same instant that hands like vices clamped on her arms and spun her around, snapping her head back.

"You little fool!" Jason snarled furiously. "You stupid little fool, you could have drowned!"

"No—no, I wasn't in any danger," Victoria gasped, frightened by the enraged glitter in his green eyes. "I'm an excellent swimmer, you see, and—"

"So is the groom who nearly drowned there last year!" he said in a terrible voice.

"Well, breaking my arms isn't going to help," she said,

but her futile efforts to free herself only made his grip tighten painfully. Victoria's chest rose and fell in agitation, but she tried desperately to appeal to his reason. "I know I've frightened you, and I'm sorry, but I wasn't in any danger. I haven't done anything wrong."

"You haven't done anything wrong? And you aren't in any danger?" he repeated ominously, his eyes dropping to her bosom as it heaved with her fearful breaths. Victoria suddenly realized she was dripping wet and scantily clad, soaking his shirt where her breasts touched him. "Suppose someone other than me were standing on this bank watching you—what do you think would happen?"

Victoria swallowed and wet her lips, remembering the time she had strolled into the house long after dark, and discovered that her father had organized a search party to comb the woods for her. First he had reacted with joy. Afterward, she had not been able to sit down with comfort for two days. "I—I don't know what would happen," she answered him, trying to brazen it out. "I suppose whoever it was would hand me my clothes and—"

Jason's gaze dropped to her moistened lips, then slid lower, following the line of her throat down to the tantalizing mounds of flesh exposed to his view above her clinging wet chemise. With her head thrown back, they quivered and thrust forward invitingly, emphasizing the undeniable fact that she was an alluring woman and not the child he had tried to convince himself she was. "This is what would happen!" he snapped suddenly, and his mouth crushed hers in a fierce, brutal kiss that was meant to punish and humiliate her.

Victoria squirmed silently against him, trying to break his hold and to drag her mouth away from the fierce possession of his lips. Her struggle only seemed to make him angrier, and the kiss more painful. "Please," she gasped tearfully against his mouth. "I'm sorry I frightened you—"

Slowly his hands loosened their grip, and then he lifted his head and stared down into her frightened eyes. Automatically, Victoria crossed her arms over her breasts, her hair spilling over her shoulders like a sheet of wet rubies overlaid with a sheen of gold, her sapphire eyes wide with fear and contrition. "Please," she whispered, her voice shaking with both emotions as she tried to maintain the truce that had existed between them for almost five days. "Don't be angry. I'm sorry I frightened you. I've been swimming since I was a child, but I shouldn't have done it today, I know that now."

Her straightforward, ungrudging admission caught Jason completely off guard. Every feminine ploy in existence had been used on him since he'd made his fortune and gained his title, but without success; Victoria's candor, combined with her beautiful, upturned face and the sensation of her alluring body pressing against him, acted on him like a powerful aphrodisiac. Desire surged through him, heating his blood, sending it singing through his veins, forcing his hands to pull her closer.

Victoria saw something primitive and terrifying flare in his eyes as his hands tightened on her arms. She jerked back, a scream rising in her throat, but his lips covered hers, stifling her voice with a demanding insistence that stunned her into immobility. Like an alarmed rabbit captured in a painless trap, she struggled until she felt his hands stroke soothingly up and down her spine and shoulders, while his lips moved on hers with inflaming expertise.

Dizzily, she slid her hands up his chest, trying to cling for support to the very object that was destroying her balance. This innocent action triggered an instant reaction from Jason. His arms tightened around her and he deepened the kiss, his lips moving on hers with hungry ardor, insistently shaping and fitting her lips to his own. Lost in a haze of nameless yearnings, Victoria leaned up on her toes, responding to the forceful pressure of his arms. He groaned as she molded her body against his, and his parted lips crushed hers, sliding insistently back and forth, urging hers to part; the moment they did, his tongue slid between them, plunging into the soft recesses of her mouth.

Victoria tore her mouth free, horrified by what he was doing, and pushed against him with all her strength. "Don't!" she cried.

He let her go so abruptly that she staggered back a step; then he drew a long, audible breath, holding it for an abnormally long time. Tearing her hostile gaze from Jason's chest, she glared at him, fully expecting him to lay the blame for this entirely unseemly kiss at her door. "I suppose this was my fault, too," she said angrily. "No doubt you'll say I was asking for such treatment!" His mobile mouth twisted into a grim smile and Victoria had the fleeting impression that he was struggling for composure.

"You made the first mistake this afternoon," he said finally. "This one was mine. I'm sorry."

"What?" she said, unable to believe her ears.

"Contrary to what you obviously think of me," he drawled, "I am not in the habit of seducing innocents—"

"I was *not* in danger of being seduced," Victoria lied proudly.

Lazy mockery lit his eyes. "Weren't you?" he asked, as amusement seemed to drain the tension from his body.

"No, I most assuredly was not!"

"Then I suggest you put your clothes on before I'm tempted to show you how wrong you are."

Victoria opened her mouth to make some suitably scathing remark about his outrageous conceit, but his bold, glinting smile was too much for her. "You're impossible!" she said lamely.

"You're right," he agreed and turned his back so she could dress.

Trying desperately to control her raging emotions and match his casual mood, Victoria hastily dressed. Andrew had kissed her a few times, but never in that way. Never like that. Jason should never have done so, nor should he be so insufferably composed about it. She was quite certain she had every right to be furious with him, but perhaps things were different in England. Perhaps ladies here took such kisses in stride. Perhaps she would only look a fool if she made an issue of it. Even if she did make an issue of it, Jason would merely shrug the kiss aside as insignificant, which he was already doing. She had nothing to gain by stirring up hostility in him, and she had everything to lose. Still, she could not entirely control her pique. "You really *are* impossible," she said again.

"We've already agreed on that."

"You're unpredictable as well."

"In what way?"

"Well, I almost thought you were going to hit me for frightening you. Instead you kissed me." Leaning down, she picked up John's boat. "I'm beginning to think you're much like your dog—you both look far more fierce than you really are."

For once she saw his complacent, knowing facade crack a bit. "My dog?" he echoed blankly.

"Willie," she clarified.

"You must be terrified of canaries if you find Willie fierce."

"I'm coming to the conclusion there's no reason to be afraid of either of you."

A smile touched the corners of his sensual lips as he took the little boat from her. "Don't mention that to anyone else, or you'll ruin my reputation."

Victoria wrapped the blanket around her, then tipped her head to the side. "Do you have one?"

"Of the worst sort," he averred flatly, shooting her a challenging look. "Shall I tell you the sordid details?"

"Certainly not," Victoria said primly. Hoping that perhaps Jason's mild contrition over the kiss would make him more pliable, Victoria summoned up the courage to broach the subject that had been bothering her for days. "There's a way you can atone for your 'mistake,' " she said tentatively as they walked toward the house.

Jason shot her a measuring look. "I would say one mistake offset the other. However, what is it you want?"

"I want my clothes back."

"No."

"You don't understand," she cried, her emotions jangled by the kiss and now by his implacable attitude. "I am in mourning for my parents."

"I do understand; however, I do not believe that grief is ever so great that it cannot be contained within, and I don't believe in the outward display of mourning. Moreover, Charles and I want you to build a new life here—one you can enjoy."

"I don't need a new life!" Victoria said desperately. "I am only here until Andrew comes for me and—"

"He isn't going to come for you, Victoria," Jason said. "He's only written you one letter in all these months."

The words stabbed through Victoria's brain like hot daggers. "He *will* come, I tell you. There was only enough time to receive one letter before I left."

Jason's expression hardened. "I hope you are right. However, I forbid you to wear black. Grieving is done in the heart."

"How would you know?" Victoria burst out, whirling on him, her hands clenched at her sides. "If you had a heart, you'd not force me to parade around in these clothes as if my parents had never existed. You don't have a heart!"

"You're right," he bit out, his voice all the more frightening because it was so low. "I don't have a heart. Remember that, and don't deceive yourself into believing that beneath my fierce exterior, I'm as tame as a lapdog. Dozens of women have made that mistake and regretted it."

Victoria walked away from him on legs that shook. How could she have imagined they might be friends! He was cold and cynical and hard; he had a vicious, unreliable temper; and besides that he was obviously unbalanced! No sane man could kiss a woman with tenderness and passion one moment, then become outrageously flirtatious, only to turn cold and hateful a mere moment later. He was no lapdog—he was as dangerous and unpredictable as the panther he resembled!

Despite the fact that she walked as quickly as she could, Jason's long strides kept him easily beside her and they arrived at the circular drive in front of the house at the same time.

The Earl of Collingwood was waiting for them, already mounted on his splendid sorrel with John comfortably ensconced in front of him.

Embarrassed and angry, Victoria bade the earl a brief good-bye, smiled lamely at John and handed him his sailboat, then rushed inside.

John watched her, looked at Jason, then turned anxiously to his father. "He didn't give Miss Tory a thrashing, did he?"

The earl lifted his amused glance from Jason's wet shirtfront to his lordship's face. "No, John, Lord Fielding did not give her a thrashing." To Jason he said, "Shall I ask Caroline to call upon Miss Seaton tomorrow?"

"Come with her, and we'll continue our business discussion."

Robert nodded. Tightening his arm protectively around

his little son, he touched his booted heel to his restive mount and the sorrel cantered off down the drive.

Jason watched them leave, his bland expression fading to one of grim displeasure as he permitted himself for the first time to face what had happened to him beside the creek.

Chapter Nine

By the next afternoon, Victoria still had not been able to put Jason's earthshaking kiss out of her mind. Sitting on the grass beside Willie, she stroked his proud head while he gnawed on the bone she had brought him. Watching him, she thought again of Jason's easy, smiling attitude when the kiss was over, and her stomach knotted as she compared her own innocence and stupidity to his sophistication and brittle worldliness.

How could he have held her and kissed her as if he were trying to devour her one moment, and then joked about it the next? And where, she wondered, had she ever found the ability to match his lighthearted mood when her senses were reeling and her knees were knocking together? And after all of that, how could he look at her with those freezing eyes of his and advise her not to make the same mistake "dozens" of other women had?

What made him behave like that? she wondered. He was impossible to cope with, impossible to understand. She had tried to befriend him, only to end up being kissed. Everything seemed so different in England; perhaps here, kisses like that were nothing out of the ordinary and she had no reason to feel guilty and angry. But she did. Loneliness for Andrew swamped her, and she shuddered with shame for her willing participation in Jason's kiss.

She glanced up as Jason rode toward the stables. He had gone hunting this morning, so she'd been able to avoid him while she tried to gather her wits, but her reprieve was coming to an end—the Earl of Collingwood's carriage was pulling up in the front drive. Reluctantly, she arose. "Come, Willie," she said tightly. "Let's go tell Lord Fielding that the earl and countess have just arrived, and spare poor Mr. O'Malley a needless trip to the stables."

The dog lifted his great head and regarded her with intelligent eyes, but he didn't move. "It's time you stopped hiding from people. I'm not your servant, you know, and I refuse to keep bringing your meals out here. Northrup told me you used to be fed at the stables. Come, Willie!" she repeated, determined to take control of this small part of her life, at least. She took two more steps and waited. The dog stood up and looked at her, his alert expression making her certain he understood the command.

"Willie," she said irritably, "I am growing excessively impatient with arrogant males." She snapped her fingers. "I said *come!*" Again she stepped forward, watching over her shoulder, fully prepared to drag the obstinate animal by the scruff of his neck if he refused. "Come!" she said sharply, and this time he followed slowly in her wake.

Buoyed up by her small victory, Victoria walked toward the stables from which Jason was emerging, his long rifle hanging loosely from his hand.

In front of the house, the Earl of Collingwood lifted his wife down from the carriage. "There they are, over there," he told his wife, nodding in the direction of the stables. Tucking her hand affectionately in the crook of his arm, he started across the lawns toward the other couple. "Smile," he teased in a whisper when her steps lagged. "You look as if you're going to face an executioner."

"Which is more or less how I feel," Caroline admitted, shooting him a sheepish smile. "I know you will laugh, but Lord Fielding rather frightens me." She nodded at her husband's astonished look. "I am not the only one who feels so—nearly everyone is in awe of him."

"Jason is a brilliant man, Caroline. I've made enormous returns on every investment he's been kind enough to recommend to me."

"Perhaps, but he is still horridly unapproachable and . . . and *forbidding,* for all that. Moreover, he is capable of giving the kind of crushing setdowns that make one positively wish to *sink.* Why, last month, he told Miss Farraday that he dislikes simpering females—particularly those who cling to his arm *while* they are simpering."

"What did Miss Farraday say to that?"

"What *could* she say? She was clinging to his arm and simpering at the time. It was most embarrassing."

Ignoring her husband's meaningful grin, she smoothed her white gloves over her long fingers. "What women see in him, *I* can't imagine, yet they continually make cakes of themselves when he is about. True, he's rich as Croesus, with six estates of his own and heaven knows how many pounds a year—and, of course, he'll be the next Duke of Atherton, too. And I'll do him the justice to admit he's uncommonly handsome—"

"But you can't understand what women see in him?" her husband teased, chuckling.

Caroline shook her head, lowering her voice as they neared the couple. "His manners are not at all nice. Quite the contrary—he is shockingly blunt!"

"When a man is relentlessly pursued for his wealth and title, he should be excused for losing his patience now and then."

"You may think so, but for my part, I have the liveliest compassion for poor Miss Seaton. Only think how terrified she must be, living in the same house with him."

"I don't know if she's terrified, but I have the impression she's lonely and in need of a friend to show her how to go on in England."

"She must be quite miserable," Caroline agreed sympathetically, watching Victoria, who had just reached Jason and was speaking to him.

"The earl and countess have arrived," Victoria was saying to Jason, her manner coolly polite.

"So I see. They've followed you here," Jason explained, "they're a few paces off to your right behind you." He glanced at her again, then froze, his attention riveted on something behind her and to her left. "Move!" he ordered, pushing her roughly aside as he swung his rifle to his shoulder. Behind her Victoria heard a low, terrible snarl, and suddenly she understood what Jason meant to do.

"No!" she screamed. Striking out wildly, she knocked the barrel of the weapon into the air and flung herself to her knees, wrapping her arms around Willie and glaring at Jason. "You're insane! Insane! What has Willie done to deserve being starved and shot?" she demanded hysterically, stroking his head. "Did he swim in your stupid creek or—or dare to disobey one of your orders—or—"

The rifle slid through Jason's numb fingers until the barrel was pointing harmlessly at the ground. "Victoria," he said in a calm voice that contradicted his taut, pale features, "that isn't Willie. Willie is a collie, and I lent him to the Collingwoods three days ago for breeding."

Victoria's hand stilled in midstroke.

"Unless I've lost my sight and my mind in the last minute, I would guess the animal you are clinging to like a mother protecting her babe is at least half wolf."

Victoria swallowed and slowly stood up. "Even if he isn't Willie, he's still a dog, not a wolf," she persisted stubbornly. "He knows the command 'Come.' "

"He's *part* dog," Jason contradicted. Intending to pull her away from the animal, he stepped forward and seized her arm—an action that brought an instantaneous reaction from the dog, which crouched down, snarling and baring its fangs, the hair standing up on its back. Jason released her arm, his fingers slowly working toward the trigger of the rifle. "Move away from him, Victoria."

Victoria's eyes were riveted on the gun. "Don't do it!" she warned hysterically. "I won't let you. If you shoot him, I'll shoot you, I swear I will. I'm a better shot than I am a swimmer—anyone at home can tell you that. Jason!" she cried brokenly. "He's a dog and he's only trying to protect me from you. Anyone could understand that! He's my friend. Please, please don't shoot him. Please . . ."

Weak with relief, she watched Jason's hand relax on the rifle and again the barrel slid harmlessly toward the grass. "Stop hovering over him," he ordered. "I won't shoot him."

114

"Will you give me your word as a gentleman?" Victoria persisted, her body still blocking Wolf as she sought to prevent a fatal confrontation between the courageous dog that was trying to protect her and the man with the deadly weapon who was prepared to kill him for doing it.

"I give you my word."

Victoria started to move away, but then she remembered something Jason had told her and quickly put herself between the two combatants again. Eyeing Jason suspiciously, she reminded him, "You told me you aren't a gentleman and you said you have no principles. How can I know you'll honor your given word as a gentleman should?"

Jason's pantherish eyes gleamed with reluctant amusement as he looked at the defenseless young woman who was simultaneously championing a wolf and mutinously defying him. "I'll honor it. Now, stop behaving like Joan of Arc."

"I'm not certain I believe you. Would you swear it to Lord Collingwood as well?"

"You're pressing your luck, my dear," Jason warned softly.

Although quietly stated, it had the undeniable ring of a threat, and Victoria heeded it, not because she feared the consequences but because she felt instinctively that Jason would do as he promised. She nodded and moved away, but the dog's huge body remained poised for attack, its threatening gaze riveted on Jason.

He, in turn, was watching the animal, the rifle still ready at his side. In desperation, Victoria turned to the dog. "Sit down!" she ordered, not really expecting he would obey the command.

The dog hesitated and then sat at her side.

"There, you see!" Victoria threw up her hands in relief. "He's been well trained by someone. And he knows your gun can hurt him—that's why he keeps watching it. He's smart."

"Very smart," Jason agreed with dry mockery. "Smart enough to live right under my nose while I, and everyone else for miles around, have been hunting for the 'wolf' that's been raiding chicken houses and terrorizing the village."

"Is that the reason you go hunting every day?" When Jason nodded, Victoria unleashed a torrent of words, all designed to forestall Jason from saying the dog couldn't remain on the estate. "Well, he isn't a wolf, he's a dog, you can see that. And I've been feeding him every day, so he'll have no reason to raid chicken houses anymore. He's very smart, too, and he understands what I say."

"Then perhaps you could mention to him that it's impolite to sit there waiting for the opportunity to bite the hand that, indirectly at least, has been feeding him."

Victoria cast an anxious look at her overeager protector and then at Jason. "I think if you reach for me again and I tell him not to snarl at you, he'll get the idea. Go ahead, reach for me."

"I'd like to wring your neck," Jason said, half-seriously, but he grasped her arm as she asked. The animal crouched, ready to spring, snarling.

"No!" Victoria said sharply, and the wolf called Willie relaxed, hesitated, and licked her hand.

Victoria expelled a breath of relief. "There, you see, it worked. I'll take excellent care of him—and he won't be the least bother to anyone if you let him stay."

Jason wasn't proof against either her courage or the imploring look in those brilliant blue eyes. "Chain your dog," he sighed. When she started to object, he said, "I'll have Northrup inform the gamekeepers that he's not to be harmed, but if he ranges onto someone else's property, they'll shoot him on sight. He hasn't tried to attack anyone, but farmers value their chickens, in addition to their families."

He prevented further argument by the simple expedient of turning to greet the Earl and Countess of Collingwood, and for the first time, Victoria remembered their presence.

Mortification made her feel hot all over as she forced herself to face the woman Jason apparently regarded as a model of propriety. Instead of the haughty disdain she expected to see on the countess's face, Lady Collingwood was regarding her with something that looked remarkably like laughing admiration. Jason made the introductions and then strolled away with the earl to discuss some sort of business dealings, heartlessly leaving Victoria to acquit herself as best she could with the countess.

Lady Collingwood was the first to break the uneasy silence. "May I walk with you while you chain your dog?"

Victoria nodded, rubbing her damp palms on her skirts. "You—you must think I'm the most ill-behaved female alive," she said miserably.

"No," Caroline Collingwood said, biting her lower lip to control her mirth, "but I think you are undeniably the *bravest* one."

Victoria was stunned. "Because I'm not afraid of Willie?"

The countess shook her head. "Because you aren't afraid of Lord Fielding," she corrected, laughing.

Victoria looked at the stunning brunette in her elegant finery, but what she saw was the mischievous gleam in those dancing gray eyes and the offer of friendship in her smile. She had met a kindred spirit in this seemingly unfriendly country, she realized, and her spirits soared. "Actually, I was terrified," Victoria admitted, turning toward the back of the house where she had decided to chain her dog until such time as she could convince Jason to let him come into the house.

"But you didn't show it, you see, and that is a very good thing, because it seems to me that once a male realizes a female is frightened of something, he uses that knowledge against her in perfectly horrid ways. For example, as soon as my brother Carlton realized I was afraid of snakes, he put one in my handkerchief drawer. And before I was quite finished having hysterics over that, my brother Abbott put one in my dancing slippers."

Victoria shuddered. "I loathe snakes. How many brothers do you have?"

"Six and they all did perfectly wretched things to me until I learned to retaliate in kind. Do you have any brothers?"

"No—a sister."

By the time the gentlemen finished their business discussion and joined the ladies for an early supper, Victoria and Caroline Collingwood were on a first-name basis and well on the way to becoming fast friends. Victoria had already explained that her betrothal to Lord Fielding was an error made by Charles—but with the best of intentions—and she had talked about Andrew; Caroline had confided that her parents had chosen Lord Collingwood as her husband, but from the things she said and the way her eyes lit up whenever she spoke of him, it was perfectly obvious to Victoria that she adored him.

The meal sparkled with their laughing conversation as Victoria and Caroline continued exchanging confidences and comparing some of their childhood exploits. Even Lord Collingwood contributed stories about his boyhood, and it soon became apparent to Victoria that all three of them had enjoyed carefree childhoods and the security of loving parents. Jason, however, refused to discuss his own youth, though he seemed to genuinely enjoy listening to the stories they were telling of theirs.

"Can you really shoot a gun?" Caroline asked Victoria admiringly while two footmen served trout sautéed in butter and herbs and covered with a delicate sauce.

"Yes," Victoria admitted. "Andrew taught me how because he wanted someone to give him competition when he shot at targets."

"And did you? Give him competition, I mean."

Victoria nodded, the candleglow catching the fiery lights in her hair and turning it into a molten halo. "A great deal of it. It was the most peculiar thing imaginable, but the very first time he put the gun in my hand, I followed his instructions, aimed, and hit the target. It didn't seem very hard."

"And after that?"

"It became easier," Victoria said with a twinkle.

"I liked sabers," Caroline confessed. "My brother Richard used to let me be his fencing partner. All it takes is a good arm."

"And a steady eye," added Victoria.

Lord Collingwood chuckled. "I used to pretend I was a knight of old and joust with the grooms. I did quite well in the lists—but then, the grooms were undoubtedly reluctant to knock a fledgling earl off his horse, so I probably wasn't as good as I thought I was at the time."

"Did you play tug-of-war in America?" Caroline asked eagerly.

"Yes, and it was invariably the boys against the girls."

"But that isn't fair at all—boys are always stronger."

"Not," Victoria said with a laughing, rueful look, "if the girls manage to choose a place where there is a tree and then contrive—very casually—to wrap the rope partway around the tree as they're pulling."

"Shameless!" Jason chuckled. "You were cheating."

"True, but the odds were against us otherwise, so it wasn't really cheating."

"What do you know of 'odds'?" he teased.

"As they pertain to cards?" Victoria asked, her face lit with infectious merriment. "To tell you the shameful truth, I am nearly as adept at calculating the odds of various hands as I am at dealing the cards in such a way as to produce those particular hands. In short," she admitted baldly, "I know how to cheat."

Jason's dark brows drew together in a slight frown. "Who taught you to cheat?"

"Andrew. He said they were 'card tricks' he learned when he was away at school."

"Remind me never to put this Andrew up for membership at any of my clubs," Collingwood said dryly. "He wouldn't live to see the next day."

"Andrew never cheats," Victoria corrected loyally. "He felt it was important to know how cheating is done, so one can't be cheated by an unscrupulous gambler—but he was only sixteen at the time, and I don't think he realized yet he was unlikely ever to meet such a person. . . ."

Jason leaned back in his chair, watching Victoria with fascinated interest, amazed by the gracious ease with which she conducted herself with his guests and the way she effortlessly charmed Robert Collingwood into participating in the dinner table conversation. He noticed the way her face glowed with fondness whenever she spoke of her Andrew, and the way she brought the dining room to life with her smile.

She was fresh and alive and unspoiled. Despite her youth, there was a natural sophistication about her that came from an active mind, a lively wit, and a genuine interest in others. He smiled to himself, remembering her courageous defense of her dog, which she had announced would henceforth be called Wolf, not Willie. Jason had known a few men with

true courage in his lifetime, but he had never met a courageous woman. He remembered her shy responsiveness to
his kiss and the incredible surge of hot desire she had ignited
in his body.

Victoria Seaton was full of surprises, full of promise, he
thought, studying her surreptitiously. Vivid beauty was
molded into every flawlessly sculpted feature of her face,
but her allure went much further than that; it was in her
musical laughter and her graceful movements. There was
something deep within her that made her sparkle and glow
like a flawless jewel, a jewel that needed only the proper
background and setting: elegant clothes to complement her
alluring figure and exquisite features; a magnificent home
where she could reign as its queen; a husband to curb
her wilder impulses; a baby at her breast to cuddle and
nourish. . . .

Sitting across from her, Jason remembered his old, long
since abandoned dream of having a wife to light up his table
with her warmth and laughter . . . a woman to fill his arms in
bed and banish the dark emptiness within him . . . a woman
who would love the children he gave her. . . .

Jason caught himself up short, disgusted with his naive,
youthful dreams and unfulfilled yearnings. He had carried
them into adulthood and married Melissa, foolishly believing
that a beautiful woman could make those dreams come true.
How stupid he had been, how incredibly gullible to let
himself believe a woman cared about love or children or
anything but money and jewels and power. He scowled as he
realized Victoria Seaton was suddenly bringing all those old,
stupid yearnings back to torment him.

Chapter Ten

THE MOMENT THE COLLINGWOODS LEFT, JASON headed straight for the library, where Charles had vanished an hour before.

Charles laid his book aside at once and beamed at Jason. "Did you observe Victoria's demeanor at supper tonight?" he asked eagerly. "Isn't she splendid? She has such charm, such poise, such understanding. I nearly burst with pride watching her! Why, she's—"

"Take her to London tomorrow," Jason cut in shortly. "Flossie Wilson can join you there for the season."

"London!" Charles sputtered. "But why? Why must we hurry?"

"I want her away from Wakefield and off my hands. Take her to London and find her a husband. The season begins in a fortnight."

Charles paled, but his voice was determined. "I think I'm entitled to an explanation for this sudden decision of yours."

"I gave you one—I want her away from here and permanently off my hands. That's explanation enough."

"It isn't as easy as that," Charles protested desperately. "I can't simply advertise in the newspaper for a husband for

121

her. We have to go about it properly—by entertaining and formally introducing her to society."

"Then take her there and get started."

Raking his hand through his gray hair, Charles shook his head, trying to dissuade Jason. "My house isn't in any condition to give lavish parties—"

"Use mine," Jason said.

"Then *you* can't stay there," Charles objected, searching wildly for obstacles to throw in the way of the plan. "If you do, everyone will assume Victoria is another one of your conquests—and a brazen one, to boot. The fact that you're supposedly betrothed to her won't carry any weight."

"Whenever I'm in the city, I'll stay at your house," Jason said briskly. "Take my staff from here with you—they can be ready for a party at a day's notice. They've done so before."

"What about gowns and vouchers to Almack's and—"

"Have Flossie Wilson take Victoria to Madame Dumosse and tell Madame that I want Victoria to have the best— immediately. Flossie will know how to go about getting vouchers to Almack's. What else?"

"What else?" Charles burst out. "To begin with, Dumosse is so famous even *I've* heard of her. She won't have time to outfit Victoria, not with the season almost upon us."

"Tell Dumosse I said to use her own judgment on Victoria's wardrobe and to spare no expense. Victoria's red hair and petite height will be a challenge for her; she'll outfit Victoria so that she outshines every insipid blonde and willowy brunette in London. She'll do it if she has to go without sleep for the next two weeks, and then she'll charge me double her usual exorbitant price to compensate herself for the inconvenience. I've been through all this before," he finished briskly. "Now, since everything is settled, I have work to do."

Charles expelled a long, frustrated sigh. "Very well, but we'll leave in three days, not one. That will give me time to notify Flossie Wilson to join us in London, not here. As an unmarried man, I cannot live in the same house with Victoria unless a suitable chaperone is present—particularly in London. Send your staff ahead to see to your house and I'll send word to Flossie Wilson to join us in London the day after tomorrow. Now I have a favor to ask of you."

"What is it?"

Carefully phrasing his answer, Charles said, "I don't want anyone to know your engagement to Victoria is off, not right away."

"Why not?" Jason demanded impatiently.

Charles hesitated as if at a loss, then brightened. "Well, for one thing, if members of the *ton* believe Victoria is already betrothed to you, they won't watch her so closely. She'll be able to go about with a little more freedom, and to look over the gentlemen at her leisure, before deciding on anyone in particular."

When Jason looked ready to argue, Charles added quickly, "She'll be much more admired—and much more desired—if the London beaux believe she's wrung an offer from *you*, of all people. Only consider, every eligible bachelor in London will think she must be special indeed if you want to marry her. On the other hand, if they think she's your cast-off, they'll hang back."

"Your 'friend' Lady Kirby will already have told everyone that the engagement is off," Jason pointed out.

Charles dismissed that with a wave of his hand. "No one will pay any heed to Kirby if *you* don't deny the betrothal when you're in London."

"Fine," Jason said, ready to agree to almost anything in order to get Victoria married off. "Take her to London and present her. I'll provide a suitable dowry for her. Give some balls and invite every fop in Europe. I'll attend her debut myself," he added sardonically. "And I'll stay in London to interview her prospective suitors. It shouldn't be hard to find someone to take her off our hands."

He was so relieved to have settled the problem of Victoria that he didn't stop to consider the conflicting rationales behind Charles's impassioned argument in favor of letting the betrothal stand.

Victoria walked into the library just as Jason was leaving. They exchanged smiles; then he exited and she approached Charles. "Are you up to our nightly game of draughts, Uncle Charles?"

"What?" he asked absently. "Yes, of course, my dear. I've been looking forward to it all day. I always do." They settled down at the table on either side of the draughts board, a checkered expanse that contained 64 inlaid squares, half of them white and half of them black.

While she placed her twelve circular white counters on the twelve black squares nearest her, Victoria stole a thoughtful glance at the tall, elegant, gray-haired man whom she was rapidly coming to love like a true uncle. He had looked especially handsome tonight at dinner in his well-tailored dark jacket as he laughed at their childhood stories and even contributed a few of his own, but now he seemed preoccupied and worried. "Are you feeling unwell, Uncle Charles?" she asked, studying him as he placed his twelve black counters on the black squares closest to him.

"No, nothing of the sort," he assured her, but within the first five minutes of play, Victoria had jumped three of his counters and captured them.

"I don't seem to be able to concentrate on the game," he admitted when she jumped his fourth.

"Let's talk instead, then," Victoria suggested gently.

When he agreed with a relieved smile, Victoria sought for a tactful way to discover what was troubling him. Her father had been a great advocate of the theory that people should talk out the things that bothered them—particularly people with weak hearts, because doing so often relieved the sort of inner stress that could bring on another attack. Recalling that Jason had been with Charles just before she arrived to play draughts, Victoria seized on his lordship as the most likely cause of Charles's distress. "Did you enjoy yourself at dinner?" she began with forced casualness.

"Tremendously," he said, looking as if he meant it completely.

"Do you think Jason did?"

"Good heavens, yes. Very much. Why do you ask?"

"Well, I couldn't help noticing that he didn't join in when we were all telling tales of our youth."

Charles's gaze slid away from hers. "Perhaps he couldn't recall any amusing tales to tell us."

Victoria paid scant attention to that answer; she was racking her brain for a better way to bring the discussion around to Charles. "I thought perhaps he was displeased with something I said or did and came to you just now to discuss it."

Charles looked at her again, this time with a smile sparkling in his hazel eyes. "You're worried about me, my dear, is that it? And you'd like to know if something is troubling me?"

Victoria burst out laughing. "Am I as transparent as that?"

Sliding his long fingers over hers, he squeezed her hand. "You are not transparent, Victoria; you are wonderful. You care about people. I look at you and I feel hope for the world. Despite all the pain you have suffered in these last months, you still notice when an old man looks tired, and you care."

"You aren't old at all," she protested, admiring the way he looked in his evening clothes.

"Sometimes I feel a great deal older than I am," he said with a halfhearted attempt at humor. "Tonight is one of those nights. But you have cheered me up. May I tell you something?"

"By all means."

"There have been times in my life when I wished for a daughter, and you're exactly what I always imagined she would be."

A lump of tenderness swelled in Victoria's throat as he continued quietly, "I watch you sometimes when you are strolling in the gardens or talking to the servants, and my heart fills with pride. I know that must seem odd, since I had nothing to do with making you what you are, but I feel that way nonetheless. I feel like shouting to all the cynics in the world: 'Look at her, she is life and courage and beauty. *She* is what the Lord had in mind when he gave the first man his mate. She will fight for what she believes in, defend herself when she is being wronged—and yet she will accept a gesture of apology for that wrong and forgive it without rancor.' I know you've forgiven Jason more than once for his treatment of you.

"I think all those things, and then I think to myself, what can I give her to show her how much I care for her? What sort of gift does a man give a goddess?"

Victoria thought she saw the sheen of tears in his eyes, but she couldn't be certain because her own eyes were stinging with them.

"There now!" he said with a self-conscious laugh as he squeezed her hand fiercely tight, "I will soon have us weeping all over the draughts board. Since I have answered your question, will you answer one of mine? What do you think of Jason?"

Victoria smiled nervously. "He's been generous to me," she began with caution, but Charles waved her words aside. "That isn't what I meant. I mean, what do you think of him personally? Tell me the truth."

"I—I don't think I understand what you're asking me about."

"Very well, I'll be more specific. Do you find him handsome?"

Victoria gulped back an astonished giggle.

"Most women seem to think he's extremely attractive," Charles prodded, smiling—rather proudly, Victoria thought. "Do you?"

Recovering from her astonishment at his line of questioning, Victoria nodded, trying not to look as embarrassed as she felt.

"Good, good. And would you agree he is very . . . er . . . manly?"

To Victoria's horror, her mind chose that moment to replay the way Jason had kissed her at the creek, and she felt hot color run up her cheeks.

"I can see you think he is," Charles said, chuckling, misinterpreting the reason for her blush. "Excellent. Now, I shall tell you a secret: Jason is one of the finest men you will ever know. His life has not been a happy one, yet he has gone on with it because he has tremendous strength of mind and will. Leonardo da Vinci once said, 'The greater a man's soul, the deeper he loves.' That quote has always reminded me of Jason. He feels things deeply, but he rarely shows it. And," Charles added wryly, "because he is so strong, he seldom encounters opposition from anyone—and never from young ladies. Which is why you may occasionally find him somewhat . . . er . . . dictatorial."

Victoria's curiosity won out over her desire not to pry. "In what way hasn't his life been happy?"

"Jason must be the one to tell you about his life; I have no right to do so. He will tell you someday—I know it in my heart. However, I have something else to tell you: Jason has decided that you are to have a season in London, complete with all the glitter and fanfare. We'll leave for London in three days. Flossie Wilson will join us there, and in the fortnight before the season begins, she'll teach you whatever you'll need to know in order to go about in society. We'll stay at Jason's townhouse, which is far more suitable for entertaining than mine is, and Jason will stay at my house when he's in the city. It was one thing for the three of us to reside together here, in the privacy of the countryside, but that must end once we go to London."

Victoria hadn't the faintest idea what a season in London entailed, but she listened attentively as Charles described the round of balls, routs, soirées, theater parties, and Venetian breakfasts she would be attending. Her apprehension had escalated almost out of control by the time he mentioned that Caroline Collingwood would be in London for the same reason.

". . . and though you didn't seem to pay it any special note at dinner this evening," he finished, "Lady Caroline mentioned twice that she hoped you would be going to the city so that you could continue your acquaintance there. You'll enjoy that, will you not?"

Victoria thought she would enjoy at least that part of the season very much and she said so, but in her heart she hated to leave Wakefield and face hundreds of strangers, particularly if they were like the Kirby ladies.

"Since we've settled all that," Charles concluded, opening a small drawer in the table and extracting a deck of cards, "tell me something; when your friend Andrew taught you to play cards, did he happen to teach you piquet?"

Victoria nodded.

"Excellent, let's play that then." When Victoria readily agreed, Charles gave her a frown of mock ferocity. "You won't cheat, will you?"

"Absolutely not," she promised solemnly.

He slid the deck across to her, his eyes laughing. "First, show me how good you are at dealing from the bottom. We'll compare our techniques."

Victoria burst out laughing. She picked up the piquet deck and the cards leapt to life in her nimble fingers, flying into place with a graceful whoosh and snap as she shuffled and reshuffled them. "First I will gull you into thinking this is your lucky night," she explained, swiftly dealing cards two at a time until they each had twelve. Charles looked at the hand she had dealt him, then raised his eyes, regarding her with fascinated admiration. "Four kings. I'd bet a fortune on this hand."

"You'd lose," Victoria promised with a jaunty smile, and turned over her own cards which included four aces.

"Now let's see how well you deal from the bottom," Charles suggested. When she showed him, he threw back his head, laughing.

The card game they'd intended to play degenerated into a farce, with each of them taking turns dealing themselves outrageous winning hands, and the library rang with their mirth as each tried to dupe the other.

His concentration sorely disrupted by the peals of laughter coming from the library, Jason strolled in to investigate just as the ornate grandfather clock was chiming the hour of nine. Upon entering the library, he found Charles and Victoria slumped in their chairs wiping tears of hilarity from their eyes, a deck of cards on the table between them. "The stories you two are trading must be even funnier than those you told at dinner," Jason remarked, shoving his hands into the pockets of his snug-fitting trousers and regarding them with a slightly disgruntled expression. "I can hear you laughing from my study."

"It's my fault," Charles lied, shooting Victoria a sly wink as he stood up. "Victoria wishes to play a serious game of piquet and I've been distracting her with jokes. I can't seem to be serious tonight. Would you sit in for a game with her?"

Victoria expected Jason to refuse but, after glancing curiously at Charles, he sat down across from her, and Charles positioned himself behind Jason's chair. Charles stood there until Victoria glanced at him, then he gave her a laughing, eager look that clearly said, "Beat him soundly—cheat!"

Victoria was so giddy from their outrageous card tricks, including the new ones Charles had taught her, that she fell into the plan without further urging. "Would you prefer to deal or shall I?" she asked Jason innocently.

"You, by all means," he said courteously.

Taking care to lull him into a false sense of security, Victoria shuffled the cards without any show of deftness, then began dealing them out. Jason glanced over his shoulder at Charles and asked for a glass of brandy, then he lounged back in his chair, indifferent. He lit one of the thin cheroots he occasionally enjoyed and accepted the glass Charles handed him.

"Aren't you going to look at your cards?" Victoria asked.

Jason shoved his hands into his pockets, the cheroot clamped between his even white teeth, and leveled a speculative glance at her. "Normally, I prefer mine dealt from the top of the deck," he drawled.

Impaled on his gaze, Victoria stifled a horrified giggle and tried to bluff. "I don't know what you mean."

One dark brow lifted, challenging her. "Do you know what happens to card-cheats?"

Victoria gave up all pretense of innocence. Propping her elbows on the table, she put her chin in her hands and regarded him with laughing blue eyes. "No, what?"

"The party who has been cheated issues a challenge to the party who has done the cheating, and frequently a duel is fought to settle the matter."

"Would you like to challenge me to a duel?" Victoria ventured daringly, enjoying herself immensely.

Jason lazed in his chair, studying her laughing face and sparkling eyes while he appeared to consider the matter. "Are you as good a shot as you said you were when you threatened my life this afternoon?"

"Better," she declared baldly.

"How are you with sabers?"

"I've never held one, but perhaps Lady Caroline would stand in for me. *She* is excellent at that sort of thing."

The dazzling charm of Jason's lazy white smile did odd things to Victoria's pulse as he remarked, "I wonder what possessed me to think you and Caroline Collingwood would be safe companions." Then he added what sounded to Victoria like a lovely compliment. "God help the London beaux this season. There isn't going to be a heart left intact when you're through with them."

Victoria was still trying to recover from her astonishment at his high opinion of her effect on gentlemen when Jason straightened in his chair and became brisk. "Now, shall we have that game you were so eager for?"

When she nodded, he took the cards from her hand. *"I'll deal, if you don't mind,"* he joked. He had won three hands before Victoria saw him deftly stealing a card he needed from those he'd already discarded and shouldn't have touched.

"You wretch!" she burst out with indignant laughter. "I've fallen in with a pair of bandits! I saw what you just did—*you've* been cheating while we played this hand."

"You're wrong," Jason said, grinning as he rose to his feet with that pantherish grace of his. "I've been cheating during *all three* hands." Without warning, he leaned down and pressed a kiss on the top of her head, affectionately rumpled her long hair, and strolled out of the library.

Victoria was so stunned by his actions that she didn't notice the expression of pure joy on Charles's face as he watched Jason leave.

Chapter Eleven

THE *GAZETTE* AND THE *TIMES* REPORTED TWO DAYS
later that Lady Victoria Seaton, Countess Langston—whose
betrothal to Jason Fielding, Marquess of Wakefield, had
been previously announced—would be making her formal
bow to society at a ball to be given in a fortnight by her
cousin, the Duke of Atherton.

No sooner had London's *ton* digested that exciting news
than they witnessed a sudden burst of activity at the Marquess of Wakefield's palatial London home at #6 Upper
Brook Street.

First came two coaches accommodating, in addition to
lesser servants, Northrup, the butler; O'Malley, the head
footman; and Mrs. Craddock, the cook. These vehicles were
soon followed by a large fourgon, which contained the
housekeeper, several housemaids, three kitchen porters,
four subordinate footmen, and a mountain of trunks.

Shortly thereafter another coach arrived bearing Miss
Flossie Wilson, the duke's maiden aunt, a plump elderly lady
with a cherubic, pink-cheeked face framed by blond curls.
Perched upon her head was a delightful little mulberry-

colored bonnet that would have been more appropriate for a much younger lady and that made Miss Flossie look very much like a cuddly, elderly doll. Miss Flossie, who was a well-known figure among the Quality, climbed down from the coach, waved gaily to two of her friends who were passing by, and rushed up the front steps of her great-nephew's Brook Street mansion.

All of this activity was duly noted by the elegant ladies and gentlemen who paraded leisurely along Upper Brook Street in their gorgeous finery, but none of it created the wild stir of attention that was generated the next day when witnesses observed Jason Fielding's sleek burgundy coach, drawn by four prancing grays, pulling up smartly before the house at #6.

From the sumptuous interior of the crested coach emerged Charles Fielding, Duke of Atherton, followed by a young lady who could only be Jason Fielding's promised wife. The young lady stepped gracefully down the coach steps, tucked her hand in the crook of the duke's arm, and paused, gazing in smiling disbelief at the lavish four-story mansion with its wide bow windows.

"Good God, that's her!" young Lord Wiltshire exclaimed from his vantage point across the street. "That's Countess Langston," he added, enthusiastically digging his elbow into his companion's chest for emphasis.

"How d'you know?" Lord Crowley demanded, smoothing a nonexistent wrinkle from his injured jacket.

"It's plain to the humblest intelligence who she is—look at her, she's a beauty. An Incomparable."

"You can't see her face," his friend pointed out reasonably.

"I don't have to, nodcock. If she weren't beautiful, she'd never have wrung an offer out of Wakefield. Have you ever seen him with a woman who wasn't a raving beauty?"

"No," Lord Crowley admitted. Raising his quizzing glass, he squinted through it and emitted a low, surprised whistle. "She has red hair. Wouldn't have expected that in a million years."

"It ain't red, it's more to the gold than the red."

"No, it's titian," Lord Crowley argued. After a moment's

additional consideration, he declared, "Titian is an enchanting color. Always preferred it, myself."

"Rubbish! You've never gone in for titian hair. It's not at all the rage."

"It is now," Lord Crowley predicted, grinning. Lowering his glass he sent a smug look at his friend. "I believe my Aunt Mersley is acquainted with Atherton—she'll get an invitation to Countess Langston's come-out ball. Think I'll tag along with her to it and—" He stopped speaking and gaped as the young lady under discussion turned back to the coach and called out something. An instant later, a huge silver and gray beast hurtled out and bounded to her heel, whereupon the trio proceeded up the front steps. "Damn my eyes if that wasn't a wolf!" Lord Crowley breathed in awe.

"She's stylish," the other young man decreed when he recovered his voice. "Never heard of a woman with a wolf for a pet. Very stylish, is the countess. An Original, to be sure." Eager to spread the word that they had been the first to glimpse the mysterious Lady Victoria Seaton, the two young men separated and rushed off to their respective clubs.

By the next evening, when Jason arrived in London and strolled into White's for the first time in months, intending to enjoy a few hours of relaxation at cards before attending the theater, it was already a widely known, accepted fact that his betrothed was a dazzling beauty and an acclaimed trendsetter. As a result, instead of being able to gamble in peace, Jason was repeatedly confronted by acquaintances who interrupted his game to compliment him on his excellent taste and good fortune, and to press upon him congratulations and best wishes for his future happiness.

After enduring two hours of this farce, of having his hand shaken and his shoulder patted, it occurred to him that, despite what Charles seemed to think, it was not wise for the *ton* to believe that Victoria was betrothed to him. Jason based this conclusion on the simple observation that none of the eligible bachelors who were congratulating him would dare to risk offending him by courting his affianced bride. Therefore, he set about encouraging them to pursue her by thanking them for their good wishes but adding a disclaimer.

"The matter is not entirely settled between us yet," he murmured, or, "Lady Seaton is not completely certain her affections are permanently fixed on me—she doesn't know me well enough."

He said those things because they were necessary, but he was thoroughly disgusted with the entire farce and completely incensed at being forced to play the role of a prospective bridegroom whose fiancée was on the verge of jilting him.

By nine o'clock, when his carriage drew up in front of the elegant house in Williams Street that he provided for his mistress, Jason was in a black mood. He strode up the steps and rapped impatiently on the door.

The maid who opened it took one look at his hard features and stepped back in nervous alarm. "M—Miss Sybil instructed me to tell you she doesn't wish to see you again."

"Oh?" Jason said in a silky voice. "Is that right?"

The little maid, who knew full well her wages were paid by the terrifyingly tall, powerful man looming in front of her, nodded, swallowed, and added apologetically, "Yes, my lord. You—you see, Miss Sybil read about your fiancée's ball and how you'll be there attending it, and she took to her bed. She's there now."

"Excellent!" Jason said crudely. In no mood to tolerate a tantrum from Sybil tonight, he stalked past the maid, bounded up the staircase, and flung open the door to Sybil's bedchamber.

His eyes narrowed on the ravishingly beautiful woman who was reclining on the bed amid a mountain of satin pillows. "Having an attack of the vapors, my sweet?" he inquired coolly, leaning his shoulder against the closed door.

Sybil's green eyes shot sparks of fury at him, but she did not deign to reply.

Jason's temper, already sorely strained, was about to explode. "Get out of that bed and get dressed," he ordered in a dangerously quiet voice. "We're going to a party tonight. I sent you a note."

"I'm not going anywhere with you! Ever!"

Casually Jason began unbuttoning his jacket. "In that case, move over. We'll spend the evening right where you are."

"You rutting beast!" the tempestuous beauty exploded, leaping off the bed in a flurry of pale pink chiffon as he came toward her. "How dare you! How dare you think you can come near me after that article in the *Times!* Get out of my house!"

Jason regarded her impassively. "Must I remind you that this is *my* house? I own it."

"Then *I'll* leave it," she shot back. Despite her show of defiance her chin trembled and, covering her face, she burst into tears. "Jason, how could you," she wept, her body shaking with heart-wrenching sobs. "You told me your engagement was a sham and I believed you! I—I'll never f-forgive you for this. Never. . . ."

The anger drained from Jason's face and was replaced by a touch of surprised regret as he listened to what sounded like genuine, heartbroken weeping. "Will this help you forgive me?" he asked quietly. Reaching into his pocket, he withdrew a flat velvet box, flipped it open with his thumb, and held it toward her.

Sybil peeked between her fingers and gasped as she beheld the glittering diamond bracelet resting upon a bed of black velvet. Reverently, she lifted it from its velvet nest and hugged it to her cheek. Raising her glowing eyes to his, she said, "Jason, for the matching necklace, I would forgive you for *anything!*"

Jason, who had been about to reassure her that he had no intention of marrying Victoria, threw back his head and roared with laughter. "Sybil," he chuckled, shaking his head as if he was as amused at himself as he was at her, "I think that is your most endearing quality."

"What is?" she asked, forgetting about the bracelet as she studied his sardonic features.

"Your honest, unabashed greed," he said without a hint of malice. "All women are greedy, but you, at least, are honest about it. Now, come here and show me how pleased you are with your new trinket."

Sybil obediently walked into his arms, but her eyes were faintly troubled as she raised her face for his kiss. "You—you don't have a very high opinion of women, do you, Jason? It isn't just me you hold in secret contempt—it's all of us, isn't it?"

135

"I think," he murmured evasively, untying the satin ribbons at her breasts, "that women are delightful creatures in bed."

"And out of bed? What about then?"

He ignored her question and slid her gown off her shoulders, his fingers expertly teasing her nipples into quick response. Taking her lips in a wildly demanding kiss, he swung her up into his arms and carried her to the bed. Sybil forgot that he had never answered her question.

Chapter Twelve

VICTORIA SAT UPON THE SETTEE IN HER BEDCHAMBER, surrounded by stacks of newly arrived boxes from Madame Dumosse containing yet more gowns to add to the stunning variety of walking dresses, riding habits, ball gowns, bonnets, shawls, long French kid gloves, and slippers that already filled every available storage space in her suite. "My lady!" Ruth gasped excitedly as she unwrapped a royal blue satin cloak with a wide hood, lined in ermine. "Have you ever seen anything so beautiful?"

Victoria glanced up from Dorothy's letter. "It's lovely," she agreed weakly. "How many cloaks does that make?"

"Eleven," Ruth answered, stroking the soft white fur. "No, twelve. I forgot about the yellow velvet lined with sable. Or is it thirteen? Let me think—there are four velvet cloaks, five satin ones, two furs, and three woolen ones. Fourteen in all!"

"It's difficult to believe that I used to manage quite nicely with two," Victoria sighed, smiling. "And when I go back home, three or four will be more than enough. It seems such a waste for Lord Fielding to squander his money on clothing I won't be able to use after a few weeks. In Portage, New

York, ladies don't dress in such finery," she finished, her attention returning to Dorothy's letter.

"When you go back home?" Ruth whispered in alarm. "Whatever do you mean? I beg your pardon, my lady, forgive my asking."

Victoria didn't hear her; she was rereading the letter, which had arrived today.

Dearest Tory,

I received your letter a week ago and was very excited to learn you were coming to London, for I hoped to see you at once. I told Grandmama I wished to do so, but instead of remaining in London, we left the very next day for Grandmama's country house, which is little more than an hour's ride from the place called Wakefield Park. Now I am in the country and you are in the city. Tory, I think Grandmama means to keep us apart, and it makes me very sad and quite angry. We must contrive some way to meet, but I will leave that to you, for you are much better at thinking of schemes than I am.

Perhaps I am only imagining Grandmama's intentions. I cannot be certain. She is stern, but she has not been cruel to me. She wishes for me to make what she calls "a brilliant match" and to that end she has in mind a gentleman named Winston. I have dozens of splendid new gowns of every color, although I cannot appear in most of them until I make my come-out, which seems a very odd tradition. And Grandmama said I cannot make my come-out until you are betrothed to someone, which is another tradition. Things were so much simpler at home, were they not?

I've explained to Grandmama innumerable times that you are practically betrothed to Andrew Bainbridge and that I wish to pursue a musical career, but she does not seem to listen.

She never mentions you, but I speak of you anyway, for I am determined to make her relent and ask you to stay with us. She does not forbid me to speak of you; it is only that she never *says* anything when I do, which makes me think she prefers to pretend you do not exist.

She merely listens to me with an expression on her face that can best be described as *blank* and says nothing at all.

Actually, I have quite badgered her to death about you—but *discreetly,* as I promised you I would. At first I merely spoke of you, injecting your name into the conversation whenever possible. When Grandmama remarked that I had a fine face, I told her you are much prettier; when she commented on my skill at the piano, I told her your talent is greater; when she remarked that my manners were acceptable, I told her yours are exquisite.

When all of that failed to make her understand how close we are and how much I miss you, I was forced to take more drastic measures, and so I carried the small portrait of you that I cherish down to the drawing room and put it upon the mantel there. Grandmama said nothing, but the next day she sent me off for a tour of London, and when I returned, the portrait was back in my own room.

A few days later, she was expecting some of her friends to call upon her, so I sneaked into her favorite salon and set up a lovely display of your sketches of the scenes around Portage—the ones you gave me to remind me of home. When the ladies saw them, they all exclaimed over your talent, but Grandmama said nothing. The next day she sent me off to Yorkshire, and when I returned two days later, the sketches were back in my room in a closet.

Tonight, she entertained once again, and I was asked to play the piano for her friends. I played, but while I did, I sang the song you and I wrote when we were children—we called it "Sisters Forever," remember? I could tell from the blank expression on Grandmama's face that she was most annoyed with me. When her friends left, she informed me that she had decided to send me to Devonshire for an entire week.

If I provoke her again, I've a notion she'll send me off to Brussels or somewhere for an entire month. Still, I shall persevere. Enough about that for now.

How shocked you must have been to learn that your

engagement to Lord Fielding had been announced. How upset Andrew would be if he but knew it. However, since all that is settled now and nothing is to come of it, you must enjoy your new gowns and not feel badly that you haven't been able to observe a proper period of mourning for Mama and Papa. I wear black gloves, which Grandmama says is the proper way of mourning in England, although there are some who dress in black for six months and then in gray for the next six months.

Grandmama does not believe in flouting propriety, and even if she accepted my assurances that you are already betrothed to Andrew, which you are, I would not be able to make my come-out until next spring. She says a full year must pass after a close family member dies before one is permitted to attend anything except quiet, informal affairs. I do not mind in the least, because the prospect of balls and all that goes with them seems very frightening. You must write and tell me if it is quite as bad as it seems.

Grandmama will be going to London from time to time to attend the theater, which she likes very well, and she promised I may accompany her now and then. I will send word to you as soon as I know when that will be, and we will contrive a way to meet.

I must go now, for Grandmama has hired a tutor to teach me how to go on in society when I do make my come-out. There is so much to learn that it makes my head spin. . . .

Victoria put the letter in a drawer, glanced at the clock on the mantel and sighed. She knew very well what Dorothy meant by her last paragraph, because Miss Flossie Wilson had been drilling rules of comportment and propriety into her own head for nearly two weeks, and it was time now for another lesson.

"There you are," Miss Flossie beamed as Victoria entered the salon. "Today, I think we ought to go over the correct forms of address as they apply to members of the peerage. We can't risk your making a mistake at your ball tomorrow night."

Suppressing the wild urge to snatch up her skirts and flee

from the house, Victoria sat down near Charles, across from Miss Flossie. For nearly two weeks, Miss Flossie had dragged her from dressmaker to milliner to mantua-maker in between seemingly interminable lessons on comportment, dancing, and French. During these lessons, Miss Flossie listened to Victoria's diction, observed her every mannerism, and questioned her on her accomplishments and interests, all the while nodding her curly head and fluttering her fingers in a manner that reminded Victoria of a fidgety little bird.

"Now, then," Miss Flossie chirped. "I shall begin with dukes. As I told you yesterday, a duke is the highest nonroyal title in the British peerage. Dukes are technically 'princes,' but although it may seem to you that a prince is higher in rank, you must remember that royal sons are born princes, but are *raised* to the rank of duke. Our dear Charles," she finished triumphantly and unnecessarily, "is a duke!"

"Yes," Victoria agreed, returning Uncle Charles's sympathetic smile.

"After a duke comes a marquess. A marquess is the heir to a dukedom. And that is why our dear Jason is called a marquess! Then comes an earl, a viscount, and lastly a baron. Shall I write all this down for you, dear?"

"No," Victoria assured her hastily. "I have it in my mind."

"You are such a clever child," Miss Flossie said approvingly. "Now, then, on to forms of address. When you speak to a duke, you must call him 'your grace'; *never*," she warned in dire tones, "address a duke as 'my lord.' A duchess is also addressed as 'your grace.' However, you may call all the other peers 'my lord' and their wives 'my lady,' which is the proper form of address for them. When you are a duchess, you will be addressed as 'your grace,' " she finished triumphantly. "Isn't that exciting."

"Yes," Victoria mumbled uncomfortably. Uncle Charles had explained to her why it was necessary for society to think her betrothal to Jason was real and, since Flossie Wilson was such a chatterbox, he had decided that Flossie must believe as everyone else did.

"I have obtained permission from the patronesses of

141

'Almack's for you to dance the waltz at your come out, my dear. But enough on that subject. Now, shall we look over a section of Debrett's Peerage?" But Victoria was spared that agony by Northrup, who stepped into the salon, cleared his throat, and announced the arrival of Countess Collingwood.

"Show her in, Northrup," Uncle Charles said jovially.

Caroline Collingwood walked into the salon, noted the open etiquette books and the volume of Debrett's Peerage, and cast a conspiratorial smile at Victoria. "I was hoping you might accompany me for a drive in the park," she told Victoria.

"I'd love it above everything!" Victoria exclaimed. "Would you mind terribly, Miss Flossie? Uncle Charles?" Both gave their permission and Victoria rushed upstairs to tidy her hair and fetch her bonnet.

Waiting for her, Caroline turned politely to the two older occupants of the salon. "I imagine you must be very eager for tomorrow night."

"Oh, yes, very," Miss Flossie averred, nodding her blond curls energetically. "Victoria is a delightful young lady, which I don't have to tell you, who are already acquainted with her. Such charming manners she has, so easy and conversable. And what eyes! Such a lovely figure, too. I have every confidence she'll be a great success. I can't help wishing she was blond, however." Miss Flossie sighed and bobbed her head dejectedly, oblivious to Lady Collingwood's mahogany tresses. "Blond is all the rage, you know." Her birdlike gaze darted to Charles. "Do you recall Lord Hornby as a youth? I used to think he was the handsomest man alive. He had red hair and such *nice* address. His brother was so very short . . ." And so she continued, leaping from topic to topic as though from branch to branch.

Victoria looked around at the park and leaned back in the open carriage, closing her eyes in sheer bliss. "How peaceful it is here," she said to Caroline, "and how kind you've been to come to my rescue so many afternoons with these drives in the park."

"What were you studying when I arrived?"

"The correct forms of address for members of the peerage and their wives."

"And have you mastered it?" Caroline asked.

"Absolutely," Victoria said, suppressing a tired, irreverent giggle. "All I have to do is call the men 'my lord,' as if they are God, and their wives 'my lady,' as if I am their maid."

Caroline's laughter brought an answering chuckle from Victoria. "The thing I find hardest is French," she admitted. "My mother taught Dorothy and me to read it, and I do that well enough, but I cannot call the right words to mind when I try to speak it."

Caroline, who spoke fluent French, tried to help. "Sometimes it is best to learn a language in useful phrases, rather than single words; then you needn't think how to put them together, and the rest can come later. For example, how would you ask me for writing materials in French?"

"Mon pot d'encre veut vous emprunter votre stylo?" Victoria ventured.

Caroline's lips trembled with mirth. "You have just said, 'My inkpot wishes to borrow your pen.' "

"At least I was close," Victoria said, and they both burst into gales of mirth.

The occupants of the other carriages in the park turned at the musical sound of their gaiety and it was again noted that the dashing Countess Collingwood was showing *particular* partiality for Lady Victoria Seaton—a fact that had already added considerably to Victoria's growing prestige amongst the *ton* who had yet to meet her.

Victoria reached over to Wolf, who regularly accompanied them on their outings, and stroked his head. "Amazing, is it not, that I learned mathematics and chemistry from my father easily enough, but French defies me? Perhaps I can't grasp it because learning it seems so pointless."

"Why is it pointless?"

"Because Andrew will arrive soon and take me home."

"I shall miss you," Caroline said wistfully. "Most friendships take years before they feel as comfortable and easy as ours is now. When, exactly, do you think your Andrew is likely to arrive?"

"I wrote him within a week of my parents' death," Victoria replied, absently tucking a strand of hair into place beneath the pleated brim of her lemon yellow bonnet. "The letter would take about six weeks to reach him, and it would take him six weeks to come home. It will take him another four to six weeks to sail from America back here. That totals somewhere between sixteen and eighteen weeks. Tomorrow will be exactly eighteen weeks since I wrote him."

"You're assuming that he received that first letter in Switzerland, but mail to Europe is not always reliable. Besides, suppose he had already left for France, where you said he was going next?"

"I gave Mrs. Bainbridge—Andrew's mother—a second letter to mail to France, just in case that happened." Victoria sighed. "If I had known when I wrote to him then that I was going to be in England now, he could have stayed here in Europe, which would have been much more convenient. Unfortunately, I didn't know it, so all I told him in the first letters was that my parents had died in an accident. I'm certain he started for America as soon as he discovered that."

"Then why didn't he arrive in America before you left for England?"

"There probably wasn't quite enough time. I would guess he arrived within a week or two of my departure."

Caroline slanted Victoria a thoughtful, hesitant look. "Victoria, have you told the Duke of Atherton you are certain Andrew is coming for you?"

"Yes, but he doesn't believe me. And because he doesn't, he's determined I must have this season."

"But doesn't it seem odd that he wants you and Lord Fielding to pretend to be betrothed? I don't mean to pry," Caroline apologized quickly. "If you'd rather not discuss this with me, I'll understand."

Victoria shook her head emphatically. "I've been longing to talk to you about it, but I didn't want to take advantage of our friendship by unburdening myself to you."

"I've unburdened myself to you," Caroline said simply. "And that is what friends are for—to talk things out. You can't imagine how wonderful and how unusual I find it to have a friend in the *ton* who I know will not breathe a word I say to anyone else."

Victoria smiled. "In that case . . . Uncle Charles says the reason he wants everyone to believe I'm betrothed is because it will make it possible for me to remain free of other 'entanglements' and 'complications.' As an engaged woman, he says, I'll be able to enjoy all the excitement of my comeout without feeling the slightest pressure from suitors, or from society, to make an eligible match."

"In a way, he is right," Caroline remarked, her expression faintly puzzled, "but he is going to a deal of trouble just to keep the gentlemen from pressing offers on you."

Victoria stared thoughtfully at the neat beds of daffodils blooming beside the path. "I know that, and I've wondered about it. Uncle Charles is fond of me, and I sometimes have the feeling he still harbors the hope Lord Fielding and I might eventually wed if Andrew doesn't come for me."

Concern clouded Caroline's gray eyes. "Do you think there's such a chance?"

"None at all," Victoria said with smiling earnest.

Breathing a sigh of relief, Caroline sat back against the squabs. "Good. I should worry about you if you married Lord Fielding."

"Why?" Victoria asked, her curiosity thoroughly aroused.

"I wish I hadn't said that," Caroline murmured miserably, "but since I have, I suppose I ought to tell you. If your Andrew doesn't come for you, you ought to know what sort of man Lord Fielding really is. There are drawing rooms where he is admitted but not really welcome. . . ."

"Whyever not?"

"For one thing, there was some sort of scandal four years ago. I don't know the details because I was too young at the time to be privy to any really scandalous gossip. Last week, I asked my husband to tell me, but he is a friend of Lord Fielding's and he won't talk about it. He says it was all trumped-up nonsense circulated by a spiteful woman, and he forbade me to ask anyone else because he said it would stir up the old gossip again."

"Miss Flossie says the *ton* is always on fire with some sort of gossip and that most of it is flummery," Victoria commented. "Whatever it was, I'm certain to hear all about it in the next few weeks."

"You won't," Caroline predicted emphatically. "In the first place, you are a young, unmarried female, so no one will tell you anything even slightly scandalous for fear of offending your sensibilities or sending you into a swoon. Secondly, people gossip about others, but they rarely tell their tales to the people involved. It is the nature of gossip to be carried on behind the backs of those most intimately concerned in the story."

"Where it does the most damage and provides the most titillation," Victoria agreed. "Gossip was not unknown in Portage, New York, you know, and it was mostly flummery there, too."

"Perhaps, but there's more I wish to warn you about," Caroline continued, looking guilty but determined to protect her friend. "Because of his rank and his fortune, Lord Fielding is still considered a splendid catch, and there are a great many ladies who also find him extremely handsome. For those three reasons, they've hung out for him. However, *he* hasn't been at all nice in his treatment of *them*. In fact, there've been times he's been positively rude! Victoria," she concluded in a tone of the direst condemnation, "Lord Fielding is *not* a gentleman."

She waited for some reaction from her friend, but when Victoria merely looked at her as if that defect in Lord Fielding's character was no more significant than a wrinkled neckcloth, Caroline sighed and plunged ahead. "The men are nearly as afraid of him as many of the ladies are, not only because he's so very cold and aloof, but because there've been rumors about his duels in India. They say he's fought dozens of them and killed his opponents in cold blood, without a flicker of emotion or regret—they say he'll challenge a man to a duel for the most minor offense—"

"I don't believe that," Victoria put in with unconscious loyalty to Jason.

"You may not, but others do, and people are afraid of him."

"Do they ostracize him, then?"

146

"Just the opposite," Caroline said. "They positively *pander* to him. No one would dare give him the cut direct."

Victoria looked at her incredulously. "Surely *everyone* who knows him isn't afraid of him?"

"Almost everyone. Robert genuinely likes him and he laughs when I say there is something sinister about Lord Fielding. However, I once heard Robert's mother tell a group of her friends that Lord Fielding is wicked, that he uses women and then discards them."

"He can't be as bad as all that. You said yourself he is considered a splendid catch—"

"Actually, he's rated the best catch in England."

"There, you see! If people thought he was as terrible as you think they do, no young lady, nor her mama, would ever seek marriage to him."

Caroline snorted indelicately. "For a dukedom and a magnificent fortune, there are those who would marry Bluebeard!"

When Victoria merely chuckled, Caroline's face clouded with confusion. "Victoria, doesn't he seem strange and frightening to you?"

Victoria carefully considered the answer to that as the driver turned their carriage back toward Jason's townhouse. She remembered the biting lash of Jason's tongue when she first arrived at Wakefield and his awesome anger when he caught her swimming in the creek. She also remembered the way he had smoothly outcheated her at cards, consoled her the night she cried, and laughed at her attempt to milk the cow. She also remembered the way he had held her close against his body and kissed her with fierce, demanding tenderness, but she immediately cast that recollection out of her mind.

"Lord Fielding's temper is quick," she began slowly, "but I have noticed that he is soon over his anger and willing to let bygones be bygones. I am much like him in that respect, although I don't become angry as easily as he does. And he didn't challenge *me* to a duel when I threatened to shoot him," she added humorously, "so I cannot believe he is so very eager to shoot people. If you asked me to describe him," Victoria concluded, "I would probably say that he is an exceedingly generous man who might even be gentle underneath his—"

"You're joking!"

Victoria shook her head, trying to explain. "I see him differently than you do. I try to see people as my father taught me I should."

"Did he teach you to be blind to their faults?" Caroline asked desperately.

"Not at all. But he was a physician who taught me to look for causes of things, not merely symptoms. Because of that, whenever someone behaves oddly, I start wondering *why* they are doing so, and there is always a reason. For example, have you ever noticed that when people don't feel well, they are frequently ill-tempered?"

Caroline nodded instantly. "My brothers were cross as crabs if they felt even slightly unwell."

"That's what I mean: your brothers aren't mean people, but when they don't feel well, they become bad-tempered."

"Do you think, then, that Lord Fielding is ill?"

"I don't think he's very happy, which is the same thing as not feeling well. Regardless of that, my father also taught me to place more importance on the things a person does than on what he says. If you view Lord Fielding in that way, he has been very kind to me. He's given me a home and more beautiful clothes than I could use in a lifetime, and he's even let me bring Wolf into the house."

"You must have a superior understanding of people," Caroline said quietly.

"No, I don't," Victoria contradicted ruefully. "I lose my temper and am hurt just as easily as anyone else. Not until *afterward* do I remember to try to understand why the person might have treated me in such a way."

"And you aren't afraid of Lord Fielding, not even when he's angry?"

"Only a little," Victoria admitted ruefully. "But then, I haven't seen him since we came to London, so perhaps I'm only feeling brave because there's a distance between us."

"Not anymore," Caroline remarked, nodding meaningfully toward the elegant black-lacquered coach with a gold seal emblazoned on the door that was waiting in front of #6

Upper Brook Street. "That is Lord Fielding's crest on the black coach," she explained when Victoria looked blank. "And the coach drawn up behind that one is ours—which means my husband must have finished his business early and decided to fetch me himself."

Victoria felt a funny little leap of her heart at the knowledge that Jason was here—a reaction she immediately put down to nervous guilt for having discussed him with Caroline.

Both gentlemen were in the drawing room, listening politely as Miss Flossie tortured them with a lengthy, disjointed monologue on Victoria's progress during the last two weeks, liberally interspersed with rapturous comments about her own debut almost fifty years ago. Victoria took one glance at Jason's strained features and concluded he was mentally strangling the lady.

"Victoria!" Miss Flossie said, gleefully clapping her little hands. "At last you are back! I've been telling these gentlemen of your talent at the piano, and they are anxious beyond anything to hear you play." Cheerfully oblivious to Jason's sardonic expression when he heard himself described as "anxious beyond anything," Miss Flossie marched Victoria over to the piano and insisted that she play something at once.

Helplessly, Victoria sat down on the bench and glanced at Jason, who was concentrating on picking a piece of lint from the leg of his beautifully tailored dark blue trousers. He could not have looked more bored unless he yawned. He also looked incredibly handsome, Victoria realized, and she felt another tremor of nervousness, which was amplified a dozen times by his lazy, mocking smile when he looked up at her. "I've never known a female who could swim, shoot, tame wild animals, *and*," he concluded, "play the piano. Let's hear you do it."

Victoria could tell from his tone that he expected her to play poorly, and she longed to avoid giving a recital now, when she was so inexplicably nervous. "Mr. Wilheim gave Dorothy and me lessons as a way of repaying my father for treating his ailment of the lungs, but Dorothy is a much better musician than I. Until two weeks ago, I hadn't played in months, and I'm still out of practice," she said, hastily trying to excuse herself. "My Beethoven is barely mediocre and—"

Her lame hope for a reprieve was dashed when Jason lifted a challenging eyebrow and nodded meaningfully at the keyboard.

Victoria sighed and capitulated. "Is there anything in particular you would like to hear?"

"Beethoven," he said dryly.

Victoria sent him an exasperated look, which only made his grin widen, but she bent her head and prepared to do as he asked. Tentatively, she ran her fingers over the keyboard, then stopped, her hands poised over the keys. When she brought them down again, the room resounded with the vibrant, sweeping melody and triumphant crescendos of Beethoven's Piano Sonata in F Minor, exploding with all the power and might and lilting sweetness of the passage.

In the hall beyond the drawing room, Northrup stopped polishing a silver bowl and blissfully closed his eyes, listening enraptured. In the foyer, O'Malley stopped scolding a subordinate and tilted his head toward the drawing room, smiling at the uplifting sound of music being played in Lord Fielding's house.

When Victoria finished, everyone in the drawing room burst into spontaneous applause—except Jason, who leaned back in his chair, a wry smile on his lips. "Do you possess any other 'mediocre' skills?" he teased, but there was a sincere compliment in his eyes, and when Victoria saw it, it filled her with an absurd amount of pleasure.

Caroline and her husband left soon thereafter, promising to see Victoria at her ball tomorrow night, and Miss Flossie escorted them to the door. Left alone with Jason, Victoria felt unaccountably self-conscious, and she promptly burst into speech to hide it. "I—I'm surprised to see you here."

"Surely you didn't think I'd stay away from your debut?" he teased, with a dazzling smile. "I'm not entirely lost to the proprieties, you know. We're supposed to be betrothed. How would it look if I didn't appear here?"

"My lord—" she began.

"That has a nice ring to it," he remarked, chuckling. "Very respectful. You've never called me that before."

Victoria gave him a look of laughing severity. "And I wouldn't have done so now, except that Miss Flossie has been drilling titles and forms of address into my head for days on end. However, what I started to say was that I'm not very good at deceit, and the idea of telling people we're betrothed makes me monstrously uneasy. Uncle Charles won't listen to my objections, but I don't think this pretense is a good idea at all."

"It isn't," Jason agreed flatly. "The reason for giving you this season is to introduce you to prospective husbands—"

Victoria opened her mouth to insist that Andrew was going to be her husband, but Jason held up a hand and amended his last statement. "The purpose is to introduce you to prospective husbands, *in the event* Ambrose doesn't rush to your rescue."

"Andrew," Victoria corrected him. "Andrew Bainbridge."

Jason dismissed him with a shrug. "When the subject of our betrothal comes up, I want you to say what I've been saying."

"What is that?"

"I say that everything is not quite settled, or that you don't know me well enough to be certain your affections are fixed on me. That will leave the door open for your other suitors, and even Charles can't object."

"I'd much rather tell the truth and say we aren't betrothed."

Jason ran his hand across the back of his neck, irritably massaging the tense muscles. "You can't. If either of us cries off now—so soon after your arrival in England—there will be a great deal of unpleasant speculation about which of us cried off, and why."

Victoria remembered Caroline's description of the *ton*'s attitude toward Jason and she immediately guessed what people would think if *she* cried off. When she viewed it in that way, she was willing to continue the pretense of their betrothal. Not for the world would she repay Jason's kindness and generosity to her by letting anyone think she found him repugnant or frightening as a prospective husband. "Very well," she said. "I'll say things aren't quite settled between us yet."

"Good girl," he said. "Charles has already had one near-fatal attack and his heart is weak. I don't want to worry him needlessly, and he is utterly determined to see you well married."

"But what will happen to him when Andrew comes to take me home?" Her eyes widened as a new problem occurred to her. "And what will people here think when I—I toss you over to marry Andrew?"

Amusement gleamed in Jason's eyes at her choice of expressions. "*If* that happens, we'll say you're honoring a former betrothal arranged by your father. In England, it is a daughter's duty to marry to suit her family, and everyone will understand. Charles will miss you, but if he believes you're happy, it will soften the blow. However," he added, "I don't think that's going to happen. Charles has told me about Bainbridge, and I agree that he is probably a weak man who is under his widowed mother's thumb. Without your presence in America to reinforce his courage and determination, he's not likely to get up the gumption to defy his mother and come after you."

"Oh, for heaven's—" Victoria burst out, exasperated at his misconception of Andrew.

"I'm not finished," Jason interrupted authoritatively. "It's also apparent to me that your father wasn't particularly eager for the two of you to wed—not if he insisted on a trial separation to test your feelings for each other, when you've already known each other all your lives. You were not betrothed to Bainbridge at the time of your father's death, Victoria," Jason finished implacably. "Therefore, if he does arrive on our doorstep, he will have to gain *my* approval before I will permit you to marry him and return to America."

Victoria was torn between anger and laughter at his gall. "Of all the nerve!" she sputtered, her thoughts tumbling over themselves. "You've never met him and you've already decided what sort of man he is. And now you are saying I can't leave with him unless he passes muster with *you,* you who practically tossed me out on my ear the day I arrived at Wakefield!" It was all so absurd that Victoria started to laugh. "Do you know, I never have the faintest idea what you are going to do or say next to astound me. I don't know what to do where you're concerned."

"All you have to do," Jason said, an answering smile tugging at his lips, "is look over the current crop of London fops during the next few weeks, choose the one you want, and bring him to me for my blessing. Nothing could be easier—I'll be working here in my study nearly every day."

"Here?" Victoria uttered, choking back a horrified giggle at his description of the way she ought to go about choosing a husband. "I thought you were going to stay at Uncle Charles's house."

"I'm going to sleep there, but I'm going to work here. Charles's house is damned uncomfortable. The furniture is old and the rooms are mostly small and dark. Besides, no one will think anything of it if I'm here during the day, so long as you're properly chaperoned, which you are. There's no reason for me to be inconvenienced when I work. Speaking of chaperones, has Flossie Wilson chattered you into a coma yet?"

"She's very sweet," Victoria said, trying again not to laugh.

"I've never heard a woman talk so much and say so little."

"She has a kind heart."

"True," he agreed absently, his attention shifting to the clock. "I'm engaged for the opera tonight. When Charles returns, tell him I was here and that I'll be here tomorrow night in time to greet the guests."

"Very well." Giving him an impudent, laughing look Victoria added, "But I warn you I shall take the greatest pleasure when Andrew arrives and you're forced to admit how wrong you've been about everything."

"Don't count on it."

"Oh, but I am counting on it. I shall ask Mrs. Craddock to fix a crow pie and I shall force you to eat it while I watch."

In surprised silence, Jason gazed down at her laughing, upturned face. "You're not afraid of anything, are you?"

"I am not afraid of you," she announced blithely.

"You ought to be," he said, and on that enigmatic remark he left.

Chapter Thirteen

"NEARLY EVERYONE HAS ARRIVED," MISS FLOSSIE bubbled excitedly as Ruth finished putting the last touches to Victoria's coiffure. "It's time to make your grand entrance, my dear."

Victoria rose obediently but her knees were trembling. "I would much rather have stood in the receiving line with Uncle Charles and Lord Fielding, so I could meet the guests separately. It would have been much less nerve-racking."

"But not nearly as effective," Miss Flossie said airily.

Victoria took a last critical glance at her reflection, accepted the fan that Ruth gave her, and picked up her skirts. "I'm ready," she said shakily. As they passed across the landing, Victoria paused to look down upon the foyer below, which had been turned into a wondrous flower garden in honor of her ball, with giant pots of airy ferns and huge baskets of white roses. Then she drew a nervous breath and climbed the curving staircase that led upward to the next story, where the ballroom was located. Footmen dressed in formal, green velvet livery trimmed with gold braid stood at attention along the staircase beside tall silver stands of more white roses. Victoria smiled at the footmen she knew and nodded politely to the others. O'Malley, the head footman, was stationed at the top of the staircase and she asked him softly, "Has your tooth been bothering you? Don't fail to tell me if it pains you again—it's no trouble at all to fix another poultice."

He grinned at her with unabashed devotion. "It ain't bothered me a bit since you fixed me the last one, my lady."

"Very well, but you won't try to suffer with it if it starts up again, will you?"

"No, my lady."

He waited until Victoria had rounded the corner, then turned to the footman beside him. "She's a grand one, ain't she?"

"A lady through and through," the other footman agreed. "Just like you said she was from the start."

"She'll brighten up things for the lot of us," O'Malley predicted, "and for the master too, once she's warmin' his bed. She'll give him an heir—that'll make him happy."

Northrup stood on the balcony overlooking the ballroom, his back ramrod straight, ready to announce the names of any late-arriving guests who passed beneath the marble portal beside him. Victoria approached him on legs that felt like jelly. "Give me a moment to catch my breath," she pleaded with him. "Then you can announce our names. I'm dreadfully nervous," she confided to him.

A smile almost, but not quite, cracked his stern countenance as his expert eye flicked over the breathtaking young woman before him. "While you are catching your breath, my lady, may I say how very much I enjoyed hearing you play Beethoven's Piano Sonata in F Minor yesterday afternoon? It is a particular favorite of mine."

Victoria was so pleased, and so startled, by this unexpected cordiality from the austere servant that she nearly forgot the noisy, laughing crowd in the ballroom below. "Thank you," she said, smiling gently. "And what is your very favorite piece?"

He looked shocked by her interest, but he told her.

"I shall play it for you tomorrow," she promised sweetly.

"That is kind of you, indeed, my lady!" he replied with a stiff face and a formal bow. But when he turned to announce her name, Northrup's voice rang with pride. "Lady Victoria

155

Seaton, Countess Langston," he called out, "and Miss Florence Wilson."

A lightning bolt of anticipation seemed to shoot through the crowd, breaking off conversations and choking off laughter as some 500 guests turned in near-unison for their first real look at the American-born girl who now bore her mother's title and who was soon to receive an even more coveted one from Jason, Lord Fielding.

They saw an exotic, titian-haired goddess draped in a shimmering Grecian-style gown of sapphire silk that matched her lustrous eyes and clung to every curve of her slender, voluptuous body. Long gloves encased her arms, and her shining hair was caught up at the crown in a mass of thick, glossy curls entwined with ropes of sapphires and diamonds. They saw a sculpted face of unforgettable beauty with high, delicately molded cheekbones, a perfect nose, generous lips, and a tiny, intriguing cleft at the center of her chin.

No one looking at her would have believed that the regal young beauty's knees were nearly knocking together with panic.

The sea of nameless faces staring up at her seemed to part as Victoria descended the steps, and Jason suddenly strode forward from among the crowd. He held his hand out to her and Victoria automatically placed her hand in his, but the eyes she turned up to his were wide with fright.

Bending low as if to murmur some intimate compliment, Jason said, "You're scared to death, aren't you? Do you want me to begin the hundreds of introductions now, or would you rather dance with me and let them finish giving you a thorough look-over that way?"

"What a choice!" Victoria whispered on a choked laugh.

"I'll start the music," Jason decided wisely, and signaled the musicians with a nod of his head. He led her onto the dance floor and took her in his arms as the musicians struck up a dramatic waltz. "Can you waltz?" he said suddenly.

"What a time to ask!" she said, laughing, on the verge of nervous hysteria.

"Victoria!" Jason said severely, but with a dazzling smile for the benefit of their watchful audience, "you are the selfsame young woman who coolly threatened to blow my brains out with a gun. Do not dare turn cowardly now."

"No, my lord," she replied, desperately trying to follow him as he began to guide her through the first steps of the waltz. He waltzed, she thought, with the same relaxed elegance with which he wore his superbly tailored black evening clothes.

Suddenly his arm tightened around her waist, forcing her into nerve-racking proximity with his powerful body, and he warned in a low voice, "It is customary for a couple to engage in some form of conversation or harmless flirtation when they are dancing, otherwise onlookers perceive that the two dislike one another."

Victoria stared at him, her mouth as dry as sawdust.

"Say something to me, dammit."

The curse, uttered with *such* a brilliant, attentive smile, wrung an involuntary laugh from her, and she temporarily forgot about their audience. Trying to do as he bade her, she said the first thing that came to mind. "You waltz very well, my lord."

Jason relaxed and smiled down at her. "That is what *I* am supposed to say to *you*."

"You English have rules to govern absolutely everything," Victoria countered in mock admiration.

"You happen to be English too, ma'am," he reminded her, then added, "Miss Flossie has taught you to waltz very well. What else have you learned?"

A little stung by his assumption that she hadn't known how to waltz before, Victoria gave him a jaunty smile and said, "You may rest assured that I now possess all the skills which the English deem necessary for a young lady of birth and refinement."

"And those are?" Jason inquired, grinning at her tone.

"Besides playing the piano, I can carry a tune, waltz without falling, and embroider a fine stitch. In addition, I can read French and execute a throne-room curtsy with great aplomb. It seems to me," she observed with an impertinent smile, "that in England it is quite desirable for a female to be utterly useless."

Jason threw back his head and laughed at her observation.

She was, he thought, an amazing combination of intriguing contrasts—of sophistication and innocence, femininity and courage, lush beauty and irrepressible humor. She had a body that was created for a man's hands, a pair of eyes that could drive a man to lust, a smile that could be sunny or sensual, and a mouth—a mouth that positively invited a man to kiss it.

"It's impolite to stare," Victoria said, her mind more on keeping up the appearance of enjoying herself than on the direction of his gaze.

Jason jerked his gaze from her mouth. "Sorry."

"You said we're expected to engage in some sort of flirtation while we dance," she reminded him teasingly. "I haven't any experience with that at all—have you?"

"More than enough," he replied, admiring the glowing color highlighting her cheekbones.

"Very well—go ahead and show me how it's done."

Startled at the invitation, Jason gazed down into her dark-lashed, laughing blue eyes and momentarily lost himself in them. Desire surged through his body and his arm automatically pulled her closer. "You don't need lessons," he murmured huskily. "You're doing very well at it right now."

"At what?"

Her obvious confusion restored Jason's sanity and he relaxed his hold on her. "At getting yourself into a great deal more trouble than you ever bargained for."

On the sidelines, young Lord Crowley raised his quizzing glass and inspected Lady Victoria from head to toe. "Exquisite," he said to his friend. "Told you she was the moment we laid eyes on her, that day she arrived in Brook Street. I've never seen the equal to her. She's divine. Heavenly. An angel."

"A beauty, a true beauty!" young Lord Wiltshire agreed.

"If it weren't for Wakefield, I'd court her myself," said Crowley. "I'd lay siege to her defenses, battle off her other suitors, and then I'd give chase!"

"You could," Lord Wiltshire stated drolly, "but in order to *catch* her, you'd need to be ten years older and twenty times richer. Although, from what I hear, the marriage thing isn't entirely settled."

"In that case, I mean to get an introduction to her tonight."

"So do I," Lord Wiltshire retorted challengingly, and they both hastened off in search of their respective mothers so that introductions could be properly procured.

For Victoria, the night was an unqualified success. She had feared that the rest of the *ton* would be much like Lady Kirby, but for the most part they seemed to welcome her into their exclusive ranks. In fact, some of them—particularly the gentlemen—were almost humorously effusive in their compliments and attentions. They surrounded her, requesting introductions and dances with her, then staying by her side, vying for her attention and asking for permission to call upon her. Victoria took none of it seriously, but she treated them all with impartial friendliness.

Occasionally, she caught glimpses of Jason and smiled fondly to herself. He looked breathtakingly handsome tonight in the raven black evening clothes that matched his hair and contrasted sharply with his snowy frilled shirt and flashing white smile. Beside him, other men seemed pale and insignificant.

Many other ladies thought so too, Victoria realized four hours later as she danced with yet another of her partners. Several of those ladies were flirting outrageously with him, despite the fact that he was supposedly betrothed to her. With secret compassion, she watched a beautiful, sultry blonde trying to hold his attention by gazing invitingly into his eyes while Jason stood with his shoulder propped negligently against a pillar, an expression of bored condescension on his tanned face.

Until tonight, Victoria had assumed he treated only her with that infuriating, mocking attitude, but she realized now that Jason seemed to treat all females with cool tolerance. No doubt this attitude was what Caroline meant when she said Jason was rude and ungentlemanly. Even so, the ladies were attracted to him like pretty moths to a dangerous flame. And why not, Victoria decided philosophically, watching him gently disengage his arm from the blonde's hand and move toward Lord Collingwood. Jason was compellingly, irresistibly, magnetically . . . manly.

Robert Collingwood looked at Jason and nodded his head in the direction of Victoria's beaux, who were clustered around Flossie Wilson awaiting Victoria's return from the dance floor. "If you still intend to marry her off to someone else, Jason," he said, "you won't have long to wait. She's just become the new rage."

"Good," Jason replied, glancing at the throng of Victoria's beaux and dismissing them with a shrug.

Chapter Fourteen

ROBERT'S PREDICTION ABOUT VICTORIA'S SUCCESS turned out to be true. The day following her ball, twelve gentlemen and seven young ladies came to call upon Lady Victoria, pressing invitations on her and begging for a closer look at Wolf. Northrup was in his glory, ushering callers in and out of the salons and snapping instructions at the footmen who carried tea trays into the various salons.

By the time supper was served at nine o'clock, Victoria was too exhausted to consider going to any of the evening's balls and soirées she'd been invited to by her callers. She hadn't gone to bed last night until nearly dawn and she could scarcely keep her eyes open as she picked idly at the dessert on her plate. Jason, on the other hand, looked as fresh and vital as usual, despite having worked in his study all afternoon.

"Victoria, you were a dazzling success last night," he said, turning his attention from Charles to her. "It's obvious Crowley and Wiltshire are already besotted with you. So is Lord Makepeace, and he is considered the season's best catch."

Her sleepy eyes filled with laughter. "That particular expression calls to mind a halibut!"

A moment later she excused herself to go up to bed. Jason bade her good night, a smile lingering on his lips at her quip. She could light up a room with her smile, albeit a sleepy one. Beneath her artless sophistication, there was sweetness and intelligence, too. He sipped his brandy, remembering how she had charmed the *ton* last night with her beauty and laughter. She had won over Northrup completely, by playing Mozart especially for him tonight. When she was finished, the elderly butler had tears in his eyes. She had followed that up by sending for O'Malley and playing a rousing Irish jig for him. By the end of it, a dozen servants had gathered outside the drawing room, loitering about in order to eavesdrop on her impromptu concert. Instead of ordering them to disperse and go about their duties—as Jason had been about to do— Victoria turned to them and asked if *they* had any special favorites she could play for them. She knew all their names; she asked about their health and their families. And tired though she obviously was, she kept up her performance at the piano for more than an hour.

All the servants were devoted to her, Jason realized. Footmen smiled and bent over backward to please her. Housemaids rushed to do her tiniest bidding. And Victoria thanked each of them prettily for every service they performed. She had a way with people; she could win over barons and butlers with equal ease—perhaps because she treated them both with the same sincere, smiling interest.

Idly, Jason twisted the stem of his brandy glass in his fingertips. Without her, the dining room suddenly seemed gloomy and empty. Unaware that Charles was watching him with a gratified twinkle in his eyes, Jason continued to sit there, frowning at her empty chair.

"She's an extraordinary young woman, is she not?" Charles prodded finally.

"Yes."

"Ravishingly beautiful, and witty to boot. Why, you've laughed more since Victoria came to England than I've seen you laugh in a year! Don't deny it—the girl's unique."

"I don't deny it," Jason replied, remembering her intriguing ability to look like a countess, a milkmaid, a forlorn child, or a sophisticated woman, depending upon her mood and surroundings.

"She's charming and innocent, but she has spirit and fire, as well. The right man could turn Victoria into a passionate, loving woman—a woman to warm his bed and his life." Charles paused, but Jason said nothing. "Her Andrew has no intention of marrying her," Charles continued meaningfully. "I have no doubt of that. If he did, he'd have contacted her by now." He paused again, and again Jason said nothing.

"I feel sorrier for that Andrew fellow than for Victoria," Charles added with sly determination. "I pity *any* man who is fool enough to ignore the one woman in a thousand who could make him truly happy. Jason," Charles demanded, "are you paying any heed to all this?"

Jason sent him an impatient, puzzled look. "I've heard every word. What has all this to do with me?"

"What has all—?" Charles sputtered in frustration. Catching himself, he continued more cautiously. "It has everything to do with you, and with me too. Victoria is a young, unmarried female. Even with Miss Flossie here as her chaperone, Victoria can't continue indefinitely to live in a house with one bachelor, and another bachelor who spends every day here. If we go on like this for more than a few weeks, people will assume the betrothal's a hum and that she's really another of your conquests. When that happens, they'll cut her dead. You don't want to cause the girl humiliation, do you?"

"No, of course not," Jason said absently, staring at the brandy in his glass.

"Then there's only one solution—she'll have to marry, and quickly." He waited, but Jason was silent. "Won't she, Jason?" he urged.

"I suppose so."

"Then *who* should she marry, Jason?" Charles demanded triumphantly. "*Who* could turn her into a loving, passionate woman? *Who* needs a wife to warm his bed and give him an heir?"

Jason shrugged irritably. "How the hell should I know? I'm not the matchmaker in this family, you are."

Charles gaped at him. "Do you mean to tell me you can't think of the one man she ought to marry?"

Jason tipped the brandy glass to his lips and quickly drained it, then put the glass on the table with a decisive thud and abruptly stood up. "Victoria can sing, play the piano, curtsy, and sew," he summarized decisively. "Find a man with a good ear for music, an eye for beauty, and a love of dogs. But make certain he has a placid disposition—otherwise she'll drive him to distraction. It's as simple as that."

When Charles stared at him openmouthed, Jason said impatiently, "I have six estates to run, a fleet of ships to keep track of, and a hundred other details to concentrate on. I'll take care of those things. You take care of finding a husband for Victoria. I'll cooperate by escorting her to a few balls and soirées during the next week or two. She's already caused a sensation. With a little more exposure at a few more functions about town, she'll have more suitors than you'll know what to do with. Look them over when they call on her and draw up a list of the most likely candidates. I'll go over the list and pick one."

Charles's shoulders slumped with weary defeat. "As you wish."

Chapter Fifteen

"I HAVEN'T SEEN A YOUNG WOMAN CREATE A STIR like this since Caroline made her bow," Robert Collingwood said, grinning at Jason as they stood watching Victoria at a ball a week later. "She's set every tongue in the city wagging. Did she really tell Roddy Carstairs she could outshoot him with his own pistol?"

"No," Jason said dryly. "She told him that if he made one more improper advance to her, she would shoot him—and that if she missed, she would turn Wolf loose on him. And that if Wolf didn't finish the job, she had every faith *I* would." Jason chuckled and shook his head. "It's the first time I've ever been nominated for the role of hero. I was a little crushed, however, to be second choice after her dog."

Robert Collingwood shot him an odd look, but Jason didn't notice. He was watching Victoria. Almost completely surrounded by beaux who were vying for her attention, she stood serenely in their midst—a titian-haired queen holding court with her worshipful subjects. Draped in an ice blue satin gown with matching elbow-length gloves, her hair spilling over her shoulders in a lush, wanton mass, she dominated the entire ballroom with her enchanting presence.

As he watched, he noticed Lord Warren hovering at her elbow, his eyes delving down the low, rounded bodice of Victoria's gown. Jason's face whitened with anger. "Excuse me," he said tightly to Robert. "Warren and I are going to have a little talk."

It was the first of many times to come during the next fortnight that the *ton* witnessed the staggering spectacle of the Marquess of Wakefield swooping down like an angry hawk upon some overeager swain whose attentions toward Lady Victoria became too marked.

Three weeks after Victoria's come-out, Charles walked into Jason's study. "I have made up the list of candidates for Victoria's husband that you wanted to review," he announced in the voice of one who has been forced to perform a repugnant task and now wishes to be done with it. "I'd like to go over it with you."

Jason glanced up from the report he was reading, and his eyes narrowed on the sheet of paper in Charles's hand. "I'm busy at the moment."

"Nevertheless, I'd like to get this over with. I've found the chore of preparing it singularly unpleasant. I've selected several acceptable candidates, but the task has not been an easy one."

"I'm certain it hasn't," Jason agreed sardonically. "Every fop and fool in London has been here sniffing after her." Having said that, Jason returned his attention to the report. "Go ahead and read off the names, if you must."

Frowning in surprise at Jason's dismissive attitude, Charles took the seat across the desk from him and put on his spectacles. "First, there is young Lord Crowley, who has already asked my permission to court her."

"No. Too impulsive," Jason decreed flatly.

"What makes you say so?" Charles said with a bewildered look.

"Crowley doesn't know Victoria well enough to want to 'court' her, as you so quaintly phrased it."

"Don't be ridiculous. The first four men on this list have already asked my permission to do the same thing—providing, of course, that your claim on her is not unbreakable."

"No, to all four of them—for the same reason," Jason said

curtly, leaning back in his chair, absorbed in the report in his hand. "Who's next?"

"Crowley's friend, Lord Wiltshire."

"Too young. Who's next?"

"Arthur Landcaster."

"Too short," Jason said cryptically. "Next?"

"William Rogers," Charles shot back in a challenging voice, "and *he's* tall, conservative, mature, intelligent, and handsome. He's also heir to one of the finest estates in England. I think he would do very well for Victoria."

"No."

"No?" Charles burst out. "Why not?"

"I don't like the way Rogers sits a horse."

"You don't like—" Charles bit out in angry disbelief; then he glanced at Jason's implacable face and sighed. "Very well. The last name on my list is Lord Terrance. *He* sits a horse extremely well, in addition to being an excellent chap. He is also tall, handsome, intelligent, and wealthy. Now," he finished triumphantly, "what fault can you find with him?"

Jason's jaw tightened ominously. "I don't *like* him."

"*You* aren't going to marry him!" Charles shot back, his voice rising.

Jason lurched forward in his chair and slammed his hand on his desk. "I said I don't like him," he said through clenched teeth. "And that's the end of it."

The anger on Charles's face slowly gave way to surprise, then to a mirthless smile. "You don't want her, but you don't want anyone else to have her—is that it?"

"Right," Jason replied acidly. "I don't want her."

Victoria's low, furious voice sounded from the doorway behind them. "I don't want you either!"

Both men's heads snapped around, but as she came forward, her magnificent blue eyes were trained exclusively on Jason's impassive face. She braced her palms on his desk, her chest heaving with angry hurt. "Since you're so worried about getting me off your hands if Andrew doesn't come for me, I'll make every effort to find several substitutes for him, but you would *never* be one of them! You aren't worth a tenth of him. He's gentle and kind and good, while you are cold and cynical and conceited and—and a bastard!"

The word "bastard" ignited a leaping fury in Jason's eyes. "If I were you," he retaliated in a low, savage voice, "I'd start looking for those substitutes, because good old Andrew doesn't want you any more than I do."

Humiliated past bearing, Victoria whirled on her heel and stalked out of the room, only one thought in her mind: somehow she was going to show Jason Fielding that other men *did* want her. And she was never, never going to let herself trust him again. In the last weeks, she had been lulled into thinking they were friends. She had even thought he liked her. She remembered the name she had just called him, and her humiliation doubled. How could she have let him provoke her into calling him names!

When she had gone, Charles turned to Jason. "Congratulations," he said bitterly. "You've wanted her to despise you since the day she arrived at Wakefield, and now I know why. I've seen the way you watch her when you think no one is looking. You want her and you're afraid that in a weak moment you'll ask her to marr—"

"That's enough!"

"You want her," Charles continued furiously, "you want her, and you care for her, and you hate yourself for that weakness. Well, now you don't have to worry—you've humiliated her so thoroughly she'll never forgive you for it. Both of you were right. You *are* a bastard, and Andrew *isn't* going to come for her. Gloat away, Jason. You don't have to worry about weakening anymore. She'll hate you even more as soon as she realizes Andrew isn't coming. Enjoy your triumph."

Jason picked up the report he had been reading earlier, his expression glacial. "Make out another list during the next week and bring it to me."

Chapter Sixteen

THE TASK OF SELECTING THE BEST PROSPECTS FROM amongst the increasing number of Victoria's suitors, in order to prepare that list, became far more difficult for Charles than the last time. By the end of the following week, the house on Upper Brook Street was overflowing with bouquets of flowers brought there by a parade of eager gentlemen all hopeful of gaining the distinction of winning her favor.

Even the elegant Frenchman the Marquis de Salle fell under her spell, not despite the language barrier, but because of it. He appeared at the house one day in the company of his friend, Baron Arnoff, and another friend who had stopped to pay a morning call on Victoria.

"Your French is excellent," the marquis lied with suave, meaningless gallantry as he wisely switched to English and sat down in the appointed chair.

Victoria looked at him in laughing disbelief. "It is dismal," she declared ruefully. "I find the nasal tones one uses in French almost as difficult to imitate as the guttural ones used in Apache."

"Apache?" he inquired politely. "What is that?"

"It is the language spoken by a tribe of American Indians."

"American savages?" echoed the Russian baron, a legendary horseman in the Russian army. His expression of boredom changed to one of rapt interest. "I have heard that these savages are superb horsemen. Are they?"

"I've only known one Indian, Baron Arnoff, and he was quite old and very polite, rather than savage. My father came upon him in the woods and brought him home to nurse him back to health. His name was Rushing River, and he stayed on as a sort of helper to my father. However, to answer your question, although he was only half Apache, he was indeed a superb horseman. I was twelve when I first saw him do tricks, and I was speechless with wonder. He used no saddle and—"

"No saddle!" the baron exclaimed.

Victoria shook her head. "Apaches don't use them."

"What sort of tricks could he do?" asked the marquis, far more interested in her intoxicating face than her words.

"Once Rushing River had me place a handkerchief in the middle of a field; then he rode toward it, his horse running full-out. When he was nearly there, he let go of the rope bridle completely, leaned way down and to the side, and scooped up the handkerchief while his horse was still running. He taught me how to do it, too," she admitted, laughing.

Impressed despite himself, the baron said, "I would have to see this before I believed it. I don't suppose you could show me how it is done?"

"No, I'm sorry. The horse must be trained in the Apache style first."

"Perhaps you could teach me a word or two of Apache," the marquis teased with a coaxing smile, "and I could tutor you on your French?"

"Your offer is very kind," Victoria replied, "but it would not be at all fair, for I have much to learn and little to teach. I remember very few of the words Rushing River taught me."

"Surely you could teach me one phrase?" he prodded, smiling into her sparkling eyes.

"No, really—"

"I insist."

"Very well," Victoria capitulated with a sigh, "if you insist." She spoke a phrase in guttural accents and looked at the marquis. "Now, try to repeat it."

The marquis got it perfect on the second try and smiled with pleasure. "What does it mean?" he asked. "What did I say?"

"You said," Victoria replied with an apologetic look, " 'That man is treading upon my eagle.' "

"Treading upon my—" The marquis, the baron, and everyone else gathered in the gold salon dissolved into laughter.

The following day, the Russian baron and the French marquis returned to join the ranks of Victoria's beaux, adding immensely to her prestige and increasing her popularity.

Wherever Victoria was in the house, there was laughter and the sound of animated gaiety. Throughout the rest of the house, however, there was a vibrating, ominous tension that sprang from Lord Fielding and stretched its tentacles around everyone else. As week drifted into week and the number of Victoria's suitors doubled and redoubled, Jason's mood went from menacing to murderous. Wherever he went, he saw something that displeased him. He berated the cook for preparing his favorite meal too often; he chastised a housemaid for a speck of dust he found under the banister; he threatened to dismiss a footman who had a loose button on his jacket.

In the past, Lord Fielding had been a demanding, exacting employer, but he had also been reasonable. Now, nothing seemed to satisfy him, and any servant who crossed his path was likely to feel the lash of his caustic tongue. Unfortunately, the more impossible he became, the faster and more furiously they worked, and the more nervous and clumsy it made them.

Once his households had run as efficiently as well-oiled machines. Now servants scurried about, colliding with one another in their desperate haste to complete their tasks and avoid their employer's smoldering wrath. As a result of their nervous frenzy, a priceless Chinese vase was dropped, a bucket of wash water was spilled onto the Aubusson carpet in the dining room, and general chaos reigned throughout the house.

Victoria was aware of the tension among the staff, but when she cautiously tried to broach the subject with Jason he accused her of "trying to incite insurrection," then launched into a scathing tirade about the noise her visitors were making while he was trying to work and the nauseating smell of the flowers they brought her.

Twice Charles tried to discuss the second list of suitors with him, only to be rudely told to get out of his study and stay out.

When Northrup himself received a stinging reprimand from Jason, the entire household began to crackle with terrified tension. It ended abruptly late one afternoon, five weeks after Victoria had made her come-out. Jason was working in his study and called for Northrup, who was about to place a newly arrived bouquet of Victoria's flowers in a vase.

Rather than keep his ill-tempered master waiting, Northrup rushed into the study, the bouquet in his hand. "Yes, my lord?" he inquired apprehensively.

"How nice," Jason sneered sarcastically. "More flowers? For me?" Before Northrup could answer, Jason said bitingly, "The whole damned house stinks of flowers! Get rid of that bouquet, then tell Victoria I want to see her, and bring me that damned invitation to the Frigleys' affair tonight. I can't remember what time it begins. Then tell my valet to lay out formal clothes for it, whenever it is. Well?" he snapped. "What are you waiting for? Get moving!"

"Yes, my lord. At once." Northrup rushed into the hall and slammed into O'Malley, whom Jason had just chastised for not having a proper shine on his boots.

"I've never seen him like this," O'Malley gasped to Northrup, who was plunging the bouquet into a vase before going to summon Lady Victoria. "His lordship sent me for tea, and then he shouted at me because I should have brought him coffee."

"His lordship," Northrup remarked haughtily, "does not drink tea."

"I told him that when he asked for it," O'Malley replied bitterly, "and he said I was insolent."

"You are," Northrup replied, furthering the animosity that had been thriving between himself and the Irish footman for twenty years. With a smirk at O'Malley, Northrup strode off.

In the small salon, Victoria stared blindly at the letter she had just received from Mrs. Bainbridge, the words blurring before her burning eyes.

> . . . I cannot find any gentle way to tell you that Andrew married his cousin in Switzerland. I tried to warn you of this likely event before you left for England, but you chose not to believe it. Now that you must accept it, I suggest you look about for a more suitable husband for a girl of your station.

"No! Please!" Victoria whispered as her hopes and dreams crumbled and fell at her feet, along with her faith in all men. In her mind she saw Andrew's handsome, laughing face as she raced beside him on horseback: *"No one rides like you, Tory. . . ."* She remembered his first light kiss on her sixteenth birthday: *"If you were older,"* he whispered huskily, *"I'd be giving you a ring, instead of a bracelet. . . ."*

"Liar!" Victoria whispered brokenly. "Liar!" Hot tears stung her eyes and spilled down her cheeks, dripping slowly onto the paper.

Northrup entered the salon and intoned, "Lord Fielding would like to see you in his study, my lady, and Lord Crowley has just arrived. He asked if you could spare him a . . ." Northrup's voice trailed off into shocked silence as Victoria raised haunted, tear-drenched blue eyes to his; then she shot to her feet, covering her face with her hands, and rushed past him. A low, anguished sob escaped her as she fled into the hall and up the stairs.

Northrup's alarmed gaze followed her up the long staircase, and then he automatically bent down and picked up the letter that had fallen from her lap. Unlike the other servants, who only heard bits and pieces of family talk, Northrup was privy to much more of it, and he had never believed, as the rest of the staff did, that Lady Victoria was going to wed Lord Fielding. Moreover, he had heard her say several times that she intended to marry a gentleman in America.

Spurred by a sense of alarm, not curiosity, he glanced at the letter to see what dire news had arrived to bring such heartbreaking distress to her. He read it, and closed his eyes with shared sorrow.

"Northrup!" Lord Fielding thundered from his study down the hall.

Like an automaton, Northrup obeyed the summons.

"Did you tell Victoria I want to see her?" Jason demanded. "What have you there—is that Lady Frigley's note? Here, give it to me." Jason stretched his hand out, his eyes narrowing impatiently as the stiff-backed butler walked very, very slowly toward his desk. "What the devil is the matter with you?" he said, snatching the letter from the servant's hand. "What are these spots all over it?"

"Tears," Northrup clarified, standing rigidly erect, his eyes averted and focused on the wall.

"Tears?" Jason repeated, his gaze narrowing on the blurred words. "This isn't the invitation, it's—" Silence fell on the room as Jason finally realized what he was reading, and he sucked in his breath. When he was finished, Jason raised his wrathful gaze to Northrup. "He had his *mother* tell her he married someone else. That spineless son-of-a-bitch!"

Northrup swallowed. "My sentiments exactly," he said hoarsely.

For the first time in nearly a month, Jason's voice was without an angry edge. "I'll go talk to her," he said. Pushing back his chair, he went up to Victoria's bedchamber.

As usual, she didn't answer his knock, and as usual, Jason took matters into his own hands and went in without her permission. Instead of weeping into her pillow, Victoria was staring out the window, her face deathly pale, her shoulders so stiff and straight that Jason could almost feel her painful effort to hold herself erect. He closed the door behind him and hesitated, hoping she would issue one of her usual tart reprimands about his entering her room uninvited, but when she finally spoke, her voice was alarmingly calm and emotionless. "Please go away."

Jason ignored that and went to her. "Victoria, I'm sorry—" he began, but he stopped at the blazing anger that leapt into her eyes.

"I'll bet you are! But don't worry, my lord, I don't intend to stay here and continue to be a burden to you."

He reached for her, trying to draw her into his arms, but she recoiled from his touch and jumped back as if she had been scorched. "Don't touch me!" she hissed. "Don't you dare touch me! I don't want to be touched by any man, especially you." She drew a long, quivering breath, obviously striving for control, and then continued haltingly. "I've been thinking about how I can take care of myself. I— I'm not quite as helpless as you think," she told him bravely. "I'm an excellent seamstress. Madame Dumosse who made my gowns mentioned more than once how difficult it is to find willing workers with the right skills. She may be able to give me work—"

"Don't be ridiculous!" Jason snapped, angry at himself for having told her she was helpless when she first came to Wakefield, and angry at her for throwing it in his face now, when he wanted to comfort her.

"Oh, but I *am* ridiculous," she choked. "I am a countess without a shilling, or a home, or any pride left. I don't even know if I'm clever enough with a needle to—"

"Stop it!" Jason interrupted tightly. "I won't permit you to work like a common seamstress, and that's the end of it." When she started to argue, Jason cut her short. "Would you repay my hospitality by embarrassing Charles and me in front of all London?"

Victoria's shoulders drooped and she shook her head.

"Good. Then let's hear no more nonsense about working for Madame Dumosse."

"Then what am I to do?" she whispered, her pain-filled eyes searching his.

An odd emotion flickered across Jason's features, and his jaw tightened as if he was holding himself back from saying something. "Do what women always do," he said harshly after a long pause. "Marry a man who'll be able to provide for you in the manner to which you want to become accustomed. Charles has already received a half dozen tentative offers for your hand. Marry one of those men."

"I don't want to marry someone I don't care anything about," Victoria retorted with a brief flare of spirit.

"You'll change your mind," Jason said with cold certainty.

"Perhaps I should," Victoria said brokenly. "Caring for someone hurts too much. B-because then they betray you and—oh, Jason, tell me what's wrong with me," she cried, her wounded eyes huge and pleading. "You hate me, and Andrew—"

Jason's restraint broke. He wrapped his arms around her and gathered her tightly against his chest. "Nothing's wrong with you," he whispered, stroking her hair. "Andrew is a spineless fool. And I'm a bigger fool than he is."

"He wanted someone else more than me," she wept in his arms. "And it hurts so much to know it."

Jason closed his eyes and swallowed. "I know," he whispered.

She soaked his shirtfront with her hot tears, and they in turn finally began to melt the ice that had surrounded Jason's heart for years. Holding Victoria protectively in his arms, he waited until her weeping finally abated; then he brushed his lips against her temple and whispered, "Do you remember when you asked me at Wakefield if we could be friends?"

She nodded, unthinkingly rubbing her cheek against his chest.

"I would like that very much," Jason murmured huskily. "Could I have a second chance?"

Lifting her head, Victoria stared dubiously at him. Then she nodded.

"Thank you," he said with a ghost of a smile.

Chapter Seventeen

In the weeks that followed, Victoria experienced the full impact of Andrew's defection. At first she was hurt, then she was angry, and finally she felt a dull, aching sense of loss. But with strength and determination, she made herself come to grips with his betrayal and face the painful knowledge that her former life was permanently over. She learned how to cry lonely, private tears for all she had left behind—and then put on her best gown and her brightest smile for her friends and acquaintances.

She managed to keep her emotions well hidden from all but Jason and Caroline Collingwood, who both came to her aid in different ways—Caroline by keeping Victoria busy with a ceaseless round of social activities, and Jason by escorting her to almost all of them.

For the most part, he treated her like a patronizing older brother, escorting her to parties, the theater, the opera, and then, once there, leaving her to enjoy her own friends while he spent the evening with his. He was watchful, though, and protective—ready to swoop down and run off any beau he disapproved of. And he disapproved of several. To Victoria, who was now aware of his reputation as a shocking libertine,

177

it was rather funny to watch Jason turn the icy blast of his gaze on some overly avid admirer and stare the unfortunate gentleman into mumbled apologies and a hasty retreat.

To the rest of the *ton*, the Marquess of Wakefield's behavior was not only amusing, it was odd, and even a trifle suspect. No one believed that the couple intended to marry—not when Jason Fielding continued to welcome Lady Victoria's beaux into his home and to state repeatedly that their betrothal wasn't actually finalized. Because of those things, and because their betrothal had been announced before the countess ever set foot in England, it was generally believed the betrothal had been arranged prematurely by the ailing duke (who was openly fond of both of them) and that the couple was merely keeping up the pretense of being betrothed for his sake.

Now, however, that theory was beginning to be supplanted by a less kind one. From the very beginning, there had been a few sticklers who had voiced objections to Victoria's living arrangement, but because she had seemed such a sweet girl and because Lord Fielding had shown her no real partiality, no one else had listened to their objections. However, as the number of Jason's public appearances with Victoria increased, so did the gossip that the notorious Lord Fielding had decided to make a conquest of her—if he hadn't already.

Some of the most vicious gossips even went so far as to intimate that the betrothal was nothing but a convenient disguise for a licentious liaison being carried on right beneath poor Miss Flossie Wilson's nose. This piece of slander was repeated, but very little credited, for the simple reason that, although Lord Fielding frequently acted as her escort, he did not behave in a proprietary, loverlike way. Moreover, Lady Victoria had acquired a great many staunch defenders, including Countess Collingwood and her influential husband, both of whom took extreme personal offense whenever anyone dared breathe a word of criticism about Countess Langston.

Victoria was not unaware of the curiosity her relationship with Jason was generating, nor was she blind to the fact that many among the *ton* seemed to mistrust him. As the strangeness of her elegant new acquaintances wore off, she became much more alert to the subtle nuances of expression that crossed people's faces whenever Jason was nearby. They were suspicious of him, wary, alert. At first she thought she was only imagining the way people stiffened in his presence and became more formal, but it was not her imagination. Sometimes she heard things—snatches of whispered gossip, a word here and there—that had an undertone of malice or at least of disapproval.

Caroline had warned her that people were fearful and mistrustful of him. One night Dorothy tried to warn her too.

"Tory, Tory, it *is* you!" Dorothy said, bursting through a crowd of people surrounding Victoria outside Lord and Lady Potham's house, where there was a ball under way.

Victoria, who hadn't seen Dorothy since they left the ship, gazed at her with misty fondness as Dorothy enfolded her in a tight, protective hug. "Where have you been!" Victoria chided fondly. "You write so seldom, I thought you were still 'rusticating' in the country."

"Grandmama and I returned to London three days past," she explained quickly. "I would have come to see you straightaway, but Grandmama doesn't want me to have more than the slightest contact with you. I've been watching for you everywhere I go. But never mind about that. I haven't much time. My chaperone will be looking for me any moment. I told her I thought I saw a friend of Grandmama's and wished to convey a message to her." She threw an apprehensive look over her shoulder, too worried about her chaperone to notice the way Victoria's young admirers were curiously studying her. "Oh, Tory, I've been beside myself with worry! I know Andrew did a wretched thing to you, but you mustn't let yourself *think* of marrying Wakefield! You can't marry that man. You can't! No one likes him, you must know it. I heard Lady Faulklyn—Grandmama's companion—talking to Grandmama about him, and do you know what Lady F said?"

Victoria turned her shoulder to their avidly interested audience. "Dorothy, Lord Fielding has been very kind to me. Don't ask me to listen to unpleasant gossip, because I won't. Instead, let me introduce you to—"

"Not now!" Dorothy said desperately, too distraught to care about anything else. She tried to whisper, but it was impossible to do so and still be heard above the din, so she was forced to speak more loudly. "Do you know the kinds of things people say about Wakefield? Lady Faulklyn said he wouldn't even be *received* if it weren't for his being a Fielding. His reputation is beneath reproach. He uses women for his own nefarious ends and then turns his back on them! People are afraid of him and you should be too! They say—" She broke off as an aging lady climbed down from a carriage that was waiting in the street and wended her way through the crowd, obviously in search of someone. "I have to leave. That's Lady F."

Dorothy rushed away to head off the old woman and Victoria watched them climb back into the carriage.

Beside her, Mr. Warren helped himself to a pinch of snuff. "The young lady is quite right, you know," he drawled.

Torn from her lonely thoughts of Dorothy, Victoria glanced with distaste at the foppish young man, who looked as if he would jump in fright at his own shadow, then at the apprehensive faces of her other beaux, who had obviously overheard much of what Dorothy said.

Angry contempt burst in her breast for the lot of them. Not one of them ever did an honest day's work as Jason did. They were silly, shallow, overdressed manikins who relished hearing Jason criticized for the obvious reason that he was far wealthier than they, and far more desired by the ladies, despite his reputation.

Her bright, flirtatious smile was belied by the dangerous sparkle in Victoria's eyes as she said, "Why, Mr. Warren, are *you* afraid for my well-being?"

"Yes, my lady, and I am not the only one."

"How utterly absurd!" Victoria scoffed. "If you're interested in truth, rather than foolish gossip, I shall tell it to you. The truth is I came here, alone in the world, without close family or any fortune, a virtual dependent upon his grace and Lord Fielding. Now," she continued with a fixed smile, "I want you to look at me very closely."

Genuine mirth bubbled in her as the foolish young man put his quizzing glass to his eye, following her instructions to the letter. "Do I look misused?" Victoria demanded impatiently. "Have I been murdered in my bed? No, sir, I have not! Instead, Lord Fielding has given me the comfort of his beautiful home and offered me the protection of his name. In all honesty, Mr. Warren, I believe many women in London secretly long to be 'misused' in just such a way and, from what I have observed, by exactly *that* man. Furthermore, I believe it is jealousy of him that gives birth to all this ridiculous gossip.''

Mr. Warren flushed, and Victoria turned to the others and added flamboyantly, "If you knew Lord Fielding as I know him, you would discover that he is the very soul of kindness, consideration, refinement, and—and amiability!" she finished.

Behind her, Jason's laughter-tinged voice said, "My lady, in your attempt to whitewash my black reputation, you are making me sound like a dead bore, instead.''

Victoria whirled around, her embarrassed gaze flying to his. "However," he continued with a brief smile, "I will forgive you for it, if you will honor me with a dance?" Victoria placed her hand upon his proffered arm and walked into the crowded house beside him.

The sense of proud, triumphant elation she felt for having got up the courage to speak out on Jason's behalf began to fade when he silently took her in his arms on the crowded dance floor. She still knew very little about him, but she had learned from her own experience whenever she vainly tried to coax him into talking about himself that Jason valued his privacy. Uneasily, she wondered if he was annoyed with her for discussing him with others. When he continued to dance with her in silence, she glanced uncertainly into his thoughtful, heavy-lidded eyes. "Are you angry with me?" she asked. "For discussing you in public, I mean?"

"Was it *me* you were discussing?" he countered with lifted brows. "I couldn't tell from the description you were giving. Since when am I kind, considerate, refined, and amiable?"

"You're angry," Victoria concluded on a sigh.

A low chuckle rumbled in his chest and his arms tightened, drawing her close to his lean, muscular body. "I'm not angry," he said in a husky, gentle voice. "I'm embarrassed."

"Embarrassed?" she echoed in surprise, studying the melting warmth in his jade eyes. "Why?"

"For a man of my age, height, and wicked reputation, it's a little embarrassing to have a tiny young woman trying to defend me against the world."

Mesmerized by the tenderness in his eyes, Victoria fought the absurd impulse to lay her cheek against his claret velvet jacket.

Word spread of Victoria's public defense of Lord Fielding, whom she apparently admired but did not quite wish to wed, and the *ton* concluded that a marriage date might be imminent after all—a possibility that so distressed Victoria's other suitors that they redoubled their efforts to please her. They vied with each other for her attention, they argued amongst themselves over her, and, in the end, Lord Crowley and Lord Wiltshire dueled over her.

"She don't want either of us," young Lord Crowley angrily informed Lord Wiltshire late one afternoon as they rode away from the mansion on Upper Brook Street after a brief, unsatisfactory visit with Victoria.

"Yes, she does," Lord Wiltshire argued heatedly. "She's shown me a particular partiality!"

"You jackanapes! She thinks we're dandified Englishmen, and she don't like Englishmen," he said sulkily. "She prefers colonial bumpkins! She ain't as sweet as you think, she's laughing at us behind her hand—"

"That's a lie!" his hot-blooded friend retorted.

"Are you calling me a liar, Wiltshire?" Crowley demanded furiously.

"No," Wiltshire replied between clenched teeth, "I am calling you *out*."

"Fine," Crowley returned. "Tomorrow at dawn at my place. In the grove." Wheeling his horse around, he galloped off toward his club, whence news of his forthcoming duel spread until it finally reached the exclusive gentlemen's gaming establishment where Marquis de Salle and Baron Arnoff were rolling dice for very high stakes. "Damned young fools," de Salle remarked with an irritated sigh when informed of the planned duel. "Lady Victoria will be deeply distressed when she learns of this."

Baron Arnoff chuckled. "Neither Crowley nor Wiltshire

can shoot straight enough to do any damage. I witnessed their lack of skill myself when a group of us were hunting at Wiltshire's seat in Devon."

"Perhaps I ought to try to put a stop to it," the Marquis said.

Baron Arnoff shook his head, looking amused. "I do not see why you should. The worst that can happen is that one of them will succeed in shooting the other's horse."

"I was considering Lady Victoria's reputation. A duel fought over her will not do it any good."

"Excellent," Arnoff chuckled. "If she is less popular, I will have a better chance with her."

Several hours later, at another table, Robert Collingwood heard the news of the duel, but he did not take it so lightly. Excusing himself from the company of his friends, he left the club and went to the Duke of Atherton's London residence, where Jason had been staying. After waiting nearly an hour for Jason to return, Robert coerced the sleepy butler into awakening Jason's valet. As a result of much urging and persuasion, the valet reluctantly imparted the intelligence that his master had returned earlier from escorting Lady Victoria to a rout, and had then gone to visit a certain female at #21 in Williams Street.

Robert bounded into his carriage and gave his driver the Williams Street address. "Make it quick," he ordered.

His loud knocking finally awakened a sleepy French maid, who opened the door and discreetly denied any knowledge of Lord Fielding. "Fetch your mistress to me at once," Robert ordered her impatiently. "I haven't much time." The maid cast a quick look beyond him, saw the crest upon his coach, hesitated, and then went upstairs.

After another long wait, a lovely brunette wrapped in a filmy dressing gown came down the stairs. "What on earth is amiss, Lord Collingwood?" Sybil asked.

"Is Jason here?" Robert demanded.

Sybil nodded immediately.

"Tell him Crowley and Wiltshire are dueling over Victoria at dawn in the grove at Crowley's place," Robert told her.

Jason stretched out his hand as Sybil sat down beside him on the bed. With his eyes closed, his hand sought and found the opening of her gown, stroking seductively up her bare thigh. "Come back to bed," he invited huskily. "I have need of you again."

A wistful smile touched her eyes as she stroked his bronzed shoulder. "You don't 'need' anyone, Jason," she whispered sadly. "You never have."

A low, sensuous chuckle rumbled in Jason's chest as he rolled onto his back and swiftly pulled her down on top of his naked, aroused body. "If *that* isn't need, what do you call it?"

"That isn't what I meant by 'need,' and you know it," she whispered, pressing a kiss to his warm lips. "Don't," she said hastily as his knowledgeable hands pulled her to him. "You haven't time. Collingwood is here. He said to tell you Crowley and Wiltshire are going to duel at dawn at Crowley's place."

Jason's green eyes opened, their expression alert but not overly concerned.

"They're dueling over Victoria," she added.

In an instant Jason was a flurry of efficient motion, thrusting her aside, lunging out of bed, and swiftly pulling on his pants and boots. Cursing savagely under his breath, he jerked on his shirt. "What time is it?" he said shortly, glancing toward the window.

"About an hour before dawn."

He nodded, leaned down and pressed a brief, apologetic kiss on her brow, and then left, the sound of his boots echoing sharply against the polished wood floor.

The sky was already lightening when Jason finally located the grove on the Crowley estate and spotted the two duelists standing beneath the shadowy oaks. Fifty yards to the left of the pair, the physician's black carriage was pulled up ominously beneath another tree, a horse tied at its rear. Jason dug his heels savagely into his mount, sending the black stallion flying down the grassy knoll, its hooves throwing huge clumps of wet sod high into the air.

He skidded to a halt near the combatants and hurtled out of the saddle, running. "What the hell is going on here!" he demanded of Crowley when he reached his side, then he whirled around in surprise as the Marquis de Salle stepped out of the shadows twenty yards away and positioned himself next to young Wiltshire. "What are *you* doing here, de Salle?" Jason said angrily. "You, at least, should have more sense than these two puppies."

"I'm doing the same thing you are," de Salle drawled with a faint grin, "but without much success, as you'll soon discover."

"Crowley fired at me," Wiltshire burst out accusingly. His face was twisted with angry surprise, and his words were slurred from the liquor he had consumed to bolster his courage. "Crowley din—din't delope like a gen—genleman. Now, I'm going to *shoot* him."

"I didn't fire *at* you," Crowley boomed furiously from beside Jason. "If I had, I'd have *hit* you."

"You din't aim in—in the air," Wiltshire yelled back. "You aren—aren't a genleman. You deserve to die, and I'm gonna shoot you!" Wiltshire's arm shook as he raised it and leveled the pistol at his opponent, and then everything happened at once. The gun exploded just as the Marquis de Salle sprang forward and tried to knock it out of Wiltshire's hand and as Jason dived at Crowley, sending the rigid boy sprawling to the ground. The ball whined past Jason's ear as he fell, ricocheted off the trunk of the tree, and ripped across his upper arm.

After a stunned moment, Jason slowly sat up, his expression incredulous. He put his hand to the fiery pain in his arm and then stared at the blood that covered his fingers with an expression of almost comical disbelief.

The physician, the Marquis de Salle, and young Wiltshire all ran forward. "Here, let me have a look at that arm," Dr. Worthing said, waving the others aside and squatting down on his heels.

Dr. Worthing ripped Jason's shirt open and young Wiltshire emitted a strangled groan when he saw the blood running from Jason's wound. "Oh, God!" he wailed. "Lord Fielding, I never meant—"

"Shut up!" Dr. Worthing bit out. "Someone hand me that whiskey in my case." To Jason he said, "It's only a flesh wound, Jason, but it's fairly deep. I'll have to clean it and stitch it." He took the bottle of whiskey that the Marquis de Salle handed him, and glanced apologetically at Jason. "This is going to burn like the fires of Hades."

Jason nodded and clenched his teeth, and the physician swiftly upended the bottle, drenching the torn flesh with the fiery alcohol. Then he handed the bottle to Jason. "If I were you, Jason, I'd drink the rest of this. You're going to need plenty of stitches."

"*I* didn't shoot him," Wiltshire burst out in an attempt to avoid giving Lord Fielding, the legendary duelist, the satisfaction he had every right to demand at a later date. Four pairs of eyes looked at him in disgust. "I didn't!" Wiltshire argued desperately. "It was the tree that made it happen. I shot at the tree, and the ball hit the tree, *then* it hit Lord Fielding."

Jason raised his dark, glittering eyes to his terrified assailant and said in an ominous voice, "If you're very lucky, Wiltshire, you'll be able to stay out of my sight until I'm too old to horsewhip you."

Wiltshire backed away, turned on his heel, and started running. Jason turned his head, impaling the other petrified duelist on his gaze. "Crowley," he warned softly, "your presence offends me."

Crowley turned and fled to his horse.

When they had galloped away, Jason raised the whiskey bottle and took a long swallow, gasping as Dr. Worthing's threaded needle pierced his swollen flesh, pulling it tightly, joining flesh to flesh, then piercing again. Holding the bottle out to de Salle, he said dryly, "I regret the lack of a suitable glass; however, if you would care to join me, help yourself."

De Salle unhesitatingly reached for the proffered bottle, explaining as he did so, "I went to your house when I learned of the duel earlier this evening, but your man said you were out for the evening and wouldn't tell me where you'd gone." He took a long swallow of the strong whiskey and handed the bottle back to Jason. "So I went after Dr. Worthing and we came here, hoping to stop them."

"We should have let them shoot themselves," Jason said disgustedly, then clenched his teeth and stiffened as the needle again pierced his jagged flesh.

"Probably so."

Jason took two more long swallows of liquor and felt the stuff begin to numb his senses. Leaning his head back against the hard bark of the tree, he sighed with amused exasperation. "Exactly what did my little countess do to cause this duel?"

De Salle stiffened at Jason's affectionate phrasing and his voice lost its polite friendliness. "As nearly as I could tell, Lady Victoria supposedly called Wiltshire a dandified English bumpkin."

"Then Wiltshire should have called *her* out," Jason said with a chuckle, taking another swig of whiskey. "She wouldn't have missed her shot."

De Salle didn't smile at the joke. "What do you mean, 'your little countess'?" he demanded tersely. "If she is yours, you're taking your time making it official—you said yourself the matter wasn't settled. What kind of game are you playing with her affections, Wakefield?"

Jason's gaze shot to the other man's hostile features; then he closed his eyes, an exasperated smile on his lips. "If *you're* planning to call me out, I hope to hell you can shoot. It's damned humiliating for a man of my reputation to be shot by a tree."

Victoria tossed and turned in her bed, too exhausted to sleep and unable to still her churning thoughts. At daybreak she gave up trying and sat up in bed, watching the sky change from dark gray to pale gray, her thoughts as dismal and bleak as the morning promised to be. Propped up against the pillows, she plucked idly at the satin coverlet, while her life seemed to stretch before her like a dark, lonely, frightening tunnel. She thought about Andrew, who was married to another and lost to her now; she thought about the villagers she had loved from childhood and who had loved her in return. Now there was no one. Except Uncle Charles, of course, but even his affection couldn't still her restlessness or fill the aching void inside her.

She had always felt needed and useful; now her life was an endless round of frenzied frivolity with Jason paying all the expenses. She felt so—so unnecessary, so useless and burdensome.

She'd tried to take Jason's callous advice and choose another man to marry. She'd tried, but she simply couldn't imagine herself married to any of the shallow London blades who were trying so hard to win her. They didn't need her as a wife; she would merely be an ornament, a decoration in their lives. With the exception of the Collingwoods and a few others, *ton* marriages were superficial conveniences, nothing more. Couples rarely appeared together at the same function and, if they did, it was unfashionable for them to remain in each other's company once there. The children born of these marriages were promptly dumped into the hands of nannies and tutors. How different the meaning of "marriage" was here, Victoria thought.

Wistfully she recalled the husbands and wives she'd known in Portage. She remembered old Mr. Prowther sitting on the porch in the summers, determinedly reading to his palsied wife, who scarcely knew where she was. She remembered the look on Mr. and Mrs. Makepeace's faces when Victoria's father informed them that, after twenty years of childless marriage, Mrs. Makepeace had conceived. She remembered the way the middle-aged couple had clung to each other and wept with unashamed joy. *Those* were marriages as marriage was surely meant to be—two people working together and helping each other through good times and bad; two people laughing together, raising children together, and even crying together.

Victoria thought of her own mother and father. Although Katherine Seaton hadn't loved her husband, she had still made a cozy home for him and been his helpmate. They did things together too, like playing chess before the fire in the winter and taking walks in the summer twilight.

In London, Victoria was desired for the simple, silly reason that she was "in fashion" at the moment. As a wife she would have no use, no purpose, except as a decoration at the foot of the dining table when guests were expected for supper. Victoria knew she could never be content if that was her life. She wanted to share herself with someone who needed her, to make him happy and be important to him. She wanted to be useful, to have a purpose other than an ornamental one.

The Marquis de Salle truly cared for her, she could sense that—but he didn't love her, regardless of what he said.

Victoria bit her lip against the pain as she recalled Andrew's tender avowals of love. He hadn't really loved her.

The Marquis de Salle didn't love her either. Perhaps wealthy men, including Andrew, were incapable of feeling real love. Perhaps—

Victoria sat bolt upright as heavy, dragging footsteps sounded in the hall. It was too early for the servants to be about, and besides, they practically *ran* through the house in their haste to satisfy their employer. Something thudded against a wall and a man moaned. Uncle Charles must be ill, she thought, and flung back the covers, hurtling out of bed. Racing to the door, she jerked it open. "Jason!" she said, her heart leaping into her throat as he sagged against the wall, his left arm in a makeshift sling. "What happened?" she whispered, then quickly amended, "Never mind. Don't try to talk. I'll get a servant to help you." She whirled around, but he caught her arm in an amazingly strong grip and hauled her back, a crooked grin on his face.

"I want *you* to help me," he said, and threw his right arm over her shoulders, nearly sending her to her knees beneath his weight. "Take me to my room, Victoria," he ordered in a thick, cajoling voice.

"Where is it?" Victoria whispered as they started awkwardly down the hall.

"Don't you know?" he chided thickly in a hurt tone. "I know where *your* room is."

"What difference does that make?" Victoria demanded a little frantically as she tried to shift his weight.

"None," he said agreeably, and stopped before the next door on the right. Victoria opened it and helped him inside.

Across the hall, another bedroom door opened and Charles Fielding stood in the doorway, his face anxious and worried as he pulled on a satin dressing robe. He stopped with only one arm in its sleeve as Jason said expansively to Victoria, "Now, li'l countess, escort me to my bed."

Victoria caught the odd way Jason was slurring his words; she even thought there was a flirtatious tone in his voice, but she blamed his queer speech on either pain or possibly loss of blood.

When they reached his big four-poster bed, he pulled his arm away and waited docilely while Victoria swept the covers back; then he sat down and looked at her with a foolish grin. Victoria looked back at him, hiding her anxiety. Using her father's gentle, matter-of-fact tone, she said, "Can you tell me what happened to you?"

"Certainly!" he said, looking affronted. "I'm not an imbecile, you know."

"Well, what happened?" Victoria repeated when he made no attempt to tell her.

"Help me take off my boots."

Victoria hesitated. "I think I ought to get Northrup."

"Never mind about the boots then," he said magnanimously, and with that, he lay down and carelessly crossed his booted feet upon the maroon coverlet. "Sit down beside me and hold my hand."

"Don't be silly."

He gave her a hurt look. "You ought to be nicer to me, Victoria. After all, I have been wounded in a duel over your honor." He reached out and captured her hand.

Horrified at the mention of a duel, Victoria obeyed the increasing pressure of his hand and sat down beside his prone body. "Oh, my God—a duel! Jason, why?" She searched his pale features, saw his brave, lopsided smile, and her heart melted with contrition and guilt. For some reason, he had actually fought for her. "Please tell me why you dueled," she implored.

He grinned. "Because Wiltshire called you an English bumpkin."

"A what? Jason," she asked anxiously, "how much blood have you lost?"

"All of it," he averred outrageously. "How sorry do you feel for me?"

"Very," she answered automatically. "Now, will you please try to make sense? Wiltshire shot you because—"

He rolled his eyes in disgust. "Wiltshire din't shoot me— he couldn't hit a stone wall at two paces. A *tree* shot me." Reaching up, he cradled her shocked face between his two hands, drawing her closer to him, and his voice dropped to a whisper. "Do you know how beautiful you are?" he said hoarsely, and this time pungent whiskey fumes blasted her in the face.

"You're foxed!" Victoria accused, lurching back.

"Yer right," he agreed genially. "Got drunk with yer friend de Salle."

"Dear God!" Victoria gasped. "Was he there too?"

Jason nodded but said nothing as his fascinated gaze moved over her. Her shining hair tumbled over her shoulders in a gloriously untidy mass of molten gold, framing a face of heartbreaking beauty. Her skin was as smooth as alabaster, her brows delicately arched, her lashes thick and curly. Her eyes were like large luminous sapphires as they worriedly searched his face, trying to assess his condition. Pride and courage showed in every feature of her face, from her high cheekbones and stubborn little nose to her small chin with its tiny, enchanting cleft at the center. And yet her mouth was vulnerable and soft—as soft as the breasts that swelled at his eye level above the bodice of her lace-edged cream satin nightdress, practically begging for his touch. But it was her mouth Jason wanted to taste first. . . . He tightened his hand on her upper arm, drawing her closer.

"Lord Fielding!" she warned darkly, trying to pull back.

"A moment ago, you called me Jason. I heard you, don't deny it."

"That was a mistake," Victoria said desperately.

His lips quirked in a faint smile. "Then let's make another one." As he spoke his hand went to the nape of her neck, curving around it and inexorably pulling her face down to his.

"Please don't," Victoria begged, her face only inches from his. "Don't make me fight you—it will hurt your wound." The pressure on her nape eased very slightly, not enough to let her up, but not forcing her closer either as Jason studied her in thoughtful silence.

Victoria waited patiently for him to let her go, knowing his senses were confused by loss of blood, pain, and a goodly quantity of liquor. Not for a moment did she believe he felt the slightest genuine desire for her, and she gazed down at him with something akin to amusement.

"Have you ever been kissed, really kissed, by anyone besides old Arnold?" he asked hazily.

"Andrew," Victoria corrected, her lips twitching with laughter.

"Not all men kiss alike, did you know that?"

A giggle escaped before Victoria could stop it. "Really? How many men have you kissed?"

An answering smile tugged at his sensuous lips, but he ignored her quip. "Lean down to me," he ordered huskily, subtly increasing the pressure of his hand on her nape again, "and put your lips on mine. We'll do it my way."

Victoria's complaisance vanished and she began to panic. "Jason, stop this," she pleaded. "You don't want to kiss me. You don't even like me more than a little when you aren't foxed."

A harsh laugh escaped him. "I like you too damned much!" he whispered bitterly, then pulled her head down and captured her lips in a demanding, scalding kiss that took everything and gave nothing in return. Victoria struggled in appalled, frightened earnest, bracing her hands on either side of him and shoving hard, trying to free her mouth from his. Jason swiftly plunged his fingers into the thick hair at her nape and twisted hard. "Don't struggle!" he said through clenched teeth, "you're hurting me."

"You're hurting *me*," Victoria choked, her lips less than an inch from his. "Let me go."

"I can't," he said hoarsely, but his grip on her hair loosened and his long fingers slid downward, curving around her nape while his mesmerizing green eyes gazed deeply into hers. As if the confession were being tortured out of him, he said raggedly, "I've tried a hundred times to let you go, Victoria, but I can't." And while Victoria was still reeling from that incredible statement, Jason pulled her head down and took her mouth in an endless, drugging kiss that stole her breath and stunned her into immobility. His lips moved against hers with tender, hungry yearning, tasting and shaping them, fitting them to his own, then sliding back and forth as if he wanted more of her. Something deep within her sensed his lonely desperation and, helplessly, Victoria responded to it. Her lips softened and melted against his. Instantly, the demanding heat of Jason's kiss increased. His tongue slid over her lips, urging them to part, and the moment they yielded to the sensual pressure, his tongue plunged gently between them.

Jolt after jolt of wild sensation rocketed through Victoria

as his tongue explored her mouth, until, in a fever of dazed yearning, she touched her own tongue timidly to his lips. Jason's response was immediate; he groaned and wrapped his uninjured arm around her, crushing her breasts against his chest, his tongue plunging deeply into her mouth, then retreating to plunge again and again in a wildly exciting, forbidden rhythm.

An eternity later, he pulled his mouth from hers and slid his lips along her hot cheek, kissing her jaw and temple. And then, without warning, he stopped.

Sanity slowly came back to Victoria, bringing with it an awful realization of her shameless behavior. Her cheek was pressed to his hard chest and she was half-lying atop him like a—a shameless wanton! Shaking inside, she forced herself to raise her head, fully expecting to see Jason regarding her with either triumph or contempt—which was nothing more than she deserved. Reluctantly she opened her eyes and forced herself to meet his gaze.

"My God," he whispered hoarsely, his green eyes smoldering. Victoria flinched instinctively as he lifted his hand, but instead of shoving her away, he laid his palm against her flushed cheek, his fingertips softly tracing the delicate bones of her face. Confused by his inexplicable mood, she stared searchingly into his sultry eyes.

"Your name doesn't suit you," he whispered thoughtfully. " 'Victoria' is too long and icy for such a small, fiery creature."

Completely captivated by the intimate look in his eyes and the compelling gentleness in his voice, Victoria swallowed and said, "My parents called me Tory."

"Tory," he repeated, smiling. "I like that—it suits you perfectly." His hypnotic gaze held hers as his hand continued its seductive stroking, sliding over her shoulder and up and down her arm. "I also like the way the sun shines on your hair when you drive off in the carriage with Caroline Collingwood," he continued. "And I like the sound of your laughter. I like the way your eyes flash when you're angry. . . . Do you know what else I like?" he asked as his eyes drifted closed.

Victoria shook her head, mesmerized by his voice and the sweetness of his words.

With his eyes closed and a smile on his lips, he murmured, "Most of all . . . I like the way you fill out that nightdress you're wearing. . . ."

Victoria lurched back in offended modesty and his hand fell away, landing limply beside his head on the pillow. He was fast asleep.

With wide, disbelieving eyes, she stared at him, not knowing what to think or how to feel. He really was the most arrogant, bold— The outrage she was trying to summon absolutely refused to come forth, and a reluctant smile touched her lips as she gazed at him. The hard planes of his face were softer in sleep and, without a cynical twist to his mouth, he looked vulnerable and incredibly boyish.

Her smile deepened as she noticed how outrageously thick his eyelashes were—long, spiky lashes that any girl would yearn to have. Watching him, she began to wonder what he had been like as a little boy. Surely he hadn't been cynical and detached and unapproachable as a child. "Andrew ruined all my childhood dreams," she thought aloud. "I wonder who ruined yours." He turned his head on the pillow and a stray lock of crisp, dark hair fell across his forehead. Feeling strangely maternal and slightly wicked, Victoria reached out and smoothed it away with her fingertips. "I'll tell you a secret," she confessed, knowing he wouldn't hear her. "I like you, too, Jason."

Across the hall a door clicked shut and Victoria jumped up guiltily, straightening her nightdress and smoothing her hair. But when she peeked into the hall, no one was there.

Chapter Eighteen

WHEN VICTORIA WENT DOWN TO BREAKFAST, SHE was amazed to find Uncle Charles already seated at the table, long before he normally arose, and seeming absolutely overjoyed about something.

"You're looking as lovely as usual," Charles said, beaming, as he stood up and pulled out her chair for her.

"And you're looking even better than usual, Uncle Charles," Victoria returned, smiling as she poured her tea and measured in some milk.

"I've never *felt* better," he declared expansively. "Tell me, how is Jason feeling?"

Victoria dropped her spoon.

"What I mean is," he explained smoothly, "I heard him moving about in the hall early this morning and I heard your voice too. Jason sounded," he paused delicately, "a trifle disguised. Was he?"

Victoria nodded cheerfully. "Drunk as a wheelbarrow!"

Instead of commenting on that, Charles said, "Northrup informed me your friend Wiltshire was here an hour ago, inquiring rather desperately about Jason's health." He gave her an amused, speculative look. "Wiltshire seemed to believe Jason had fought a duel this morning and been injured."

Victoria realized it was useless to try to keep the matter from him. She nodded, laughing. "According to what Jason told me, he fought a duel with Lord Wiltshire because Lord Wiltshire called me 'an English bumpkin.' "

"Wiltshire's been plaguing me to distraction for permission to formally pay his addresses to you. I can't believe he called you that."

"I'm certain he did not. For one thing, it doesn't make the least bit of sense."

"None at all," Charles agreed cheerfully. "But whatever the provocation for the duel was, Wiltshire apparently shot Jason?"

Merriment sparkled in Victoria's eyes. "According to Lord Fielding, he was shot in the arm by a *tree*."

"Oddly enough," said Uncle Charles, amused, "that is *exactly* the story that Northrup had from young Wiltshire!" After a moment, he added, "No matter. I understand Dr. Worthing attended to Jason. He is a friend of Jason's and mine, and an excellent physician. If Jason's health was in any real danger, he would be here right now, caring for him. Moreover, Worthing can be depended upon to keep the matter quiet—dueling is illegal, you know."

Victoria paled, and Uncle Charles reached across and covered her hand with his own, giving it a reassuring squeeze. "There's nothing whatever to worry about." An inexplicable tenderness shook his voice as he added, "I can't tell you how—how profoundly happy I am to have you with us, my child. There is so much I want to tell you about Ja—about everything," he amended lamely. "The time will soon come when I can."

Victoria took the opportunity to again urge him to tell her about the days when he knew her mother, but Uncle Charles only shook his head, his expression turning solemn. "Someday soon," he promised as he always did. "But not yet."

The rest of the day seemed to drag as Victoria waited nervously for Jason to appear, wondering how he would act toward her after last night. Her mind revolved around the possibilities, unable to leave them alone. Perhaps he would despise her for letting him kiss her. Perhaps he would hate himself for admitting he liked her and didn't want to let her go. Perhaps he hadn't meant any of the sweet things he said.

She was quite certain that most of his actions last night had been induced by strong spirits, but she wanted very much to believe some sort of closer friendship, rather than their tentative one, would result from letting the barriers down between them last night. In the past weeks, she had come to care very much for him; she liked and admired him. Beyond that, she . . . Beyond that, she refused to think.

As the day crept forward, her hopes began to die and her tension continued to mount—a state that was only worsened by the two dozen callers who appeared at the house, all of them anxious to learn the truth about Jason's duel. Northrup informed everyone that Lady Victoria was out for the day, and Victoria continued to wait.

At one o'clock in the afternoon, Jason finally came downstairs only to go directly into his study, where he remained closeted in a meeting with Lord Collingwood and two other men who came to discuss some sort of business investment.

At three o'clock, Victoria went to the library. Thoroughly disgusted with herself for worrying herself to distraction, she sat there, trying to concentrate on her book, unable to carry on any sort of intelligent conversation with Uncle Charles, who was seated near the windows across the room from her, thumbing through a periodical.

By the time Jason finally strolled into the library, Victoria was so unstrung she nearly jumped to her feet when she saw him.

"What are you reading?" he inquired casually, stopping in front of her and shoving his hands into the pockets of his tight tan trousers.

"A volume of Shelley's," she said after a long, embarrassing moment during which she couldn't remember the particular poet's name.

"Victoria," he began, and for the first time Victoria noticed the tension around his mouth. He hesitated, as if searching for the right words, then said, "Did I do anything last night I should apologize for?"

Victoria's heart sank; he didn't recall any of it. "Nothing that I remember," she said, trying to keep her disappointment from showing.

The ghost of a smile hovered at his mouth. "Usually, the person who can't remember is the one who overindulged—not the other way round."

"I see. Well, no, you didn't."

"Good. In that case, I'll see you later when we leave for the theater—" With a glinting grin, he added meaningfully, "—Tory." Then he turned to leave.

"You said you didn't remember anything," Victoria burst out before she could stop herself.

Jason turned back to face her, his grin downright wolfish. "*I* remember everything, Tory. I merely wanted to know if, in *your* opinion, I did anything I ought to apologize for."

Victoria's breath came out in an embarrassed, choking laugh. "You are the most exasperating man alive!"

"True," he admitted unrepentantly, "but you *like* me anyway."

Hot color raced to her face as she watched him walk away. Never, not in her worst imaginings, had she thought he might have been awake when she said that. She sank back against her chair and closed her eyes, mortified to the very core. And that was before a movement across the room reminded her that Uncle Charles was there. Her eyes snapped open, and she saw him watching her, an expression of joyous triumph on his face.

"Very nicely done, child," he remarked softly. "I always hoped you would come to care for him, and I can see you do."

"Yes, but I don't understand him, Uncle Charles."

Her admission only seemed to gratify the duke that much more. "If you can care for him now, without understanding him, you will care for him a hundred times more when you finally do, that much I can promise you." He stood up. "I suppose I'd best be on my way. I'm engaged for the rest of the afternoon and evening with an old friend."

When Victoria walked into the drawing room that evening, Jason was waiting for her, his tall frame exquisitely attired in a wine-colored coat and trousers, a ruby winking in the folds of his pristine white neckcloth. Two matching rubies glinted in the cuffs of his shirt as he stretched out his arm, reaching for his wineglass.

"You've left off the sling!" Victoria said as she realized it was missing.

"You haven't dressed for the theater," he countered. "And the Mortrams are giving a ball. We'll go there afterward."

"I really don't wish to go to either place. I've already sent a note to the Marquis de Salle, asking him to excuse me from going down to supper with him at the Mortrams'."

"He'll be devastated," Jason predicted with satisfaction. "Particularly when he hears you went down to supper with me, instead."

"Oh, but I can't!"

"Yes," he said dryly, "you can."

"I wish you would wear the sling," Victoria evaded.

He gave her a look of exasperated amusement. "If I appear in public wearing a sling, that infant Wiltshire will have everyone in London convinced I was felled by a tree."

"I doubt he'll say that," Victoria said with a twinkle. "He's very young and therefore more likely to boast of having bested you himself in a duel."

"Which is more embarrassing than being hit by a tree. Wiltshire," he explained in disgust, "doesn't know which end of his pistol to point at the target."

Victoria swallowed a giggle. "But why must I go out with you if all you need do is appear in public looking uninjured?"

"Because if you aren't at my side, some woman who longs to be a duchess is bound to hang on my sore arm. Besides, I want to take you."

Victoria wasn't proof against his teasing persuasion. "Very well," she laughed. "I couldn't live with myself if I was responsible for ruining your reputation as an invincible duelist." She started to turn, then paused, an impudent smile on her lips. "Have you really killed a dozen men in duels in India?"

"No," he said bluntly. "Now run along and change your gown."

It seemed as if everyone in London was at the theater tonight—and every pair of eyes seemed to shift to them as they entered Jason's box. Heads turned, fans fluttered, and whispers began. At first, Victoria assumed they were surprised to see Jason looking perfectly well, rather than wounded, but she began to change her mind later. As soon as she left the box with Jason between the acts of the play, she realized that something was different. Young ladies and older ones alike, people who had been friendly in the past, were now eyeing her with stiff faces and censorious eyes. And Victoria finally realized why: Jason had reportedly fought a duel for her. Her reputation had just suffered a telling blow.

Not far away, an old woman wearing a white satin turban with an enormous amethyst at the front observed Jason and Victoria with narrowed eyes. "So," the Duchess of Claremont hissed under her breath to her elderly companion, "Wakefield has fought a duel for her."

"So I've heard, your grace," Lady Faulklyn agreed.

The Duchess of Claremont leaned upon her ebony cane, watching her great-granddaughter. "She is the image of Katherine."

"Yes, your grace."

The duchess's faded blue eyes moved over Victoria from head to toe, then shifted to Jason Fielding. "Handsome devil, isn't he?"

Lady Faulklyn paled as if afraid to risk answering in the affirmative.

Ignoring her silence, the duchess tapped her fingertips upon the jeweled handle of her cane and continued to study the Marquess of Wakefield through narrowed eyes. "He looks like Atherton," she said.

"There is a slight resemblance," Lady Faulklyn ventured hesitantly.

"Nitwit!" the duchess snapped. "Wakefield looks exactly as Atherton did when he was young."

"Exactly!" declared Lady Faulklyn.

A smile of malicious glee spread across the duchess's thin face. "Atherton thinks he's going to pull off a marriage between our two families against my wishes. He's waited twenty-two years to spite me, and he actually believes he's going to succeed." A low cackle grated in her chest as she watched the beautiful couple standing a few yards away. "Atherton's wrong," she said.

Victoria nervously averted her gaze from the stern-faced old woman wearing the peculiar turban. *Everyone* seemed to be watching Jason and her, even elderly women she'd never laid eyes upon before, like that one. She glanced apprehensively at Jason. "My coming here with you was a dreadful mistake," she told him as he handed her a glass of ratafia.

"Why? You've enjoyed watching the play." He grinned into her worried blue eyes. "And I've enjoyed watching you."

"Well, you mustn't watch me, and you particularly mustn't look as if you enjoy doing so," Victoria said, trying to ignore the surge of pleasure she felt at his casual compliment.

"Why not?"

"Because everyone is watching us."

"They've seen us together before," Jason said with an indifferent shrug, and ushered her back to his private box.

Things were worse, much worse, when they arrived at the Mortrams' ball. The moment they walked in together, everyone in the crowded ballroom seemed to turn and stare in a decidedly unfriendly fashion.

"Jason, this is horrid! It's worse than the theater. There, at least some of the people were watching the stage. Here, everyone is staring at *us,* and will you please," she implored, switching topics, "stop smiling at me in that charming way—everyone is watching us!"

"Am I being charming?" he teased, but his gaze made a swift, sweeping appraisal of the faces in the ballroom. "What I see," he drawled mildly, nodding his head to her right, "is a half dozen of your besotted admirers standing over there, looking as if they would all like to devise a way to slit my throat and dispose of my body."

Victoria could have stamped her foot in frustration. "You're deliberately ignoring what's happened. Caroline Collingwood is privy to all the *on dits,* and she told me no one believed we had any real interest in each other. Gossip had it that we were merely keeping up the charade of a betrothal for Uncle Charles's sake. But now you've fought a duel because of something someone said about me, which changes everything. They're thinking about how much time you spend at the house when I'm there—"

"It happens to be my house," Jason drawled, his brows snapping together over ominous green eyes.

"I know, but it's the principle of the thing that counts. Now everyone—particularly the ladies—is wondering all sorts of vile things about us. If you were anyone but you, it wouldn't matter so much," she said, meaning only that their confused betrothal status only added more fuel for the gossip. "It's the principle of the—"

Jason's voice dropped to a low, icy whisper. "You're mistaken if you think I give a damn what people think—including you. Don't bother lecturing me on principles, because I don't have any, and don't mistake me for a 'gentleman,' because I'm not. I've lived in places you've never heard of and I've done things in all of them that would offend all your puritanical sensibilities. You're an innocent, foolish child. I was never innocent. I was never even a child. However, since you're so concerned about what people think, the problem is relatively easy to remedy. You can spend the rest of the evening with your simpering beaux, and I'll find someone to amuse me."

Victoria was so confused and hurt by Jason's unprovoked attack that she could scarcely think after he walked away. Nevertheless, she did *exactly* as he had so rudely suggested, and despite the lessening of the nasty looks cast in her direction, she had a perfectly dreadful time. Her hurt pride compelled her to act as if she enjoyed dancing with her partners and listening to their flattering conversation, but her ears seemed to be tuned to the sound of Jason's deep voice, and her heart seemed to sense when he was near her.

With growing misery, Victoria realized Jason had coolly surrounded himself with three beautiful blondes who were vying with each other for his attention and turning themselves inside out to win one of his lazy smiles. Not once since last night had she permitted herself to dwell on the pleasure his lips had given her. Now she couldn't seem to think of anything else, and she longed to have him back at her side, instead of flirting with those other women, and the devil fly with public opinion!

Beside her, a handsome young man of about twenty-five reminded her that she had promised him the next dance.

"Yes, of course," Victoria said, politely but not enthusiastically. "Do you happen to know the time, Mr. Bascomb?" she asked as he led her onto the dance floor.

"Yes, indeed," he declared proudly. "It is half past eleven." Victoria stifled a groan. It would be hours yet before the evening's ordeal would come to an end.

Charles fitted his key into the lock and opened the door just as Northrup hurried into the entrance hall. "There was no need for you to wait up for me, Northrup," Charles said kindly, handing him his hat and cane. "What time is it?"

"Half past eleven, your grace."

"Jason and Victoria won't be home much before dawn, so don't try to wait up for them," he advised. "You know how late these affairs go on."

Northrup bade him good night and vanished in the direction of his rooms. Charles turned in the opposite direction and started toward the salon, intending to relax with a glass of port and savor at leisure thoughts of the romance between Jason and Victoria that had finally burst into full bloom last night in Jason's bedroom. He started across the foyer, but a loud, imperative knocking upon the front door made him stop and turn back. Thinking that Jason and Victoria must have forgotten their key and come home early, he opened the door, his smile fading to a look of mild inquiry when he beheld a tall, well-dressed man of about thirty.

"Forgive my intrusion at this late hour, your grace," the gentleman said. "I am Arthur Winslow, and my firm has been employed by another firm of solicitors in America, with instructions to see that this letter is delivered to you at once. I have another one for Miss Victoria Seaton."

An uncontrollable premonition of disaster began to thunder in Charles's brain as he accepted his letter. "Lady Seaton is out for the evening."

"I know that, your grace." The young man gestured ruefully over his shoulder at the carriage in the street. "I've been waiting there for one or both of you to return since early this evening, when these letters were placed in my hands. "In the event Lady Seaton was not here, our instructions were to deliver her letter into your hands and to ask you to be certain she receives it at once." He placed the second letter in Charles's clammy palm and tipped his hat. "Good evening, your grace."

Icy dread racked his body as Charles closed the door and opened his letter, searching for the identity of the sender. The name "Andrew Bainbridge" leapt out at him. He stared at it, his heart beginning to hammer in painful jerks; then he forced himself to read what was written. As he read, the color drained from his face and the words swam before his blurring eyes.

When he was finished, Charles's hands fell to his sides and his head dropped forward. His shoulders shook and tears trickled down his face, falling to the floor, as his dreams and hopes collapsed with an explosion that made the blood roar in his ears. Long after his tears stopped, he stood staring blindly at the floor. Finally, very slowly, his shoulders straightened and he lifted his head. "Northrup," he called as he started walking up the stairs, but his voice was a choked whisper. He cleared his throat and called again, "Northrup!"

Northrup rushed into the foyer, pulling on his jacket. "You called, your grace?" he said, his alarmed gaze on the duke, who had stopped halfway up the staircase, his hand gripping the railing for support.

Charles turned his head and looked down at him. "Summon Dr. Worthing," he said. "Tell him to come at once. Tell him it's urgent."

"Shall I send for Lord Fielding and Lady Victoria?" Northrup asked quickly.

"No, dammit!" Charles ground out, and then he recovered control of his voice. "I'll let you know, after Dr. Worthing arrives," he amended, continuing slowly up the staircase.

It was nearly dawn when Jason's coachman pulled the spirited grays up before the house at #6 Upper Brook Street. Neither Jason nor Victoria had spoken a word since leaving the Mortrams' ball, but at Jason's sudden intake of breath, Victoria straightened and looked around. "Whose carriage is that?" she asked.

"Dr. Worthing's. I recognize the bays." Jason flung open the door, leapt out of the carriage and unceremoniously hauled her down, then vaulted up the steps toward the house, leaving Victoria to fend for herself. Victoria snatched up her long skirts and ran after him, panic throbbing in her throat as a haggard Northrup opened the front door.

"What's wrong?" Jason snapped.

"Your uncle, my lord," Northrup replied grimly. "He's had an attack—his heart. Dr. Worthing is with him."

"Dear God!" Victoria said, clutching Jason's sleeve in a grip of terror.

Together they ran up the staircase, while behind them Northrup called, "Dr. Worthing asked that you not go in until I informed him of your arrival!"

Jason lifted his hand to knock on Charles's door, but Dr. Worthing was already opening it. He stepped out into the hall, firmly closing the door behind him. "I thought I heard you come in," he explained, combing his fingers through his white hair in a harassed gesture.

"How is he?" Jason demanded tightly.

Dr. Worthing removed his wire-rimmed spectacles and carefully concentrated on polishing the lenses. After an endless moment, he drew a long breath and raised his eyes. "He's suffered a very grave setback, Jason."

"Can we see him?" Jason asked.

"Yes, but I must warn you both not to do or say anything to upset him."

Victoria's hand flew to her throat. "He isn't—isn't going to die, is he, Dr. Worthing?"

"Sooner or later, everyone must die, my dear," he told her, his expression so grim that Victoria began to shake with terror.

They entered the dying man's room and went to stand beside his bed, Victoria on one side, Jason on the other. A brace of candles was lit on the table beside the bed, but to Victoria the room already seemed as dark and frightening as a waiting tomb. Charles's hand was lying limply on the coverlet and, swallowing her tears, she reached out and took it tightly in hers, trying desperately to infuse some of her strength into him.

Charles's eyes fluttered open and focused on her face. "My dear child," he whispered. "I didn't intend to die so soon. I wanted so much to see you happily settled first. Who will care for you when I am gone? Have you anyone else who can take you in and provide for you?''

Tears raced down Victoria's cheeks. She loved him so, and now she was going to lose him. She tried to speak, but the lump of anguish and fear in her throat strangled her voice and she could only squeeze Charles's frail hand even tighter.

Charles turned his head on the pillow and looked at Jason. "You are so like me," he whispered, "so stubborn. And now you will be as alone as I have always been."

"Don't talk," Jason warned him, his voice harsh with sorrow. "Rest."

"I *can't* rest," Charles argued weakly. "I can't die in peace, knowing that Victoria will be alone. You will both be alone in different ways. She cannot remain under your protection, Jason. Society would never forgive . . ." His voice trailed off. Visibly fighting for enough strength to continue, he turned his head to Victoria.

"Victoria, you're named after me. Your mother and I loved each other. I—I was going to tell you about all that someday. Now there is no more time."

Victoria could no longer restrain her tears, and she bent her head, her shoulders shaking with wrenching sobs.

Charles dragged his gaze from her weeping form and looked at Jason. "It was my dream that you and Victoria would wed. I wanted you to have each other when I was gone. . . ."

Jason's face was a taut mask of controlled grief. He nodded, the muscles working in his throat. "I'll take care of Victoria—I'll marry her," he clarified quickly as Charles started to argue.

Victoria's shocked, teary gaze flew to Jason's face; then she realized that he was merely trying to ease Charles's dying hour.

Wearily, Charles closed his eyes. "I don't believe you, Jason," he whispered.

Stricken with terror and desperation, Victoria dropped to her knees beside the bed, clutching Charles's hand. "You mustn't worry about us, Uncle Charles," she wept.

Feebly turning his head on the pillow, Charles opened his eyes and stared at Jason. "Do you swear it?" he whispered.

"Swear to me that you will wed Victoria, that you will care for her always."

"I swear it," Jason said, and the fierce look in his eyes convinced Victoria that this was no charade on his part, after all. He was giving his oath to a dying man.

"And you, my child?" he said to Victoria. "Do you solemnly swear you will have him?"

Victoria tensed. This was no time to argue over former grievances and petty technicalities. The brutal fact was that without Jason, without Charles, she had no one else in the world, and she knew it. She remembered the heady delight of Jason's kisses, and although she feared his surface coldness, she knew he was strong and he would keep her safe. What little was left of her half-formed plans to someday return on her own to America gave way to the more pressing need to survive and to ease Charles's worry in his dying hours.

"Victoria?" Charles prodded feebly.

"I will have him," she whispered brokenly.

"Thank you," Charles murmured with a pathetic attempt at a smile. He pulled his left hand out from beneath the blanket, and grasped Jason's hand. "Now I can die in peace."

Suddenly Jason's entire body tensed. His eyes jerked to Charles's and his face became a cynical mask. With biting sarcasm, he agreed, "Now you can die in peace, Charles."

"No!" Victoria burst out, weeping. "Don't die, Uncle Charles. Please don't!" Trying desperately to give him a reason to fight for his life, she sobbed, "If you die, you won't be able to give me away at our wedding. . . ."

Dr. Worthing stepped forward from the shadows and gently helped Victoria to her feet. Nodding to Jason to follow him, he led her out into the hall. "That's enough for now, my dear," he said soothingly. "You'll make yourself ill."

Victoria raised her tear-streaked face to the physician. "Do you think he will live, Dr. Worthing?"

The kindly middle-aged physician soothingly patted her arm. "I'll stay with him and let you know the moment there is any change." And without a word of any real reassurance, he retreated back into the bedchamber, closing the door behind him.

Victoria and Jason went downstairs to the salon. Jason sat down beside her and, in a gesture of comfort, he put his arm around her, easing her head onto his shoulder. Victoria turned her face into his hard chest and sobbed out her grief and terror until there were no more tears left in her to shed. She spent the rest of the night in Jason's arms, keeping a silent, prayerful vigil.

Charles spent the rest of the night playing cards with Dr. Worthing.

Chapter Nineteen

EARLY THE FOLLOWING AFTERNOON, DR. WORTHING was able to report that Uncle Charles was "still holding his own." The next day, he came downstairs to the dining room where Jason and Victoria were having dinner and informed them that Charles "appeared to be much improved."

Victoria could scarcely contain her joy, but Jason merely quirked a brow at the physician and invited him to join them for dinner.

"Er—thank you," Dr. Worthing said, shooting a sharp look at Jason's inscrutable features. "I believe I can leave my patient unattended for a short time."

"I'm certain you can," Jason replied blandly.

"Do you think he'll recover, Dr. Worthing?" Victoria burst out, wondering how Jason could appear so utterly unemotional.

Carefully avoiding Jason's assessing stare, Dr. Worthing directed his uneasy gaze at Victoria and cleared his throat. "It's difficult to say. You see, he says he wants to live to see you two married. He's most determined to do so. You might say that he's clinging to that as a reason to live."

Victoria bit her lip and glanced uneasily at Jason before

asking the doctor, "What will happen if he starts to recover and we—we tell him we've changed our minds?"

Jason answered her in a bland drawl. "In that case, he'll undoubtedly have a relapse." Turning to the physician, he said coolly, "Won't he?"

Dr. Worthing's gaze skittered away from Jason's steely eyes. "I'm sure you know him better than I, Jason. What do you think he'll do?"

Jason shrugged. "I think he'll have a relapse."

Victoria felt as if life were deliberately tormenting her, taking away her home and the people she loved, forcing her to come to a strange foreign land, and now propelling her into a loveless marriage with a man who didn't want her.

Long after both men left, she remained at the table, listlessly toying with the food on her plate, trying to find a way out of this dilemma for Jason's sake and her own. Her dreams of a happy home, with a loving husband at her side and a baby gurgling in her arms, came back to mock her, and she allowed herself a bout of self-pity. After all, she hadn't asked very much of life; she hadn't yearned for furs and jewels, for seasons in London or palatial homes where she could play reigning queen. She had wanted no more than what she'd had in America—except that she had wanted a husband and children to go with it.

A wave of dizzying homesickness washed over her and she bent her head. How she longed to set time back a year and keep it there, to have her parents' smiling faces before her, to listen to her father speak of the hospital he wanted to build, and to be surrounded by the villagers who had been her second family. She would do anything, anything to go back home again. An image of Andrew's handsome, laughing face appeared to taunt her, and Victoria thrust it away, refusing to shed any more tears for the faithless man she had adored.

She pushed her chair back and went looking for Jason. Andrew had abandoned her to her own fate, but Jason was here and he was obliged to help her think of some way out of a marriage neither of them wanted.

She found him alone in his study—a solitary, brooding man standing with his arm draped on the mantel, staring into the empty fireplace. Compassion swelled in her heart as she realized that, although he had pretended to be cold and unemotional in front of Dr. Worthing, Jason had come in here to worry in lonely privacy.

Suppressing the urge to go to him and offer sympathy, which she knew he would only reject, she said quietly, "Jason?"

He lifted his head and looked at her, his face impassive.

"What are we going to do?"

"About what?"

"About this outrageous idea Uncle Charles has of seeing us married."

"Why is it outrageous?"

Victoria was amazed by his answer, but determined to discuss the matter, calmly and frankly. "It's outrageous because I don't want to marry you."

His eyes hardened. "I'm well aware of that, Victoria."

"You don't want to be married either," she answered reasonably, lifting her hands in a gesture of appeal.

"You're right." Shifting his gaze back to the fireplace, he lapsed into silence. Victoria waited for him to say something more; when he didn't, she sighed and started to leave. His next words made her turn back and stare. "However, our marriage could give each of us something we *do* want."

"What is that?" she asked, peering at his ruggedly chiseled profile, trying to fathom his mood. He straightened and turned, shoving his hands deep in his pockets, his eyes meeting hers. "You want to go back to America, to be independent, to live among your friends and perhaps build the hospital your father dreamed of building. You've told me all that. If you're honest with yourself, you'll admit you'd also like to go back there to show Andrew, and everyone else, that his desertion meant nothing to you—that you forgot about him as easily as he forgot about you, and you went on with your life."

Victoria was so humiliated by his reference to her plight that it took a moment before his next words registered on her. "And," he finished matter-of-factly, "I want a son."

Her mouth fell open as he continued calmly, "We could give each other what we both want. Marry me and give me a son. In return, I'll send you back to America with enough money to live like a queen and build a dozen hospitals."

Victoria stared at him in stricken disbelief. "Give you a son?" she echoed. "Give you a son, and then you'll send me back to America? Give you a son and *leave* him here?"

"I'm not completely selfish—you could keep him with you until he is . . . say, four years old. A child needs his mother until he is that age. After that, I would expect to have him with me. Perhaps you will choose to stay here with us when you bring him back. Actually, I'd prefer that you stay here permanently, but I will leave that up to you. There is one thing, however—a condition to all this—that I would insist upon."

"What condition?" Victoria asked dazedly.

He hesitated as if framing his answer with care, and when he finally spoke, he looked away, studying the landscape above the fireplace as if he wished to avoid meeting her eyes. "Because of the way you leapt to my defense the other night, people have assumed you do not despise or fear me. If you agree to this marriage, I will expect you to reinforce that opinion and not do or say anything to make them think differently. In other words, no matter what may transpire between us in private, when we are in public I would expect you to behave as if you married me for more than my money and title. Or to put it simply—as if you care for me."

For no reason at all, Victoria recalled his caustic remarks at the Mortrams' ball: *"You're mistaken if you think I give a damn what people think. . . ."* He had been lying, she realized with a pang of tenderness. He obviously cared what they thought or he wouldn't ask her to do this.

She gazed at the cool, dispassionate man standing before her. He looked powerful, aloof, and completely self-assured. It was impossible to believe he wanted a son, or her, or anyone—as impossible as it was to believe that it bothered him that people feared and mistrusted him. Impossible, but true. She remembered how boyish he had seemed the night of his duel, when he had teased her and coaxed her to kiss him. She remembered the hungry yearning in his kiss and the lonely desperation of his words: *"I've tried a hundred times to let you go. But I can't."*

Perhaps beneath his cool, unemotional facade, Jason felt as lonely and empty as she did. Perhaps he needed her, and couldn't make himself say so. Then again, perhaps she was only trying to fool herself into believing it. "Jason," she said, voicing part of her thoughts aloud. "You can't expect me to have a child and then hand him over to you and go my own way. You can't be as cold and heartless as your proposition makes you sound. I—I can't believe you are."

"You won't find me a cruel husband, if that's what you mean."

"That is *not* what I mean," Victoria burst out a little hysterically. "How can you speak of marrying me as if you're discussing a—a common business arrangement— without any feeling, without any emotion, without even a pretense of love or—"

"Surely you have no illusions left about love," he scoffed with stinging impatience. "Your experience with Bainbridge should have taught you that love is only an emotion used to manipulate fools. I neither expect nor want your love, Victoria."

Victoria grasped the back of the chair beside her, reeling under his words. She opened her mouth to refuse his offer, but he shook his head to forestall her. "Don't answer me before you consider what I've said. If you marry me, you'll have the freedom to do whatever you like with your life. You could build one hospital in America and another near Wakefield, and stay in England. I have six estates and a thousand tenants and servants. My servants alone could provide you with enough sick people to fill up your hospital. If not, I'll pay them to get sick." A ghost of a smile tugged at his lips, but Victoria was too heartsore to see any humor in the situation.

When he saw that his quip had won no response, he added lightly, "You can cover the walls of Wakefield with your sketches, and if you run out of room, I'll add on to the house." Victoria was still trying to absorb the startling information that he knew she sketched when he reached out and ran his fingertips across her taut cheek and said matter-of-factly, "You'll find me a very generous husband, I promise you."

The finality of the word "husband" sent a chill skidding through Victoria's body and she clasped her arms, rubbing them in a futile effort to warm herself. "Why?" she whispered. "Why me? If you want sons, there are dozens of females in London who are nauseatingly eager to marry you."

"Because I'm attracted to you—surely you know that," he said. "Besides," he added, his eyes teasing as his hands went to her shoulders and he tried to draw her near, "you like me. You told me so when you thought I was asleep—remember?"

Victoria gaped at him, unable to absorb the amazing revelation that he was actually attracted to her. "I liked Andrew, too," she retorted with angry impertinence. "I have poor judgment in the matter of men."

"True," he agreed, amusement dancing in his eyes.

She felt herself being drawn relentlessly closer to his chest. "I think you've taken leave of your senses!" she said in a strangled voice. "I think you're quite mad!"

"I have and I am," he agreed as he angled his arm across her back, holding her close.

"I won't do it. I can't—"

"Victoria," he said softly, "you have no choice." His voice turned husky and persuasive as her breasts finally came into contact with his shirt. "I can give you everything a woman wants—"

"Everything but love," Victoria choked.

"Everything a woman *really* wants," he amended, and before Victoria could fathom that cynical remark, his firmly chiseled lips began a slow, deliberate descent toward hers. "I'll give you jewels and furs," he promised. "You'll have more money than you've ever dreamed of." His free hand cupped the back of her head, crumpling the silk of her hair as he tilted her face up for his kiss. "In return, all you have to give me is this. . . ."

Oddly, Victoria's one thought was that he was selling himself too cheaply, asking too little of her. He was handsome and wealthy and desired—surely he had a right to expect more from his wife than this. . . . And then her mind went blank as his sensual mouth seized possession of hers in an endless, stirring kiss that slowly built to one of demanding insistence and left her trembling with hot sensations. He touched his tongue to her lips, sliding it between them, coaxing them, then forcing them to part, and when they did his tongue plunged between them, sending shock waves of dizzying emotions jolting through her. Victoria moaned and his arms tightened protectively around her, pulling her against his hard length while his tongue began a slow, wildly erotic seduction and his hands shifted possessively over her sides and shoulders and back.

By the time he finally lifted his head, Victoria felt dazed and hot and inexplicably afraid.

"Look at me," he whispered, putting his hand beneath her chin and tipping it up. "You're trembling," he said as her wide blue eyes lifted to his. "Are you afraid of me?"

Regardless of all the raw emotions quivering through her, Victoria shook her head. She wasn't afraid of him; she was suddenly, inexplicably afraid for herself. "No," she said.

A smile hovered about his lips. "You are, but you've no reason to be." He laid his hand against her heated face, slowly running it back to smooth her heavy hair. "I will hurt you only once, and then only because it's unavoidable."

"What—why?"

His jaw tensed. "Perhaps it won't hurt after all. Is that it?"

"Is what it?" Victoria cried a little hysterically. "I wish you wouldn't speak in riddles when I'm already so confused I can scarcely think."

With one of his quicksilver changes of mood, he dismissed the matter with a cool shrug. "It doesn't matter," he said curtly. "I don't care what you did with Bainbridge. That was before."

"Before?" Victoria repeated in rising tones of frustrated incomprehension. "Before what?"

"Before me," he said in a clipped tone. "However, I think you ought to know in advance that I won't tolerate being cuckolded. Is that clear?"

Victoria's mouth dropped open. "Cuckolded! You're mad. Utterly mad."

His lips quirked in a near-smile. "We've already agreed on that."

"If you continue speaking in insulting innuendos," she warned, "I'm going upstairs to the sanctuary of my room."

Jason looked down into her stormy blue eyes and repressed the sudden urge to gather her into his arms and again devour her mouth with his. "Very well, we'll talk about something mundane. What is Mrs. Craddock preparing?"

Victoria felt as if the world, and everyone in it, was revolving in one direction, while she was constantly turning in the opposite direction, dizzy and lost. "Mrs. Craddock?" she uttered blankly.

"The cook. See, I have learned her name. I also know that O'Malley is your favorite footman." He grinned. "Now, what is Mrs. Craddock preparing for supper?"

"Goose," Victoria said, trying to recover her balance. "Is—is that acceptable?"

"Perfectly. Are we dining at home?"

"I am," she replied, deliberately noncommittal.

"In that case, naturally, so am I."

He was playing the role of husband already, she realized dazedly. "I'll inform Mrs. Craddock then," she said, and turned away in a trance of confusion. Jason said he was attracted to her. He wanted to marry her. Impossible. If Uncle Charles died, she would *have* to marry him. If she married him now, perhaps Uncle Charles would find the will to live. And children—Jason wanted children. She wanted them too, very much. She wanted *something* to love. Perhaps they could be happy together; there were times when Jason could be charming and engaging, times when his smile made her feel like smiling. He had said he wouldn't hurt her. . . . She was halfway across the room when Jason's calm voice stopped her.

"Victoria—"

Automatically, Victoria turned toward him.

"I think you've already made your decision about our marriage. If it is yes, we ought to see Charles after supper and tell him we're setting the date for our wedding. He'll like that, and the sooner we tell him, the better."

Jason was insisting on knowing if she intended to marry him, Victoria realized. She stared across the room at the handsome, forceful, dynamic man—and the moment seemed to freeze in time. Why did she think he was tense as he waited for her answer? Why did he have to ask her to marry him as if it was a business proposition?

"I—" Victoria began helplessly, while Andrew's sweet,

216

formal proposal suddenly tolled through her mind. *"Say you will marry me, Victoria. I love you. I'll always love you. . . ."*

Her chin came up in angry rebellion. At least Jason Fielding didn't mouth words of love he didn't feel. Neither, however, had he proposed to her with any show of sentimental affection, so she accepted his proposal in the same unemotional way it had been offered. She looked at Jason and nodded stiffly. "We'll tell him after supper."

Victoria could have sworn the tension seemed to leave Jason's face and body.

Technically, it was the evening of her engagement, and Victoria decided to use the occasion to try to set a better pattern for their future. The morning of the duel, Jason had said he enjoyed her laughter. If, as she suspected, he was as lonely and empty inside as she herself often felt, then perhaps they could brighten each other's lives. Barefoot, she stood in front of the open wardrobe, surveying her loveliest gowns, trying to decide what to wear for this mock-festive occasion. She finally decided on an aqua chiffon gown with an overskirt dusted with shimmering gold spangles and a necklace of gold-encrusted aquamarines Jason had given her as a gift the night of her come-out. Ruth brushed her hair until it shone, then parted it at the center and let it fall in gleaming waves that framed Victoria's face and spilled over her shoulders and back. When Victoria was satisfied with her appearance, she left her room and went down to the drawing room. Jason had evidently followed the same impulse, for his tall frame was formally clad in an immaculately tailored claret velvet coat and trousers with a white brocade waistcoat and ruby studs winking in his shirtfront.

He was pouring champagne into a glass when he looked up and saw her, and his bold eyes moved over her with unhidden masculine appreciation. Pride of ownership was evident in his possessive gaze and Victoria's stomach jumped nervously when she saw it. He had never looked at her like this before—as if she were a tasty morsel he was planning to devour at his leisure.

"You have the most disconcerting ability to look like an enchanting child one moment, and an incredibly alluring woman, the next," he said.

"Thank you," Victoria said uncertainly, "I think."

"It was intended as a compliment," he assured her, smiling slightly. "I'm not usually so clumsy with compliments that you can't identify them. I'll be more careful in future."

Touched by this small indication that he intended to try to change to please her, Victoria watched as he deftly poured the sparkling liquid into two glasses. He handed her one and she started to turn toward the settee, but he put a restraining hand on her bare arm and drew her back. With his other hand he opened the lid of a large velvet jeweler's box lying beside his glass and withdrew a triple strand of the largest, most magnificent pearls Victoria had ever seen. Wordlessly he turned her toward the mirror above the side table and pushed her long hair aside. His fingers sent tiny tremors down her spine as he removed the aquamarines and laid the wide, heavy pearl choker around her slim neck.

In the mirror, Victoria watched his expressionless features as he fastened the diamond clasp at the back of her neck, then lifted his eyes to hers, studying the pearl choker at her throat. "Thank you," she began awkwardly, turning around. "I—"

"I'd rather be thanked with a kiss," Jason instructed patiently.

Victoria leaned up on her toes and obediently but self-consciously pressed a kiss on his smooth, freshly shaven cheek. Something about the way he gave her pearls and coolly expected a kiss in return bothered her very much—it was as if he was purchasing her favors, beginning with a kiss in exchange for a necklace. That notion was rather frighteningly confirmed when he said about her kiss: "That isn't much of a kiss for so beautiful a necklace," and took her lips with sudden, demanding insistence.

When he let her go, he smiled quizzically into her apprehensive blue eyes. "Don't you like pearls, Victoria?"

"Oh, I do—truly!" Victoria said nervously, angry with herself for her inability to control her foolish, fanciful fears. "I've never seen such beautiful ones as these. Even Lady Wilhelm's weren't so huge. These are fit for a queen."

"They belonged to a Russian princess a century ago," he

said, and Victoria was oddly touched that he apparently thought her worthy of such a priceless necklace.

After supper, they went upstairs to see Charles. His delight when they quietly told him of their decision to go ahead with the wedding plans took years off his face, and when Jason fondly put his arm around Victoria's shoulders, the bedridden invalid actually laughed with joy. He looked so happy, so confident that they were doing the right thing, that Victoria almost believed they were, too.

"When's the wedding to be?" Charles asked suddenly.

"In one week," Jason said, earning a surprised glance from Victoria.

"Excellent, excellent!" Charles averred, beaming at them. "I intend to be well enough by then to attend myself."

Victoria started to protest, but Jason's fingers tightened on her arm, warning her not to argue.

"And what have you there, my dear?" Charles asked, beaming at the necklace at her throat.

Her hand went automatically to the object of his gaze. "Jason gave me these tonight, to seal our barg—betrothal," she explained.

When the interview with Charles was finished, Victoria pleaded exhaustion and Jason walked her to the door of her bedroom suite. "Something is bothering you," he said calmly. "What is it?"

"Among other things, I feel wretched about being married before my mourning period for my parents is past. I've felt guilty every time I've gone to a ball. I've had to be evasive about when my parents died so people wouldn't realize what a disrespectful daughter I am."

"You've done what you had to do, and your parents would understand that. By marrying me immediately, you're giving Charles a reason to live. You saw how much better he looked when we told him we've set the date for the wedding. Besides, the original decision to cut short your mourning period was mine, not yours, and so you had no choice in the matter. If you must blame someone, blame me."

Logically, Victoria knew he was right, and she changed the subject. "Tell me," she said, her smile lightly accusing, "now that I've just discovered *we* decided to be married in one week, could you tell me *where* we decided to be married?"

"Touché," he grinned. "Very well; we've decided to be married here."

Victoria shook her head emphatically. "Please, Jason, can't we be married in church—in the little village church I saw near Wakefield? We could wait a little longer until Uncle Charles can make the trip." Astonished, she watched a look of cold revulsion flash through his eyes at the mention of a church, but after a moment's hesitation, he acquiesced with a curt nod. "If a church wedding is what you want, we'll have it here in London at a church large enough to accommodate all the guests."

"Please, no—" Victoria burst out, unconsciously laying her hand on his sleeve. "I'm very far from America, my lord. The church near Wakefield would be better—it reminds me of home, and ever since I was a little girl, I've dreamed of being married in a little village church—" She'd dreamed of being married in a little village church to Andrew, Victoria realized belatedly, and wished she'd never thought of the church at all.

"I want our marriage to take place in London, before the *ton*," Jason said with absolute finality. "However, we'll compromise," he offered. "We'll be married in church here, and then we'll go to Wakefield for a small celebration."

Victoria's hand slid from his sleeve. "Forget I mentioned a church at all. Invite everyone here to the house. It would be little short of blasphemy to enter a church and seal what is nothing more than a cold business arrangement." With a lame attempt at humor, she added, "While we were vowing to love and honor one another, I'd be waiting for lightning to strike."

"We'll be married in a church," Jason said curtly, cutting short her diatribe. "And if lightning strikes, I'll bear the expense for a new roof."

Chapter Twenty

"GOOD AFTERNOON, MY DEAR," CHARLES SAID cheerfully, patting the edge of the bed beside him. "Come sit down. Your visit last night with Jason has restored my health beyond belief. Now, tell me more about your wedding plans."

Victoria sat down beside him. "Truthfully, it's all very confusing, Uncle Charles. Northrup has just told me Jason packed the things from his study this morning and has moved back to Wakefield."

"I know," Charles said, smiling. "He came in to see me before he left and told me he'd decided to do it 'for the sake of appearances.' The less time he spends in close proximity to you, the less chance there is for any further gossip."

"So that's why he left," Victoria said, her worried expression clearing.

Laughter shook Charles's shoulders as he nodded. "My child, I think this is the first time in his life that Jason has ever made a concession to propriety! It irked him to do it, but he did it anyway. You have a decidedly good influence on him," Charles finished merrily. "Perhaps you can teach him next to stop scoffing at principles."

Victoria smiled back at him, relieved and quite suddenly very happy. "I'm afraid I don't know anything about the wedding arrangements," she admitted, "except that it's to take place in a big church here in London."

"Jason is taking care of everything. He took his secretary with him to Wakefield, along with the main staff from here, so they can make the preparations. After the ceremony, a wedding celebration will take place at Wakefield for your close friends and some of the villagers. I believe the invitation list and the invitations are already in the process of being prepared. So you have nothing to do except remain here and enjoy everyone's surprise when they realize you are well and truly to be the next Duchess of Atherton."

Victoria dismissed that and hesitantly brought up something that was much more important to her. "The night you were so very ill, you mentioned something about my mother and you—something you had intended to tell me."

Charles turned his head away, gazing out the window, and Victoria said quickly, "You needn't tell me if it will upset you to speak of it."

"It's not that," he said, slowly returning his gaze to her face. "I know how understanding and sensible you are, but you're still very young. You loved your father, probably as much as you loved your mother. Once I tell you what I have to say, you might begin to think of me as an interloper in their marriage, although I swear to you I never communicated with your mother after she married your papa. Victoria," he explained miserably, "I'm trying to tell you I don't want you to despise me, and I fear you might when you hear the story."

Victoria took his hand in hers and said gently, "How could I possibly despise someone with the good sense to love my mother?"

He looked down at her hand and his voice was choked with emotion. "You inherited your mother's heart as well, do you know that?" When Victoria remained silent, his gaze returned to the windows and he began the story of his involvement with Katherine. Not until he was done did he look at Victoria again, and when he did he saw no condemnation in her eyes, only sorrow and compassion. "So you see," he finished, "I loved her with all my heart. I loved her and I cut her out of my life when she was the only thing worth living for."

"My great-grandmother *forced* you to do it," Victoria said, her eyes stormy.

"Were they happy—your mother and father, I mean? I've always wondered what sort of marriage they had, but I've been afraid to ask."

Victoria remembered the awful scene she had witnessed so many Christmases ago between her parents, but it was outweighed by the eighteen years of kindness and consideration they'd shown each other. "Yes, they were happy. Their marriage wasn't at all like a *ton* marriage."

She spoke of a *"ton* marriage" with such aversion that Charles smiled curiously. "What do you mean by a *ton* marriage?"

"The sort of marriage nearly everyone here in London has—except for Robert and Caroline Collingwood and a few others. The sort of marriage where the couple is rarely in each other's company, and when they happen to meet at some affair, they behave like polite, well-bred strangers. The gentlemen are always off enjoying their own amusements, and the ladies have their cicisbeos. At least my parents lived together in a real home and we were a real family."

"I gather you intend to have an old-fashioned marriage with an old-fashioned family," he teased, looking very pleased at the idea.

"I don't think Jason wants that sort of marriage." She couldn't bring herself to tell Charles that Jason's original offer was for her to give him a son and then go away. She consoled herself with the knowledge that, even though he'd made that offer, he'd seemed to prefer that she remain with him in England.

"I doubt very much if Jason knows what he wants right now," Charles said gravely. "He needs you, child. He needs your warmth and your spirit. He won't admit that, even to himself yet—and when he finally does admit it to himself, he won't like it, believe me. He'll fight you," Charles warned gently. "But sooner or later, he'll open his heart to you, and when he does, he'll find peace. In return, he'll make you happier than you've ever dreamed of being."

She looked so dubious, so skeptical, that Charles's smile faded. "Have patience with him, Victoria. If he weren't so strong in body and mind, he'd never have survived to the age of thirty. He has scars, deep ones, but you have the power to heal them."

"What sort of scars?"

Charles shook his head. "It will be better for both of you if Jason himself is the one to finally tell you about his life, especially his childhood. If he doesn't, then you can come to me."

In the days that followed, Victoria had little time to think about Jason or anything else. No sooner had she left Charles's bedroom than Madame Dumosse arrived at the house with four seamstresses. "Lord Fielding has instructed me to prepare a wedding gown for you, mademoiselle," she said, already walking around Victoria. "He said it is to be very rich, very elegant. Individual. Befitting a queen. No ruffles."

Caught somewhere between annoyance and laughter at Jason's high-handedness, Victoria shot her a sidelong look. "Did he happen to select a color, too?"

"Blue."

"Blue?" Victoria burst out, prepared to do physical battle for white.

Madame nodded, her finger thoughtfully pressed to her lips, her other hand plunked upon her waist. "Yes, blue. Ice blue. He said you are glorious in that color—'a titian-haired angel,' he said."

Victoria abruptly decided ice blue was a lovely color to be married in.

"Lord Fielding has excellent taste," Madame continued, her thin brows raised over her bright, alert eyes. "Don't you agree?"

"Decidedly," Victoria said, laughing, and she surrendered herself to the skilled ministrations of the dressmaker.

Four hours later, when Madame finally released her and whisked her seamstresses off to the shop, Victoria was informed that Lady Caroline Collingwood was waiting for her in the gold salon.

"Victoria," her friend exclaimed, her pretty face anxious as she held out her hands, clasping Victoria's. "Lord Fielding came to our house this morning to tell us about the wedding. I'm honored to be your matron of honor, which Lord Fielding said you wished me to be, but this is all so sudden—your marriage, I mean."

Victoria suppressed her surprised pleasure at the news that Jason had thoughtfully remembered she'd need an attendant and had stopped to see the Collingwoods.

"I never suspected you were developing a lasting attachment to Lord Fielding," Caroline continued, "and I can't help wondering. You do wish to marry him, don't you? You aren't being, well, forced into it in any way?"

"Only by fate," Victoria said with a smile, sinking exhaustedly into a chair. She saw Caroline's frown and hastily added, "I'm not being forced. It's what I wish to do."

Caroline's entire countenance brightened with relief and happiness. "I'm so glad—I've been hoping this would happen." At Victoria's dubious look, she explained, "In the past few weeks, I've come to know him better, and I *quite* agree with Robert, who told me that the things people think about Lord Fielding are the result of gossip started solely by one particularly spiteful, malicious woman. I doubt anyone would have believed all the rumors if Lord Fielding himself hadn't been so aloof and uncommunicative. Of course, one doesn't particularly like people who believe terrible things about one, does one? So he probably didn't feel the slightest obligation to disabuse us. And as Robert said, Lord Fielding is a proud man, which would make it impossible for him to grovel in the face of adverse public opinion, particularly when it was so unfair!"

Victoria stifled a giggle at her friend's wholehearted endorsement of the man she had once feared and condemned, but it was typical of Caroline. Caroline refused to see any faults whatever in the people she liked, and she was conversely unwilling to admit there were any redeeming qualities in the people she didn't. That quirk in her lively personality made her the most loyal of friends, however, and Victoria was deeply grateful to her for her unswerving friendship. "Thank you, Northrup," she said as the butler came in carrying the tea tray.

"I can't think why I ever found him frightening," Caroline said while Victoria poured the tea. Breathlessly eager to absolve Jason of any blame she might have put on him in the past, she continued, "I was wrong to let my imagination run away with my sense that way. I believe the reason I thought him frightening stemmed from the fact that he is so very tall and his hair is so black, which is perfectly absurd of me. Why, do you know what he said when he left us this morning?" she asked in a voice of intense gratification.

"No," Victoria said, smothering another smile at Caroline's determination to elevate Jason from devil to saint. "What did he say?"

"He said I have always reminded him of a pretty butterfly."

"How lovely," Victoria declared sincerely.

"Yes, it was, but not nearly as lovely as the way he described *you*."

"Me? How on earth did all this come up?"

"The compliments, you mean?" When Victoria nodded, Caroline said, "I had just finished remarking on how happy I am that you are marrying an Englishman and staying here, so we can remain close friends. Lord Fielding laughed and said we complement each other perfectly, you and I, because I have always reminded him of a pretty butterfly, and you are like a wild flower that flourishes even in adversity and brightens up everyone's lives. Wasn't that utterly charming of him?"

"Utterly," Victoria agreed, feeling absurdly pleased.

"I think he is far more in love with you than he lets on," Caroline confided. "After all, he fought a duel for you."

By the time Caroline left, Victoria was half-convinced Jason actually cared for her, a belief that enabled her to be quite gay and positive the following morning, when a staggering procession of callers began arriving to wish her happy after learning of her impending marriage.

Victoria was entertaining a group of young ladies who'd come to call on her for exactly that reason when the object of their romantic discussion strolled into the blue salon. The laughter trailed off into nervous, uncertain murmurs as the young ladies beheld the dangerously impressive figure of the unpredictable Marquess of Wakefield, garbed in a coal black riding jacket and snug black breeches that made him look overwhelmingly male. Unaware of his impact on these impressionable females, many of whom had cherished secret dreams of captivating him themselves, Jason favored them with a glinting smile. "Good morning, ladies," he said; then he turned to Victoria and his smile became far more intimate. "Could you spare me a moment?"

Excusing herself at once, Victoria followed him into his study.

"I won't keep you away from your friends long," he promised, reaching into the pocket of his jacket. Without another word, he took her hand in his and slid a heavy ring onto her finger. Victoria gazed at the ring, which covered her finger all the way to her knuckle. A row of large sapphires was flanked by two rows of dazzling diamonds on both sides. "Jason, it's beautiful," she breathed. "Breathtakingly, incredibly, beautiful. Thank—"

"Thank me with a kiss," he reminded her softly, and when Victoria tipped her face up to his, his lips captured hers in a long, hungry, thorough kiss that drained her mind of thought and her body of all resistance. Shaken by his ardor and her body's helpless response to it, Victoria stared into his smoky jade eyes, trying to understand why Jason's kisses always had this shattering effect on her.

His gaze dropped to her lips. "Next time, do you think you could find it in your heart to kiss me without being asked?" It was the thread of disappointed yearning Victoria thought she heard in his voice that melted her heart. He had offered himself as her husband; in return he asked for very little—only this. Leaning up on her toes, she slid her hands up along his hard chest and twined them around his neck, and then she covered his lips with hers. She felt a tremor run through his tall frame as she innocently brushed her lips back and forth over his, slowly exploring the warm curves of his mouth, learning the taste of him, while his parted lips began to move against hers in a wildly arousing kiss.

Lost in the mounting turmoil of their kiss and unaware of the hardening pressure against her stomach, Victoria let her fingers slide into the soft hair at his nape while her body automatically fitted itself to his—and suddenly everything changed. Jason's arms closed around her with stunning force, his mouth opening on hers with fierce hunger. He parted her lips, teasing her with his tongue until he coaxed her to touch her own tongue to his lips, and when she did, he gasped, pulling her even closer, his body taut with fiery need.

When he finally lifted his head, he stared down at her with an odd expression of bemused self-mockery on his ruggedly chiseled features. "I should have given you diamonds and sapphires the other night, instead of pearls," he commented. "But don't kiss me like this again until *after* we're married."

Victoria had been warned by her mother and by Miss Flossie that a gentleman could be carried away by his ardor, which would lead him to behave in an unspecified—but very unsuitable—way to the young lady who wrongly permitted him to lose his head. She realized instinctively that Jason was telling her *he* had been very close to losing his head. And she was feminine enough to feel a tiny twinge of satisfaction because her inexperienced kiss could so affect this very experienced man—especially since Andrew had never seemed so affected by her kiss. On the other hand, she had never kissed Andrew in the way Jason liked her to kiss him.

"I see you have my meaning," he said wryly. "Personally, I have never particularly prized virginity. There are distinct advantages to marrying women who have already learned how to please a man. . . ." He waited, watching her closely as if expecting—hoping for—some sort of reaction from her, but Victoria merely looked away, her spirits drooping. Her virginity, or so it was said, should have been a highly valued gift to her husband. She certainly couldn't offer him any experience in "pleasing a man," whatever that entailed. "I—I'm sorry to disappoint you," she said, embarrassed at the subject. "Things are very different in America."

Despite the haggard strain in Jason's voice, his words were gentle. "You've no need to apologize or look so miserable, Victoria. Don't ever fear telling me the truth. No matter how bad the truth is, I can accept it and even admire you for having the courage to say it." His hand lifted to caress her cheek. "It doesn't matter," he said soothingly. Abruptly, his manner turned brisk. "Tell me if you like your ring, then run along back to your friends."

"I love it," she said, trying to keep up with his swift,

incomprehensible changes of mood. "It's so beautiful I'm already terrified of losing it."

Jason shrugged with complete indifference. "If you lose it, I'll buy you another."

He left then, and Victoria looked down at her betrothal ring, wishing he hadn't been so cavalier about its potential loss. She wished the ring was more important to him, and less easily replaced. On the other hand, as a token of his affection, it was dismally appropriate, since *she* was unimportant to him and easily replaced.

He needs you, child. Charles's words came back to reassure her and she smiled, remembering that, at least when she was in his arms, Jason seemed to need her very much. Feeling somewhat reassured, she went back to the salon, where her ring was immediately noted and duly exclaimed over by all the young ladies.

In the days that preceded her wedding, nearly three hundred people came to call on Victoria to wish her happiness. Elegant carriages paraded up and down the street, discharging their passengers and returning a correct twenty minutes later to pick them up again, while Victoria sat in the salon, listening to handsome middle-aged matrons offering advice on the difficult tasks of running large houses and entertaining on the lavish scale required of the nobility. Younger married women talked to her about the problems of finding proper governesses and the best way to locate acceptable tutors for children. And in the midst of all the cheerful chaos, a comforting sense of belonging began to take root deep in Victoria. Until now, she'd had no occasion to know these people better than slightly or to converse with them about anything other than the most superficial topics. She had been inclined to see them for the most part as wealthy, pampered females who never gave a thought to anything except gowns, jewels, and diversion. Now she saw them in a new light—as wives and mothers who also cared about performing their duties in an exemplary fashion—and she liked them much better.

Of everyone she knew, only Jason stayed away, but he did so for the sake of appearances, and Victoria had to be grateful for that, even though it sometimes gave her the uneasy feeling she was marrying an absentee stranger. Charles came downstairs often to charm the ladies with his conversation and make it clear that Victoria had his whole-hearted support. The rest of the time he remained out of sight, "to gather his strength" as he told Victoria, so that he could have the honor of giving her away. Neither Victoria nor Dr. Worthing could dissuade him from his determination to do that. Jason didn't bother to try.

As the days passed, Victoria truly enjoyed the time she spent in the salon with her callers—except on those occasions when Jason's name was mentioned and she sensed a familiar undercurrent of apprehension amongst them. It was obvious her new friends and acquaintances admired the social prestige she would enjoy as the wife of a fabulously wealthy marquess, but Victoria had the uneasy feeling there were some who still had serious reservations about her future husband. It bothered her because she was coming to like these people very much, and she wanted them to like Jason, too. Occasionally, as she chatted with one visitor, she overheard snatches of conversation about Jason from another part of the room, but the conversations always stopped abruptly when Victoria turned attentively to listen. It prevented her from coming to his defense, because she didn't know what to defend him against.

The day before they were to be married, the pieces of the puzzle finally fell into place, forming a lurid picture that nearly sent Victoria reeling to the floor. As Lady Clappeston, the last visitor of the afternoon, took her leave, she gave Victoria's arm a fond pat and said, "You're a sensible young woman, my dear. And unlike some of the foolish doomhangers who worry about your safety, *I* have every faith you'll deal well with Wakefield. You're nothing like his first wife. In my opinion, Lady Melissa deserved everything she said he did to her, and more. The woman was nothing but a trollop!"

With that, Lady Clappeston sailed out of the salon, leaving Victoria staring at Caroline. "His first wife?" she uttered, feeling as if she were in the midst of a nightmare. "Jason was married before? Why—why didn't someone tell me?"

"But I thought you knew at least that much," Caroline

burst out, anxious to acquit herself. "I naturally assumed your uncle or Lord Fielding would have told you. Surely you must have heard at least some gossip?"

"All I ever heard were snatches of conversations that always stopped as soon as people noticed I was present." Victoria returned, white with rage and shock. "I've heard the name Lady Melissa mentioned in connection with Jason, but no one ever referred to her as his *wife*. People usually spoke of her in such disapproving tones that I assumed she had been . . . involved . . . with Jason, you know," she finished awkwardly, "in the same way Miss Sybil someone-or-other was involved with him until now."

"Was involved?" Caroline repeated in surprise at Victoria's use of the past tense. She caught herself immediately, and looked down, apparently fascinated with the pattern of the upholstery on the blue silk sofa.

"Naturally, now that we are going to be married, Jason won't—or will he?" she asked.

"I don't know what he'll do," Caroline said miserably. "Some men, such as Robert, do give up their paramours when they marry, but others do not."

Victoria rubbed her temples with her fingertips, her mind in such turmoil that she was sidetracked by this discussion of mistresses. "Sometimes, England is so strange to me. At home, husbands do not give their time or affection to women other than their wives. At least, I never heard about it. Yet I've heard remarks here that make me think it is perfectly acceptable for wealthy married gentlemen to consort with—with ladies who are not their wives."

Caroline turned the conversation to a more pressing topic. "Does it matter terribly to you that Lord Fielding was married before?"

"Of course it does. At least I think it does. I don't know. What matters most right now is that no one in the family told me about it." She stood up so abruptly that Caroline jumped. "If you'll excuse me, I want to go up and talk to my Uncle Charles."

Uncle Charles's valet put his finger to his lips when Victoria tapped at Charles's door and informed her the duke was asleep. Too upset to wait for him to awaken so her questions could be answered, Victoria marched down the hall to Miss Flossie's room. In recent weeks, Miss Flossie had virtually relinquished her duties as Victoria's chaperone to Caroline Collingwood. As a result, Victoria had scarcely seen the lovable little yellow-haired woman except at an occasional meal.

Victoria tapped at her door, and when Miss Flossie cheerfully invited her to enter, she stepped into the pretty little sitting room that adjoined Miss Flossie's bedroom.

"Victoria, my dear, you're looking as radiant as a bride!" Miss Flossie said with her bright, vague smile and usual lack of discernment, for in truth Victoria was deathly pale and visibly overwrought.

"Miss Flossie," Victoria said, plunging straight in, "I've just come from Uncle Charles's room, but he was asleep. You are the only other person I can turn to. It's about Jason. Something is terribly wrong."

"Good heavens!" Miss Flossie cried, setting her needlework aside. "Whatever do you mean?"

"I've just discovered that he was married before!" Victoria burst out.

Miss Flossie tipped her head to one side, an elderly china doll in a little white lace cap. "Dear me, I thought Charles had told you—or Wakefield himself. Well, in any event, Jason was married before, my dear. So now you know." Having dispatched that problem, Miss Flossie smiled and picked up her needlework again.

"But I don't know anything. Lady Clappeston said the oddest thing—she said Jason's wife deserved everything he did to her. What did he do?"

"Do?" Miss Flossie repeated, blinking. "Why, nothing that I know of for certain. Lady Clappeston was foolish indeed to say he did anything, for she couldn't know either, unless she was married to him, which I can assure you she was not. There, does that make you feel better?"

"No!" Victoria burst out a little hysterically. "What I wish to know is *why* Lady Clappeston believes Jason did bad things to his wife. She must have reason to think so, and unless I miss my guess, a great many people think as she does."

"They may," Miss Flossie agreed. "You see, Jason's wretched wife, may she rest in peace—though I don't know how she could do so, when one considers how wickedly she behaved when she was alive—cried to everyone about Wakefield's abominable treatment of her. Some people evidently believed her, but the very fact that he didn't murder her should prove that he is a man of admirable restraint. If I had a husband, which of course I don't, and I did the things Melissa did, which of course I would never do, he would surely beat me. So if Wakefield beat Melissa, which I don't know for certain he did, he would be more than justified in it. You may take my word on that."

Victoria thought of the times she had seen Jason angry, of the leashed fury in his eyes and the awesome, predatory power she sometimes glimpsed beneath his urbane exterior. A picture flashed across her terrified mind—an image of a woman screaming as he beat her for some trivial infraction of his personal rules. "What," she whispered hoarsely, "what sort of things did Melissa do?"

"Well, there is no nice way to say it. The truth is that she was seen in the company of other men."

Victoria shuddered. Nearly every fashionable lady in London was seen in the company of other men. It was a way of life for fashionable married ladies to have their cicisbeos. "And he beat her for that?" she whispered sickly.

"We don't *know* that he beat her," Miss Flossie pointed out with careful precision. "In fact, I rather doubt it. I once heard a gentleman criticize Jason—behind his back, of course, for no one would ever have the courage to criticize him to his face—for the way he *ignored* Melissa's behavior."

A sudden idea was born in Victoria's reeling mind. "Exactly what did the gentleman say?" she asked carefully. *"Exactly,"* she emphasized.

"Exactly? Well, since you insist, he said—if I remember correctly—'*Wakefield is being cuckolded in front of all London and he damned well knows it, yet he ignores it and wears the horns. He's setting a bad example for the rest of our wives to see. If you ask me, he ought to lock the harlot up in his place in Scotland and throw away the key.*' "

Victoria's head fell back weakly against her chair, and she closed her eyes with a mixture of relief and sorrow. "Cuckolded," she whispered. "So that's it. . . ." She thought of how proud Jason was, and how much his pride must have been mangled by his wife's public infidelities.

"Now, then, is there anything else you want to know?" Miss Flossie said.

"Yes," Victoria said with visible unease.

The tension in her voice gave Miss Flossie a nervous start. "Well, I hope it isn't anything about *you-know*," she twittered nervously, "because as your nearest female relative I realize it is my responsibility to explain that to you, but the truth is I'm abysmally ignorant about it. I've cherished the hope your mother might have already explained it."

Victoria curiously opened her eyes, but she was too exhausted by all that had happened to do more than say mildly, "I don't quite understand what you're talking about, ma'am."

"I'm speaking of *'you-know'*—that is what my dearest friend, Prudence, always called it—which was very silly for I didn't know at all. However, I can repeat to you the information given my friend Prudence by *her* mother on the day before her marriage."

"I beg your pardon?" Victoria repeated, feeling stupid.

"Well, you needn't beg my pardon; I should ask yours for not having the information to give you. But ladies do not discuss *you-know*. Do you wish to hear what Prudence's mother said about it?"

Victoria's lips twitched. "Yes, ma'am," she said, without having the vaguest idea what they were discussing.

"Very well. On your wedding night, your husband will join you in your bed—or perhaps he takes you to his, I can't recall. In any event, you must not, under any circumstances, demonstrate your revulsion, nor scream, nor have vapors. You must close your eyes and permit him to do *you-know*. Whatever that may be. It will hurt and be repugnant, and there will be blood the first time, but you must close your eyes and persevere. I believe Prudence's mama suggested that while *you-know* is happening, Prudence should try to think of something else—like the new fur or gown she will soon be able to buy if her husband is pleased with her. Nasty business, is it not?"

Tears of mirth and anxiety gathered in Victoria's eyes and her shoulders shook with helpless laughter. "Thank you,

Miss Flossie," she giggled. "You've been very reassuring." Until now, Victoria hadn't let herself worry about the intimacies of marriage to which Jason would be entitled and of which he would undoubtedly avail himself, since he wanted a son from her. Although she was the daughter of a physician, her father had meticulously ensured that her eyes were never exposed to the sight of a male patient's anatomy below the waist. Still, Victoria was not completely ignorant of the mating process. Her family had kept a few chickens and she had witnessed the flapping of wings and squawking that accompanied the act, although exactly what was happening was impossible to tell. Moreover, she had always averted her eyes out of some peculiar need to allow them their privacy while they went about creating new chicks.

Once when she was fourteen, her father had been summoned to a farmer's house to look after the farmer's wife who was in labor. While Victoria was waiting for the baby to be born, she had wandered out to the small pasture where the horses were kept. There she had witnessed the frightening spectacle of a stallion mounting a mare. He had clamped his huge teeth viciously into the mare's neck, holding her helpless while he did his worst to her, and the poor mare screamed in pain.

Visions of flapping wings, squawking hens, and terrified mares paraded across her mind, and Victoria shuddered.

"My dear girl, you look quite pale, and I don't blame you," Miss Flossie put in not at all helpfully. "However, I have been given to understand that once a wife has done her duty and produced an heir, a thoughtful husband may be depended upon to get himself a paramour and do *you-know* to her, leaving his wife in peace to enjoy the rest of her life."

Victoria's gaze skittered nervously to the window. "A paramour," she breathed, knowing Jason already had one, and that he'd had a great many others in the past—all beautiful, according to what gossip she'd heard. As Victoria sat there, she began to rethink her earlier feelings toward the gentlemen of the *ton* and their mistresses. She had thought it perfidious of them to be married and still keep paramours, but perhaps it wasn't that at all. It seemed more likely that, as Miss Flossie suggested, the gentlemen of the *ton* were more civilized, refined, and considerate of their wives.

Rather than using their wives to fulfill their baser desires, they simply found another woman to do so, set her up in a nice house with servants and beautiful gowns, and left their poor wives in peace. Yes, she decided sensibly, this was probably an ideal way of handling the matter. Certainly the ladies of the *ton* seemed to think so, and they would know far better than she herself.

"Thank you, Miss Flossie," she said sincerely. "You've been very helpful and very kind."

Miss Flossie beamed, her yellow curls bouncing beneath her little white lace cap. "Thank *you*, my dear girl. You've made Charles happier than I've ever seen him. And Jason, too, of course," she added politely.

Victoria smiled, but she couldn't quite accept the notion that she had made Jason truly happy.

Wandering back to her room, she sat down before the empty fireplace and forced herself to try to untangle her emotions and stop hiding from the facts. Tomorrow morning she was going to marry Jason. She wanted to make him happy—she wanted it so much she hardly knew how to deal with her own feelings. The fact that he had been married to a faithless woman evoked sympathy and compassion in her heart, not resentment—and an even greater desire to make up for all the unhappiness in his life.

Restlessly, Victoria got up and walked about the room, picking up the porcelain music box on her dressing table, then laying it down and walking over to the bed. She tried to tell herself she was marrying Jason because she had no choice, but as she sat down upon the bed, she admitted that wasn't entirely true. Part of her *wanted* to marry him. She loved his looks and his smile and his dry sense of humor. She loved the brisk authority in his deep voice and the confidence in his long, athletic strides. She loved the way his eyes gleamed when he laughed at her and the way they smoldered when he kissed her. She loved the lazy elegance with which he wore his clothes and the way his lips felt—

Victoria tore her thoughts from Jason's lips and stared bleakly at the gold silk bed hangings. She loved many things about him—too many things. She was not a good judge of men; her experience with Andrew was proof of that. She had deceived herself into believing Andrew loved her, but she had no illusions about what Jason felt for her. He was attracted to her and he wanted a son from her. He liked her, too, Victoria knew, but beyond that, he felt nothing for her. She, on the other hand, was already in serious danger of falling in love with him. But he didn't want her love. He'd told her that in the plainest possible terms.

For weeks she'd been trying to convince herself that what she felt for Jason was gratitude and friendship, but she knew now it had already gone much deeper than that. Why else would she feel this burning need to make him happy and make him love her? Why else would she have experienced such rage when Miss Flossie spoke of his wife's public infidelities?

Fear raced through Victoria and she rubbed her damp palms against her lime-colored muslin gown. Tomorrow morning she was going to commit her entire life into the keeping of a man who didn't want her love, a man who could use the tenderness she felt for him as a weapon to hurt her. Every instinct for self-preservation that Victoria possessed warned her not to marry him. Her father's own words tolled through her mind, as they had been doing for days, warning her not to walk down that aisle tomorrow: *"Loving someone who doesn't love you is hell! . . . Don't ever let anyone convince you that you can be happy with someone who doesn't love you. . . . Don't ever love anyone more than they love you, Tory. . . ."*

Victoria bent her head, her hair falling forward in a curtain around her tense face, her hands clenched into fists. Her mind warned her not to marry him, that he would make her miserable—but her heart begged her to gamble everything on him, to reach for the happiness just beyond her grasp.

Her mind told her to run, but her heart begged her not to be a coward.

Northrup tapped upon her door, his voice vibrating with disapproval. "Excuse me, Lady Victoria," he said from the other side of her closed door. "There is a distraught, disheveled young lady downstairs, without escort or bonnet, who arrived in a hired carriage, but who claims to be . . . ahem . . . your sister? I am not aware of any young female relations of yours here in London, so naturally I suggested she leave, however—"

"Dorothy?" Victoria burst out, pulling open the door and raking her hair off her forehead. "Where is she?" Victoria said, her face radiant.

"I put her in the small salon at the front," Northrup said with visible dismay. "But if she is your sister, of course, I shall show her into the more comfortable yellow salon and . . ."

His voice trailed off as Victoria raced around the corner and down the stairs.

"Tory!" Dorothy burst out, wrapping Victoria in a fierce, protective hug, her words tumbling over themselves, her voice shaking with laughter and tears. "You should have *seen* the look your butler gave my hired carriage—it was nearly as bad as the look he gave *me*."

"Why didn't you answer my last letter?" Victoria said, hugging her tightly.

"Because I only returned from Bath today. Tomorrow I'm being sent to France for two months to acquire what Grandmama calls 'polish.' She'll be mad as fire if she discovers I've been here, but I can't just stand by and let you marry that man. Tory, what have they done to make you agree? Have they beaten you or starved you or—"

"Nothing of the sort," Victoria said, smiling and smoothing her sister's golden hair. "I want to marry him."

"I don't believe you. You're only trying to fool me so I won't worry. . . ."

Jason leaned back in his carriage, idly slapping his gloves upon his knee as he gazed out the window, watching the mansions parading past along the route to his house in Upper Brook Street. His wedding was tomorrow. . . .

Now that he had admitted to himself his desire for Victoria and made the decision to marry her, he wanted her with an urgency that was almost irrational. His growing need for her made him feel vulnerable and uneasy, for he knew from past experience how vicious, how treacherous, the "gentle sex" could be. Still, he couldn't stop himself from wanting her any more than he could stifle his naive, boyish hope that they were going to make each other happy.

Life with her would never be placid, he thought with a wry

smile. Victoria would amuse, frustrate, and defy him at every turn—he knew that as surely as he knew that she was marrying him only because she had no other choice. He knew it as surely as he knew that her virginity had already been given to Andrew.

The smile abruptly faded from his lips. He had hoped she would deny it the other afternoon; instead she had looked away and said, "I'm sorry."

He had hated hearing the truth, but he had admired her for telling it to him. In his heart, he couldn't blame Victoria for giving herself to Andrew, not when he could so easily understand how it had happened. He could well imagine how an innocent young girl, raised in the country, could have been convinced by the wealthiest man in the district that she was going to be his wife. Once Bainbridge convinced her of that, it probably hadn't been too difficult to steal her virginity. Victoria was a warm, generous girl who would probably give herself to the man she truly loved as naturally as she gave her attention to the servants or her affection to Wolf.

After the dissolute life he himself had led, for him to condemn Victoria for surrendering her virginity to the man she loved would be the height of hypocrisy, and Jason despised hypocrites. Unfortunately, he also despised the thought of Victoria lying naked in another man's arms. Andrew had taught her well, he thought tightly as the carriage drew up before #6 Upper Brook Street. He had taught her how to kiss a man and how to increase his ardor by pressing herself against him. . . .

Tearing his mind away from those painful thoughts, he alighted from the coach and strode up the steps. Victoria was over Andrew now, he told himself fiercely. She had forgotten about him in the past weeks.

He knocked on the door, feeling a little foolish for appearing on her doorstep on the night before their wedding. He had no reason for coming except to pleasure himself with the sight of her and, he hoped, to please her by telling her about the Indian pony he had arranged to have put on one of his ships from America. It was to be one of her wedding presents, but in truth he was absurdly eager to see her demonstrate her skill on it. He knew how beautiful she would look with her graceful body bent low over the horse's neck, and her wondrous hair glinting in the sunlight. . . . "Good evening, Northrup. Where is Lady Victoria?"

"In the yellow salon, my lord," Northrup replied. "With her sister."

"Her sister?" Jason said, smiling with surprise and pleasure when Northrup nodded. "Evidently the old witch has lifted the restriction against Dorothy coming here," he added, already starting down the hall. Glad to have this opportunity to meet the young sister Victoria had told him about, Jason opened the door to the yellow salon.

"I can't bear it," a young girl was weeping into her handkerchief. "I'm *glad* Grandmama won't let me attend your wedding. I couldn't stand to be there, watching you walk down the aisle, knowing you're pretending he's Andrew—"

"Evidently, I've arrived at an inconvenient time," Jason drawled. The hope he had secretly cherished that Victoria actually wanted to marry him died a swift, painful death at the discovery that she needed to pretend he was Andrew before she could force herself to walk down the aisle.

"Jason!" Victoria said, whirling around in dismay as she realized he had overheard Dorothy's foolish ramblings. Recovering her composure, she held out her hands to him and said with a gentle smile, "I'm so glad you're here. Please come and show yourself to my sister." Knowing there was no possible way to smooth things over with a compassionate lie, she tried to make him understand by telling him the truth. "Dorothy has overheard some condemning remarks made by my great-grandmother's companion, Lady Faulklyn, and because of what she overheard, Dorothy has formed the most absurd impression that you are a cruel monster." She bit her lip when Jason lifted a sardonic eyebrow at Dorothy and said absolutely nothing; then she bent over Dorothy. "Dorothy, will you please be reasonable and at least let me introduce Lord Fielding to you, so you can see for yourself that he is very nice?"

Unconvinced, Dorothy raised her gaze to the cold, implacable features of the man who loomed before her like a dark, angry giant, his arms crossed over his wide chest. Her eyes rounded and, without a word, she slowly stood up, but instead of curtsying, she glared at him. "Lord Fielding," she said defiantly, "I don't know whether you are 'very nice' or not. However, I warn you that if you ever dare to harm a hair on my sister's head I shan't scruple to—to shoot you! Do I make myself perfectly clear?" Her voice shook with angry fear, but she bravely held his cold green eyes with her own.

"Perfectly."

"Then, since I can't convince my sister to run away from you," she finished, "I shall return to my great-grandmother's house. Good evening."

She walked out with Victoria at her heels. "Dorothy, how *could* you," Victoria demanded miserably. "How could you be so rude?"

"Better he think I am rude than that he can abuse you without anyone exacting retribution."

Victoria rolled her eyes and hugged her sister good-bye, then hastened back to the salon.

"I'm sorry," she said abjectly to Jason, who was standing at the windows watching Dorothy's carriage pull away.

Glancing over his shoulder at her, Jason raised his eyebrows. "Can she shoot?"

Uncertain of his mood, Victoria smothered a nervous giggle and shook her head. When he turned back to the window and said nothing else, she tried to explain. "Dorothy has a vivid imagination and she won't believe I'm not marrying you because I'm distraught over Andrew."

"Aren't you?" he mocked.

"No, I'm not."

He turned fully around then, his eyes like shards of icy green glass. "When you walk down that aisle tomorrow, Victoria, your precious Andrew isn't going to be waiting for you, *I* am. Remember that. If you can't face the truth, don't come to the church." He had come here to tell her he had gotten her an Indian pony; he had intended to tease her and make her smile. He left without another word.

Chapter Twenty-one

◦⟶⟵◦

THE SKY WAS CLOUDY AND GRAY AS JASON'S SHINY, black-lacquered coach swayed gently through the crowded London streets, drawn by four prancing chestnut horses in magnificent silver harness. Six outriders in green velvet livery led the procession, followed by four more mounted, uniformed men behind the coach. Two coachmen sat proudly erect atop the coach and two more clung to the back of the vehicle.

Victoria huddled in the deep, luxurious squabs of Jason's coach, wrapped in a gown of incredible beauty and wildly extravagant expense, her thoughts as bleak as the day outside.

"Are you cold, my dear?" Charles asked solicitously from his place across from her.

Victoria shook her head, wondering nervously why Jason had insisted upon making such a grand spectacle of their marriage.

A few minutes later, she put her hand in Charles's and stepped down from the coach, walking slowly up the long shallow steps of the massive Gothic church like a child being led to a frightening event by her parent.

She waited beside Charles at the back of the church, trying not to think of the enormity of what she was about to do, letting her gaze wander aimlessly over the crowds of people. Her apprehensive mind fastened haphazardly on the vast differences between the London aristocrats garbed in silks and fine brocades who had come to witness her wedding and the simple, friendly villagers she had always expected to have near her on her wedding day. She scarcely knew most of these people—some she had never even seen before. Carefully averting her gaze from the altar, where Jason, not Andrew, would soon be waiting for her, she stared at the pews. An empty place, reserved for Charles, was vacant on the first bench on the right, but the rest of them were filled with guests. Directly across the aisle on the first bench, which would normally have been reserved for the bride's immediate family, there was an elderly lady leaning on an ebony cane, her hair concealed by a vivid purple satin turban.

The turbaned head seemed vaguely familiar, but Victoria was much too nervous to remember where she had seen it, and Charles diverted her attention by nodding toward Lord Collingwood, who was coming toward them.

"Has Jason arrived?" Charles asked when Robert Collingwood had reached them.

The earl, who was Jason's best man, kissed Victoria's hand, smiled reassuringly, and said, "He's here, and he's ready when you are."

Victoria's knees began to shake. She wasn't ready. She wasn't ready to do this at all!

Caroline straightened the train of Victoria's diamond-studded blue satin gown and smiled at her husband. "Is Lord Fielding nervous?"

"He says he isn't," Robert said. "But he would like to get this proceeding under way."

How cold, Victoria thought, her fear escalating to panic. How unemotional. How Jason.

Charles was fidgety, eager. "We're ready," he said enthusiastically. "Let's begin."

Feeling like a marionette whose strings were being pulled by everyone else, Victoria placed her hand on Charles's arm and began the endless walk down the candlelit aisle. She moved through the candlelight in a luxurious swirl of shimmering blue satin with diamonds sparkling like tiny twinkling lights in her hair, at her throat, and scattered across her veil. In the wide loft above, the choir sang, but Victoria didn't hear them. Behind her, moving farther away with each step, were the laughter and carefree days of her girlhood. Ahead of her . . . ahead of her was Jason, dressed in a splendid suit of rich midnight blue velvet. With his face partly shadowed, he looked very tall and dark. As dark as the unknown . . . as dark as her future.

Why are you doing this?! Victoria's panicked mind screamed at her as Charles led her toward Jason.

I don't know, she cried in silent answer. *Jason needs me.*

That's no reason! her mind shouted. *You can still escape. Turn and run.*

I can't! her heart cried.

You can. Just turn around and run. Now, before it's too late.

I can't! I can't just leave him here.

Why not?

He'll be humiliated if I do—more humiliated than he ever was by his first wife.

Remember what your father said—never let anyone convince you that you can be happy with someone who doesn't love you. Remember how unhappy he was. Run! Quick! Get out of here before it's too late!

Victoria's heart lost the battle against terror as Charles put her frozen hand in Jason's warm one and stepped away. Her body tensed for flight, her free hand grasped her skirts, her breath quickened. She started to jerk her right hand from Jason's grasp at the same moment that his fingers clamped around hers like a steel trap and he turned his head sharply, his intense green eyes locking onto hers, warning her not to try it. Then suddenly his grip slackened; his eyes became aloof, blank. He released her hand, letting it fall to her side in front of her wide skirts, and he looked at the archbishop.

He's going to stop it! Victoria realized wildly as the archbishop bowed and said, "Shall we begin, my lord?"

Jason curtly shook his head and opened his mouth.

"No!" Victoria whispered, trying to stop Jason.

"What did you say?" the archbishop demanded, scowling at her.

Victoria lifted her eyes to Jason's and saw the humiliation he was hiding behind a mask of cynical indifference. "I'm only frightened, my lord. Please take my hand."

He hesitated, searching her eyes, and relief slowly replaced the iron grimness on his features. His hand touched hers, then closed reassuringly around her fingers.

"*Now,* may I proceed?" whispered the archbishop indignantly.

Jason's lips twitched. "Please do."

As the archbishop began reading the long service, Charles gazed joyously upon the bride and groom, his heart swelling until it felt ready to burst, but a flash of purple seen from the corner of his eye combined with an eerie feeling that he was being watched suddenly drew his attention. He glanced sideways, then stiffened in shock as his eyes clashed with the pale blue ones belonging to the Duchess of Claremont. Charles stared at her, his face alive with cold triumph; then, with a final contemptuous glance, he turned from her and pushed her presence from his mind. He watched as his son stood beside Victoria, two proud, beautiful young people taking vows that would unite them forever. Tears stung his eyes as the archbishop intoned, "Do you, Victoria Seaton . . ."

"*Katherine, my love,*" Charles whispered to her in his heart, "*do you see our children here? Aren't they beautiful together? Your grandmother kept us from having children of our own, my darling—that victory was hers, but this one is ours. We shall have grandchildren instead, my sweet. My sweet, beautiful Katherine, we shall have grandchildren. . . .*" Charles bent his head, unwilling to let the old woman across the aisle see that he was crying. But the Duchess of Claremont could see nothing through the tears that were falling from her own eyes and racing down her wrinkled cheeks. "*Katherine, my love,*" she whispered to her in her heart, "*look what I have done. In my stupid, blind selfishness I prevented you from marrying him and having children with him. But now I have arranged it so that you shall have grandchildren instead. Oh, Katherine, I loved you so. I wanted you to have the world at your feet, and I wouldn't believe that all you wanted was him. . . ."*

When the archbishop asked Victoria to repeat her vows, she remembered her bargain to make it appear to everyone that she was deeply attached to Jason. Raising her face to his, she tried to speak out clearly and confidently, but when she was promising to love him, Jason's gaze suddenly lifted toward the domed ceiling of the church, and a sardonic smile tugged at his lips. Victoria realized he was watching for lightning to strike the roof, and her tension dissolved into a muffled giggle, which earned a deeply censorious frown from the archbishop.

Victoria's mirth vanished abruptly as Jason's deep, resonant voice echoed through the church, endowing her with all his worldly goods. And then it was over. "You may kiss the bride," the archbishop said.

Jason turned and looked at her, his eyes gleaming with a triumph that was so intense, so unexpected, and so terrifying that Victoria stiffened when his arms encircled her. Bending his head, he claimed her trembling lips in a long, bold kiss that caused the archbishop to glower and several guests to chuckle; then he released her and took her arm.

"My lord," she whispered imploringly as they walked up the aisle toward the doors leading from the church, "please—I can't keep up with you."

"Call me Jason," he snapped, but he slowed down. "And the next time I kiss you, pretend you like it."

His icy tone hit her like a bucketful of freezing water, but somehow Victoria managed to stand between Charles and Jason outside the church and smile tightly at all of the 800 guests who paused to wish them both happy.

Charles turned aside to talk to one of his friends just as the last guest emerged from the church, leaning heavily on the jeweled handle of her ebony cane.

Ignoring Jason completely, the duchess approached Victoria, peering steadily into her blue eyes. "Do you know who I am?" she demanded without preamble when Victoria smiled politely at her.

"No, ma'am," Victoria said. "I'm very sorry, but I do not. I believe I've seen you somewhere before, for you look familiar, and yet—"

"I am your great-grandmother."

Victoria's hand tightened spasmodically on Jason's arm. This was her great-grandmother, the woman who had refused to offer her shelter and who had destroyed her mother's happiness. Victoria's chin lifted. "I have no great-grandmother," she said with deadly calm.

This flat denouncement had a very odd effect on the dowager duchess. Her eyes glowed with admiration and a hint of a smile softened her stern features. "Oh, but you do, my dear," she said. "You do," she repeated almost fondly. "You are very like your mother in looks, but that defiant pride of yours came from me." She chuckled, shaking her head as Victoria started to argue. "No—do not bother to disavow my existence again, for my blood flows in your veins and it is my own stubbornness I see in your chin. Your mother's eyes, my willfulness—"

"Stay away from her!" Charles hissed furiously, his head jerking around. "Get out of here!"

The duchess stiffened and her eyes snapped with anger. "Don't you dare use that tone on me, Atherton, or I'll—"

"Or you'll what?" Charles bit out savagely. "Don't bother to threaten me. I have everything I want now."

The Dowager Duchess of Claremont regarded him down the full length of her aristocratic nose, her expression triumphant. "You have it because I *gave* it to you, you fool." Ignoring Charles's stunned, furious stare, she turned to Victoria again and her eyes warmed. Reaching out, she laid her frail hand against Victoria's cheek while moisture misted her eyes. "Perhaps you will come to Claremont House to see Dorothy when she returns from France. It has not been easy keeping her away from you, but she would have spoiled everything with her foolish chatter about old scand—old gossip," the duchess corrected quickly.

She turned to Jason then and her expression became very severe. "I am entrusting my great-granddaughter into your keeping, Wakefield, but I shall hold you personally responsible for her happiness, is that clear?"

"Quite clear," he said in a solemn voice, but he eyed the tiny woman who was issuing vague threats to him with thinly veiled amusement.

The duchess scrutinized his tranquil features sharply, then

nodded. "So long as we understand one another, I will take my leave." She lifted her wrist. "You may kiss my hand."

With perfect equanimity, Jason took her upraised hand in his and pressed a gallant kiss to the back of it.

Turning to Victoria, the duchess said bleakly, "I suppose it would be too much to ask—?" Victoria could make little sense of what had transpired in the minutes since her great-grandmother had walked up to her, but she knew beyond any doubt that the emotion she saw in the old woman's eyes was love—love, and a terrible regret.

"Grandmama," she whispered brokenly, and found herself wrapped tightly in her great-grandmother's arms.

The duchess drew back slightly, her smile gruff and self-conscious; then she bent an imperious look on Jason. "Wakefield, I've decided not to die until I've held my great-great-grandson in my arms. Since I cannot live forever, I shall not countenance any delays on your part."

"I will give the matter prompt attention, your grace," Jason said, straight-faced, but with laughter lurking in his jade eyes.

"I shall not countenance any shilly-shallying about on your part either, my dear," she warned her blushing great-granddaughter. Patting Victoria's hand, she added rather wistfully, "I've decided to retire to the country. Claremont is only an hour's ride from Wakefield, so perhaps you will visit me from time to time." So saying, she beckoned to her solicitor, who was standing at the church doors, and said grandly, "Give me your arm, Weatherford. I've seen what I wished to see and said what I wished to say." With a final, triumphant look at a dazed Charles, she turned and walked away, her shoulders straight, her cane barely brushing the ground.

Many of the wedding guests were still milling about, waiting for their carriages, when Jason guided Victoria through the throngs and into his own luxurious vehicle. Victoria automatically smiled as people waved and watched them leave, but her mind was so battered by the emotion-charged day that she did not become aware of her surroundings again until they were approaching the village near Wakefield. With a guilty start, she realized she hadn't spoken more than a dozen words to Jason in over two hours.

Beneath her lashes she stole a swift glance at the handsome man who was now her husband. His face was turned away from her, his profile a hard, chiseled mask, devoid of all compassion or understanding. He was angry with her for trying to leave him at the altar, she knew—angry and unforgiving. Fear of his possible revenge jarred through her nervous system, adding more tension to her already overburdened emotions. She wondered frantically if she had created a breach between them that might never heal. "Jason," she said, timidly using his given name, " I'm sorry about what happened in the church."

He shrugged, his face emotionless.

His silence only increased Victoria's anxiety as the coach rounded a bend and descended into the picturesque little village near Wakefield. She was about to apologize again when church bells suddenly began tolling, and she saw villagers and peasants lining the road ahead, dressed in their holiday best.

They smiled and waved as the coach passed by, and little children, holding bouquets of wild flowers clutched tightly in their fists, ran forward, offering their posies to Victoria through the open coach window.

One little boy of about four years caught his toe on a thick root at the side of the road and landed in a sprawled heap atop his bouquet. "Jason," Victoria implored, forgetting about the uneasiness between them, "tell the driver to stop—please!"

Jason complied, and Victoria opened the door. "What lovely flowers!" she exclaimed to the little boy, who was picking himself up from the road beside their coach while some older boys jeered and shouted at him. "Are those for me?" she asked enthusiastically, nodding to the bedraggled flowers.

The little boy sniffed, rubbing the tears from his eyes with a grimy little fist. "Yes, mum—they was for you afore I falled on 'em."

"May I have them?" Victoria prodded, smiling. "They would look lovely right here in my own bouquet."

The little boy shyly held out the decapitated stems to her. "I picked 'em myself," he whispered proudly, his eyes wide as Victoria carefully inserted two stems into her own lavish bouquet. "My name's Billy," he said, looking at Victoria with his left eye, his right eye skewing up toward the corner near his nose. "I live at the orphanage up there."

Victoria smiled and said gently, "My name is Victoria. But my very closest friends call me Tory. Would you like to call me Tory?"

His little chest swelled with pride, but he shot a cautious look at Jason and waited for the lord's nod before he nodded his head in an exuberant yes.

"Would you like to come to Wakefield someday soon and help me fly a kite?" she continued, while Jason watched her in thoughtful surprise.

His smile faded. "I don't run so good. I fall down a lot," he admitted with painful intensity.

Victoria nodded understandingly. "Probably because of your eye. But I may know a way to make it straight. I once knew another little boy with an eye like yours. One day when we were all playing Settlers and Indians, he fell and hurt his good eye, and my father had to put a patch on it until it healed. Well, while the good eye was covered up, the bad eye began to straighten out—my father thought it was because the bad eye had to work while the good eye was covered up. Would you like me to visit you, and we'll try the patch?"

"I'll look queer, mum," he said hesitantly.

"We thought Jimmy—the other little boy—looked exactly like a pirate," Victoria said, "and pretty soon we were all trying to wear patches on one eye. Would you like me to visit you and we'll play pirate?"

He nodded and turned to smile smugly at the older children. "What did the lady say?" they demanded as Jason signaled the driver to continue.

Billy shoved his hands into his pockets, puffed out his chest, and proudly declared, "She said *I* can call her Tory."

The children joined in with the adults, who formed a procession and followed the coach up the hill in what Victoria assumed must be some sort of festive village custom when the lord of the manor married. By the time the horses trotted through the massive iron gates of Wakefield Park, a small army of villagers was following them and more people were awaiting them along the tree-lined avenue that ran through the park. Victoria glanced uncertainly at Jason, and she could have sworn he was hiding a smile.

The reason for his smile became obvious as soon as their coach neared the great house. She had told Jason that she had always planned to be married in a little village with all the villagers there to help celebrate the occasion, and in a strangely quixotic gesture, the enigmatic man she had just married was trying to fulfill at least part of her dream. He had transformed the lawns of Wakefield into a fairy-tale bower of flowers. Enormous canopies of white orchids, lilies, and roses stretched above huge tables laden with silver plate, china, and food. The pavilion at the far end of the lawns was covered in flowers and strung with gaily colored lamps. Torches burned brightly everywhere she looked, driving off the encroaching dusk and adding a festive, mysterious glow to the scene.

Instead of being annoyed at leaving most of the wedding guests in London, Jason had obviously spent a fortune turning the estate into a haven of whimsical beauty for her, and then he had invited all the village to come and celebrate their marriage. Even nature had collaborated with Jason's scheme, for the clouds began to vanish, driven away by the setting sun, which decorated the sky in splashes of vivid pink and purple.

The coach came to a stop in front of the house, and Victoria looked around at this evidence of Jason's thoughtfulness—a thoughtfulness that was in direct opposition to his normal facade of callous indifference. She glanced at him, seeing the little smile that crinkled the corners of his eyes despite his best efforts to hide it, and she laid her hand softly on his arm. "Jason," she whispered, her voice shaky with emotion. "I—I thank you." Recalling his admonition to thank him with a kiss, she laid her hand against his hard chest and kissed him, with shy tenderness pouring through her veins.

A man's laughing Irish voice jerked Victoria back to reality. "Jason, my boy, are you going to get out of that coach and introduce me to your bride, or must I introduce myself?"

Jason swung around and a look of surprised pleasure

broke across his tanned features as he bounded down from the coach. He reached out to shake the brawny Irishman's hand, but the man enfolded him in a great bear hug. "So," the stranger said finally, grasping Jason's shoulders and beaming at him with unhidden affection, "you've finally gotten yourself a wife to warm up this big, cold palace of yours. At least you could've waited until my ship put into port, so I could've attended the wedding," he teased.

"I didn't expect to see you until next month," Jason said. "When did you get back?"

"I stayed to see the cargo unloaded, then I came home today. I rode over here an hour ago, but instead of finding you hard at work, I learned you were busy getting yourself married. Well, are you going to introduce me to your wife?" he demanded good-naturedly.

Jason turned to help Victoria down and then he introduced the seaman to her as Captain Michael Farrell. Captain Farrell was about fifty, Victoria guessed, with thick auburn hair and the merriest hazel eyes she had ever seen. His face was tanned and weathered, with tiny lines feathering out from the corners of his eyes, attesting to a life spent on the deck of a ship. Victoria liked him on sight, but hearing herself referred to for the first time as Jason's wife shook her composure so badly that she greeted Mike Farrell with the reserved formality she had been required to maintain since coming to England.

When she did so, Captain Farrell's expression altered. The warm approval vanished from his eyes, and his manner far surpassed hers in rigidity. "It is a pleasure to meet you, Lady Fielding," he intoned with a brief, cool bow. "You'll pardon my lack of proper attire. I had no idea when I came here that a party was soon to commence. Now, if you'll excuse me, I've been at sea for six months and I'm eager for my own hearth."

"Oh, but you can't leave!" Victoria said, reacting with the unaffected warmth that was far more natural to her than regal formality. She could see that Captain Farrell was an especially good friend of Jason's, and she wanted desperately to make him feel welcome. "My husband and I are overdressed for this time of day," she teased. "Besides, when I was at sea for only six weeks, I positively longed to dine on a table that didn't tilt and sway, and I'm certain our tables will stay just where they are."

Captain Farrell scrutinized her as if uncertain what to make of her. "I gather you did not enjoy your voyage, Lady Fielding?" he asked noncommittally.

Victoria shook her head, her smile infectious. "Not as much as I enjoyed breaking my arm or having measles—at least then I didn't retch, which I did for an entire week at sea. I am not a good sailor, I fear, for when a storm blew up before I'd recovered from mal de mer, I was shamefully afraid."

"Good Lord!" Captain Farrell said, his smile regaining some of its original warmth. "Don't call yourself a coward on that account. Seasoned seamen have been afraid of dying during an Atlantic storm."

"But I," Victoria contradicted, laughing, "was afraid I was *not* going to die."

Mike Farrell threw back his head and laughed; then he grasped both Victoria's hands in his huge, calloused paws and grinned at her. "I'll be delighted to stay and join you and Jason. Forgive me for being so . . . er . . . hesitant before."

Victoria nodded happily. Then she helped herself to a glass of wine from the tray being passed by a footman and went off to visit the two farmers who had brought her to Wakefield the day of her arrival.

When she was gone, Mike Farrell turned to Jason and said quietly, "When I saw her kissing you in the coach, I liked the look of her right off, Jason. But when she greeted me in that prim, proper way—with that blank look in her eyes as if she weren't really seeing me—I feared for a moment you'd married another haughty bitch like Melissa."

Jason watched Victoria putting the awkward farmers at ease. "She's anything but haughty. Her dog is part wolf and she's part fish. My servants dote on her, Charles adores her, and every stupid fop in London fancies himself in love with her."

"Including you?" Mike Farrell said pointedly.

Jason watched Victoria finish her wine and reach for another glass. The only way she could make herself marry him this morning was by pretending he was Andrew, and, even so, she'd damned near left him standing at the altar in front of 800 people. Since he had never seen her drink more than a sip of wine before, and she was already on her second glass, Jason assumed she was now trying to dull her revulsion at having to couple with him tonight.

"You don't quite look like the happiest of bridegrooms," Mike Farrell said, observing Jason's dark frown.

"I've never been happier," Jason replied bitterly, and went to greet guests whose names he didn't know so that he could introduce them to the woman he was beginning to regret having married. He performed the function of host and acted the part of bridegroom with an outward appearance of smiling cordiality, all the while remembering that Victoria had nearly fled from him in the church. The memory was searingly painful and belittling, and he couldn't get it out of his mind.

Stars were twinkling in the sky as Jason stood on the sidelines, watching her dance with the local squire and Mike Farrell and then several of the villagers. She was deliberately avoiding him, he knew, and on those rare occasions when their eyes met, Victoria quickly looked away.

She had long since removed her veil and asked the orchestra to play more lively tunes, then charmed the villagers by asking them to teach her the local dances. By the time the moon was riding high in the sky, everyone was dancing and clapping and thoroughly enjoying themselves, including Victoria, who had now finished five glasses of wine. Evidently she was trying to drink herself into a stupor, Jason thought sarcastically, noting the flush on her cheeks. Disgust knotted his stomach as he thought of his hopes for tonight, for their future. Like a fool, he had believed happiness was finally within his grasp.

Lounging against a tree, he watched her, wondering why women were so attracted to him until he married them, and then they loathed him. He had done it again, he thought furiously. He had made the same idiotic mistake twice—he had married a woman who agreed to have him because she wanted something *from* him, not because she wanted him.

Melissa had wanted every man she saw, except him. Victoria wanted only Andrew—good, gentle, kind, *spineless* Andrew.

The only difference between Melissa and Victoria was that

Victoria was a much better actress, Jason decided. He had known Melissa was a selfish, calculating bitch from the start, but he had thought Victoria was closer to an angel . . . a fallen angel, of course—thanks to Andrew—but he hadn't held that against her. Now he did. He despised her for having given herself freely to Andrew, yet wanting to avoid giving herself to her husband, which was exactly what she was trying to do by consuming enough wine to render her insensible. He hated the way she had trembled in his arms and avoided his gaze when he danced with her a few minutes ago, and then she had shuddered when he suggested it was time to go inside.

Dispassionately, Jason wondered why he could make his mistresses cry out in ecstasy, but the women he married wanted nothing to do with him the moment the vows were said. He wondered why making money came so easily to him, but happiness always eluded him. The vicious old bitch who had raised him had evidently been right—he was the spawn of the devil, undeserving of life, let alone happiness.

The only three women who had ever been part of his life—Victoria, Melissa, and his foster mother—had all seen something in him that made him loathsome and ugly in their sight, although both his wives had hidden their revulsion until after the wedding, when his wealth was finally theirs.

With implacable resolve, Jason approached Victoria and touched her arm. She jumped and pulled away as if his touch burned her. "It's late and it's time to go in," he said.

Even in the moonlight her face turned noticeably pale and a trapped, haunted look widened her eyes. "B-but it's not really late—"

"It's late enough to go to bed, Victoria," he told her bluntly.

"But I'm not the least bit sleepy!"

"Good," Jason said with deliberate crudity. He knew she understood because her whole body began to tremble. "We made a bargain," he said harshly, "and I expect you to keep your part of it, no matter how distasteful you find the prospect of going to bed with me."

His icy, authoritative voice chilled her to the bone. Nodding, Victoria walked stiffly into the house and up to her new rooms, which adjoined Jason's.

Sensing her withdrawn mood, Ruth silently helped Victoria remove her wedding gown and put on the cream satin and lace negligee Madame Dumosse had created especially for use on her wedding night.

Bile rose in Victoria's throat and terror clutched at her insides when Ruth went over to turn the bed down. The wine she had drunk, hoping to quiet her fears, was now making her dizzy and sick. Instead of calming her as it had earlier, it was making her feel violently ill and horribly unable to control her emotions. She wished devoutly she hadn't touched it. The only other time she'd had more than a sip of the stuff was after her parents' funeral, when Dr. Morrison insisted she have two glasses. It had made her retch that time, and he had told her she might be one of those people whose systems couldn't tolerate it.

With Miss Flossie's lurid description screaming through her mind, Victoria walked toward the bed. Soon her blood would be spilled on these sheets, she thought wildly. How much blood? How much pain? She broke out in a cold sweat, and dizziness swept over her as Ruth plumped up the pillows. Like a puppet she climbed in, trying to control her quaking panic and rising nausea. She mustn't scream or show her revulsion, Miss Flossie had told her, but when Jason pulled the connecting door open and strode into the room wearing a maroon brocade dressing robe that showed much of his bare chest and legs, Victoria couldn't stifle her gasp of fear. "Jason!" she burst out, pressing back into the pillows.

"Who were you expecting—Andrew?" he asked conversationally. His hands went to the satin belt that held the sides of his dressing robe together, and Victoria's fear escalated to panic. "D-don't do that," she pleaded wildly, unable to speak or think coherently. "A gentleman surely doesn't disrobe in front of a lady, even if they *are* m-married."

"I think we've had this conversation before, but in case you've forgotten, I'll remind you again that I'm no gentleman." His hands pulled at the ends of the satin belt. "However, if the sight of my ungentlemanly body offends your sensibilities, you can solve that problem by closing your eyes. The only other solution is for me to get into bed and *then* remove my robe, and *that* option offends *my* sensibilities." He opened the robe, shrugging out of it and Victoria's eyes widened in mute terror on his huge, muscular body.

Whatever tiny, secret hope Jason had harbored that she might yet submit willingly to his advances vanished when she closed her eyes and averted her face from him.

Jason stared at her and then, with deliberate crudity, he yanked the sheets from her fists and swept them away. He got into bed beside her and wordlessly untied the bow at the low bodice of her satin and lace negligee; then he sucked in his breath as he beheld the nude perfection of her body.

Victoria's breasts were full and ripe, her waist tiny, her hips gently rounded. Her legs were long and incredibly shapely, with slim thighs and trim calves. As his gaze roved over her, a blush stained her smooth ivory skin and when he laid his hand tentatively against one voluptuous breast, her whole body lurched and stiffened, rejecting his touch.

For an experienced woman, she was as cold and unyielding as a stone, lying there, her averted face twisted with revulsion. Jason considered trying to seduce her into cooperating, then tossed the idea aside with contempt. She had nearly left him at the altar this morning, and she obviously had no desire to suffer his prolonged caresses.

"Don't do this," she pleaded frantically as he caressed her breast. "I'm going to be sick!" she cried, trying to lunge out of bed. "You're going to make me sick!"

Her words hammered into his brain like sharp nails, and black rage exploded inside him. Shoving his hands into her luxurious hair, Jason rolled onto her. "In that case," he growled on a raw, infuriated breath, "we'd better get this over with in a hurry."

Visions of blood and terrible pain roared through Victoria, adding their horror to the nausea the wine was causing. "I don't want to!" she cried piteously.

"We made a bargain, and as long as we're married, you'll keep it," he whispered as he pried her stiff thighs apart. Victoria whimpered as his rigid manhood probed boldly at her, but somewhere in the depths of her stricken mind, she knew he was right about the bargain and she stopped fighting him. "Relax," he warned bitterly in the darkness above her, "I may not be as considerate as your dear Andrew, but I don't want to hurt you."

His vicious mention of Andrew at a time like this cut her to the heart, and her anguish erupted in a scream of pain as Jason rammed into her. Her body writhed beneath his, and tears poured from her eyes in hot, humiliated streaks as her husband used her without kindness or caring.

The instant his weight lifted from her, Victoria turned onto her side, burying her face in the pillow, her body racked with sobs that were part horror, part shock. "Get out," she choked, pulling her knees up to her chest and curling into a ball of anguish. "Get out, get out!"

Jason hesitated, then rolled from the bed, picked up his robe, and walked into his room. He closed the door, but the sounds of her weeping followed him. Nude, he went over to his dresser, snatched up a crystal decanter of brandy and half-filled a glass with the potent brew. He swallowed all of the burning liquid, trying to drown out the memory of her resistance and the sound of her heartbroken revulsion, to blot out the thought of her stricken face when she tried to pull her hand free of his at the altar.

How stupid he'd been to believe he'd felt warmth from Victoria when she kissed him. She'd told him when he first suggested they marry that she didn't want to marry him. Long ago, when she discovered they were supposedly betrothed, she'd told him what she really thought of him: *"You are a cold, callous, arrogant monster. . . . No woman in her right mind would marry you. . . . You aren't worth a tenth of Andrew. . . ."*

She'd meant every word.

How stupid he'd been to convince himself she actually cared for him. . . . Jason turned to put the glass down on the dresser and caught his reflection in the mirror. Traces of blood were smeared on his thighs.

Victoria's blood.

Her heart might have belonged to Andrew, but not her beautiful body—that she had given only to Jason. He stared at himself while self-loathing poured through his veins like acid. He had been so damned jealous, so wounded by her attempt to leave him at the altar, that he hadn't even noticed she was a virgin.

He closed his eyes in agonizing remorse, unable to bear the sight of himself. He had shown Victoria no more tenderness or consideration than a drunken seaman shows a paid doxy.

He thought of how dry and tight her passage had been, how small and fragile she had felt in his arms, how viciously he had used her, and a fresh surge of sickening regret ripped through him.

Opening his eyes, he stared at himself in the mirror, knowing he had turned her wedding night into a nightmare. Victoria was indeed the gentle, courageous, spirited angel he had thought she was from the very beginning. And he—he was exactly what his foster mother had called him as a child: the spawn of the devil.

Shrugging into his robe, Jason took a velvet box from a drawer and went back into Victoria's room. He stood beside her bed, watching her sleep. "Victoria," he whispered. She flinched in her slumber at the sound of his voice and he ached with remorse. How vulnerable and hurt she looked; how incredibly beautiful she was with her hair spilling over the pillows and gleaming in the candlelight.

Jason watched her in tormented silence, unwilling to disturb her. Finally he reached down and gently drew the covers over her slim bare shoulders, then smoothed her heavy hair off her forehead. "I'm sorry," he whispered to his sleeping wife.

He blew out the candle and put the velvet box on the little table beside the bed where she would be certain to see it when she awoke. Diamonds would soothe her. Women would forgive anything for diamonds.

Chapter Twenty-two

VICTORIA OPENED HER EYES AND STARED BLANKLY out the windows at a dark, overcast sky. Sleep hung over her like a thick web, tangling her waking thoughts as she gazed aimlessly past the unfamiliar rose and gold silk draperies hanging from the corners of her bed.

She felt sluggish and dull, as if she hadn't slept at all, yet she had no particular urge to go back to sleep or to fully awaken. Her mind floated aimlessly, and then it suddenly began to clear.

Dear God, she was married! Truly married. She was Jason's wife.

She stifled a cry of stricken protest at the thought and jerked upright as the full recollection of last night hit her. So this was what Miss Flossie had tried to warn her about. No wonder women didn't discuss it! She started to hurtle from the bed in response to some belated instinct to flee; then she checked herself, straightened the pillows, and fell back against them, gnawing on her lower lip. The humiliating details of her wedding night came back in painful clarity and she cringed, remembering the way Jason had crudely disrobed in front of her. She shuddered as she recalled the way he had taunted her about Andrew, and then he had used her. He had used her as if she were an animal, a dumb animal without feeling or emotion, unworthy of tenderness or kindness.

A tear trickled down her cheek as she thought of tonight, and tomorrow night, all the nights that lay ahead of her until Jason could finally get her with child. How many times would it take? A dozen? Two dozen? More? No, please, not more. She couldn't bear much more of it.

Angrily she dashed the tear away, furious with herself for succumbing to fear and weakness. Last night he had said he intended to continue doing that ugly, humiliating thing to her—it was her part of their bargain. Now that she knew what the bargain really entailed, she wanted out of it immediately!

She flung the bedcovers aside and climbed out of the silken cocoon that was supposed to be her compensation for a lifetime of misery imposed on her by a cynical, heartless man. Well, she was no simpering English girl, afraid to stand up for herself or face the world. She would rather face a firing squad than another night like the last one! She could live without luxury, if this was the way she was expected to pay for it.

She glanced around the room, trying to plan her next step, and her gaze fell on a black velvet box on the table beside the bed. She picked it up and opened the clasp, then ground her teeth in rage at the sight of the spectacular diamond necklace that lay within it. It was two inches wide and fashioned to look like a delicate cluster of flowers, with diamonds cut in various shapes to make up the petals and leaves of tulips, roses, and orchids.

Rage billowed in her in a red mist as she picked up the necklace by its clasp, holding it up with two fingers as if it were a poisonous snake, then dropped it into the box in an unceremonious pile.

Now she understood what had bothered her all along about the gifts Jason gave her and the way he wanted to be thanked with a kiss. He was buying her. He actually believed she could be bought—purchased like a cheap dockside harlot. No—not a cheap one, an expensive one, but a harlot, nonetheless.

After last night, Victoria already felt used and injured; the necklace added another insult to her growing list of Jason's offenses. She could hardly believe she'd deceived herself into thinking he cared for her, that he needed her. He cared for no one, needed no one. He didn't want to be loved and he had no love to give anyone. She should have known—he'd said as much.

Men! Victoria thought furiously, her temper adding bright spots of color to her pale cheeks. What monsters they were—Andrew with his false declarations of love, and Jason who thought he could use her and then pay her off with a stupid necklace.

Wincing at the pain between her legs, she climbed out of bed and marched into the marble bath that adjoined her suite on the opposite side of Jason's. She would get a divorce, she decided. She'd heard of them. She would tell Jason she wanted one, now.

Ruth came in just as Victoria emerged from the bath.

The little maid's face was wreathed in a secretive smile as she tiptoed into the room and glanced about her. Whatever she expected to see, it obviously was not her mistress striding militantly across the room, already up and bathed, wrapped in a towel, ruthlessly brushing her hair. Nor did she expect to hear the new bride of Jason Fielding, who was rumored to be an irresistible lover, say in a tone of dripping ice, "There's no reason to creep about in here as if you're afraid of your shadow, Ruth. The monster is in the next room, not this one."

"M-monster, miss?" the poor maid stammered blankly. "Oh," she giggled nervously, thinking she was mistaken, "you must have said 'the master,' but I thought you said—"

"I said *'monster,'* " Victoria almost snapped. The sound of her waspish voice made her instantly contrite. "I'm sorry, Ruth. I'm just a little . . . well, tired, I guess."

For some reason, that made the little servant blush and giggle, which irritated Victoria, who was already teetering on the verge of hysteria, despite her efforts to tell herself how cold and logical and determined she was. She waited, drumming her fingers, until Ruth was finished tidying the room. The clock on the mantel showed the hour as eleven as she walked to the door of her suite through which Jason had come last night. She paused with her hand on the handle, trying to compose herself. Her body was shaking like jelly at the thought of confronting him and demanding a divorce, but she meant to do exactly that, and nothing was going to deter her. Once she informed him that their marriage was over, Jason would have no more marital rights. Later, she would decide where she was going and what she would do. For now, she needed to get him to agree to a divorce. Or did she even need his permission? Since she wasn't certain, she decided it was wise not to alienate him unnecessarily or anger him into refusing. But then, she shouldn't beat about the bush too long, either.

Victoria straightened her shoulders, tightened the belt of her velvet robe, turned the handle, and marched into Jason's room.

Suppressing the desire to hit him over the head with the porcelain pitcher beside his bed, she said very civilly, "Good morning."

His eyes snapped open, his expression instantly alert, wary almost, and then he smiled. That sleepy, sensual smile of his, which before might have melted her heart, now made her grind her teeth in rage. Somehow, she kept her expression polite, almost pleasant.

"Good morning," Jason said huskily, his eyes running over her voluptuous figure, clad in the sensuous softness of shimmering gold velvet. Recalling the way he had ravaged her last night, Jason dragged his eyes from the low vee of her robe and shifted his body to make room for her beside him on the bed. Deeply touched that she would come in to bid him good morning when she had every right to despise him for last night, he patted the space he had vacated and said gently, "Would you like to sit down?"

Victoria was so busy trying to think of a way to ease into what she had to say that she automatically accepted Jason's invitation. "Thank you," she said politely.

"For what?" he teased.

It was exactly the opening Victoria was searching for. "Thank you for everything. In many ways, you've been extraordinarily kind to me. I know how displeased you were when I showed up at your door months ago, but even though you didn't want me here, you let me stay. You bought me beautiful clothes, and you took me to parties, which was excessively kind of you. You fought a duel for me, which wasn't necessary at all, but was very gallant on your part. You married me in a church, which you didn't in the least wish to do, and you gave me a lovely party here last night and invited people you didn't know, just to please me. Thank you for all that."

Jason reached up, idly rubbing his knuckles against her pale cheek. "You're welcome," he said softly.

"Now I'd like a divorce."

His hand froze. "You *what?*" he said in an ominous whisper.

Victoria clenched and unclenched her hands in her lap, but she kept her resolve strong. "I want a divorce," she repeated with false calm.

"Just like that?" he said in an awful, silky voice. Although Jason was very willing to concede he had treated her badly last night, he had not expected anything like this. "After one day of marriage, you want a divorce?"

Victoria took one look at the anger kindling in his glittering eyes and hastily stood up, only to have Jason's hand clamp about her wrist and jerk her back down. "Don't manhandle me, Jason," she warned.

Jason, who had left her last night looking like a wounded child, was now confronted with a woman he didn't recognize—a coldly enraged, beautiful virago. Instead of apologizing, as he'd intended to do a minute ago, he said, "You're being absurd. There've only been a handful of divorces in England in the last fifty years, and there'll be no divorce between us."

Victoria pulled her arm free with a wrenching tug that nearly dislocated her shoulder, then stepped back, well out of his reach, her chest rising and falling in fury and fright. "You are an animal!" she hissed. "I am not absurd, and I won't be used like an animal ever again!"

She stalked into her room and slammed the door, then locked it with a loud snap.

She had taken only a few steps when the door burst open behind her with an explosive crack and came flying out of its frame, hanging drunkenly from one hinge. Jason stood in the gaping hole of the doorway, his face white with rage, his voice hissing between his teeth. "Don't you ever bar a door to me again as long as you live," he snarled. "And don't ever threaten me with divorce again! This house is my property, under the law, just as you are my property. Do you understand me?"

Victoria nodded jerkily, mentally recoiling from the blinding violence flashing in his eyes. He turned on his heel and stalked out of the room, leaving her shaking with fear. Never had she witnessed such volcanic rage in a human being. Jason wasn't an animal, he was a crazed monster.

She waited, listening to the sounds of his drawers abruptly opening and closing as he dressed, her mind working frantically for some way to extricate herself from the nightmare her life had become. When she heard his door slam and knew he had gone downstairs, she walked over to her bed and sank down. She remained where she was, thinking, for nearly an hour, but there was no way out. She was trapped for a lifetime. Jason had spoken the truth—she was his chattel, just like his house and his horses.

If he wouldn't agree to a divorce, she couldn't imagine how she could possibly go about obtaining one on her own. She wasn't even certain she had adequate reason to convince a court to give her a divorce, but she was perfectly certain she couldn't possibly explain to a group of bewigged male judges what Jason had done to her last night to make her want a divorce.

She had been grasping wildly at straws when she conceived the idea of divorce this morning. The whole idea was impossibly radical, she realized with a despondent sigh. She was trapped here until she gave Jason the son he wanted. Then she would be bound to Wakefield by the existence of the very child who might have set her free, because she knew she could never go away and leave a baby of hers.

Victoria looked aimlessly about the luxurious room. Somehow she was going to have to learn to adapt to her new life, to make the best of things until fate might intervene to help her somehow. In the meantime, she would have to take steps to keep her sanity, she decided as a numbing calm stole over her. She could spend time with other people, leave the house and go about her own business or amusements. She would have to devise pleasant diversions to distract herself from dwelling upon her problems. Beginning immediately. She hated self-pity and she refused to wallow in it.

She had already made friends in England; soon she would have a child to love and to love her in return. She would make the best of an empty life by filling it with anything she could find to keep her sane.

She raked her hair back away from her pale face, and stood up resolved to do exactly that. Even so, her shoulders dropped as she rang for Ruth. Why did Jason hold her in such contempt, she wondered miserably. She ached for someone to talk to, to confide in. Always before she'd had her mother, or her father, or Andrew to talk with and listen to. Talking things out always helped. But since she came to England, there was no one. Charles's health was poor and she'd had to put on a brave, cheerful face for him from the very first day she came here. Besides, Jason was his nephew, and she couldn't possibly discuss her fears about Jason with his own uncle, even if Charles were here at Wakefield. Caroline Collingwood was a good and loyal friend, but she was miles away, and Victoria doubted if Caroline could understand Jason, even if she herself tried to discuss him.

There was nothing for it, Victoria decided, but for her to continue holding everything inside herself, to pretend to be happy and confident, until—someday—she might actually feel that way again. There would come a time, she promised herself grimly, when she could face the night without dread of Jason walking into her room. There would come a time when she could look at him and feel nothing—not fear or hurt or humiliation or loneliness. That day would come—somehow, it would! As soon as she conceived a child, he would leave her alone, and she prayed it would happen soon.

"Ruth," she said tightly when the little maid appeared. "Would you ask someone to harness one of the horses to the smallest carriage we have—one I can easily drive? And please ask whoever does it to choose the gentlest horse we have—I'm not very familiar with driving a carriage. When you've done that, please ask Mrs. Craddock to pack several baskets of leftover food from the party last night so I may take them with me."

"But, my lady," Ruth said hesitantly, "only look out the window. It's turned chilly and there's a storm comin'. See for yourself how dark the sky is."

Victoria glanced out the windows at the leaden skies. "It doesn't look as if it will rain for hours, if at all," she decided a little desperately. "I'd like to leave in half an hour. Oh, has Lord Fielding gone out, or is he downstairs?"

"His lordship's gone out, my lady."

"Do you happen to know if he's left the estate, or is merely outdoors somewhere?" Victoria asked, unable to disguise the desperate anxiety in her voice. Despite her resolve to think of Jason as a complete stranger and to treat him as one, she did not relish the idea of confronting him again right now, when her emotions were still so raw. Besides, she was rather certain he would order her to stay at home, rather than permitting her to go out when a storm could be coming on. And the truth was, she had to get out of this house for a while. She had to!

"Lord Fielding ordered the horses put to the phaeton and he drove off. He said he had some calls to make. I saw him leave with my own eyes," Ruth assured her.

The carriage was loaded with food and waiting in the drive when Victoria came downstairs.

"What shall I tell his lordship?" Northrup said, looking exceedingly distressed when Victoria insisted upon leaving despite his dire prediction of an impending storm.

Victoria turned, allowing him to place a lightweight mauve cloak over her shoulders. "Tell him I said good-bye," Victoria said evasively.

She walked outside, went around to the back of the house and unsnapped Wolf's chain, then came around to the front again. The head groom assisted her into the carriage and Wolf bounded up beside her. Wolf looked so happy to be unchained that Victoria smiled and patted his regal head. "You're free at last," she told the huge animal. "And so am I."

Chapter Twenty-three

VICTORIA SNAPPED THE REINS WITH MORE ASSUR-
ance than she felt, and the spirited horse bounded forward,
its satiny coat glistening in the gloom. "Easy, now," Victoria whispered in fright. Jason obviously did not believe in
keeping sedate carriage horses in his stables—the flashy
mare harnessed to Victoria's carriage was incredibly hard to
control. She pranced and danced until Victoria's hands were
blistered and red from trying to hold her to a slow trot.

As Victoria was nearing the village, the wind picked up
and lightning flashed in blue streaks, splitting the sky into
jagged slices while thunder boomed an ominous warning and
the sky turned almost as black as night. Minutes later, the
sky opened up and rain came down in blinding sheets,
driving into her face, obscuring her vision, and turning her
cloak to a sodden mass.

Straining to see the road ahead, Victoria shoved her
dripping hair off her face and shivered. She had never seen
the orphanage, but Captain Farrell had told her where the
road was that led to it, as well as the road that led to his own
house. Victoria strained her eyes, and then she saw what
looked like one of the roads he had described. It forked off to

her left and she turned the horse onto it, not certain whether she was heading toward the orphanage or Captain Farrell's house. At the moment she didn't care, so long as she was going to a warm, dry place where she could get out of the downpour. The road rounded a bend and began to climb upward through increasingly dense woods, passed two deserted cottages, then narrowed until it was scarcely more than a dirt track, which was rapidly becoming a quagmire in the torrential downpour.

Mud sucked at the wheels of the carriage and the mare began to labor with the effort of freeing her hooves from the deep slime every time she took a step. Up ahead Victoria saw a dim light coming through the trees. Shivering with relief and cold, she turned onto a little lane that was sheltered by a thick stand of ancient oak trees, their branches meeting overhead like a dripping umbrella. Suddenly lightning rent the sky, illuminating a cottage large enough for a small family but certainly not large enough to house twenty orphans. Thunder cracked deafeningly overhead and the mare shied, half-rearing in the traces. Victoria jumped down from the carriage. "Easy now," she told the mare soothingly as she reached for the nervous animal's bridle. Her feet sank into the mud as she led the horse to the post in front of the cottage and tied her there.

With Wolf protectively at her side, she lifted her sodden skirts, walked up the front steps of the cottage, and knocked.

A moment later the door was flung open and Captain Farrell's rugged face was silhouetted in the light from the cheerful fire behind him. "Lady Fielding!" he gasped, reaching out to pull her quickly inside. A low, vicious snarl from Wolf stopped his hand in midmotion and his eyes widened as he beheld the wet gray beast that was snarling at him, its lip curled back above white fangs.

"Wolf, stop it!" Victoria commanded wearily, and the animal subsided.

Keeping a wary eye on the ferocious-looking beast, Captain Farrell cautiously drew Victoria inside. Wolf followed close at her heels, his tawny eyes riveted warningly on Mike Farrell. "What in heaven's name are you doing out in this weather?" he asked worriedly.

"S-swimming," Victoria tried to joke, but her teeth were chattering and her body was trembling with cold as he pulled her cloak off and tossed it over the back of a chair near the fire.

"You'll have to get out of those wet garments or you'll catch your death. Will that great beast let you out of his sight long enough to put on some warm clothes?"

Victoria wrapped her arms around herself and nodded, glancing at her fierce canine guardian. "S-stay here, Wolf."

The dog flopped down in front of the fireplace and put his head on his big paws, his eyes trained on the doorway into the bedroom through which they disappeared.

"I'll stoke up the fire," Captain Farrell said kindly in the bedroom, handing her a pair of his own trousers and one of his shirts. "These clothes are the best I can offer." Victoria opened her mouth to speak, but he forestalled her. "I'll not listen to any foolish arguments about the impropriety of wearing men's clothes, young woman," he said authoritatively. "Use the water in the pitcher to wash and then put on these clothes and wrap yourself up in that blanket. When you're ready, come out by the fire and get warm. If you're worried about whether Jason might disapprove of your wearing my clothes, you can stop worrying—I've known him since he was a very small lad."

Victoria's head came up defensively. "I am not at all concerned with what Jason might think," she said, unable to keep the rebellious note out of her voice. "I have no intention of freezing to death to suit him. Or anyone," she amended quickly, realizing how much she was giving away in her beleaguered discomfort.

Captain Farrell shot her an odd, narrow look, but he only nodded. "Good. That's very sensible thinking."

"If I were sensible, I would have stayed home today." Victoria smiled wanly, trying to hide her misery over her abortive effort to brighten her life.

When she emerged from the bedroom, Captain Farrell had already put her horse in the small barn beyond the house, stoked up the fire, and made her a cup of tea. He handed her a big cloth. "Use this to dry your hair," he commanded kindly, indicating that she should sit in the chair he'd drawn up close to the fire.

"Do you mind if I smoke this?" he asked, holding up a pipe as he sat down across from her.

"Not at all," Victoria said politely.

He filled the bowl with tobacco and lit it, puffing idly, his disconcertingly direct gaze focused on Victoria's face. "Why didn't you do that?" he asked finally.

"Why didn't I do what?"

"Stay at home today."

Wondering if she looked as guilty and unhappy as she felt at the moment, Victoria gave a light, evasive shrug. "I wanted to bring food to the orphanage. There was so much of it left after our party last night."

"Yet it was obviously going to rain, and you could have sent a servant to the orphanage—which, by the way, is another mile past here. Instead, you decided to brave the weather and try to find the place yourself."

"I needed—wanted, I mean—to get away, to get out of the house for a while, that is," Victoria said, paying unnecessary attention to the act of stirring her tea.

"I'm surprised Jason didn't insist you stay home," he persisted pointedly.

"I didn't think it was necessary to ask his permission," Victoria replied, uneasily conscious of Captain Farrell's searching questions and intent gaze.

"He must be worried sick about you by now."

"I very much doubt if he'll discover I've been gone." Or that he'd care, even if he knew, she thought miserably.

"Lady Fielding?"

There was something about the bluntness beneath his polite tone that made Victoria certain she did not want to continue this conversation. On the other hand, she had little choice. "Yes, Captain?" she said warily.

"I saw Jason this morning."

Victoria's unease grew. "Oh, yes?" She had the worst feeling that for some reason Jason might have come here to discuss her with his old friend, and she felt as if all the world was turning against her.

Apparently Captain Farrell sensed her suspicion, because he explained, "Jason owns a large fleet of ships. I have command of one of them, and he wanted to discuss the success of this last voyage with me."

Victoria seized on that remark to try to shift the conversation away from herself. "I didn't know Lord Fielding knew anything about ships, or that he was involved with them," she said in a bright, inquiring voice.

"That's odd."

"What is?"

"Perhaps I am simple and old-fashioned, but I find it rather odd that a woman wouldn't know that her husband spent years of his life aboard a ship."

Victoria gaped at him. As far as she knew, Jason was an English lord—an arrogant, wealthy, world-weary, spoiled aristocrat. The only thing that distinguished him from the rest of the noblemen she'd met was that Jason spent a great deal of time in his study working, while the other wealthy gentlemen she'd met in England seemed to spend all their time in the pursuit of pleasure and diversion.

"Perhaps you simply aren't interested in his accomplishments?" Captain Farrell prodded, his manner chilling. He puffed on his pipe for a moment, then said bluntly, "Why did you marry him?"

Victoria's eyes flew wide open. She felt like a trapped rabbit—a feeling she was beginning to experience very often and which was beginning to grate terribly on her pride. She raised her head and regarded her inquisitor with ill-concealed resentment. With as much dignity as she could muster, she replied evasively, "I married Lord Fielding for the usual reasons."

"Money, influence, and social position," Captain Farrell summarized with scathing disgust. "Well, you have all three now. Congratulations."

This unprovoked attack was too much for Victoria to bear. Tears of fury sprang to her eyes as she stood up, clutching the blanket to herself. "Captain Farrell, I am not wet enough or miserable enough or desperate enough to sit here and feel obliged to listen to you accuse me of being mercenary and—and selfish and—a social parasite—"

"Why not?" he bit out. "Evidently, you're all those things."

"I don't care what you think of me. I—" Her voice cracked and Victoria started toward the bedroom, intending to get her clothes, but he rolled to his feet and blocked her way, angrily searching her face as if he were trying to look into her soul.

"Why do you want a divorce?" he demanded sharply, but his expression gentled slightly as he stared down at her beautiful, fragile features. Even wrapped in a plain woolen blanket, Victoria Seaton was an incredibly lovely sight, with the firelight glinting in her red-gold hair and her magnificent blue eyes flashing with helpless resentment. She had spirit, but it was evident from the tears glistening in her eyes that her spirit was nearly broken. In fact, she looked as if she were about to splinter apart.

"This morning," he persisted, "I jokingly asked Jason if you'd left him yet. He said you hadn't left him, but you'd asked for a divorce. I assumed he meant that to be humorous, but when you walked in here just now, you certainly didn't look like a happy new bride."

Teetering on the brink of utter despair, Victoria gazed into her tormentor's implacable, sun-bronzed face, fighting back her tears and trying to hold onto her dignity. "Will you please step out of my way," she said hoarsely.

Instead of moving aside, he caught her by the shoulders. "Now that you have everything you married him for—the money, the influence, the social position—why do you want a divorce?" he demanded.

"I have nothing!" Victoria burst out, perilously close to tears. "Now, let go of me!"

"Not until I understand how I could have misjudged you so much. Yesterday, when you spoke to me, I thought you were wonderful. I saw the laughter in your eyes when you talked, and I saw the way you treated the villagers. I thought to myself that you were a real woman—one with heart and spirit, not some mercenary, spoiled little coward!"

Hot tears filled Victoria's eyes at this unfair condemnation from a perfect stranger, and a friend of Jason's to boot. "Leave me alone, damn you!" she demanded brokenly, and tried to shove him out of her way.

Amazingly, his arms wrapped around her, hauling her against his broad chest. "Cry, Victoria!" he ordered gruffly. "For God's sake, cry."

Victoria shuddered as he whispered, "Let the tears come, child." He stroked her back with his broad hand. "If you try to hold all this inside you, you'll shatter."

Victoria had learned to deal with tragedy and adversity; she could not, however, cope with kindness and understanding. The tears rushed to her eyes and poured out of her in wrenching sobs that shook her body and tore themselves from her in painful torrents. She had no idea when Captain Farrell coaxed her to sit beside him on the plain sofa across from the fire, or when she began to tell him about her parents' deaths and the events leading up to Jason's cold-blooded offer of marriage. With her face buried against his shoulder, she answered his questions about Jason and why she had married him. And when she was finished, she felt better than she had in weeks.

"So," he said with a slight, admiring smile. "Despite Jason's unemotional proposal, despite the fact that you actually know nothing about him, you still thought he truly needed you?"

Victoria self-consciously wiped her eyes and nodded sheepishly. "Obviously, I was foolish and fanciful to think that, but there were times he seemed so alone—times when I would look at him in a crowded ballroom, surrounded by people—usually women—and I would have this queer feeling that he felt as lonely as I did. And Uncle Charles said Jason needed me, too. But we were both wrong. Jason wants a son, it's as simple as that. He doesn't need me or want me."

"You're wrong," Captain Farrell said with gentle finality. "Jason has needed a women like you since the day he was born. He needs you to heal wounds that are deep, to teach him how to let himself love and be loved in return. If you knew more about him, you'd understand why I say that." Getting up, Captain Farrell walked over to a small table and picked up a bottle. He poured some of its contents into two glasses, then handed one to her.

"Will you tell me about him?" Victoria asked as he went to the fireplace and stood looking down at her.

"Yes."

Victoria glanced at the potent-smelling whiskey he'd handed her and started to put it down on the table.

"If you want to hear about Jason, I suggest you drink that first," Captain Farrell said grimly. "You're going to need it."

Victoria took a sip of the burning stuff, but the burly Irishman lifted his glass and gulped down half the liquid in it as if he, too, needed it.

"I'm going to tell you things about Jason that only I know, things he obviously doesn't want you to know or he would have told you. By telling you these things, I'm betraying Jason's trust, and until this moment, I was one of the few people close to him who had never betrayed him in some way or another. He is like a son to me, Victoria, so it hurts me to do this; yet I feel it is imperative that you understand him."

Victoria slowly shook her head. "Perhaps you shouldn't tell me anything, Captain. Lord Fielding and I are at outs most of the time, but I would not like to see either of you hurt by the things you tell me."

A smile flickered briefly across Captain Farrell's grim features. "If I thought you might use what I tell you as a weapon against him, I'd keep my silence. But you won't do that. There is a gentle strength about you, a compassion and understanding that I witnessed firsthand last night when I saw you mingling with the villagers. I watched you laughing with them and putting them at their ease, and I thought then that you were a wonderful young woman—and the perfect wife for Jason. I still think that."

He drew a long breath and began. "The first time I saw your husband, I was in Delhi. It was many years ago, and I was working for a wealthy Delhi merchant named Napal who shipped goods back and forth from India all over the world. Napal not only owned the goods he traded, he owned four ships that carried them across the seas. I was first mate on one of those ships.

"I'd been away for six months on an extremely profitable voyage, and when we returned to port, Napal invited the captain and myself to come to his home for a small, private celebration.

"It's always hot in India, but it seemed even hotter that day, especially because I got lost trying to find Napal's home. Somehow I ended up in a maze of alleyways and when I finally worked my way out of them, I found myself in a squalid little square filled with filthy, ragged Indians—the poverty there is beyond imagination. At any rate, I looked around, hoping against hope to find someone I could speak to in French or English in order to ask directions.

"I saw a small crowd of people gathered at the end of the square, watching something—I couldn't see what—and I went over to them. They were standing outside a building, watching what was going on inside it. I started to turn back, to try to retrace my steps, when I saw a crude wooden cross nailed up outside the building. Thinking it was a church and that I might find someone I could speak to in my own language, I pushed through the crowd and went in. I elbowed my way past a hundred ragged Indians toward the front of the place, where I could hear a woman screaming like a fanatic, in English, about lust and the vengeance of the Almighty.

"I finally got to where I could see, and there she was, standing on this wooden scaffold with a little boy beside her. She was pointing to the child and screaming that he was the devil. She shrieked that he was 'the seed of lust' and 'the product of evil,' and then she jerked the child's head up and I saw his face.

"I was stunned when I realized the boy was white, not Indian. She shouted at everyone to 'Look upon the devil and see what vengeance the Lord takes'; then she turned the boy around to show the 'vengeance of the Lord.' When I saw his back, I thought I would be sick."

Captain Farrell swallowed audibly. "Victoria, the little boy's back was black and blue from his last beating and it was scarred from God knows how many other beatings. From the looks of it, she'd just finished beating him in front of her 'congregation'—the Indians don't object to that sort of barbaric cruelty.

His face contorted as he continued. "While I stood there, the demented hag screamed at the child to get down on his knees, to pray for forgiveness from the Lord. He looked her right in the eye, not saying anything, but he didn't move, and she brought her whip down across his shoulders with enough force to send a grown man to his knees. The child went down to his. *'Pray, you devil,'* she screamed at the kneeling child, and she hit him again. The child said nothing, he just looked straight ahead; and it was then I saw his eyes . . . His eyes were dry. There wasn't a single tear in them. But there was pain there—God, they were filled with such pain!''

Victoria shuddered with pity for the unknown child, wondering why Captain Farrell was telling her this hideous story before telling her about Jason.

Captain Farrell's face twisted. "I'll never forget the torment in his eyes," he whispered hoarsely, "or how green they seemed at that moment."

Victoria's glass crashed to the floor and shattered. She shook her head wildly, trying to deny what he was telling her. "No," she cried in anguish. "Oh, please, no—"

Seemingly oblivious to her horror, Captain Farrell continued, staring straight ahead, lost in the memories. "The little boy prayed then, he clasped his hands together and recited, 'I kneel to the Lord and ask his forgiveness.' The woman made him say it louder, over and over again, and when she was satisfied, she hauled him to his feet. She pointed at the dirty Indians and told him to beg the righteous for their forgiveness. Then she handed him a little bowl. I stood watching as the little boy went into the crowd to kneel at the feet of her 'congregation' and kiss the hems of their dirty robes and 'beg them for their forgiveness.' ''

"No," Victoria moaned, wrapping her arms around her and closing her eyes as she tried to blot out the image of a little boy with curly black hair and familiar green eyes being subjected to such demented evil.

"Something inside of me went crazy," Farrell continued. "The Indians are a fanatic lot and I take no interest in their ways. But to see a child of my own race so abused did something to me. It was more than that, though. There was something about that little boy that reached out to me—he was filthy and ragged and undernourished, but there was a proud, defiant look in those haunted eyes of his that broke my heart. I waited while he kneeled to the Indians around me and kissed the hems of their robes, asking for their forgiveness while they dropped coins into the wooden bowl. Then he brought the bowl to the woman, and she smiled. She took the bowl and smiled at him; she told him he was 'good' now, smiling that fanatic, demented smile of hers.

"I looked at that obscene woman standing on the make-shift altar, holding a cross, and I wanted to kill her. On the other hand, I didn't know how loyal her congregation was to her and, since I couldn't fight them off single-handedly, I asked if she would sell the boy to me. I told her I thought he needed a man to punish him properly."

Pulling his gaze from its distant focus, Captain Farrell looked at Victoria, a mirthless smirk on his face. "She sold him to me for the six months' pay I was carrying in my pocket. Her husband had died a year before and she needed money as much as she needed a whipping boy. But before I was out of the place, she was showering my money on her congregation and shouting about God sending His gifts to them through her. She was insane. Utterly insane."

Victoria's voice was a pleading whisper. "Do you think things were better for Jason before his father died?"

"Jason's father is still alive," Captain Farrell answered stiffly. "Jason is Charles's illegitimate son."

The room began to whirl and Victoria clamped her hand over her mouth, fighting down the nausea and dizziness that assailed her.

"Does it disgust you so much to discover you're married to a bastard?" he asked, watching her reaction.

"How could you think such a stupid thing!" Victoria burst out indignantly.

He smiled at that. "Good. I didn't think you'd care, but the English are very fastidious about such things."

"Which," Victoria retorted hotly, "is extremely hypocrit-ical on their part, since three royal dukes I could name are direct descendants of three of King Charles's bastards. Besides that, I am not English, I am American."

"You are lovely," he said gently.

"Would you tell me the rest of what you know about Jason?" she asked, her heart already full to bursting with compassion.

"The rest isn't quite as important. I took Jason to Napal's home that same night. One of Napal's servants cleaned him up and sent him in to see us. The child didn't want to talk, but once he did, it was obvious he was bright. When I told Napal the story, he felt pity for Jason and took him into his business as a sort of errand boy. Jason received no money, but he was given a bed in the back of Napal's office, decent food, and clothes. He taught himself to read and write—he had an insatiable desire to learn.

"By the time Jason was sixteen, he'd learned all he could from Napal about being a merchant. Besides being clever and quick, Jason had an incredible drive to succeed—I imagine that came from being forced to beg with a wooden bowl as a child.

"At any rate, Napal grew more mellow as he grew older and, since he had no children of his own, he began to think of Jason more as a son than a poorly paid, overworked clerk. Jason convinced Napal to let him sail on one of Napal's ships so that he could learn the shipping business at first-hand. I had become a captain by then, and Jason sailed with me for five years."

"Was he a good sailor?" Victoria asked softly, feeling terribly proud of the little boy who had grown into such a successful man.

"The best. He started as a common seaman, but he learned navigation and everything else from me in his free time. Napal died two days after we returned from one of our voyages. He was sitting in his office when his heart stopped. Jason tried everything to bring him back, he even bent over him and tried to breathe his own air into his lungs. The others in the office thought Jason had gone crazy, but you see, he loved the old miser. He grieved for him for months. But he didn't shed a single tear," Mike Farrell said quietly. "Jason can't cry. The witch who raised him was convinced that 'devils' can't cry, and she beat him worse if he did. Jason finally told me that when he was about nine years old.

"Anyway, when Napal died he left everything to Jason. During the next six years, Jason did what he'd tried to convince Napal to do—he bought an entire fleet of ships and he eventually multiplied Napal's wealth many times over."

When Captain Farrell stood staring silently into the fire, Victoria said, "Jason married, too, didn't he? I discovered that only a few days ago."

"Ah, yes, he married," Mike said, grimacing as he walked over to the bottle of whiskey and poured himself another drink. "Two years after Napal's death, Jason had become one of the richest men in Delhi. That distinction won him the mercenary interest of a beautiful, amoral woman named Melissa. Her father was an Englishman living in Delhi and working for the government. Melissa had looks and breeding and style, she had everything but what she needed most— money. She married Jason for what he could give her."

"Why did Jason marry *her?*" Victoria wanted to know.

Mike Farrell shrugged. "He was younger than she was and dazzled by her looks, I suppose. Then too, the lady— and I use the term loosely—had a . . . er . . . look about her that would make any man expect to find warmth in her arms. She sold that warmth to Jason in return for everything she could wheedle from him. He gave her plenty, too—jewels that would please a queen. She took them and smiled at him. She had a beautiful face, but for some reason when she smiled at him like that, it reminded me of that demented old witch with the wooden bowl."

Victoria had a sharp, painful vision of Jason giving her the pearls and the sapphires and asking her to thank him with a kiss. She wondered sadly if he thought he had to bribe a woman to care for him.

Lifting his glass, Mike took a long swallow. "Melissa was a slut—a slut who spent her life going from bed to bed after she was married. The funny thing was, she had a fit when she found out Jason was a bastard. I was at their house in Delhi when the Duke of Atherton appeared and demanded to speak with his son. Melissa went wild with fury when she realized Jason was Charles's *illegitimate* son. It seems it offended her principles to mingle her bloodline with a bastard's. It did not, however, offend her principles to bestow her body on any man of her own class who invited her into his bed. Odd code of ethics, wouldn't you say?"

"Extremely!" Victoria agreed.

Captain Farrell grinned at her loyal reply, then said, "Whatever tenderness Jason felt for her when he married her was soon destroyed by living with her. She gave him a son, though, and for that reason, he kept her in the height of fashion and ignored her affairs. Frankly, I don't think he cared what she did."

Victoria, who had been unaware that Jason had a son, sat bolt upright, staring in dazed shock at Captain Farrell as he went on. "Jason adored that child. He took him nearly everywhere he went. He even agreed to come back here and spend his money restoring Charles Fielding's run-down estates so that Jamie could inherit a proper kingdom. And in the end, it was all for nothing. Melissa tried to run away with her latest lover, and she took Jamie with her, intending to ransom him back to Jason later. Their ship sank in a storm."

Captain Farrell's hand tightened on his glass and the muscles in his throat worked convulsively. "I was the first to discover Melissa had taken Jamie with her. I was the one who had to tell Jason his son was dead. I cried," he said hoarsely. "But Jason didn't. Not even then. He can't cry."

"Captain Farrell," Victoria said in a suffocated voice, "I would like to go home now. It's getting late, and Jason may be worried about me."

The sorrow vanished from the captain's face and a smile broke across his rugged features. "An excellent idea," he agreed. "But before you go, I want to tell you something."

"What is it?"

"Don't let Jason fool you or himself into believing he wants nothing from you but a child. I know him better than anyone else does, and I saw the way he watched you last night. He's already more than half in love with you, though I doubt he wants to be."

"I can't blame him for not wanting to love any woman," Victoria said sadly. "I can't imagine how he's survived everything that's happened to him and stayed sane."

"He's strong," Captain Farrell replied. "Jason is the strongest human being I've ever known. And the finest. Let yourself love him, Victoria—I know you want to. And teach him how to love you. He has a great deal of love to give, but first, he'll have to learn to trust you. Once he trusts you, he'll lay the world at your feet."

Victoria stood up, but her eyes were cloudy with trepidation. "What makes you so certain this will all work out the way you think it will?"

The Irishman's voice was soft and there was a faraway look in his eyes. "Because I knew another lass like you long ago. She had your warmth and your courage. She taught me how it feels to trust, to love, and to be loved. I don't fear dying because I know she's there, waiting for me. Most men love easily and often, but Jason is more like me. He will love only once—but it will be for always."

Chapter Twenty-four

❦

WHILE VICTORIA PUT ON HER STILL-DAMP CLOTHES, Captain Farrell brought the horse and carriage around from his small barn. He helped her into it, and mounted his own horse. The downpour had subsided to a gloomy, persistent drizzle as he rode beside her in the early darkness toward Wakefield.

"There's no reason for you to ride all the way back with me," she said. "I know the way."

"There's every reason," Captain Farrell warned. "The roads aren't safe for a woman alone after dark. Last week a coach was stopped just the other side of the village, the occupants robbed, and one of them shot. A fortnight before that, one of the older girls at the orphanage wandered too far abroad at night and was found dead in the river. She was an addled girl, so there's no telling whether foul play was involved, but you can't take chances."

Victoria heard him, but her mind was on Jason, her heart filled with warmth for the man who had sheltered her when she came to England, given her beautiful things, teased her when she was lonely, and ultimately married her. True, he was frequently distant and unapproachable, but the more she contemplated the matter, the more convinced she became that Captain Farrell was right—Jason must care for her, or he'd never have risked another marriage.

She remembered the hungry passion of his kisses before they were married and she became even more convinced. Despite the torment he had suffered as a child in the name of "religion," he had gone into a church and married her there, because she asked him to.

"I think you'd better not come any farther," Victoria said when they neared the iron gates of Wakefield.

"Why?"

"Because if Jason knows I've spent the afternoon with you, he's bound to suspect you told me about him as soon as I act differently toward him."

Captain Farrell lifted his brows. *"Are* you going to act differently toward him?"

Victoria nodded in the darkness. "I rather think I will." In a soft underbreath she said, "I'm going to try to tame a panther."

"In that case, you're right. It's best not to tell Jason you came to my place. There were two deserted cottages before you reached mine. I suppose you could say you stopped there—but I warn you, Jason has an aversion to deceit. Don't get caught up in the lie."

"I have an aversion to deception, too," Victoria said with a little shiver. "And an even greater aversion to being caught in one by Jason."

"I'm very much afraid he'll be worried and angry if he's returned and discovered you've been out in this storm alone."

Jason had returned, and he was worried. He was also furious. Victoria heard his raised voice coming from the front of the house as soon as she entered it from the rear, after tying Wolf outside. With a mixture of alarm and eagerness to see him, she walked down the hall and stepped into his study. He was pacing back and forth, his back to her, addressing a group of six terrified servants. His white shirt was soaked, clinging wetly to his broad shoulders and tapered back, and his brown riding boots were covered in mud. "Tell me again what Lady Fielding said," he raged at

Ruth. "And stop that damned weeping! Start from the beginning and tell me her words *exactly*."

The maid wrung her hands. "She—she said to have your gentlest horse harnessed to the smallest carriage, because she said she weren't—wasn't too good at driving carriages. Then she told me to have Mrs. Craddock—the cook—pack baskets with food left over from the party last night, and to have the baskets put in the carriage. I w-warned her it was comin' on to storm, but she said it wouldn't start for hours. Then she asked me if I was certain-sure you'd left the house and I told her I was. Then she left."

"And you let her go?" Jason exploded at the servants, passing a contemptuous glance over all of them. "You let an overemotional woman, who's completely inept at the reins, take off in a storm with enough food to last her for a month, and not one of you had the brains to stop her!" His eyes sliced over the groom. "You heard her tell the dog they were 'free at last' and you didn't think that was peculiar?"

Without waiting for a reply, he turned his dagger gaze on Northrup, who was standing like a proud man before a firing squad, prepared to meet a terrible and unjust fate. "Tell me again, *exactly* what she said to you," Jason snapped.

"I asked her ladyship what I should tell you when you returned," Northrup said stiffly. "She said, 'Tell him I said good-bye.'"

"And that didn't sound a damned bit odd to you?" Jason bit out. "A new bride leaves the house and says to tell her husband good-bye!"

Northrup flushed to the roots of his white hair. "Considering other things, my lord, it did not seem 'odd.'"

Jason stopped pacing and stared at him in blank fury. "Considering what 'other things'?" he demanded.

"Considering what you said to me when you left the house an hour before her ladyship did, I naturally assumed the two of you were not in accord, and that her ladyship was distressed about it."

"Considering what *I* said when I left?" Jason demanded murderously. "What the hell did *I* say?"

Northrup's thin lips quivered with resentment. "When you left the house this morning, I bade you have a good day."

"And?" Jason gritted.

"And you told me you had already made *other plans*. I naturally assumed that meant you did not intend to have a good day and so, when her ladyship came down, I assumed you were not in accord."

"It's too damn bad you didn't 'assume' she was leaving me and try to stop her."

Victoria's heart ached with remorse. Jason thought she had left him, and for a man as proud as he to admit such a thing to his servants, he must be beside himself. Never in her wildest dreams had she imagined he would jump to that conclusion, but now that she knew what Melissa had done, she could understand why he had. Determined to save his pride, she summoned up a bright, conciliatory smile and crossed the thick Aubusson carpet to his side. "Northrup would never be so silly as to think I would leave you, my lord," she said brightly, tucking her hand in Jason's arm.

Jason whirled around so violently that he nearly pulled her off her feet. Victoria recovered her balance and said softly, "I may be 'overemotional,' but I hope I'm not a complete fool."

Jason's eyes blazed with relief—a relief that was instantly replaced by fury. "Where in hell have you been?" he hissed.

Victoria took pity on the mortified servants and said contritely, "You've every right to scold me, and I can tell you intend to, but I hope you won't do it in front of the servants."

Jason clamped his jaws together so tightly that a nerve pulsed in his cheek as he bit back his wrath and nodded his head in the general direction of the servants, curtly dismissing them. In the charged silence that followed, the servants rushed out of the room, the last one closing the door behind him. The instant the door closed, Jason's wrath erupted. "You idiot!" he bit out between clenched teeth. "I've turned the countryside upside down looking for you."

Victoria looked at his handsome, ruggedly hewn face with its stern, sensual mouth and hard jaw, but what she saw was a helpless, dirty little boy with dark curly hair being whipped because he was "evil." A lump of poignant tenderness swelled in her throat and she unthinkingly laid her hand against his cheek. "I'm sorry," she whispered achingly.

Jason jerked away from her touch, his brows snapping together over biting green eyes. "You're sorry?" he mocked scathingly. "Sorry for what? Sorry for the men who are still out there, searching for a trace of you?" He turned away as if he couldn't bear her closeness and walked over to the windows. "Sorry for the horse I rode into the ground?"

"I'm sorry you thought I was leaving you," Victoria interrupted shakily. "I would never do that."

He turned back to her, regarding her ironically. "Considering that yesterday you tried to leave me at the altar, and this morning you demanded a divorce, I find your last announcement somewhat astonishing. To what shall I attribute your freakish streak of fidelity this evening?"

Despite his outward attitude of sarcastic indifference, Victoria heard the clipped terseness in his voice when he referred to her leaving him at the altar, and her heart sank. Evidently that had bothered him very much.

"My lord—" she began softly.

"Oh, for God's sake!" he snapped. "Stop calling me your lord and don't grovel. I despise groveling."

"I was not groveling!" Victoria said, and in her mind saw him kneeling beneath a black, uncoiling whip. She had to clear the tears from her throat before she could go on. "What I started to say was that I only tried to take the extra food to the orphanage today. I'm sorry I worried you, and I won't do it again."

He stared at her, the anger draining out of him. "You're free to do whatever you want to do, Victoria," he said wearily. "This marriage was the greatest mistake of my life."

Victoria hesitated, knowing nothing she could say would change his mind when he was in this mood, and finally excused herself to change her gown. He did not have supper with her, and she went to bed that night thinking he would surely join her there—if for no other reason than to hold her to her bargain to give him a son.

Jason did not join her that night, nor for the next three. In fact, he went out of his way to completely avoid her. He worked in his study all day, dictating letters to his secretary, Mr. Benjamin, and meeting with men who came from London to talk to him about investments and shipping and all sorts of unfathomable business transactions. If he encountered Victoria at meals or passed her in the halls, he greeted her politely but without familiarity, as if she were a stranger to him.

When he was finished working, he went upstairs, changed his clothes, and drove off to London.

Since Caroline had gone to the south of England to visit one of her brothers whose wife was soon to give birth, Victoria spent most of her time at the orphanage, organizing games for the children, and paying calls upon the villagers so that they would continue to feel easy in her company. But no matter how busy she kept, she still missed Jason very much. In London, he had spent a good deal of time with her. He had escorted her nearly everywhere she went, to balls and parties and plays, and although he didn't remain by her side, she had known he was there—watchful, protective. She missed his teasing remarks, she even missed his scowl. In the weeks since Andrew's mother's letter had come, Jason had become her friend, and a very special one.

Now he was a civil stranger who might need her, but who was purposely and effectively keeping her at arm's length. She knew he was no longer angry with her; he had simply locked her out of his heart and mind as if she didn't exist.

On the fourth night, Jason went to London again and Victoria lay awake, staring at the rose silk canopy above her bed, stupidly longing to dance with him again as she had done so many times before. Jason was wonderful to dance with; he moved with such natural grace. . . .

She wondered what he did during these long nights in London before he came home. She decided he probably spent his time gambling in the exclusive gentlemen's clubs to which he belonged.

On the fifth night, Jason didn't bother coming home at all. The next morning at breakfast Victoria glanced at the gossipy section of the *Gazette* that reported on the doings of the *haute ton,* and she discovered what Jason had been doing while in London. He had not been gambling or meeting with more businessmen. He had been at Lord Muirfield's ball— dancing with the elderly lord's exquisite, voluptuous wife. It also mentioned that on the prior evening, Lord Fielding had attended the theater and been seen in the company of an unnamed brunette opera dancer. Victoria knew three things about Jason's mistress—her name was Sybil, she was an opera dancer, and she was a brunette.

Jealousy bloomed in Victoria—full-bodied, frustrated, sick jealousy. It caught her completely off guard, for she had never experienced the bitter agony of it before.

Jason chose that untimely moment to stroll into the dining room wearing the same clothes he had left for London in the night before. Except that now his beautifully tailored black evening jacket was carelessly slung over his left shoulder, his neckcloth was untied and hanging loose, and his white lawn shirt was open at the throat. Obviously, he had not spent the night at his own house in London, where he kept a full wardrobe.

He nodded distantly to her as he went over to the sideboard and helped himself to a cup of steaming black coffee.

Victoria slowly arose from her chair, trembling with hurt fury. "Jason," she said, her voice cool and stiff.

He glanced inquiringly over his shoulder at her, then saw her stony features and turned fully around. "Yes?" he said, lifting the cup to his lips and watching her over its rim.

"Do you remember how you felt when your first wife was in London, engaging in all sorts of salacious affairs?"

The coffee cup lowered an inch, but his features remained impassive. "Perfectly," he said.

Amazed and a little impressed with her own bravery, Victoria glanced meaningfully at the paper, then lifted her chin. "Then I hope you won't make me feel that way again."

His gaze flicked to the open paper, then back to her. "As I recall, I didn't particularly care what she did."

"Well, I do care!" Victoria burst out because she couldn't stop herself. "I understand perfectly that considerate husbands have—have paramours, but you are supposed to be discreet. You English have rules for everything and discretion is one of them. When you flaunt your—your lady friends, it's humiliating and it hurts." She strode out of the room, feeling like an undesirable, cast-off shoe.

She looked like a beautiful young queen, with her long hair swaying in molten waves and thick curls at her back, her body moving with unconscious grace. Jason watched her in silence, the coffee cup forgotten in his hand. He felt the familiar, hot need for her rising in his loins, the longing he'd felt for months to gather her into his arms and lose himself in her. But he didn't move toward her. Whatever she felt for him, it was not love or even desire. She thought it was "considerate" of him to keep a mistress discreetly tucked away so he could satisfy his disgusting lust with her, Jason realized bitterly. But Victoria's pride was piqued at the idea of his being seen in public with that same woman.

Her pride was suffering, nothing more. But when he remembered the terrible beating her pride had already received from her beloved Andrew, he discovered he didn't have the heart to hurt her more. He understood about pride; he remembered how shattered and enraged he had felt when he first discovered Melissa's perfidy.

He stopped in his study to retrieve some documents and then walked up the staircase, reading the documents and carrying his jacket.

"Good morning, my lord," his valet said, casting a look of reproof at the abused jacket hooked over his master's thumb.

"Good morning, Franklin," Jason said, handing over the jacket without taking his eyes from the newly arrived documents.

Franklin laid out Jason's shaving mug, razor, and strop, then whisked the jacket to the wardrobe, where he began brushing it. "Is your attire for this evening to be formal or informal, my lord?" he inquired politely.

Jason turned to the second page of the document. "Informal," he said absently. "Lady Fielding thinks I've been spending too much time away from home at night."

He strolled toward the marble bath adjoining his bedchamber, unaware of the expression of pleasure dawning across his valet's face. Franklin watched until Jason had disappeared into the bath, then laid the jacket aside and hastened down the stairs to share the happy news with Northrup.

Until Lady Victoria had burst into the house months ago and disrupted the orderly, disciplined tedium of everyone's lives, Mr. Franklin and Mr. Northrup had jealously guarded their individual positions of trust. In fact, they had scrupulously avoided one another for four long years. Now, however, these two former adversaries were allied in their mutual concern for, and interest in, the well-being of the lord and lady of the house.

Mr. Northrup was in the front hall near the salon, polishing a table. Glancing about to ensure that there were no lesser menials around to overhear, Mr. Franklin hurried forward, eager to impart his news about this latest development in his lordship's tumultuous romance—or more accurately, his *lack* of romance—and to hear in return any news that Mr. Northrup might wish to confide in him. He leaned near his confidant, blissfully unaware of O'Malley, who was in the salon pressing his ear to the wall in order to hear their conversation. "His lordship intends to dine at home this evening, Mr. Northrup," the valet advised in a conspiratorial stage whisper. "I believe that is a good sign. A very good sign indeed."

Northrup straightened, his expression unimpressed. "It is an unusual event, considering his lordship's absences these five nights past, but I do not find it particularly encouraging."

"You don't understand—his lordship specifically said he was staying at home because her ladyship wished for him to do so!"

"Now, that *is* encouraging, Mr. Franklin!" Northrup leaned back, casting a cautious glance around to make certain no one was near enough to overhear, then said, "I believe the reason for her ladyship's request may lie in a particular article in the *Gazette* that she saw this morning, which led her to believe that his lordship was possibly entertaining a certain lady of a certain class—an opera dancer, I believe."

O'Malley pulled his ear from the wall, rushed to the side door of the salon, and sprinted down the back hall that was used by the servants to carry refreshments to the salon from the kitchen. "She's done it!" he crowed triumphantly to the kitchen servants as he burst into the room.

Mrs. Craddock straightened from her task of rolling out pastry dough, so eager to hear what he had to say that she ignored the fact that he snatched an apple from her worktable. "What has she done?"

O'Malley leaned against the wall and helped himself to a large bite of the juicy apple, waving the uneaten portion in the air for emphasis as he spoke. "She gave his lordship what-for, that's what! I heard it all from Franklin and Northrup. Her ladyship read in the paper that his lordship was with Miss Sybil, and her ladyship told Lord Fielding to stay home where he belongs. He's goin' t'do it, too. I told the lot of you the lass could handle the master. Knew it as soon as she told me she was Irish! But she's a true lady, too," he added loyally. "All gentle-like and smiling."

"She's been a sad lady these last days, poor thing," Mrs. Craddock said, still looking a little worried. "She scarcely eats when he isn't here, and I've made all her favorites. She always thanks me so politely, too. It's enough to make a body weep. I can't think why he isn't in her bed at night where she belongs. . . ."

O'Malley shook his head glumly. "He hasn't been there since their weddin' night. Ruth says she's certain-sure of it. And her ladyship ain't sleeping in *his* bed neither, because the upstairs maids are keeping an eye on his chambers, and there's never more than one pillow on his bed with a crease in it." In morose silence, he finished his apple and reached for another, but this time Mrs. Craddock whacked his hand with her towel. "Snop snitching my apples, Daniel, they're for a pie I'm makin' for dessert." A sudden smile flickered across her kindly features. "No, go ahead and take the apples. I've decided to make something else for them tonight. Something more festive than a pie."

The youngest scullery maid, a homely, buxom girl of about sixteen, piped up, "One of the laundry maids was tellin' me about a certain powder you can put in a man's wine that gets him into the mood for having a woman, if his manhood's what's causin' the problem. The laundry maids all think mebbe his lordship ought to have a little speck o' that powder—just to help things along."

The kitchen servants all murmured agreement, but O'Malley exclaimed derisively, "Lord, girl! Where do you get such ideas? His lordship don't need them powders, and you can tell everyone in the laundry I said so! Why, John coachman's nose runs year-round from a permanent chill he got while spendin' nearly every night last winter waitin' atop the coach, out in the elements, for his lordship to leave Miss

Hawthorne's bed. Miss Hawthorne," he finished informatively, "was his ladybird afore Miss Sybil."

"Was he with Miss Sybil last night?" Mrs. Craddock asked, already measuring out flour for her "festive" dessert. "Or was that just newspaper talk?"

O'Malley's cheerful face sobered. "He was there, right enough. I heerd it from one of the grooms. Course, we don't know fer shure that anythin' happened whilst he was there. Mebbe he was payin' her off."

Mrs. Craddock sent him a weak, unconvinced smile. "Well, at least he's stayin' home for supper with his wife tonight. That's a good start."

O'Malley nodded agreement and headed off to share his latest news with the groom who'd provided him with the master's exact whereabouts last night.

Which was why, of the 140 people at Wakefield Park, only Victoria was surprised when Jason strolled into the dining room that night to join her for supper.

"You're staying home tonight?" she burst out in amazed relief as he sat down at the head of the table.

He sent her a measuring look. "I was under the distinct impression that was what you wanted me to do."

"Well, I did," Victoria admitted, wondering if she looked her best in the emerald green gown she was wearing and wishing he wasn't so far away from her at the opposite end of the long table. "Only I didn't really expect you to do it. That is—" She broke off as O'Malley turned from the sideboard, carrying a tray with two sparkling crystal glasses filled with wine. It was nearly impossible to carry on a conversation with Jason so far away, both emotionally and physically.

She sighed as O'Malley headed straight toward her, an odd, determined gleam in his eye. "Your wine, my lady," he said and swept a glass from the tray, plunking it on the table with a queer, exaggerated flourish that inevitably tipped the glass and spilled wine all over the linen tablecloth in front of her place.

"O'Malley—!" Northrup bit out from his station near the sideboard where he routinely supervised the serving of meals.

293

O'Malley sent him a look of ignorant innocence and made a great fuss of pulling back Lady Victoria's chair, helping her to stand, and guiding her down to Jason's end of the table. "There now, my lady," he said, positively emanating anxious contrition as he pulled out the chair on Jason's immediate right. "I'll have more wine for ye in a trice. Then I'll clean up that mess down there. Smells awful, it does, spilled wine. Best to stay far away from it. Can't think how I came to spill yer wine thataway," he added, whisking up a linen napkin and placing it across Victoria's lap. "Me arm's been painin' me of late and that's prob'ly what did it. Nothin' serious fer ye to worry 'bout—just an old bone what was broken years ago."

Victoria straightened her skirts and looked at him with a sympathetic smile. "I'm sorry your arm pains you, Mr. O'Malley."

O'Malley then turned to Lord Fielding, intending to utter more false excuses, but his mouth went dry when he met Jason's piercing, relentless gaze and saw him rubbing his finger meaningfully along the edge of his knife as if he were testing its sharpness.

O'Malley ran his forefinger between his collar and neck, cleared his throat, and hastily mumbled to Victoria, "I-I'll get yer ladyship another glass of wine."

"Lady Fielding doesn't drink wine with dinner," Jason drawled, stopping him in his tracks. He glanced at her as an afterthought. "Or have you changed your habits, Victoria?"

Victoria shook her head, puzzled by the unspoken communication that seemed to be flying back and forth between Jason and poor O'Malley. "But I think I'd like some tonight," she added, trying to soothe over a situation she didn't understand.

The servants withdrew, leaving them to dine in the oppressive splendor of the ninety-foot-long dining room. Heavy silence hung over the entire meal, punctuated only by the occasional clink of gold flatware against Limoges porcelain as they ate—a silence that was made more awful for Victoria because she was acutely aware of the dazzling gaiety that would be surrounding Jason right now if he'd gone to London, rather than remaining here with her.

By the time the plates were being cleared away and dessert brought in, her misery had turned to desperation. Twice she had tried to break through the barrier of silence by commenting on such nonabrasive topics as the weather and the excellence of their ten-course meal. Jason's replies to these conversational gambits were polite but unencouragingly brief.

Victoria fidgeted with her spoon, knowing she had to do something, and quickly, because the gap between them was widening with every moment, growing deeper with every day, until soon there would be no way to bridge it.

Her dismal anxiety was temporarily forgotten when O'Malley marched in with dessert and, with an ill-concealed smile, set before them a small, beautiful cake, decorated with two intertwined, colorful flags—one British, the other bearing the stars and stripes of America.

Jason glanced at the cake and lifted his sardonic gaze to the meddlesome footman. "Am I to assume Mrs. Craddock was in a patriotic mood today?" O'Malley's face fell, his eyes taking on a wary look as his master regarded him with cold displeasure. "Or is this supposed to remind me, symbolically, that I'm married?"

The footman blanched. "Never, milord." He waited, impaled on Jason's gaze, until Jason finally dismissed him with a curt nod.

"If this was supposed to represent our marriage," Victoria said with unintentional humor, "Mrs. Craddock should have decorated the cake with two crossed swords, not two flags."

"You're right," Jason agreed blandly, ignoring the beautiful little cake and reaching for his wineglass.

He sounded so infuriatingly uninterested in the terrible state of their marriage that Victoria panicked and plunged into the topic she'd been trying to bring up all evening. "I don't want to be right!" She dragged her gaze to his unreadable face. "Jason, please—I want things to be different between us."

He looked mildly surprised as he leaned back in his chair and studied her impassively. "Exactly what sort of arrangement do you have in mind?"

His manner was so distant and unconcerned that Victoria's nervousness doubled. "Well, I'd like us to be friends, for one thing. We used to laugh together and talk about things."

"Talk away," he invited.

"Is there anything in particular you'd like to talk about?" she asked earnestly.

Jason's eyes moved over her intoxicating features. He thought, *I want to talk about why you need to drink yourself into oblivion before you can face going to bed with me. I want to talk about why my touch makes you sick.* He said, "Nothing in particular."

"Very well, then, I'll start." She hesitated, and then said, "How do you like my gown? It is one you had Madame Dumosse make for me."

Jason's gaze dropped to the creamy flesh swelling invitingly above the low green bodice of the gown. She looked ravishing in green, he thought, but she should have had emeralds to wear around her slim throat to complement the gown. If things were different, he would have dismissed the servants and pulled her onto his lap, and then he would have unfastened the back of her gown, exposing her intoxicating breasts to his lips and hands. He would have kissed each one, then carried her upstairs and made love to her until they were both too weak to move. "The gown is fine. It needs emeralds," he said.

Victoria's hand flew self-consciously to her bare throat. She did not have any emeralds. "I think you look very nice, too," she said, admiring the way his expensively tailored dark blue jacket clung to his splendid shoulders. His face was so tanned, his hair so dark, that his white shirt and neckcloth stood out in dazzling contrast. "You're very handsome," she said wistfully.

A glimmer of a startled smile appeared at his lips. "Thank you," he said, visibly taken aback.

"You're welcome," Victoria replied and, because she thought he seemed pleased by her compliment to his looks, she seized on that as an acceptable topic of conversation. "When I first saw you, I thought you were frightening-looking, did you know that? Of course, it was nearly dark and I was nervous, but—well—you're so huge that it was frightening."

Jason choked on his wine. "To what are you referring?"

"To our first meeting," Victoria clarified innocently. "Remember—I was outside in the sunlight, holding that piglet, which I gave to the farmer, and then you dragged me inside the house and it was dark compared to outdoors—"

Jason stood up abruptly. "I'm sorry I treated you uncivilly. Now, if you don't mind, I think I'll spend the evening doing some work."

"No," Victoria said hastily, also standing up, "please don't work. Let's do something else—something we can do together. Something you'd like."

Jason's heart slammed into his ribs. He gazed down at her flushed cheeks and saw the invitation in her imploring blue eyes. Hope and disbelief collided in his chest, exploding, as he laid his hand tenderly against her flushed cheek, slowly running it back, smoothing her heavy silken hair.

Victoria trembled with pleasure because he was finally treating her with warmth. She should have tried to draw him out days ago, rather than suffering in silence. "We could play chess if you like," she said happily. "I'm not very good at it, but if you have cards—"

His hand jerked away from her, and his face became a closed mask. "Excuse me, Victoria. I have work to do." He moved around her and disappeared into his study, where he remained for the rest of the evening.

Victoria's heart sank with bewildered disappointment, and she spent the evening trying to read. By bedtime, she was absolutely resolved not to let him fall back into their former pattern of being polite strangers, no matter what it took to change things. She remembered the way he had looked at her just before she suggested playing chess—it was the same way he looked at her before he kissed her. Her body had recognized it instantly, turning warm and shaky in that unexplainable way it always did when Jason touched her. He may have wanted to kiss her, rather than play chess. Dear God, he may have wanted to do that awful thing to her again—

Victoria shuddered at the thought, but she was willing to do even that if harmony could be restored. Her stomach turned over at the thought of Jason fondling her when she was naked, studying her body in that awful, detached way as

297

he'd done on their wedding night. Perhaps it wouldn't have been so terrible if he'd been nice to her while he did it—nice in the way he was when he kissed her.

She waited in her room until she heard Jason moving about in his, then put on a turquoise satin dressing robe trimmed with wide strips of beige lace at the hem and full sleeves. She opened the connecting door to Jason's suite, which had been rehung—minus its lock—and walked in. "My lor—Jason," she said abruptly.

He was shrugging out of his shirt, his chest almost completely exposed, and his head snapped up.

"I'd like to talk to you," she began firmly.

"Get out of here, Victoria," he said with icy annoyance.

"But—"

"I do not want to talk," he bit out sarcastically. "I do not want to play chess. I do not want to play cards."

"Then what *do* you want?"

"I want you out of here. Is that clear enough?"

"I'd say it's very clear," she replied with unbending dignity. "I won't bother you again." She walked back into her room and closed the door, but she was still angrily determined to make her marriage happy and solid. She didn't understand what he expected from her. Most particularly she did not understand *him*. But she knew someone who did. Jason was thirty, much older and more worldly than she, but Captain Farrell was older than Jason, and he would be able to advise her about what to do next.

Chapter Twenty-five

Victoria walked determinedly down to the stables the next morning and waited while a horse was saddled for her. Her new black riding habit was beautifully cut, with a tight, fitted jacket that accentuated her full breasts and tiny waist. The snowy white stock of her shirt set off her vivid coloring and high cheekbones, and her titian hair was caught up at the nape in an elegant chignon. The chignon made her feel older and more sophisticated; it bolstered her flagging confidence.

She waited at the stables, idly tapping her riding crop against her leg; then she smiled brightly at the groom who led out a prancing gelding, its ebony coat shimmering like satin.

Victoria gazed in admiring wonder at the magnificent horse. "He's beautiful, John. What's his name?"

"This here's Matador," the groom said. "He's from Spain. His lordship picked him for you to ride until your new horse gets here in a few weeks."

Jason had bought her a horse, Victoria realized as the groom gave her a leg up into the saddle. She couldn't imagine why Jason had felt the need to buy another horse for her when his stable reportedly housed the finest horseflesh in England; still, it was a generous thing for him to do, and perfectly typical of the man not to bother mentioning it.

She slowed Matador to a walk as they turned up the steep, winding lane that led to Captain Farrell's house and breathed a sigh of relief when the Captain stepped out onto the porch to help her down from the sidesaddle. "Thank you," she said when her feet were safely on the ground. "I was hoping you'd be here."

Captain Farrell grinned at her. "I intended to ride over to Wakefield today, to see for myself how you and Jason were coming along."

"In that case," Victoria said with a sad smile, "it's just as well you didn't put yourself to the trouble."

"No improvement?" he said in surprise, ushering her into his house. He filled a kettle with water for tea and put it over the fire.

Victoria sat down and morosely shook her head. "If anything, things are worse. Well, not worse, exactly. At least Jason stayed home last night instead of going to London and visiting his, er . . . well, you know what I mean," she said. She hadn't planned on such an intimate topic. She only wanted to discuss Jason's mood, not their most personal relationship.

Captain Farrell took two cups from a shelf and glanced over his shoulder, his expression perplexed. "No, I don't. What do you mean?"

Victoria gave him an acutely uneasy look.

"Out with it, child. I confided in you. You must know you can confide in me. Who else can you talk to?"

"No one," Victoria said miserably.

"If what you're trying to say is as difficult as that, suppose you think of me as your father—or Jason's father."

"You aren't either one. And I'm not certain I could tell my own father what you're asking."

Captain Farrell put the teacups down and turned slowly, watching her across the room. "Do you know the only thing I dislike about the sea?" When she shook her head, he said, "The solitude of my cabin. Sometimes I enjoy it. But when I'm worried about something—like a bad storm I can feel brewing—there's no one I can confide my fears to. I can't let my men know I'm afraid or they'll panic. And so I have to keep it bottled up inside of me, where the fear grows all out of proportion. Sometimes I'd be out there and I'd get a feeling my wife was ill or in peril, and the feeling would haunt me because there was no one there to reassure me that I was being foolish. If you can't talk to Jason and you won't talk to me, then you'll never find the answers you're looking for."

Victoria gazed at him with affection. "You are one of the kindest men I've ever known, Captain."

"Then why don't you just imagine I'm your father and talk to me in that way?"

Many people, including women, had confided all sorts of things to Dr. Seaton with very little embarrassment and no shame, Victoria knew. And if she was ever going to understand Jason, she had to talk to Captain Farrell.

"Very well," she said, and was relieved when he was thoughtful enough to turn his back and busy himself with the preparations for tea. It was easier to talk to his back. "Actually, I came here to ask you if you were certain you told me everything you knew about Jason. But to answer your question, Jason stayed home last night for the first time since I last saw you. He's been going to London, you see, to visit his . . . ah . . ." She drew a long breath and said firmly, "His paramour."

Captain Farrell's back stiffened, but he did not turn around. "What makes you think a thing like that?" he said, slowly taking down a bowl of sugar.

"Oh, I'm certain of it. The papers hinted at it yesterday morning. Jason was gone all night, but when he returned I was at breakfast and I'd just read the paper. I was upset—"

"I can imagine."

"And I nearly lost my temper, but I tried to be reasonable. I told him I realized that considerate husbands kept mistresses, but that I thought he ought to be discreet and—"

Captain Farrell lurched around, gaping at her with a bowl of sugar in one hand and a pitcher of milk in the other. "You told him that you thought it was *considerate* of him to keep a mistress, but that he ought to be *discreet?*"

"Yes. Shouldn't I have said that?"

"More importantly, *why* did you say it? Why did you even *think* it?"

Victoria heard the criticism in his voice and stiffened slightly. "Miss Wilson—Flossie Wilson explained that in England it is the custom for considerate husbands to have—"

"Flossie Wilson?" he burst out in appalled disbelief. "Flossie Wilson?" he repeated as if he couldn't believe his ears. "Flossie Wilson is a spinster, not to mention a complete henwit! An utter peagoose! Jason used to keep her at Wakefield to help look after Jamie so that when he was away, Jamie would have a loving female with him. Flossie was loving, all right, but the ninnyhammer actually misplaced the baby one day. You asked a woman like *that* for advice on keeping a husband?"

"I didn't *ask* her, she offered the information," Victoria replied defensively, flushing.

"I'm sorry for shouting at you, child," he said, rubbing the back of his neck. "In Ireland a wife takes a skillet to her husband's head if he goes to another woman! It's much simpler, more direct, and far more effective, I'm sure. Please go on with what you were trying to tell me. You said you confronted Jason—"

"I'd really rather not continue," Victoria said warily. "I don't think I should have come. Actually, it was a dreadful idea. I only hoped you could explain to me why Jason has become so distant since our wedding—"

"What," Captain Farrell said tensely, "do you mean by 'distant'?"

"I don't know how to explain it."

He poured tea into two cups and picked them up. "Victoria," he said, frowning as he turned, "are you trying to tell me he doesn't come to your bed very often?"

Victoria blushed and stared at her hands. "Actually, he hasn't been there since our wedding night—although I greatly feared that, after he broke the door down the next morning when I locked it—"

Without a word, Captain Farrell turned back to the cupboard, put down the teacups, and filled two glasses with whiskey.

He walked over and thrust one at her. "Drink this," he

ordered firmly. "It will make it easier to talk, and I intend to hear the rest of this tale."

"Do you know, before I came to England I'd never tasted spirits of any kind, except wine after my parents died," she said, shuddering at the contents of the glass and then looking at him as he sat down. "But ever since I came here, people have been giving me wine and brandy and champagne and telling me to drink it because I'll feel better. It doesn't make me feel better in the least."

"Try it," he ordered.

"I did try it. You see, I was so nervous the day we got married that I tried to pull away from Jason at the altar. So when we arrived at Wakefield, I thought some wine might help me face the rest of the night. I drank five glasses at our wedding celebration, but all it did was make me sick when we—I went to bed that night."

"Am I to understand that you nearly left Jason at the altar in front of a churchful of his acquaintances?"

"Yes, but they didn't realize it. Jason did, though."

"Good God," he whispered.

"And on our wedding night I nearly threw up."

"Good God," he whispered again. "And the next morning you locked Jason out of your room?"

Victoria nodded, feeling miserable.

"And then you told him yesterday that you thought it was *considerate* of him to go to his mistress?" When Victoria nodded again, Captain Farrell stared at her in mute fascination.

"I did try to make up for it last night," she informed him defensively.

"I'm relieved to hear that."

"Yes, I offered to do anything he would like."

"That should have improved his disposition immensely," Captain Farrell predicted with a faint smile.

"Well, for a moment it seemed to. But when I said we could play chess or cards, he became—"

"You suggested he play *chess*? For God's sake, why chess?"

Victoria looked at him in quiet hurt. "I tried to think of the things my mother and father used to do together. I would have suggested a walk, but it was a little chilly."

303

Visibly torn between laughter and distress, Captain Farrell shook his head. "Poor Jason," he said in a laughing underbreath. When he looked at her again, though, he was in deadly earnest. "I can assure you that your parents did . . . er . . . other things."

"Such as what?" Victoria said, thinking of the nights her parents had sat across from each other before the fire, reading books. Her mother cooked her father's favorite dishes for him, too, and she kept his house neat and his clothes mended, but Jason had an army of people to perform those wifely tasks for him, and they did it to perfection. She glanced at Captain Farrell, who had lapsed into uneasy silence. "What sort of things are you referring to?"

"I'm referring to the sort of intimate things your parents did when you were in your own bed," he said bluntly, "and they were in theirs."

A long-ago memory paraded across her mind—a memory of her parents standing outside her mother's bedroom door, and her father's pleading voice as he tried to hold his wife in his arms—*"Don't keep denying me, Katherine. For God's sake, don't!"*

Her mother had been denying her father her bed, Victoria realized weakly. And then she remembered how hurt and desperate her father had seemed that night and how furious she had been with her mother for hurting him. Her parents were friends, true enough, but her mother did not love her father. Katherine had loved Charles Fielding, and because she did, she had barred her husband from her bed after Dorothy was born.

Victoria bit her lip, remembering how lonely her father had often seemed. She wondered if all men felt lonely—or perhaps what they felt was rejected—if their wives refused them their bed.

Her mother had not loved her father, she knew, but they had been friends. Friends . . . She was trying to make Jason into her friend, she realized suddenly, exactly as she'd seen her mother do to her father.

"You're a warm woman, Victoria, full of life and courage. Forget about the sorts of marriages you've seen amongst the *ton*—they're empty and unsatisfying and superficial. Think about your parents' marriage instead. They were happy, weren't they?"

Her prolonged silence made Captain Farrell frown and abruptly change his tack. "Never mind about your parents' marriage. I know about men, and I know Jason, so I want you to remember one thing. If a woman locks her husband out of her bedroom, he will lock her out of his heart. At least he will if he has any pride. And Jason has a great deal of it. He won't grovel at your feet or beg you for your favors. You've withheld yourself from him; now it's up to you to make certain he understands you don't wish to do so any longer."

"How am I supposed to do that?"

"Not," he said succinctly, "by suggesting that he play chess. And not by thinking it's considerate of him to go to another woman, either." Captain Farrell rubbed the muscles at the back of his neck. "I never realized how difficult it must be for a man to raise a daughter. There are some things that are very hard to discuss with the opposite sex."

Victoria stood up restlessly. "I'll think about everything you said," she promised, trying to hide her embarrassment.

"May I ask you something," he said hesitantly.

"I suppose it's only fair," Victoria said with a winsome smile, hiding her dread. "After all, I've asked you a great deal."

"Didn't anyone ever talk about married love with you?"

"It isn't the sort of thing one discusses with anyone except one's mother," Victoria said, flushing again. "One hears about one's marital duty, of course, but somehow you don't really understand—"

"Duty!" he said in disgust. "In my country, a lass is eager for her wedding night. Go home and seduce your husband, my girl, and he'll take care of the rest. You won't look upon it as a duty after that. I know Jason well enough to assure you of that fact!"

"And if I—I do what you say, then will he be happy with me?"

"Yes," Captain Farrell said gently, smiling. "And he'll make *you* happy in return."

Victoria put down her untouched glass of whiskey. "I

know little about marriage, less about being a wife, and absolutely nothing about seduction."

Captain Farrell looked at the exotic young beauty standing before him, and his shoulders shook with silent laughter. "I don't think you'll have to try very hard to seduce Jason, my dear. As soon as he realizes you want him in your bed, I feel certain he'll be more than happy to oblige."

Victoria turned pink as roses, smiled weakly, and headed for the door.

She rode home on Matador, so lost in thought that she was scarcely aware of the magnificent gelding's progress. By the time she galloped to a stop in front of Wakefield Park, she was certain of at least one thing: she did not want Jason to have a marriage that left him as lonely as her father had been.

Submitting to Jason in bed would not be such a terrible thing, especially if—at other times—he might kiss her again in that bold, intimate way of his, pressing his mouth to hers and doing those shocking things with his tongue that made her senses swim and her body hot and weak. Instead of thinking of new gowns, as Miss Flossie had suggested, when Jason was in her bed, she would think of the way he used to kiss her. Having come that far, she even admitted to herself that she had loved his kisses. A pity men didn't do that sort of thing when they were in bed, she thought. It would have made the whole thing so much nicer. Evidently, kissing was done when one was out of bed, but in bed, men did what they'd had in mind all along.

"I don't care!" Victoria said with great determination as a groom ran out and helped her alight. She was resolved to endure anything to make Jason happy and restore their former closeness. According to Captain Farrell, all she had to do now was hint to Jason that she wanted to share her bed with him.

She went into the house. "Is Lord Fielding at home?" she asked Northrup.

"Yes, my lady," he said, bowing. "He is in his study."

"Is he alone?"

"Yes, my lady." Northrup bowed again.

Victoria thanked him and went down the hall. She opened

the door to the study and quietly slipped inside. Jason was seated at his desk at the opposite end of the long room, his profile turned to her, a sheaf of papers at his elbow, another in his hand. Victoria looked at him, at the little boy who had risen from his squalid childhood and grown into a handsome, wealthy, powerful man. He had amassed a fortune and bought estates, forgiven his father, and housed an orphan from America. And he was still alone. Still working, still trying.

"I love you," she thought, and the unbidden thought nearly sent her to her knees. She had loved Andrew forever. But if that was true, why hadn't she ever felt this driving desperation to make Andrew happy? She loved Jason, despite her father's warning, despite Jason's own warning that he didn't want her love, only her body. How odd that Jason should have the very thing he didn't want, and not what he did. How determined she was to make him want both.

She crossed the room, her footsteps silenced by the thick Aubusson carpet, and went to stand behind his chair. "Why do you work so hard?" she asked softly.

He jumped at the sound of her voice but did not turn around. "I enjoy working," he said shortly. "Is there something you want? I'm very busy."

It was not an encouraging beginning, and for a split second Victoria actually considered saying, very bluntly, that she wanted him to take her to bed. But the truth was that she was not that bold, and not that eager to actually go upstairs either—particularly when he was in a mood that was even colder than the mood he'd been in on their wedding day. Hoping to improve his spirits, she said softly, "You must get horrid backaches, sitting all day like this." She summoned all her courage and put her hands on his wide shoulders, intending to knead them with her fingers.

Jason's whole body stiffened the instant she touched him. "What are you doing?" he demanded.

"I thought I would rub your shoulders."

"My shoulders are not in need of your tender ministrations, Victoria."

"Why are you snapping at me?" she asked, and went around to the front of his desk, watching his hand as it moved swiftly across the page, his handwriting bold and firm. When he ignored her, she perched on the side of his desk.

Jason threw down his quill in disgust and leaned back in his chair, studying her. Her leg was beside his hand, swinging slightly as she read what he had been writing. Against his volition, his eyes moved upward over her breasts, riveting on the inviting curve of her lips. She had a mouth that begged to be kissed, and her eyelashes were so long they cast shadows on her cheeks. "Get off my desk and get out of here," he snapped.

"As you wish," his wife said cheerfully, and stood up. "I just came in to say good-day. What would you like for dinner?"

You, he thought. "It doesn't matter," he said.

"In that case, is there anything special you'd like for dessert?"

The same thing I'd like for dinner, he thought. "No," he said, fighting down the instantaneous, clamoring demands of his body.

"You're awfully easy to please," she said teasingly, and reached out to trace the line of his straight eyebrows.

Jason seized her hand in midair and held it away, his grip like iron. "What the hell do you think you're doing?" he bit out.

Victoria quailed inwardly, but she managed a light shrug. "There are always doors between us. I thought I'd open your study door and see what you were doing."

"There is more separating us than doors," he retorted, dropping her hand.

"I know," she agreed sadly, looking down at him with melting blue eyes.

Jason jerked his gaze from hers. "I am very busy," he said curtly, and picked up his papers.

"I can see that," she said with an odd softness in her voice. "Much too busy for me right now." She left quietly.

At suppertime she walked into the drawing room wearing a peach chiffon gown that clung to every curve and hollow of her voluptuous body and was nearly transparent. Jason's eyes narrowed to slits. "Did I pay for that?"

Victoria saw his gaze rivet on the daringly low vee of the

chiffon bodice, and smiled. "Of course you did. I don't have any money."

"Don't wear it out of the house. It's indecent."

"I knew you'd like it!" she said with a chuckle, sensing instinctively that he liked it very much or his eyes wouldn't have flared like that.

Jason looked at her as if he couldn't believe his ears, then turned to the crystal decanters on the table. "Would you like some sherry?"

"Lord, no!" she said and laughed. "As you must already have guessed, wine does not agree with me. It makes me ill. It always has. Look what happened when I drank it on our wedding day." Unaware of the importance of what she had just said, Victoria turned to examine a priceless Ming Dynasty vase reposing on a gilt table inlaid with marble, her mind turning over an idea. She decided to do it. "I'd like to go to London tomorrow," she said, walking toward him.

"Why?"

She perched on the arm of the chair he had just sat in. "To spend your money, of course."

"I wasn't aware I'd given you any," he murmured, distracted by the sight of her thigh beside his chest. In the romantic candlelight, the sheer chiffon appeared to be translucent and flesh-colored.

"I still have most of the money you've been giving me as an allowance all these weeks. Will you go to London with me? After I shop, we could see a play and stay at the townhouse."

"I have a meeting here, the morning after next."

"That's even better," she said without thinking. Alone for several hours in the coach, there would be ample time for lazy conversation. "We'll come home together tomorrow night."

"I can't spare the time," he said shortly.

"Jason—" she said softly, reaching out to touch his crisp dark hair.

He shot up out of the chair, looming over her, his voice ringing with contempt. "If you need money to use in London, say so! But stop acting like a cheap strumpet or I'll treat you like one, and you'll end up on that sofa with your skirts tossed over your head."

Victoria stared at him in humiliated fury. "For your information I would rather be a cheap strumpet than a complete, blind fool like you, who mistakes every gesture someone makes and leaps to all the wrong conclusions!"

Jason glared at her. "Just exactly what is that supposed to mean?"

Victoria almost stamped her foot in frustrated wrath. "You figure it out! You're very good at figuring me out, except you're always *wrong!* But I'll tell you this—if I were a strumpet, I'd starve to death if things were left up to you! Furthermore, you can dine alone tonight and make the servants miserable instead of me. Tomorrow I am going to London without you." With that, Victoria swept out of the room, leaving Jason staring after her, his brows drawn together in bafflement.

Victoria stormed up to her room, flung off the sheer chiffon dress, and put on a satin robe. She sat down at her dressing table and, as her ire cooled, a wry smile touched the generous curve of her lips. The look of amazement on Jason's face when she told him she would starve to death if she was a strumpet and things were left up to him had been almost comical.

Chapter Twenty-six

◁◦▷

VICTORIA LEFT FOR LONDON VERY EARLY THE NEXT morning and started back to Wakefield at dusk. Cradled lovingly in her hands was the object she'd seen in a shop when she first came to the city weeks ago. It had reminded her of Jason then, but it had looked terribly expensive, and besides, it wouldn't have been proper to buy him a gift at that time. The memory of it had lingered in her mind all these weeks, nagging at her, until she was afraid to wait any longer and risk having it sold to someone else.

She had no idea when she would give it to him; certainly not now, when things were so hostile between them—but soon. She shuddered at the recollection of its price. Jason had given her an outrageously huge allowance, which she had scarcely touched, but the gift had cost every shilling of it, plus a good deal more, which the proprietor of the exclusive little shop was more than happy to put on the account that he eagerly opened in the name of the Marchioness of Wakefield.

"His lordship is in his study," Northrup advised Victoria as he opened the front door.

"Does he want to see me?" Victoria asked, puzzled by

Northrup's quick, unsolicited information on Jason's where-abouts.

"I don't know, my lady," Northrup replied uncomfortably. "But he has . . . er . . . been inquiring whether you were home yet."

Victoria looked at Northrup's harassed expression and remembered Jason's anxiety when she had disappeared for an afternoon to Captain Farrell's. Since her trip to London had taken twice as long as it would have had she remembered the exact location of the shop, she assumed that Northrup had been called up on the firing line again by Jason.

"How many times has he inquired?" she asked.

"Three," Northrup replied. "In the last hour."

"I see," Victoria said with an understanding smile, but she felt absurdly pleased to know Jason had thought about her.

After allowing Northrup to divest her of her pelisse, she went to Jason's study. Unable to knock with the gift in her hands, she turned the handle and put her shoulder gently to the door. Instead of working at his desk where she expected him to be, Jason was standing at the window, his shoulder propped against the frame, his expression bleak as he gazed out across the terraced lawns at the side of the house. He glanced around at the first sound of her approach and instantly straightened.

"You're back," he said, shoving his hands into his pockets.

"Didn't you think I would be?" Victoria asked, scanning his features.

He shrugged wearily. "Frankly, I have no idea what you're going to do from one moment to the next."

Considering her actions of late, Victoria could understand why he must think her the most impulsive, unpredictable female alive. Yesterday alone she had treated him flirtatiously, tenderly, and then furiously walked out on him in the drawing room. And now she had an insane urge to put her arms around him and ask him to forgive her. Rather than do that and risk another cutting rejection like the last, she quelled the urge and instead reversed her earlier decision and decided to give him the gift now. "There was something I had to buy in London," she said brightly, showing him the wrapped package in her hands. "I saw it weeks ago, only I didn't have enough money."

"You should have asked me for it," he said, already heading toward his desk with the obvious intention of burying himself in work again.

Victoria shook her head. "I couldn't very well ask you for money when the thing I wished to buy was for you. Here," she said, holding out her hands. "It's for you."

Jason stopped in his tracks and looked at the oblong object wrapped in silver paper. "What?" he said blankly, as if she had spoken words he didn't understand.

"The reason I went to London was to buy this for you," Victoria explained, her smile quizzical as she held the heavy package closer to him.

He stared at the gift in confusion, his hands still in his pockets. With a sudden wrench of her heart, Victoria wondered if he had ever been given a gift before. Neither his first wife nor his mistresses were likely to have done so. And it was a foregone conclusion that the cruel woman who raised him hadn't.

The compulsion to wrap her arms around him was almost uncontrollable as Jason finally pulled his hands from his pockets. He took the gift and turned it in his hands, looking at it as if uncertain what to do with it next. Hiding her throbbing tenderness behind a bright smile, Victoria perched on the edge of the desk and said, "Aren't you going to open it?"

"What?" he said blankly. Recovering his composure, he said, "Do you want me to open it now?"

"What better time could there be?" Victoria asked gaily, and patted the spot on his desk beside her hip. "You can set it here while you open it, but be careful—it's fragile."

"It's heavy," he agreed, shooting her a quick, uncertain smile as he carefully untied the slender cord and removed the silver paper. He took the cover off the large leather box and reached into the velvet-lined interior.

"It reminded me of you," Victoria said, smiling as he gingerly removed an exquisitely carved panther made of solid onyx, its eyes a pair of glittering emeralds. As if a living cat had been captured by magic while running, and then magically transformed into onyx, there was vibrant motion in every sleek line of its smooth body, power and grace in its flanks, danger and intelligence in its fathomless green eyes.

Jason, whose collection of paintings and rare artifacts was said to be one of the finest in Europe, examined the panther with a reverence that nearly brought tears to Victoria's eyes as she watched him. It was a lovely piece, she knew, but he was treating it as if it were a priceless treasure.

"He's very fine," Jason said softly, running his thumb along the panther's back. With infinite care, he put the animal down on his desk and turned to Victoria. "I don't know what to say," he admitted with a lopsided grin.

Victoria looked up at his ruggedly chiseled face with its boyish smile and she thought he had never looked so endearingly handsome. Feeling incredibly lighthearted herself, she said, "You don't have to say a thing—except 'thank you,' if you want to say that."

"Thank you," he said in an odd, hoarse voice.

Thank me with a kiss. The thought leapt from nowhere into Victoria's mind and the words flew out of her mouth before she could stop them. "Thank me with a kiss," she reminded him with a gay smile.

Jason drew a long, unsteady breath as if he was bracing himself for something difficult; then he flattened his hands on the desk on either side of her and leaned down. He touched his lips to hers, and the sweetness of his touch was almost past bearing. Victoria's head tipped back under the brief pressure of his mouth, upsetting her balance, and, as Jason lifted his head to draw away, she clutched at his arms for leverage. To Jason, having her hands on his arms, holding him in his bent position, was like inviting a starving man to a banquet. His mouth swooped down on hers, moving with tender fierceness, and when she began kissing him back, his kiss became more insistent. He parted her lips with his tongue, teasing her, urging her to respond.

Timidly, her tongue touched his, and Jason lost control. He groaned and wrapped his arms around her, lifting her from the desk and pulling her body tight against his. He felt her hands slide up his chest and curve eagerly around his neck, holding his face to hers, and the encouragement he sensed in her gesture ignited a blaze of passion in him that nearly obliterated his reason. Against his will, his hand slid from her back to her midriff, then moved upward, cupping the intoxicating ripeness of her full breast. Victoria trembled at the intimacy of his touch, but instead of pulling away, as Jason expected her to do, she fitted her body tightly against his rigid arousal, as lost in the passionate kiss as he was.

Captain Farrell's cheerful voice sounded in the hallway, just outside the study: "Don't bother, Northrup, I know the way." The door to the study was flung open and Victoria jerked free of Jason's embrace. "Jason, I—" Captain Farrell began as he strode into the study. He stopped short, an apologetic grin on his face as his gaze took in Victoria's pink cheeks and Jason's dark frown. "I should have knocked."

"We're finished," Jason said dryly.

Unable to meet her friend's eyes, Victoria sent a fleeting smile in Jason's direction and mumbled something about going upstairs to change her clothes for supper.

Captain Farrell put out his hand. "How are you, Jason?"

"I'm not certain," Jason replied absently, watching Victoria leave.

Mike Farrell's lips twitched with laughter, but his amusement faded to concern as Jason turned away and walked slowly over to the windows. As if he was incredibly weary, Jason ran his hand across the back of his neck massaging the tense muscles as he stood staring out across the lawns.

"Is anything wrong?"

Jason's answer was a grim laugh. "Nothing is wrong, Mike. Nothing I don't deserve. And nothing I can't take care of."

When Mike left an hour later, Jason leaned back in his chair and closed his eyes. The desire Victoria had ignited in him was still eating at him like fire licking at his belly. He wanted her so badly that he ached with it. He wanted her so badly he had to grit his teeth and fight against the urge to bound up the stairs and take her right now. He felt like strangling her for telling him to be a "considerate" husband and keep a mistress.

His child-bride was twisting him into knots. She had wanted to play chess and cards with him; now she was trying her hand at a more titillating game—teasing him. Victoria had become a tease, and she was superbly, instinctively effective. She sat on his desk, she sat on the arm of his chair,

she brought him a present, she asked him for a kiss. Brutally
he wondered if she had pretended he was Andrew when he
was kissing her a few minutes ago, as she had pretended he
was Andrew when they got married.

Disgusted with his body's relentless craving for her, he
surged to his feet and walked swiftly up the wide, winding
staircase. He had known he was marrying another man's
woman—only he hadn't expected it to bother him so much.
Pride alone prevented him from forcing her to go to bed with
him again. Pride, and the knowledge that, when it was over,
he would feel no more satisfaction than he had felt on their
wedding night.

Victoria heard him moving about in his room and she
knocked on the connecting door. He called to her to come
in, but her smile faded abruptly when she walked in and saw
Franklin, his valet, packing a bag, while Jason stuffed papers
from the pile on the table in front of the fireplace into a
leather case. "Where are you going?" Victoria gasped.

"To London."

"But—why?" she persisted, so disappointed she could
hardly think.

Jason glanced at his valet. "I'll finish packing, Franklin."
He waited until the valet withdrew and closed the door, then
said shortly, "I can work better there."

"But last night you said you couldn't come to London and
stay there with me tonight, because you had to be *here* to
meet with some people early tomorrow."

Jason stopped shoving papers into his case and straightened. With deliberate crudity he said, "Victoria, do you
know what happens to a man when he is kept in a state of
unrelieved sexual arousal for days at a time?"

"No," Victoria said weakly, and shook her head for
emphasis.

"In that case, I'll explain it to you," he snapped.

Victoria apprehensively shook her head. "I-I don't think
you should—not when you're in one of your moods."

"I did not have 'moods' before I met you," Jason bit out.
Turning his back to her, he braced his hands on the mantel,
and stared down at the floor. "I'm warning you, go back to
your room before I forget what a 'considerate' husband I'm
supposed to be and I don't bother going to London."

Victoria felt sick. "You're going to your mistress, aren't you?" she demanded chokingly, remembering unbelievingly how sweet he had seemed when she gave him his gift.

"You are beginning to sound unpleasantly like a jealous wife," he said between his teeth.

"I can't help it, I *am* a wife."

"You have a very peculiar idea of what being a wife means," he mocked savagely. "Now, get out of here."

"Damn you!" Victoria blazed. "I don't *know* how to be a wife, can't you see that? I know how to cook and sew and look after a husband, but you don't need me for that, because you have other people to take care of you. And I'll tell you something else, Lord Fielding," she continued, working herself into a fine rage, "I may not be a very good wife, but you're an *impossible* husband! When I offer to play chess with you, you get angry. When I try to seduce you, you get nasty—"

She saw Jason's head jerk up, but she was so angry she didn't pay any heed to the stunned expression on his face. "And when I bring you a gift, you go off to London to see your mistress!"

"Tory," he said achingly, "come here."

"No, I'm not finished!" Victoria burst out in humiliated fury. "Go off to your mistress, if that's what you want, but don't blame *me* when you never have a son. I may be naive, but I'm not stupid enough to believe I'm supposed to produce a baby without—without some cooperation from you!"

"Tory, please come here," he repeated hoarsely.

The raw emotion in his voice finally registered on Victoria and abruptly neutralized her anger, but she was still afraid of another rejection if she went to him. "Jason, I don't think you *know* what you want. You said you wanted a son, but—"

"I know exactly what I want," he contradicted, opening his arms to her. "If you'll come here, I'll show you. . . ."

Mesmerized by the seductive invitation in those green eyes and the velvet roughness of his deep voice, Victoria walked slowly forward and found herself wrapped in a crushing embrace. His mouth opened over hers, slanting back and forth in a fierce, wildly arousing kiss that sent heat racing through her. She felt the intimate, rising pressure of his body against hers as his hands stroked possessively over her back and breasts, soothing her fears, igniting flames of need wherever he touched her. "Tory," he breathed in a ragged whisper, sliding his lips down her neck and sending shivers of delight up her spine. "Tory," he repeated achingly and buried his lips on hers again.

He kissed her slowly, deeply, and then with urgent hunger, running his hands down her sides, cupping her bottom and pulling her tightly against his rigid arousal, wringing a moan of pure, primitive desire from her.

With his lips still locked to hers, he put his arm beneath her knees and swept her into his arms. Lost in the vibrant, heated magic of his hands and mouth, Victoria felt the world tilt as he gently laid her on the bed. Clinging desperately to that special, beautiful universe where nothing existed except her husband, she closed her eyes tightly while he stripped off his clothes. She felt his weight settle onto the bed, and she fought back her panic as she waited for him to untie her robe.

Instead, he tenderly kissed her closed eyes and put his arms around her, gently drawing her against him. "Princess," he whispered, the huskiness of his voice as sweet to her ears as the endearment, "please open your eyes. I'm not going to pounce on you, I promise."

Victoria swallowed and opened her eyes, relieved beyond anything when she realized he had thoughtfully extinguished all but the candles on the mantel across the room.

Jason saw the fear in her wide blue eyes and he leaned up on his elbow, reaching out with his free hand to tenderly smooth the tousled red-gold curls that were spread luxuriantly across his pillow. No man but he had ever touched her, he thought reverently. Pride surged through him at the thought. This beautiful, brave, unspoiled girl had given herself to him, and him alone. He wanted to make up to her for their wedding night, to make her moan with rapture and cling to him.

Ignoring the urgent throbbing in his loins, he touched his lips to her ear. "I don't know what you're thinking," he said softly, "but you look frightened to death. Nothing is different from how it was a few minutes ago when we were kissing each other."

"Except that you don't have any clothes on," Victoria reminded him shakily.

He bit back a smile. "True. But you do."

Not for long, she thought, and she heard his deep sensuous chuckle, as if he read her thoughts.

He kissed the corner of her eye. "Would you like to keep your robe on?"

The wife whose virginity he had taken with brutal, uncaring swiftness looked into his eyes, laid her hand against his cheek, and whispered softly, "I want to please you. And I don't think you want me to keep it on."

With a low groan, Jason leaned down and kissed her with fierce tenderness, shuddering uncontrollably when she kissed him back with an innocent ardor that sent desire roaring through him like wildfire. He pulled his mouth from hers. "Tory," he said wryly, "if you pleased me any more than you do when you kiss me, I'd die of pleasure."

He drew a shaky breath and untied the velvet rope at her waist, but when he started to part her robe, her hand clamped convulsively over his. "I won't open it if you don't want me to, sweet," he promised, his hand unmoving beneath hers. "Only I hoped there wouldn't be any more things separating us—not misunderstandings, not doors, not even clothes. I took mine off to show you myself, not to frighten you."

She shivered at his tender explanation and took her hand from his; then, to his intense joy, Victoria slid her hand around his neck and offered herself up to him.

Her robe fell away beneath his questing fingers and he bent his head and kissed her, his fingers rubbing her nipple, his tongue sliding across her lips, urging them to part for his probing tongue. Instead of merely submitting to his intimate kiss, Victoria drew his tongue into her mouth, wrapped her arms fiercely around his neck, and welcomed his thrusting tongue. Against his palm her nipple rose up proudly, and Jason tore his mouth from hers, bending his head to her breast.

Victoria jumped in startled resistance, and he looked up at her in wonder as he again realized that no man had ever touched or kissed her as he was doing. "I won't hurt you, darling," he whispered reassuringly, and pressed his lips to the hardened little bud, kissing it, nuzzling until he felt her relax, then he slowly parted his lips, drawing her nipple into his mouth.

Victoria's dazed amazement that he would wish to suckle at her breast gave way to a startled moan of intense pleasure as her nipple was pulled into his mouth and the drawing pressure of his mouth began to increase, tightening relentlessly on her nipple until quick, piercing stabs of desire were shooting rhythmically through her entire body. Her finger slid into his crisp black hair, holding his head to her as if she wanted him never to leave—until she felt his hand suddenly slide downward between her legs.

"No!" The terrified whisper burst out of her, and she clamped her legs together. Instead of making Jason angry, a she feared, her resistance won a muffled, hoarse laugh from him.

In one smooth motion he shifted upward and kissed her lips with raw, dizzying hunger. "Yes," he whispered, his lips moving back and forth against hers. "Oh, yes . . ." His hand delved down again, teasing softly at the triangle between her legs, his fingers toying with her until the stiffness flowed out of her legs and her thighs relaxed, surrendering to his gentle insistent persuasion. Jason pressed his fingers to her and the wet warmth of her welcome there almost broke his control. He could not believe the ardor in her, nor the natural ease with which she drove him wild—for as Victoria surrendered each separate part of her body to him, she gave it up wholly, holding nothing back. He moved his fingers in her and her hips lifted, arching sweetly against his hand while she clung to his shoulders, her nails digging into his flesh. Bracing his hands on either side of her, he moved partially atop her.

Victoria's heart leapt with a mixture of pulsing pleasure and stark terror when she felt the demanding heat of his maleness pressing between her legs, but instead of entering her, Jason circled his hips against her in a gently grinding rhythm that slowly drove her frantic with fierce, throbbing pleasure, until there was no more fear—only an exquisite aching need to have him fill her.

His knee wedged between her legs. "Don't be afraid," he said hoarsely. "Don't be afraid of me."

Victoria slowly opened her eyes and gazed at the man

above her. His face was hard and dark with passion, his shoulders and arms taut with the strain of holding back, his breathing fast and labored. Trancelike, she touched her fingertips to his sensual lips, realizing instinctively how desperately he wanted her and how much control he was exerting to stop himself from taking her. "You are so gentle," she whispered brokenly, "so gentle . . ."

A low groan erupted from Jason's chest and his restraint shattered. He plunged into her partway and eased out, plunging deeper the next time, and the next, until she arched her hips beneath him and he drove his full length into her incredible warmth. Sweat dampened his forehead as he fought down the tormenting demands of his own body and began to move slowly within her, watching her face. Her head tossed on the pillows as she strained toward him in trembling need, pressing her hips hard against his pulsing thighs, reaching for the bursting fulfillment he was determined to give her. He heard her low, frantic gasp and began to steadily increase the tempo of his deep, driving thrusts. "Reach for it, Tory," he rasped out hoarsely. "I'll give it to you. I promise."

A shivering ecstasy pierced Victoria's entire body, sending streaks of pleasure curling through her that came faster and faster until they erupted in an explosion that tore a scream from her throat. Jason bent his head and kissed her one last desperate time, and then he drove into her, joining her in sweet oblivion.

Afraid his weight would crush her, he moved onto his side, pulling her with him, his body still intimately joined with hers. When his labored breathing finally evened out, he kissed her forehead and smoothed her rumpled, satiny hair off her forehead. "How do you feel?" he asked softly.

Victoria's long curly lashes fluttered up and eyes like deep blue pools of languid wonder gazed into his. "I feel like a wife," she whispered.

He laughed huskily at that, tracing his finger along the elegant curve of her cheek, and she snuggled against him. "Jason," she said, her voice throbbing with emotion as she raised her eyes to his. "There's something I want to tell you."

"What?" he asked, smiling tenderly.

Very simply, and without embarrassment, she said, "I love you."

His smile faded.

"I do. I lov—"

He pressed his finger to her lips, silencing her, and shook his head. "No, you don't," he said with quiet, implacable firmness. "Nor should you. Don't give me more than you already have, Tory."

Victoria averted her eyes and said nothing, but his rejection hurt her more than she imagined possible. Lying in his arms, his words came back to haunt her . . . *I don't need your love. I don't want it.*

Outside in the hall, Franklin tapped on the door, intending to see if Lord Fielding desired help with the packing. When there was no answer to his knock, Franklin assumed his lordship must be elsewhere in the suite and, as was his custom, he opened the door unbidden.

He took one step into the dimly lit room and blinked, his startled gaze riveting on the couple lying in the huge four-poster, then bouncing in horror to the pile of clothes that Jason had been removing from his armoire and that were now lying in an ignominious heap upon the floor beside the bed. The diligent valet bit his lip against the overwhelming impulse to tiptoe forward and disentangle his lordship's exquisitely tailored evening jacket from the pants legs of his buckskins. Instead, Franklin wisely backed out of the room, closing the door with a soft click.

Once out in the hall, his distress over Lord Fielding's abused garments gave way to delayed joy at what he had just witnessed. Turning, he rushed down the hall and out onto the balcony overlooking the foyer below. "Mr. Northrup!" he whispered loudly, leaning precariously over the railing and beckoning frantically to Northrup, who was standing near the front door. "Mr. Northrup, I have news of great import! Come closer so we shan't be overheard. . . ."

Down the hall on Franklin's left, two alert maids rushed out of the rooms they'd been cleaning, crashed into each other, and elbowed each other aside in their urgency to hear what news Franklin had. On his right a footman suddenly materialized in the hall and began enthusiastically polishing a mirror with beeswax and lemon oil.

"It has happened!" Franklin hissed at Northrup, cleverly disguising his news in terms so vague he was certain no one could possibly understand even if they overheard.

"Are you certain?"

"Of course I am," said Franklin, affronted.

A momentary grin cracked Northrup's rigid features, but he recovered quickly, retreating behind his customary mask of aloof formality. "Thank you, Mr. Franklin. In that case, I shall order the coach back to the stables."

So saying, Northrup turned and proceeded to the front door. Opening it, he walked outside into the night, where a luxurious, maroon-lacquered coach with the gold Wakefield seal emblazoned on the door was waiting, its lamps glowing brightly in the darkness. Four gleaming matched chestnuts stamped fitfully in the traces, tossing their heavy manes and rattling their harnesses in restless eagerness to be off. Unable to attract the attention of the liveried drivers sitting erectly atop the coach, Northrup walked down the terraced steps to the drive.

"His lordship," he said to the coachman in his coolest, most authoritative voice, "will not require your services this evening. You may put the horses away."

"He won't be needin' the coach?" John coachman burst out in surprise. "But he sent me word himself an hour ago that he wanted the horses put to, and quick!" .

"His plans," Northrup said frostily, "have changed."

John coachman expelled a sigh of frustrated irritation and glowered at the uncommunicative butler. "I tell you, there's been a mistake. He means to go to London—"

"Idiot! He *meant* to go to London. He has now retired for the night instead!"

"At half past seven in the—" As Northrup turned and marched into the house, a wide, understanding smile suddenly dawned across the coachman's face. Nudging his companion in the ribs, the coachman sent him a sly, laughing look, and said, "Methinks Lady Fielding has decided brunettes are out o' fashion." Then he sent the horses wheeling toward the stables so he could share the news with the grooms.

Northrup walked directly into the dining room, where O'Malley was whistling cheerfully under his breath and putting away the fragile porcelain place setting he had earlier laid out for Victoria's solitary meal, when he first learned of the master's sudden intention to visit London. "There has been a change, O'Malley," Northrup said.

"Aye, Mr. Northrup," the insolent footman cheerfully agreed, "there certainly has."

"You may remove the covers from the table."

"Aye, I already have."

"However, Lord and Lady Fielding may wish to dine at a later hour."

"Upstairs," predicted O'Malley with a bald grin.

Northrup stiffened and then marched away. "Damned insolent Irishman!" he muttered furiously.

"Pompous stuffed shirt!" O'Malley replied to his back.

Chapter Twenty-seven

"GOOD MORNING, MY LADY," RUTH SAID, BEAMING brightly.

Victoria rolled over in Jason's huge bed, a dreamy smile in her eyes. "Good morning. What time is it?"

"Ten o'clock. Shall I bring you one of your dressing robes?" she asked, glancing around at the telltale tangle of discarded clothing and bedcovers on the floor.

Victoria's face warmed, but she was too languid, too deliciously exhausted, to feel anything but mild embarrassment at being discovered in Jason's bed with clothes strewn everywhere. He had made love to her twice more before they fell asleep, and again early this morning. "Don't bother, Ruth," she murmured. "I think I'd like to sleep a little longer."

When Ruth left, Victoria rolled onto her stomach and snuggled deeper into the pillows, a soft smile on her lips. The *ton* thought Jason Fielding was cool, cynical, and unapproachable, she remembered with a secret smile. How stunned they would be if they only knew what a tender, passionate, stormy lover he was in bed. Or perhaps it wasn't a secret after all, she thought, her smile wavering a little. She'd seen the covetous way married women often looked at Jason and, since they couldn't possibly have wanted to marry him, they must have wanted him for a lover.

As she thought about that, she remembered how many times she'd heard his name linked with certain beautiful married ladies whose husbands were old and ugly. No doubt there had been many women in his life before her, for he had known exactly how to kiss her and where to touch her to make her body quicken with need.

Victoria pushed those lowering thoughts from her mind. It didn't matter how many women had known the wild, pagan beauty of his lovemaking, because from now on, he was hers and hers alone. Her eyes were drifting closed when she finally noticed the flat black jeweler's case resting on the table beside the bed. Without much interest, she pulled her hand from beneath the silk sheets and reached out, opening the catch. A magnificent emerald necklace lay inside, along with a note from Jason that read, "Thank you for an unforgettable night."

A frown marred Victoria's smooth forehead. She wished he hadn't argued when she tried to tell him she loved him. She wished he'd told her he loved her, too. And she particularly wished he'd stop handing her jewels whenever she pleased him. This trinket, in particular, felt unpleasantly like a payment for services rendered. . . .

Victoria awoke with a start. It was nearly noon and Jason had told her his meeting this morning would be over by then. Eager to see him and bask in the warmth of his intimate smile, she dressed in a pretty lavender gown with soft full sleeves gathered into wide cuffs at the wrists. She fidgeted impatiently while Ruth fussed with her hair, brushing it until it glistened, then twisting it into thick curls bound with lavender satin ribbons.

As soon as she was finished, Victoria rushed down the hall, then forced herself to walk at a more decorous pace as she proceeded down the grand staircase. Northrup actually smiled at her when she inquired about Jason's whereabouts, and when she passed O'Malley in the hall en route to Jason's study, she could have sworn the Irish footman winked at her. She was still wondering about that when she knocked on Jason's door and went in. "Good morning," she said brightly. "I thought you might like to dine with me."

Jason scarcely glanced in her direction. "I'm sorry, Victoria. I'm busy."

Feeling rather like a bothersome child who had just been firmly, but politely, put in her place, Victoria said hesitantly, "Jason—why do you work so hard?"

"I enjoy working," he said coolly.

Obviously he enjoyed it more than her company, Victoria realized, since he certainly didn't need the money. "I'm sorry for interrupting you," she said quietly. "I won't do it again."

As she left, Jason started to call to her that he had changed his mind, then checked the impulse and sat back down at his desk. He wanted to dine with her, but it wouldn't be wise to spend too much time with her. He would let Victoria be a pleasant part of his life, but he would not let her become the center of it. That much power over him he would not give any woman.

Victoria laughed as little Billy wielded his mock saber in the field behind the orphanage and ordered one of the other orphans to "walk the plank." With a black patch over his good eye, the sturdy youngster looked adorably piratical.

"Do you think that patch will do the trick?" the vicar asked, standing beside her.

"I'm not certain. My father was as surprised as everyone else when it worked so well on the little boy back home. When his eye straightened, Papa wondered if, instead of the eye itself being at fault in these cases, perhaps the problem might lie with the muscles of the eye that control its movement. If so, then by covering the good eye, the muscles of the bad eye might strengthen if they were forced into use."

"My wife and I were wondering if you might honor us for supper tonight, after the children put on their puppet show. If I may say so, my lady, the children here at the orphanage are fortunate indeed to have such a generous and devoted patron as yourself. I daresay there isn't an orphanage in

England whose children possess better clothing or food than these children now do, thanks to your generosity."

Victoria smiled and started to decline the kindly invitation to supper; then she abruptly changed her mind and accepted it. She sent one of the older children to Wakefield with a message telling Jason she was dining at the vicar's house, then leaned against a tree, watching the children play pirates and wondering how Jason would react to her unprecedented absence tonight.

In truth, she had no way of knowing if he'd care. Life had become very strange, very confusing. In addition to the jewelry he had given her before, she now owned a pair of emerald earrings and a bracelet to match the necklace, diamond eardrops, a ruby brooch, and a set of diamond pins for her hair—something for each of the five consecutive nights he had made love to her since she had admitted trying to seduce him.

In bed each night, he made passionate love to her. In the morning, he left her an expensive piece of jewelry, then thrust her completely out of his mind and his life until he again joined her for supper and bed. As a result of this odd treatment, Victoria was rapidly acquiring a very lively resentment toward Jason and an even livelier distaste for jewelry.

Perhaps she could have borne his attitude better if he actually worked constantly, but he didn't. He made time to go riding with Robert Collingwood, to visit with the squire, and to do all sorts of other things. Victoria was granted his company only at supper and then later, when they went to bed. The realization that this was how her life was going to be made her sad, and then it made her angry. Today she was angry enough to deliberately stay away from home at suppertime.

Obviously Jason wanted the sort of marriage typical to the *ton*. She was expected to go her way and he his. Sophisticated people did not live in each other's pockets, she knew; to do so was considered vulgar and common. They didn't profess to love one another either, but in that regard, Jason was behaving very oddly. He had told her not to love him, yet he made love to her night after night, for hours at a time, drowning her senses in pleasure until she finally cried out her love for him. The harder she tried to hold back the words "I love you," the more torrid his lovemaking became until he forced the admission from her with his hands and mouth and hard, thrusting body. Then and only then did he let her find the explosive ecstasy he could give or withhold from her.

It was as if he wanted, needed to hear those words of love; yet never, not even at the peak of his own fulfillment, did Jason ever say them to her. Her body and heart were enslaved by Jason; he was chaining her to him—deliberately, cleverly, successfully, holding her in a bondage of fierce, hot pleasure—yet he was emotionally detached from her.

After a week of this, Victoria was determined to somehow force him to share what she felt and admit it. She would not, could not, believe he didn't love her—she could feel it in the tenderness of his hands on her and the fierce hunger of his lips. Besides, if he didn't want her love, why would he deliberately force her to say it?

Based on what Captain Farrell had told her, she could almost understand the fact that Jason didn't want to trust her with his heart. She could understand it, but she was resolved to change matters. Captain Farrell had said Jason would love only once. . . . Once and always. She wanted desperately to be loved that way by him. Perhaps if she wasn't so readily available to him, he would realize that he missed her, and would even admit that much to her. At least, that was her hope when she sent a polite note to him explaining that she would not be home for supper.

Victoria was on tenterhooks during the puppet show and later, during supper at the vicar's house, as she waited for the hour when she could return to Wakefield and see for herself how Jason had reacted to her absence. Despite her protest that it wasn't necessary, the vicar insisted on escorting her home that night, warning her during the entire distance about the perils that lay in wait for a woman foolish enough to venture out alone after dark.

With wonderful, if admittedly unlikely, visions of Jason going down on one knee the instant she arrived and professing his love for her because he had missed her so much at their evening meal, Victoria practically ran into the house.

Northrup informed her that Lord Fielding, upon learning

of her intention to dine elsewhere, had decided to dine with neighbors and had not yet returned.

Utterly frustrated, Victoria went up to her rooms, took a leisurely bath, and washed her hair. He still hadn't returned when she was finished, so she got into bed and disinterestedly leafed through a periodical. If Jason had meant to turn the tables on her, Victoria thought disgustedly, he couldn't have found a better way—not that she believed he'd actually gone to that much trouble merely to teach her a lesson.

It was after eleven when she finally heard him enter his room and she instantly snatched up the periodical, staring at it as if it were the most absorbing material in the world. A few minutes later, he strolled into her room, his neckcloth removed, his white shirt unbuttoned nearly to his waist, revealing the crisp mat of dark hair that covered the bronzed muscles of his chest. He looked so breathtakingly virile and handsome that Victoria's mouth went dry, but Jason's ruggedly chiseled face was perfectly composed. "You didn't come home for supper," he remarked, standing beside her bed.

"No," Victoria agreed, trying to match his casual tone.

"Why not?"

She gave him an innocent look and repeated his own explanation for ignoring her. "I enjoy the company of other people, just as you enjoy working." Unfortunately, her composure slipped a notch, and she added a little nervously, "I didn't think you'd mind if I wasn't here."

"I didn't mind at all," he said, to her chagrined disappointment, and after placing a chaste kiss upon her forehead, he returned to his own rooms.

Bleakly, Victoria looked at the empty pillows beside her. Her heart refused to believe that he didn't care whether she was here or not for supper. She didn't want to believe he intended to sleep alone tonight either, and she lay awake waiting for him, but he never came.

She felt awful when she awoke the next morning—and that was before Jason walked into her room, freshly shaven and positively exuding vitality—to casually suggest, "If you're lonely for company, Victoria, perhaps you should go to the city for a day or two."

Despair shot through her and her hairbrush slid from her

limp fingers, but stubborn pride came to her rescue and she pinned a bright smile on her face. Either he was calling her bluff or he wished to be rid of her, but whatever his reason, she was going to do as he recommended. "What a lovely idea, Jason. I think I'll do that. Thank you for suggesting it."

Chapter Twenty-eight

VICTORIA WENT TO LONDON AND STAYED FOR FOUR days, hoping against hope that Jason might come after her, growing lonelier and more frustrated by the hour when he didn't. She went to three musicales and to the opera, and visited with her friends. At night she lay awake, trying to understand how a man could be so warm at night and so cold during the day. She couldn't believe he saw her only as a convenient receptacle for his desire. That couldn't be true— not when he seemed to enjoy her company at the evening meal so much. He always lingered over each course, joking with her and urging her to converse with him on all manner of subjects. Once he had even complimented her on her intelligence and perception. Several other times he had asked her opinions on subjects as diverse as the arrangement of furniture in the drawing room and whether or not he ought to pension off the estate manager and hire a younger man.

On the fourth night, Charles escorted her to a play, and afterward she returned to Jason's townhouse in Upper Brook Street to change her clothes for the ball she'd promised to attend that night. She was going to go home tomorrow morning, she decided with a mixture of exasperation and resignation; she was ready to cede this contest of wills to Jason and to resume the battle for his affection on the home front.

Wrapped in a spectacular ball gown of swirling silver-spangled gauze, she walked into the ballroom with the Marquis de Salle on one side and Baron Arnoff on the other.

Heads turned when she entered, and Victoria noticed again the rather peculiar way people were looking at her. Last night she'd had the same uncomfortable sensation. She could scarcely believe the *ton* would find any reason to criticize her simply because she was in London without her husband. Besides, the glances she was receiving from the elegant ladies and gentlemen were not censorious. They watched her with something that resembled understanding, or perhaps it was pity.

Caroline Collingwood arrived toward the end of the evening, and Victoria pulled her aside, intending to ask Caroline if she knew why people were behaving oddly. Before she had the opportunity, Caroline provided the answer. "Victoria," she said anxiously, "is everything all right—between Lord Fielding and you, I mean? You aren't estranged already, are you?"

"Estranged?" Victoria echoed blankly. "Is that what people think? Is that why they're watching me so strangely?"

"You're not doing anything wrong," Caroline assured her hastily, casting an apprehensive glance about to make certain that Victoria's devoted escorts were out of hearing. "It's just that, under the circumstances, people are jumping to certain conclusions—the conclusion that you and Lord Fielding are not in accord, and that you've, well, you've left him."

"I've what!" Victoria burst out in a disgusted whisper. "Whyever would they think such a thing? Why, Lady Calliper isn't with her husband, and Countess Graverton isn't with hers, and—"

"I'm not with my husband either," Caroline interrupted desperately. "But you see, none of our husbands were married before. Yours was."

"And that makes a difference?" Victoria said, wondering what outrageous, unknown convention she'd broken this time. The *ton* had rules governing behavior in every category, with a long list of exceptions that made everything impossibly confusing. Still, she could not believe that first wives were permitted to go their own way in society, while second wives were not.

"It makes a difference," Caroline sighed, "because the first Lady Fielding said some dreadful things about Lord Fielding's cruelties to her, and there were people who believed her. You've been married for less than two weeks, and now you're here, and you don't look very happy, Victoria, truly you don't. The people who believed the things the first Lady Fielding said have remembered them, and now they're repeating what she said and pointing to you as confirmation."

Victoria looked at her, feeling absolutely harassed. "I never thought, never imagined, they'd do so. I was planning to go back home tomorrow anyway. If it weren't so late, I'd leave tonight."

Caroline laid her hand on Victoria's arm. "If there's something bothering you, something you don't wish to discuss, you know you can stay with us. I won't press you."

Shaking her head, Victoria hastily assured her, "I want to go home tomorrow. For tonight, there's nothing I can do."

"Except try to look happy," her friend said wryly.

Victoria thought *that* was excellent advice, and she set out to follow it with a slight modification of her own. For the next two hours, she endeavored to speak to as many people as possible, managing skillfully to bring Jason's name into her conversation each time and to speak of him in the most glowing terms. When Lord Armstrong remarked to a group of friends that it was becoming impossible to satisfy his tenants, Victoria quickly remarked that her husband was on the best of terms with his. "My Lord Fielding is so wise in the management of estates," she finished in the breathless voice of a besotted bride, "that his tenants adore him and his servants positively worship him!"

"Is that right?" said Lord Armstrong, shocked. "I shall have to have a word with him. Didn't know Wakefield gave a jot for his tenants, but there you are—I was mistaken."

To Lady Brimworthy, who complimented Victoria on her sapphire necklace, Victoria replied, "Lord Fielding showers me with gifts. He is so *very* generous, so kind and thoughtful. And he has such excellent taste, does he not?"

"Indeed," agreed Lady Brimworthy, admiring the fortune in diamonds and sapphires at Victoria's slender throat. "Brimworthy flies into the boughs when I buy jewels," she added morosely. "Next time he rings a peal over my head for being extravagant, I shall mention Wakefield's generosity!"

When elderly Countess Draymore reminded Victoria to join her tomorrow for a Venetian breakfast the countess was giving, Victoria replied, "I'm afraid I cannot, Countess Draymore. I've been away from my husband for four days now, and to tell you the truth, I miss his company. He is the very soul of amiability and kindness!"

Countess Draymore's mouth dropped open. As Victoria moved away, the old lady turned to her cronies and blinked. "The soul of amiability and kindness?" she repeated in puzzlement. "Where did I conceive the idea she was married to Wakefield?"

In his house on Upper Brook Street, Jason paced back and forth across his suite like a caged beast, silently cursing his aging London butler for giving him incorrect information about Victoria's whereabouts tonight, and cursing himself for coming to London in pursuit of her like a jealous, lovesick boy. He had gone to the Berfords' tonight, which was where the butler said Victoria was, but Jason hadn't seen her among the crush at the Berfords' ball. Nor was she at any of the other three places the butler thought she might be.

So successful was Victoria in her attempt to appear devoted to her husband that by the end of the evening, the guests were regarding her with more amusement than concern. She was still smiling about that when she entered the house shortly before dawn.

She lit the candle the servants had left for her on the table in the foyer and climbed the carpeted staircase. She was in the process of lighting the candles in her bedchamber when a stealthy sound from the adjoining suite caught her attention. Praying that the person in there was a servant and not a prowler, Victoria moved quietly toward the door. Holding her candle high in her shaking hand, she reached for the handle on the connecting door just as it was flung open, startling a scream from her. "Jason!" she said shakily, her hand on her throat. "Thank God it's you. I-I thought you were a prowler and I was about to have a look."

"Very brave," he said, glancing at the upraised candle in her hand. "What were you going to do if I was a prowler—threaten to set my eyelashes on fire?"

Victoria's giggle caught in her throat as she noticed the ominous glitter in those green eyes and the muscle leaping in his hard jaw. Behind that sardonic facade of his, there was a terrible burning anger, she realized. Automatically, she began backing away as Jason moved forward, towering over her. Despite the civilized elegance of his superbly tailored evening clothes, he had never looked more dangerous, more overpowering than he did as he came toward her with that deceptively lazy, stalking stride of his.

Victoria started backing around her bed, then stopped moving and quelled her rioting, irrational fear. She had not done anything wrong, and here she was behaving like a cowardly child! She would discuss this whole thing reasonably and rationally, she decided. "Jason," she said, with only a small quiver in her reasonable voice, "are you angry?"

He stopped a few inches from her. Brushing back the sides of his black velvet jacket, he put his hands on his hips, his booted feet planted apart, his legs spread in a decidedly aggressive stance. "You could say that," he drawled in an awful voice. "Where the hell have you been?"

"At—at Lady Dunworthy's ball."

"Until dawn?" he sneered.

"Yes. There's nothing unusual in that. You know how late these things go—"

"No, I don't know," he said tightly. "Suppose you tell me why the minute you are out of my sight you forget how to count!"

"Count?" Victoria repeated, growing more frightened by the moment. "Count what?"

"Count days," he clarified acidly. "I gave you permission to be here for two days, not four!"

"I don't need your permission," Victoria burst out unwisely. "And don't pretend you care whether I'm here or at Wakefield!"

"Oh, but I *do* care," he said in a silky voice, stripping off his jacket with slow deliberation and beginning to unbutton his white lawn shirt. "And you *do* need my permission. You've become very forgetful, my sweet—I'm your husband, remember? Take off your clothes."

Wildly, Victoria shook her head.

"Don't make me angry enough to force you," he warned softly. "You won't like what happens if you do, believe me."

Victoria believed that wholeheartedly. Her shaking hands went to the back of her dress, awkwardly fumbling with the tiny fasteners. "Jason, for God's sake, what's wrong?" she pleaded.

"What's wrong?" he repeated scathingly, tossing his shirt on the floor. "I'm jealous, my dear." His hands went to the waistband of his trousers. "I'm jealous, and I find the feeling not only novel, but singularly unpleasant."

Under other circumstances, Victoria would have been overjoyed at his admission of jealousy. Now it only made her more frightened, more tense, and her fingers more awkward.

Seeing her lack of progress, Jason reached out and roughly spun her around, his hands unfastening the tiny loops at the back of her gown with an ease that spoke of long experience in undressing women. "Get into bed," he snapped, giving her a shove in that direction.

Victoria was a mass of quivering rebellion and jellied fear by the time he joined her and pulled her roughly into his arms. His mouth came down on hers in a hard, punishing kiss and she clamped her teeth together, gasping at the harsh pressure.

"Open your mouth, damn you!"

Victoria braced her hands against his chest and averted her face from his. "No! Not this way. I won't let you!"

He smiled at that—a hard, cruel smile that chilled her blood. "You'll let me, my sweet," he whispered silkily. "Before I'm done with you, you'll *ask* me."

Furious, Victoria shoved against his chest with an unexpected strength born of fear and rolled out from under him.

She had almost got her feet to the floor when he caught her arm and yanked her back onto the bed, jerking her hands up and pinioning them above her head, then throwing his leg over both of hers. "That was very foolish," he whispered, and slowly bent his head.

Tears of fear sprang to Victoria's eyes as she lay pinned on her back like a trussed hare, watching Jason's mouth descend purposefully toward hers. But instead of a renewed, painful assault like the last one, his mouth took hers in a long, insolently thorough kiss while his free hand began roving up and down her body, his fingers cupping a rosy breast, lightly squeezing the thrusting nipple, then drifting lower down her flat abdomen, stroking and caressing the triangular mound of curly golden hair, until her traitorous body began to respond to his skillful hand. Victoria squirmed in frantic earnest as his fingers moved lower yet, but it was no use—he wedged his leg between her knees and his fingers gained entry to the place they sought.

Liquid heat began to race through her, eventually sapping her strength, melting her resistance, and her lips parted beneath his. His tongue drove into her mouth, filling it, then withdrawing, while his fingers within her began to match the slow, driving movements of his tongue. The incredibly erotic onslaught of her senses was more than Victoria could withstand. With a silent moan of surrender she gave herself up to him, turning her face fully toward him and returning his kiss, her body pliant beneath him. The moment she did, Jason released her hands.

His head dipped lower and he nuzzled her neck as he sought the rosy ripeness of her breasts. His tongue drew tiny circles on her heated skin; then his mouth closed over her nipple, wringing a gasp of pure pleasure from her as she clasped his dark, curly head and held it to her. With an odd little laugh he moved lower, his tongue tracing a hot path down her taut abdomen until Victoria realized what he meant to do and tried frantically to wriggle away. His hands caught her hips, lifting her to him as his mouth closed around her. By the time he stopped, white-hot sensations were screaming through Victoria's entire body and she was desperate for release.

He raised himself up over her, his hot engorged manhood

probing lightly, teasingly at the place his hands and mouth had been. Moaning softly, Victoria arched her hips, her hands pulling his hips to her. He eased into her wet warmth with tormenting slowness, then moved gently backward and forward, thrusting himself into her a fraction deeper each time, withdrawing slightly, then driving deeper, until Victoria was half-mad with the need to be completely filled by him. Her legs gripped him and she lifted to meet each thrust, her face flushed, her chest rising and falling in quick, shallow breaths. Suddenly he drove into her with a force that sent a scream of pure pleasure through her—and just as suddenly, he pulled out.

"No!" Victoria cried out in surprised loss, wrapping her arms around him.

"Do you want me, Victoria?" he whispered.

Her dazed eyes flew open and she saw him, his hands braced beside her head as he held himself away from her, his face hard.

"Do you?" he repeated.

"I'll never forgive you for this," Victoria choked.

"Do you want me?" he repeated, circling his hips provocatively against her sensitive softness. "Tell me."

Passion was raging through her body, battling against her weakened will, arguing in his favor. He was jealous. He cared. He was hurt by her long absence. Her lips formed the word "yes," but not even raging desire could make her voice it.

Satisfied with that, Jason gave her what she wanted. As if to atone for humbling her, he gave of himself with unselfish determination, moving his body in the ways that gave her maximum pleasure, fighting down the demands of his rampaging desire as she shuddered beneath him with each plunging stroke. He brought her to a tumultuous climax, holding her impaled on his throbbing staff as spasms of pleasure shook her. Then he crushed her to him and finally allowed himself release.

When it was over, there was complete silence between them. Jason was still for a long minute, staring at the ceiling; then he got out of bed and walked into his own rooms. Other than their wedding night, it was the first time he had ever left her after making love to her.

Chapter Twenty-nine

VICTORIA AWOKE WITH A HEAVY, ACHING HEART, feeling as if she hadn't slept at all. A lump of harsh despair grew in her throat when she remembered Jason's humiliating, unprovoked revenge on her last night. Shoving her tousled hair off her face, she leaned up on an elbow, her gaze drifting with numb abstractedness about the room. And then her eyes fell on the leather jewelry case beside the bed.

A rage unlike any she had ever experienced exploded in her brain, obliterating every other emotion within her. She hurtled out of bed, pulled on a dressing robe, and snatched up the box.

In a furious swirl of pale green satin, she flung open the door to Jason's room and stalked in. "Don't you ever give me another piece of jewelry!" she hissed.

He was standing beside his bed, his long legs encased in biscuit-colored trousers, his chest bare. He glanced up just in time to see her hurl the box at his head, but he didn't flinch, didn't move a muscle to avoid the heavy leather box that sailed by, missing his ear by a hairsbreadth.

It hit the polished floor with a loud thud and slid beneath

his bed. "I'll never forgive you for last night," Victoria blazed, her nails digging into her palms, her chest rising and falling with each furious breath. "Never!"

"I'm sure you won't," he said in a flat, expressionless voice and reached for his shirt.

"I hate your jewelry, I hate the way you treat me, and I hate you! You don't know how to love anyone—you're a cynical heartless *bastard!*"

The word flew out of her mouth before Victoria realized what she had said, but whatever reaction she expected, it was not the one she received. "You're right," he agreed tightly. "That's *exactly* what I am. I'm sorry to have to shatter any illusions you may still have about me, but the truth is, I'm the by-product of a brief, meaningless liaison between Charles Fielding and some long forgotten dancer he kept in his youth."

He pulled a shirt on over his muscular shoulders and shoved his arms into it, while it slowly began to register on Victoria that he thought he was confessing something ugly and repugnant to her.

"I grew up in squalor, raised by Charles's sister-in-law. Later, I slept in a warehouse. I taught myself to read and write; I didn't go to Oxford or do any of the things your other refined, aristocratic suitors have done. In short, I am none of the things you think I am—none of the good things or the nice things."

He began buttoning his shirt, his hooded gaze carefully lowered to his hands. "I'm not a fit husband for you. I'm not fit to touch you. I've done things that would make you sick."

Captain Farrell's words sliced through Victoria's mind: *The hag made him kneel and beg for forgiveness in front of those dirty Indians.* Victoria looked at Jason's proud, lean face, and she felt as if her heart would break. Now she even understood why he wouldn't, couldn't, accept her love.

"I'm a bastard," he finished grimly, "in the truest meaning of the word."

"Then you're in excellent company," she said, her voice shaking with emotion. "So were three sons of King Charles, and he made them all dukes."

For a moment he looked nonplussed; then he shrugged.

"The point is that you've told me you loved me, and I can't let you go on thinking that. You loved a mirage, not me. You don't even know me."

"Oh yes, I do," Victoria burst out, knowing that whatever she said now would determine their entire future. "I know everything about you—Captain Farrell told me more than a week ago. I know what happened to you when you were a little boy. . . ."

Rage blazed in Jason's eyes for a moment, but then he shrugged resignedly. "He had no right to tell you."

"*You* should have told me," Victoria cried, unable to control her voice or the tears streaming down her cheeks. "But you wouldn't because you're ashamed of the things you should be proudest of!" Brushing furiously at her tears, she said brokenly, "I wish he hadn't told me. Before he did, I only loved you a little. Afterward, when I realized how brave and—and how strong you really are, then I loved you so much more, I—"

"What?" he said in a ragged whisper.

"I never *admired* you before that day," she said hysterically, "and now I do and I can't stand what you're doing to—"

Through a blur of tears she saw him move, felt herself crushed against his hard chest, and her pent-up emotions broke loose. "I don't care who your parents are," she sobbed in his arms.

"Don't cry, darling," he whispered, "please don't."

"I hate it when you treat me like a witless doll, d-dressing me in ball gowns and—"

"I'll never buy you another gown," he tried to tease, but his voice was hoarse and raw.

"And then you drape me in j-jewels—"

"No more jewels either," he said, hugging her tighter.

"And then when you're done p-playing with me, you t-toss me aside."

"I'm an ass," he said, stroking her hair and rubbing his jaw against the top of her head.

"You've n-never told me what you think or how you feel about things, and I c-can't read your mind."

"I don't have a mind," he said harshly. "I lost it months ago."

Victoria knew she had won, but the relief was so painfully exquisite that her slim shoulders began to shake with wrenching sobs.

"Oh, God, please don't cry like this," Jason groaned, running his hands helplessly over her heaving shoulders and down her back, desperately trying to console her. "I can't bear it when you cry." Threading his hands through her hair, he turned her tear-streaked face up to his, his thumbs moving tenderly over her cheeks. "I'll never make you cry again," he whispered achingly. "I swear I won't." He bent his head, kissing her with gentle violence. "Come to bed with me," he murmured, his voice hoarse and urgent. "Come to bed with me and I'll make you forget last night. . . ."

In answer, Victoria wrapped her arms fiercely around her husband's neck and Jason swung her into his arms, driven to try to make amends to her in the only way he knew how. He put his knee on the mattress, lowering her gently and following her down, his lips clinging to hers in an unbroken, scalding kiss.

When he finally lifted himself off her to tear off his shirt and unbutton his pants, Victoria watched him unashamedly, glorying in his magnificent body—the long, muscular legs and narrow hips, the strong arms and broad shoulders, the heavily corded muscles that rippled in his back as he turned onto his side— A strangled cry tore from her chest.

Jason heard it and his whole body stiffened at the realization of what she was seeing. The scars! He had forgotten about the damned scars. Vividly he remembered the last time he had forgotten to hide them—he remembered the horror of the woman in his bed, the scorn and revulsion in her face when she saw that he had let himself be whipped like a dog. Because of that, he'd always kept his back turned away from Victoria when they were making love, and he'd always carefully extinguished the candles before they went to sleep.

"Oh, God," Victoria choked behind him, staring in horror at the white scars that crisscrossed his beautiful back. There were dozens of them. Her fingers shook as she reached out to touch them; the moment she did, his skin flinched. "Do they still hurt?" she whispered in anguished surprise.

"No," Jason said tautly. Shame washed over him in sickening waves as he waited helplessly for her inevitable reaction to the stark evidence of his humiliation.

To his utter disbelief he felt her arms encircle him from behind and the touch of her lips on his back. "How brave you must have been to endure this," she whispered achingly, "how strong to survive it and go on living. . . ." When she began kissing each scar, Jason rolled onto his side and jerked her into his arms. "I love you," he whispered agonizedly, plunging his hands into her luxuriant hair and turning her face up to his. "I love you so much. . . ."

His kisses seared her flesh like glowing brands as his mouth moved from her lips to her neck and breasts, his hands sliding along her back and sides, making her moan and writhe beneath his gentle assault. He raised up on his hands, his face above her, his voice hoarse with passion. "Please touch me—let me feel your hands on me."

It had never occurred to Victoria that he would want her to touch him as he touched her, and the knowledge was thrilling. She put her hands against his tanned chest, slowly spreading her fingers, amazed when her simple touch made his breath catch. Experimentally, she slid her hands lower, and the taut muscles of his abdomen jumped reflexively. She put her lips to his tiny nipple and kissed it as he kissed hers, flicking her tongue back and forth against it, and when she pulled it tightly into her mouth a groan ripped from his chest.

Heady with her newly discovered power over his body, she rolled him onto his back and brushed her parted lips over his, sweetly offering him her tongue. A funny little laugh that was part groan, part chuckle sounded in his throat and he drew her tongue into his mouth, one hand cradling the back of her head as he crushed his lips against hers while his free arm wrapped around her hips and lifted her fully atop his aroused length.

Without thought, Victoria moved her hips against his engorged manhood, circling herself on him, until she was faint with the pleasure she was giving him and taking for herself. She moved downward, lost in her desperate eagerness to please him, trailing kisses along his chest, nuzzling his abdomen, until his hands suddenly tangled in her hair and pulled her face back to his. Beneath her she could feel the pulsing of his rigid shaft, the fiery touch of his heated skin, the violent hammering of his heart against her breasts. But instead of taking her, as she expected, he gazed at her with desire raging in his eyes and humbly said the words he had tried to force her to say last night. "I want you," he whispered. As if he didn't think he had humbled himself enough, he added, "Please, darling."

Feeling as if her heart would break with the love bursting in it, Victoria answered him with a melting kiss. It was answer enough. Jason gathered her tightly into his arms, rolled her onto her back, and drove swiftly and surely into her. His arms wrapped around her shoulders and hips, pulling her more tightly to him, forging them into one as he drove into her again and again.

Victoria arched herself upward in a fevered need to share and stimulate his burgeoning passion, pressing her hips hard against his pulsing thighs, crushing her lips against his, while the waves of sensation shooting through her built into a frenzy and began exploding through her entire body in piercing streaks of pure, vibrant ecstasy.

A shudder shook Jason's powerful frame as he felt the spasms of her fulfillment gripping him, and he plunged into her one last time. His body jerked convulsively, shuddering again and again as Victoria's body drew from his a lifetime of bitterness and despair. She drained him of everything and replaced it all with joy. It burst in his heart and poured through his veins until he ached with the sheer bliss of it.

After all his farflung financial triumphs and aimless sexual exploits, he had finally found what he had unconsciously been searching for: He had found the place he belonged. He owned six English estates, two Indian palaces, and a fleet of ships each with a private cabin for his exclusive use, yet he had never felt he had a home. He was home now. This one beautiful girl, lying contentedly in his arms, was his home.

Still holding her, he moved onto his side, then he combed his fingers through her rumpled, satiny hair and brushed a tender kiss against her temple.

Victoria's lashes fluttered up and he felt as if he would drown in the deep blue pools of her eyes. "How do you feel?" she teased, smiling as she asked him the same question he had once asked her.

With tender solemnity, he replied, "I feel like a husband." Bending his head, he took her sweet lips in a long, lingering kiss, then gazed down into her glowing blue eyes. "To think I actually believed there were no such things as angels," he sighed, relaxing back against the pillows and reveling in the simple joy of having her in his arms, her head resting on his shoulder. "How incredibly stupid I must be—"

"You're brilliant," his wife declared loyally.

"No, I'm not," he chuckled wryly. "If I had even the slightest intelligence, I would have climbed into bed with you the first time I wanted to and then insisted you marry me."

"When was the first time you wanted to do that?" she teased.

"The day you arrived at Wakefield," he admitted, smiling at the memory. "I think I fell in love with you when I saw you standing on my doorstep with a piglet in your arms and your hair blowing in the wind like flaming gold."

Victoria sobered and shook her head. "Please—let's never lie to each other, Jason. You didn't love me then, and you didn't love me when you married me. It doesn't matter, though, truly it doesn't. All that matters is that you love me now."

Jason tipped her chin up and forced her to meet his gaze. "No, sweet—I meant what I said. I married you because I loved you."

"Jason!" she said, flattered but nevertheless determined to set a pattern of honesty and frankness for the future. "You married me because it was the wish of a dying man."

"The wish of a *dying*—" To Victoria's astonishment, Jason threw back his head and burst out laughing; then he wrapped his arms around her and pulled her up onto his naked chest. "Oh, darling," he said, chuckling, rubbing his knuckles tenderly across her cheek, "that 'dying man' who summoned us to his bedside and clung to your hand was clutching a fistful of playing cards in his other."

Victoria reared up on her elbows. "He was *what!*" she demanded, torn between laughter and fury. "Are you certain?"

"Positive," Jason averred, still chuckling. "I saw them when the blanket moved. He was holding four queens."

"But why would he do such a thing to us?"

Jason's broad shoulders lifted in a shrug. "He evidently decided we were taking too long to get around to the business of marriage."

"When I think of how I prayed he would get well, I could murder him!"

"What a thing to say," Jason teased, laughing. "Don't you like the end result of his scheming?"

"Well, yes, I do, but why didn't you tell me—or at least tell him you knew what he was up to?"

Jason nipped her ear. "What? And spoil his fun? Never!"

Victoria gave him an indignant look. "You should have told me. You had no right to keep it from me."

"True."

"Then why didn't you tell me?"

"Would you have married me if you didn't think it was an absolute necessity?"

"No."

"That's why I didn't tell you the truth."

Victoria collapsed on his chest, laughing helplessly at his unprincipled determination to get what he wanted and his complete lack of contrition for it. "Have you no principles at all?" she demanded with laughing severity.

He grinned. "Apparently not."

Chapter Thirty

VICTORIA WAS SEATED IN THE SALON LATE THAT afternoon, waiting for Jason to return from an errand, when the elderly butler who presided over the London house appeared in the doorway. "Her grace, the Duchess of Claremont wishes to see you, my lady. I told—"

"He told me you were not in to visitors," her grace said gruffly, marching into the room to the horror of the butler. "The silly fool doesn't seem to understand that I am 'family,' not 'visitors.' "

"Grandmama!" Victoria burst out, leaping to her feet in nervous surprise at the unexpected appearance of the gruff old lady.

The duchess's turbaned head swiveled to the shocked servant. "There!" she snapped, waving her cane at the butler. "Did you hear that? *Grandmama!*" she emphasized with satisfaction. Mumbling abject apologies, the butler bowed himself out of the room, leaving Victoria apprehensively confronting her relative, who sat down upon a chair and folded her blue-veined hands upon the jeweled head of her cane, scrutinizing Victoria's features minutely. "You look happy enough," she concluded, as if surprised.

"Is that why you came here from the country?" Victoria asked, sitting down across from her. "To see if I am happy?"

"I came to see Wakefield," her grace said ominously.

"He isn't here," Victoria said, taken aback by the old lady's sudden scowl.

Her great-grandmother's scowl darkened. "So I understand. All London understands he isn't here with you! I mean to run him to ground and call him to task if I have to chase him clear across Europe!"

"I find it amazing," Jason drawled in amusement as he walked into the salon, "that nearly everyone who knows me is half-afraid of me—except my tiny wife, my young sister-in-law, and you, madam, who are three times my age and one-third my weight. I can only surmise that courage—or recklessness—is passed through the bloodline, along with physical traits. However," he finished, grinning, "go ahead. I give you leave to take me to task right here in my own salon."

The duchess came to her feet and glowered at him. "So! You have finally remembered where you live and that you have a wife!" she snapped imperiously. "I told you I would hold you responsible for Victoria's happiness, and you are not making her happy. Not happy at all!"

Jason's speculative gaze shot to Victoria, but she shook her head in helpless bewilderment and shrugged. Satisfied that Victoria was not responsible for the duchess's opinion, he put his arm around Victoria's shoulders and said mildly, "In what way am I failing in my duties as a husband?"

The duchess's mouth fell open. "In what way?" she repeated in disbelief. "There you stand, with your arm about her, but I have it on the best authority that you have been to her bed only six times at Wakefield!"

"Grandmama!" Victoria burst out in horror.

"Hush, Victoria," she said, directing her dagger gaze at Jason as she continued. "Two of your servants are related to two of mine, and they tell me all Wakefield Park was in an uproar when you refused to bed your bride for a week after the ceremony."

Victoria let out a mortified moan and Jason's arm tightened supportively around her shoulders.

"Well," she snapped, "what have you to say to that, young man?"

Jason quirked a thoughtful eyebrow at her. "I would say I apparently need to have a word with my servants."

"Don't you dare make light of this! You, of all men, ought to know how to keep a wife in your bed and at your side. God knows half the married females in London have been panting after you these four years past. If you were some mincing fop with his shirtpoints holding up his chin, then I could understand why you don't seem to know how to go about getting me an heir—"

"I intend to make your heir my first priority," Jason drawled with amused gravity.

"I will not countenance any more shilly-shallying about," she warned, somewhat mollified.

"You've been very patient," he agreed drolly.

Ignoring his mockery, she nodded. "Now that we understand each other, you may invite me to dinner. I cannot stay long, however."

With a wicked grin, Jason offered her his arm. "No doubt you intend to pay us an extended visit at a later date—say, nine months hence?"

"To the day," she affirmed boldly, but when she glanced at Victoria, there was laughter in her eyes. As they headed into the dining room, she leaned toward her great-granddaughter and whispered, "Handsome devil, isn't he, my dear?"

"Very," Victoria agreed, patting her hand.

"And despite the gossip I heard, you're happy, are you not?"

"Beyond words," Victoria said.

"I would like it if you came to visit me someday soon. Claremont House is only fifteen miles from Wakefield, along the river road."

"I'll come very soon," Victoria promised.

"You may bring your husband."

"Thank you."

In the days that followed, the Marquess and Marchioness of Wakefield appeared at many of the *ton*'s most glittering functions. People no longer whispered about his alleged cruelty to his first wife, for it was plain to everyone that

Jason, Lord Fielding, was the most devoted and generous of husbands.

One had only to look at the couple to see that Lady Victoria was aglow with happiness and that her tall, handsome husband adored her. In fact, it gave rise to considerable amusement when the *ton* beheld the formerly aloof, austere Jason Fielding grinning affectionately at his new bride as he waltzed with her or laughing aloud in the midst of a play at some whispered remark of hers.

Very soon, it become the consensus of opinion that the marquess had been the most maligned, misjudged, and misunderstood man alive. The lords and ladies who had treated him with wary caution in the past now began actively to seek out his friendship.

Five days after Victoria had tried to put to rest gossip about her absent husband by speaking of him in the most admiring of terms, Lord Armstrong paid a call upon Jason to request his advice in winning over the cooperation and loyalty of his own servants and tenants. Lord Fielding had looked shocked, then grinned and suggested that Lord Armstrong speak to *Lady* Fielding about that.

At White's that same evening, Lord Brimworthy goodnaturedly blamed Jason for Lady Brimworthy's latest purchase of an extravagantly expensive set of sapphires. Lord Fielding shot him an amused look, wagered five hundred pounds on the next hand of cards, and a moment later smoothly divested Lord Brimworthy of that sum.

The following afternoon in Hyde Park, where Jason was teaching Victoria to drive the splendid new high-perch phaeton he'd purchased for her, a carriage drew to an abrupt stop and three ancient ladies peered at him. "Amazing!" said Countess Draymore to her cronies as she scrutinized Jason's features through her monocle. "She *is* married to Wakefield!" She turned to her friends. "When Lady Victoria said her husband was 'the soul of amiability and kindness,' I thought she must be talking of someone else!"

"He's not only amiable, he's brave," cackled the eldest of the old ladies, watching the couple careening precariously down the lane. "She has nearly turned that phaeton over twice!"

To Victoria, life had become a rainbow of delights. At

night, Jason made love to her and taught her to make love to him. He bathed her senses in pleasure and drew from her a stormy passion she had never known she was capable of, then shared it with her. She had taught him to trust and now he gave himself to her completely—body, heart, and soul. He withheld nothing and gave her everything—his love, his attention, and every conceivable gift he could think of from the whimsical to the extravagant.

He had his sleek yacht renamed the *Victoria* and coaxed her into sailing with him on the Thames. When Victoria commented that she enjoyed sailing on the Thames much more than on the ocean, Jason ordered another yacht to be built for her exclusive use, furnished entirely in pale blues and golds, for the comfort of Victoria and her friends. That piece of spectacular extravagance caused Miss Wilber to remark jealously to a group of friends at a ball, "One lives on tenterhooks wondering what Wakefield will buy her to surpass a yacht!"

Robert Collingwood raised his brows and grinned at the envious young woman. "The Thames, perhaps?"

To Jason, who had never before known the joy of being loved and admired not for what he possessed or for what he appeared to be but for what he really *was*, the quiet inner peace he felt was sheer bliss. At night, he could not hold her close enough or long enough. During the day, he took her on picnics and swam with her in the creek at Wakefield Park. When he was working, she was there on the perimeters of his mind, making him smile. He wanted to lay the world at her feet, but all Victoria seemed to want was him, and that knowledge filled him with profound tenderness. He donated a fortune to build a hospital near Wakefield—the Patrick Seaton Hospital—then he began arrangements for another one to be built in Portage, New York, also named for Victoria's father.

Chapter Thirty-one

ON THE ONE-MONTH ANNIVERSARY OF THEIR WED-
ding, a message arrived that required Jason to travel to
Portsmouth, where one of his ships had just put into port.

On the morning of his departure, he kissed Victoria good-
bye on the steps of Wakefield Park with enough ardor to
make her blush and the coachman smother a laugh.

"I wish you didn't have to go," Victoria said, pressing her
face to his muscular chest, her arms around his waist. "Six
days seems like forever, and I'll be dreadfully lonely without
you."

"Charles will be here to keep you company, sweet," he
said, grinning at her and hiding his own reluctance to leave.
"Mike Farrell is just down the road, and you can visit with
him. Or you could always pay another visit to your great-
grandmother. I'll be home on Tuesday in time for supper."

Victoria nodded and leaned up on her toes to kiss his
smoothly shaven cheek.

With great determination, she kept herself as busy as
possible during those six days, working at the orphanage and
supervising her household, but the time still seemed to drag.
The nights were even longer. She spent her evenings with

Charles, who had come for a visit, but when he went up to bed, the clock seemed to stop.

On the night before Jason was expected to return, she wandered around her room, trying to avoid getting into her lonely bed. She walked into Jason's suite, smiling at the contrast between his masculine, heavily carved, dark furnishings and her own room, which was done in the French style with gossamer silk draperies and bedhangings of rose and gold. Lovingly, she fingered the gold-inlaid backs of his brushes. Then she reluctantly returned to her own room and finally fell asleep.

She awakened at dawn the next day, her heart full of excitement, and began planning a special meal for Jason's homecoming.

Dusk faded into twilight and finally into chilly, starlit darkness as she waited in the salon, listening for the sound of Jason's coach in the drive. "He's back, Uncle Charles!" she said delightedly, peering out the window at the coach lamps moving along the drive toward the house.

"That must be Mike Farrell. Jason won't be here for at least another hour or two," he said, smiling fondly at her as she began smoothing her skirts. "I know how long it takes to make his journey, and he's already shaved off a day in order to get back tonight, rather than tomorrow."

"I suppose you're right, but it's only half past seven, and I asked Captain Farrell to join us for supper at eight." Her smile faded as the carriage drew up before the house, and she realized it wasn't Jason's luxurious traveling coach. "I think I'll ask Mrs. Craddock to delay supper," she was saying when Northrup appeared in the doorway of the salon, an odd, strained look upon his austere face.

"There is a gentleman here to see you, my lady," he announced.

"A gentleman?" Victoria echoed blankly.

"A Mr. Andrew Bainbridge from America."

Victoria reached weakly for the back of the nearest chair, her knuckles turning white as her grip tightened.

"Shall I show him in?"

She nodded jerkily, trying to get control over the violent surge of resentment quaking through her at the memory of his heartless rejection, praying she could face him without

354

showing how she felt. So distracted with her own rampaging emotions was she that she never noticed the sudden pallor of Charles's complexion or the way he slowly stood up and faced the door as if he were bracing to meet a firing squad.

An instant later, Andrew strode through the doorway, his steps long and brisk, his smiling, handsome face so endearingly familiar that Victoria's heart cried out in protest against his betrayal.

He stopped in front of her, looking at the elegant young beauty standing before him in a seductive silk gown that clung to her ripened curves, her glorious hair tumbling riotously over her shoulders and trim back. "Tory," he breathed, gazing into her deep blue eyes. Without warning, he reached out, pulling her almost roughly into his arms and burying his face in her fragrant hair. "I'd forgotten how beautiful you are," he whispered raggedly, holding her more tightly to him.

"Obviously!" Victoria retorted, recovering from her stunned paralysis and flinging his arms away. She glared at him, amazed at his gall in daring to come here, let alone embrace her with a passion he'd never shown her before. "Apparently you forget people very easily," she added tartly.

To her utter disbelief, Andrew chuckled. "You're angry because it's taken me two weeks longer to come for you than I wrote you in my letter it would take, is that it?" Without waiting for a reply, he continued, "My ship was blown off course a week after we sailed and we had to put in for repairs at one of the islands." Placing his arm affectionately around Victoria's stiff shoulders, he turned to Charles and put out his hand, grinning. "You must be Charles Fielding," he said with unaffected friendliness. "I can't thank you enough for looking after Victoria until I could come for her. Naturally, I'll want to repay you for any expenses you have incurred on her behalf—including this delightful gown she's wearing."

He turned to Victoria. "I hate to rush you, Tory, but I've booked passage on a ship leaving in two days. The captain of the ship has already agreed to marry—"

"Letter?" Victoria interrupted, feeling violently dizzy. "What letter? You haven't written me a single word since I left home."

"I wrote you several letters," he said, frowning. "As I explained to you in my last one, I kept writing to you in America because my meddling mother never sent your letters on to me, so I didn't know you were here in England. Tory, I told you all this in my last letter—the one I sent you here in England by special messenger."

"I did not receive any letter!" she persisted in rising tones of hysteria.

Anger thinned Andrew's lips. "Before we leave, I intend to call upon a firm in London that was paid a small fortune to make certain my letters were delivered personally to you and your cousin the duke. I want to hear what they have to say for themselves!"

"They'll say they delivered them to me," Charles said flatly.

Wildly, Victoria shook her head, her mind already realizing what her heart couldn't bear to believe. "No, you didn't receive any letter, Uncle Charles. You're mistaken. You're thinking of the one I received from Andrew's mother—the one telling me he was married."

Andrew's eyes blazed with anger when he saw the guilt on the older man's face. He seized Victoria by the shoulders. "Tory, listen to me! I wrote you a dozen letters while I was in Europe, but I sent them to you in America. I did not learn of your parents' death until I returned home two months ago. From the day your parents died, my mother stopped sending me your letters. When I came home, she told me your parents had died and that you had been whisked off to England by some wealthy cousin of yours who had offered you marriage. She said she had no idea where or how to find you here. I knew you better than to believe you would toss me over merely for some wealthy old cousin with a title. It took a while, but I finally located Dr. Morrison, and he told me the truth about your coming here and gave me your direction.

"When I told my mother I was coming here after you, she admitted the rest of her duplicity. She told me about the letter she wrote you saying I had married Madeline in Switzerland. Then she promptly had one of her 'attacks.' Except this one turned out to be real. I couldn't leave her while she was teetering at death's door, so I wrote you and your cousin, here—" He shot a murderous look at Charles. "—who for some reason did not tell you of my letters. In them, I explained what had happened, and I told each of you that I would come for you as soon as I possibly could."

His voice softened as he cradled Victoria's stricken face between his palms. "Tory," he said with a tender smile, "you've been the love of my life since the day I saw you racing across our fields on that Indian pony of Rushing River's. I'm not married, sweetheart."

Victoria swallowed, trying to drag her voice past the aching lump in her throat. "I am."

Andrew snatched his hands away from her face as if her skin burned him. "What did you say?" he demanded tightly.

"I said," Victoria repeated in an agonized whisper as she stared at his beloved face, "I am. Married."

Andrew's body stiffened as if he were trying to withstand a physical blow. He glanced contemptuously at Charles. "To him? To this old man? You sold yourself for a few jewels and gowns, is that it?" he bit out furiously.

"No!" Victoria almost screamed, shaking with rage and pain and sorrow.

Charles spoke finally, his voice expressionless, his face blank. "Victoria is married to my nephew."

"To your *son!*" Victoria hurled the words at him. She whirled around, hating Charles for his deceit, and hating Jason for collaborating with him.

Andrew's hands clamped on her arms and she felt his anguish as if it were her own. "Why?" he said, giving her a shake. "Why!"

"The fault is mine," Charles said tersely. He straightened to his full height, his eyes on Victoria, silently pleading for her understanding. "I have dreaded this moment of reckoning ever since Mr. Bainbridge's letters arrived. Now that the time is here, it is worse than I ever imagined."

"When did you receive those letters?" Victoria demanded, but in her heart she already knew the answer, and it was tearing her to pieces.

"The night of my attack."

"Your *pretended* attack!" Victoria corrected, her voice shaking with bitterness and rage.

"Exactly so," Charles confessed tightly, then turned to Andrew. "When I read that you were coming to take Victoria from us, I did the only thing I could think of—I feigned a heart attack, and I pleaded with her to marry my son so that she would have someone to look after her."

"You bastard!" Andrew bit out between clenched teeth.

"I do not expect you to believe this, but I felt very sincerely that Victoria and my son would find great happiness together."

Andrew tore his savage gaze from his foe and looked at Victoria. "Come home with me," he implored desperately. "They can't make you stay married to a man you don't love. It can't be legal—they coerced you into it. Tory, please! Come home with me, and I'll find some way out of this. The ship leaves in two days. We'll be married anyway. No one will ever know—"

"I can't!" The words were ripped from her in a tormented whisper.

"Please—" he said.

Her eyes brimming with tears, Victoria shook her head. "I can't," she choked.

Andrew drew a long breath and slowly turned away.

The hand Victoria stretched out to him in silent, helpless appeal, fell to her side as he walked out of the room. Out of the house. Out of her life.

A minute ticked by in ominous silence, then another. Clutching the folds of her gown, Victoria twisted it until her knuckles whitened, while the image of Andrew's anguished face seared itself into her mind. She remembered how she had felt when she first learned he was married, the torment of dragging herself through each day, trying to smile when she was dying inside.

Suddenly the churning pain and rage erupted inside of her and she whirled around on Charles in a frenzy of fury. "How could you!" she cried. "How could you do this to two people who never did a thing to hurt you! Did you see the look on his face? Do you know how much we've hurt him? *Do* you?"

"Yes," Charles said hoarsely.

"Do you know how I felt all those weeks when I thought

he had betrayed me and I had no one? I felt like a beggar in your house! Do you know how I felt, thinking I was marrying a man who didn't want me, because I had no choice—" Her voice failed and she looked at him through eyes so blinded by the tears she was fighting to hold back that she couldn't see the anguish in his.

"Victoria," Charles rasped, "don't blame Jason for this. He didn't know I was pretending my attack, he didn't know about the lett—"

"You're lying!" Victoria burst out, her voice shaking.

"No, I swear it!"

Victoria's head snapped up, her eyes glittering with outrage at this last insult to her intelligence. "If you think I'd believe another word either of you ever say—" She broke off, afraid of the deathly gray pallor of Charles's haunted face, and ran from the room. She ran up the stairs, stumbling in her tear-blinded haste, and raced down the hall to her rooms. Once inside, she leaned against the closed door, her head thrown back, her teeth clamped together so tightly her jaws ached as she fought for control of her rioting emotions.

Andrew's face, contorted with pain, appeared again before her tightly closed eyes and she moaned aloud with sick remorse. *"I've loved you since the day I saw you racing across our fields on that Indian pony. . . . Tory, please! Come home with me. . . ."*

She was nothing but a pawn in a game played by two selfish, heartless men, she realized hysterically. Jason had known all along that Andrew was coming, just as he had known all along that Charles had been playing cards the night of his false "attack."

Victoria pushed away from the door, ripped off her gown, and changed into a riding habit. If she stayed in this house another hour, she would go insane. She couldn't scream at Charles and risk having his death on her conscience. And Jason— He was due back tonight. She would surely plunge a knife into his heart if she saw him now, she thought hysterically. She snatched a white woolen cloak from the wardrobe and ran down the stairs.

"Victoria, wait!" Charles shouted as she raced down the hall toward the back of the house.

Victoria spun around, her whole body trembling. "Stay away from me!" she cried, backing away. "I'm going to Claremont. You've done enough!"

"O'Malley!" Charles barked desperately as she ran out the back door.

"Yes, your grace?"

"I've no doubt you 'overheard' what happened in the drawing room—"

O'Malley the eavesdropper nodded grimly, not bothering to deny it.

"Can you ride?"

"Yes, but—"

"Go after her," Charles said in frantic haste. "I don't know whether she'll take a carriage or ride, but go after her. She likes you, she'll listen to you."

"Her ladyship won't be in a mood to listen to no one, and I can't say as I blame her fer it."

"Never mind that, dammit! If she won't come back, at least follow her to Claremont and make certain she gets there in safety. Claremont is fifteen miles south of here, by the river road."

"Suppose she heads for London and tries to go away with the American gentleman?"

Charles raked his hand through his gray hair, then shook his head emphatically. "She won't. If she meant to leave with him, she'd have done it when he asked her to go with him."

"But I ain't all that handy with a horse—not like Lady Victoria is."

"She won't be able to ride her fastest in the dark. Now, get down to the stables and go after her!"

Victoria was already galloping away on Matador, with Wolf running beside her, when O'Malley dashed toward the stables. "Wait, please!" he yelled, but she didn't seem to hear him, and she bent low over the horse's neck, sending the mighty gelding racing away as if the devil were after her.

"Saddle the fastest horse we've got, and be quick!" O'Malley ordered a groom, his gaze riveted on Victoria's flashing white cloak as it disappeared down Wakefield's long winding drive toward the main road.

Three miles flew by beneath Matador's thundering hooves

before Victoria had to slow him down for Wolf's sake. The gallant dog was racing beside her, his head bent low, willing to follow her until he dropped dead from exhaustion. She waited for him to catch his breath and was about to continue her headlong flight when she heard the clatter of hooves behind her and a man's unintelligible shout.

Not certain whether she was being pursued by one of the brigands who preyed on solitary travelers at night or by Jason, who might have returned and decided to track her down, Victoria turned Matador into the woods beside the road and sent him racing through the trees on a zigzagging course meant to lose whoever was following her. Her pursuer crashed through the underbrush behind her, following her despite her every effort to lose him.

Panic and fury rose apace in her breast as she broke from the cover of the trees that should have concealed her and spurred her horse down the road. If it was Jason behind her, she would die before she'd let him run her to ground like a rabbit. He'd made a fool of her once too often. No, it couldn't be Jason! She hadn't passed his coach on the drive when she rode away from Wakefield, nor had she seen any sign of it before she turned off onto the river road.

Victoria's anger dissolved into chilling terror. She was coming to the same river where another girl had mysteriously drowned. She remembered the vicar's stories about bloodthirsty bandits who preyed on travelers at night, and she threw a petrified glance over her shoulder as she raced toward one of the bridges that traversed the winding river. She saw that her pursuer had temporarily dropped back out of sight around a bend in the road, but she could hear him coming, following her as surely as if he had a light to guide him— Her cloak! Her white cloak was billowing out behind her like a waving beacon in the night.

"Oh, dear God!" she burst out as Matador clattered across the bridge. On her right there was a path that ran along the riverbank, while the road continued straight ahead. She jerked the horse to a bone-jarring stop, scrambled out of the saddle, and unfastened her cloak. Praying wildly that her ploy would work, Victoria flung her cloak over the saddle, turned the horse down the path along the riverbank, and whacked Matador hard on the flank with her crop, sending the horse galloping down the river path. With Wolf at her side, she raced into the woods above the path and crouched down in the underbrush, her heart thundering in her chest. A minute later, she heard her pursuer clatter across the bridge. She peeked between the branches of the bush concealing her and saw him veer off on the path that ran beside the river, but she couldn't see his face.

She didn't see that Matador eventually slowed from a run to a walk, then ambled down to the river for a drink. Nor did she see the river tug her cloak free from the saddle while the horse drank, carrying it a few yards downstream, where it tangled among the branches of a partially submerged fallen tree.

Victoria didn't see any of that, because she was already running through the woods, parallel with the main road, smiling to herself because the bandit had fallen for the best trick Rushing River had ever taught her. To mislead one's pursuer, one merely sent one's horse in one direction and took off on foot in another. Tossing her cloak over the saddle had been an ingenious improvisation of Victoria's own.

O'Malley jerked his horse to a jolting stop beside Victoria's riderless gelding. Frantically, he twisted his head around to scan the steep bank behind and above him, searching for some sign of her up there, thinking her horse must have thrown her at some point between there and here. "Lady Victoria?" he shouted, his gaze sweeping in a wide arc over the bank behind him, the woods on his left, and finally the river on his right . . . where a white cloak floated eerily atop the water, hooked on a partially submerged fallen tree. "Lady Victoria!" he screamed in terror, vaulting from his horse. "The damned horse!" he panted, frantically stripping off his jacket and pulling off his boots. "The damned horse threw her off the ridge into the river . . ." He raced into the murky, rushing water, swimming toward the cloak. "Lady Victoria!" he cried and dove under. He came up, shouting her name and gasping for breath, then he dove under again.

Chapter Thirty-two

THE HOUSE WAS ABLAZE WITH LIGHTS WHEN JASON'S coach pulled to a stop in the drive. Eager to see Victoria, he bounded up the shallow terraced front steps. "Good evening, Northrup!" he grinned, slapping the stalwart butler on the back and handing over his cape. "Where is my wife? Has everyone already eaten? I was delayed by a damnable broken wheel."

Northrup's face was a frozen mask, his voice a raw whisper. "Captain Farrell is waiting for you in the salon, my lord."

"What's wrong with your voice?" Jason asked good-naturedly. "If your throat's bothering you, mention it to Lady Victoria. She's wonderful with things like that."

Northrup swallowed convulsively and said nothing.

Tossing him a mildly curious look, Jason turned and strode briskly down the hall toward the salon. He threw open the doors, an eager smile on his face. "Hello, Mike, where is my wife?" He glanced around at the cheerful room with the little fire burning in the grate to ward off the chill, expecting her to materialize from a shadowy corner, but all he saw was Victoria's cloak lying limply across the back of a

363

chair, water dripping from its hem. "Forgive my poor manners, my friend," he said to Mike Farrell, "but I haven't seen Victoria in days. Let me go and find her, then we'll all sit down and have a nice talk. She must be up—"

"Jason," Mike Farrell said tightly. "There's been an accident—"

The memory of another night like this one ripped agonizingly across Jason's brain—a night when he had come home expecting to find his son, and Northrup had acted oddly; a night when Mike Farrell had been waiting for him in this very room. As if to banish the terror and pain already screaming through his body, he shook his head, backing away. "No!" he whispered, and then his voice rose to a tormented shout. "No, damn you! Don't tell me that—!"

"Jason—"

"Don't you dare tell me that!" he shouted in agony.

Mike Farrell spoke, but he turned his head away from the unbearable torment on the other man's ravaged face. "Her horse threw her off the ridge into the river, about four miles from here. O'Malley went in after her, but he couldn't find her. He—"

"Get out," Jason whispered.

"I'm sorry, Jason. Sorrier than I can say."

"Get *out!*"

When Mike Farrell left, Jason stretched his hand toward Victoria's cloak, his fingers slowly closing on the wet wool, pulling it toward him. The muscles at the base of his throat worked convulsively as he brought the sodden cloak to his chest, stroking it lovingly with his hand, and then he buried his face in it, rubbing it against his cheek. Waves of agonizing pain exploded through his entire being, and the tears he had thought he was incapable of shedding fell from his eyes. "No," he sobbed in demented anguish. And then he screamed it.

Chapter Thirty-three

"HERE, NOW, MY DEAR," THE DUCHESS OF CLARE-
mont said, patting her great-granddaughter's shoulder. "It
breaks my heart to see you looking so wretched."

Victoria bit her lip, staring out of the window at the
manicured lawns stretching out before her, and said nothing.

"I can scarcely believe your husband hasn't come here
yet to apologize for the outrageous deceit he and Atherton
practiced on you," the duchess declared irritably. "Perhaps
he didn't arrive home the night before last, after all." Restlessly, she walked about the room, leaning on her cane, her
lively eyes darting toward the windows as if she, too,
expected to see Jason Fielding arriving at any moment.
"When he does put in an appearance, it will afford me great
satisfaction if you force him to get down on his knees!"

A wry, mirthless smile touched Victoria's soft lips. "Then
you are bound to be disappointed, Grandmama, for I can
assure you beyond any doubt that Jason will not do that.
He's more likely to walk in here and try to kiss me and,
and—"

"—and seduce you into coming home?" the duchess
finished bluntly.

"Exactly."

"And could he accomplish that?" she asked, tipping her white head to the side, her eyes momentarily amused despite her frown.

Victoria sighed and turned around, leaning her head against the windowframe and folding her arms across her midriff. "Probably."

"Well, he's certainly taking his time about it. Do you truly believe he knew about Mr. Bainbridge's letters? I mean, if he did know about them, it was utterly unprincipled of him not to tell you."

"Jason has no principles," Victoria said with weary anger. "He doesn't believe in them."

The duchess resumed her thoughtful pacing but she stopped short when she came to Wolf, who was lying in front of the fireplace. She shuddered and changed direction. "What sin I've committed to deserve having this ferocious beast as a houseguest, I don't know."

A sad giggle emitted from Victoria. "Shall I chain him outside?"

"Good God, no! He tore the seat of Michaelson's breeches when he tried to feed him this morning."

"He doesn't trust men."

"A wise animal. Ugly though."

"I think he's beautiful in a wild, predatory way—" Like Jason, she thought, and hastily cast the debilitating recollection aside.

"Before I sent Dorothy off to France, she had already adopted two cats and a sparrow with a broken wing. I didn't like them either, but at least *they* didn't watch me like this animal does. I tell you, he has every happy expectation of eating me. Even now, he's wondering how I'll taste."

"He's watching you because he thinks he's guarding you," Victoria explained, smiling.

"He thinks he's guarding his next meal! No, no," she said, raising her hand when Victoria started toward Wolf, intending to put him outside. "Don't, I beg you, endanger any more of my servants. Besides," she relented enough to admit, "I haven't felt this safe in my house since your great-grandfather was alive."

"You don't have to worry about prowlers sneaking in," Victoria agreed, returning to her vigil at the window.

"Sneaking in? My dear, you couldn't *bribe* a prowler to enter this room."

Victoria remained at the window for another minute, then turned and wandered aimlessly toward a discarded book lying upon a glossy, satinwood table.

"Do sit down, Victoria, and let me pace for a while. There's no sense in us banging into one another as we traverse the carpet. What could be keeping that handsome devil of yours from our lair?"

"It's just as well Jason hasn't come before now," Victoria said, sinking into a chair and staring at her hands. "It's taken me this long to calm down."

The duchess stomped over to the windows and peered out at the drive. "Do you think he loves you?"

"I thought so."

"Of course he does!" her grace asserted forcefully. "All London is talking about it. The man is besotted with you. Which is undoubtedly why he went along with Atherton's scheme and kept Andrew's letter a secret from you. I shall give Atherton the edge of my tongue for that shoddy piece of business. Although," she added audaciously, still peering out the window, "I probably would have done the same thing in the same circumstances."

"I can't believe that."

"Of course I would. Given a choice between letting you marry some colonial I didn't know and didn't have any faith in, versus my own wish to see you married to the premier *parti* in England—a man of wealth, title, and looks—I might well have done as Atherton did."

Victoria forebore to point out that it was exactly that sort of thinking that had caused her mother and Charles Fielding a great deal of misery.

The duchess stiffened imperceptibly. "You're quite certain you wish to return to Wakefield?"

"I never meant to leave permanently. I suppose I wanted to punish Jason for the way Andrew was forced to learn I was married—Grandmama, if you had seen the look on Andrew's face you would understand. We were the greatest of friends from the time we were children; Andrew taught me to swim and shoot and play chess. Besides, I was furious with Jason and Charles for using me like a toy—a pawn—an *object* without feelings of any importance. You can't believe how utterly alone and miserable I felt for a long time after I thought Andrew had coldly tossed me aside."

"Well, my dear," the duchess said thoughtfully, "you are not going to be alone much longer. Wakefield has just arrived—no, wait, he's sent an emissary! Who is this person?"

Victoria flew to the window. "Why, it's Captain Farrell—Jason's oldest friend."

"Hah!" said the duchess gleefully, banging her cane upon the floor. "Hah! He's sent in a second. I would never have expected that of Wakefield, but so be it!"

She flapped her hand urgently at Victoria. "Run along into the drawing room and do not show your pretty face in here unless I come for you."

"What? No, Grandmama!" Victoria burst out stubbornly.

"Yes!" the duchess replied. "At once! If Wakefield wishes to treat this as a duel and send in his second to negotiate terms, then so be it! I shall be *your* second. I shall grant no quarter," she said with a gleeful wink.

Victoria reluctantly did as she was bidden and went into the drawing room, but under no circumstances was she actually willing to let Captain Farrell leave here without talking to him. If her great-grandmother didn't summon her within five minutes, Victoria decided, she would return to the salon and speak to Captain Farrell.

Only three minutes had elapsed before the doors to the drawing room were abruptly pulled open and her great-grandmother stood in the doorway, her face an almost comical mixture of shock, amusement, and horror. "My dear," she announced, "it seems you have unwittingly brought Wakefield to his knees, after all."

"Where is Captain Farrell?" Victoria said urgently. "He hasn't left, has he?"

"No, no, he's here, I assure you. The abject fellow is reposing upon my sofa at this very moment, awaiting the refreshments that I so generously offered to him. I suspect he thinks me the most heartless creature on earth, for when he told me his news, I was so distracted that I offered him refreshment instead of commiseration."

"Grandmama! You aren't making sense. Did Jason send Captain Farrell to ask me to come back? Is that why he's here?"

"Most assuredly it is not," her grace averred with raised brows. "Charles Fielding sent him here to bring me the grievous tidings of your untimely demise."

"My *what?*"

"You drowned," the duchess said succinctly. "In the river. Or at least, your white cloak appears to have done so." She glanced at Wolf. "This mangy beast is presumed to have run off into the woods whence he came before you befriended him. The servants at Wakefield are in mourning, Charles has taken to his bed—deservedly—and your husband has locked himself into his study and will not let anyone near him."

Shock and horror nearly knocked Victoria to her knees; then she whirled around.

"Victoria!" the dowager called, hurrying as fast as she could in her great-granddaughter's wake as Victoria raced across the hall and burst into the salon with Wolf at her heels.

"Captain Farrell!"

His head jerked up and he stared at her as if seeing a ghost, then his gaze shot to the other "apparition" that skidded to a four-legged stop and began snarling at him.

"Captain Farrell, I didn't drown," Victoria said, taken aback by the man's wide-eyed stare. "Wolf, stop!"

Captain Farrell came to his feet as disbelief slowly gave way to joy and then to fury. "Is this your idea of a joke!" he bit out. "Jason is insane with grief—"

"Captain Farrell!" the duchess said in ringing tones of authority, drawing herself up to her full diminutive height. "I will thank you to keep a civil tongue in your head when addressing my great-granddaughter. She did not know until this moment that Wakefield believed her to be anywhere but here, where she specifically said she would be."

"But the cloak—"

"I was being chased by someone—I think one of the bandits you mentioned—and I tossed the cloak over my horse's saddle and sent him off down the path along the river, thinking that would divert the bandit off my trail."

The anger drained from the captain's face and he shook his head. "The 'someone' chasing you was O'Malley, who nearly drowned trying to find and rescue you from the river where he spotted your cloak."

Victoria's head fell back and she closed her eyes in remorse; then her long lashes flew open and she became a sudden flurry of motion. She hugged her great-grandmother, her words tumbling out in her haste. "Grandmama, thank you for everything. I must leave. I'm going home—"

"Not without me, you're not!" the duchess replied with a gruff smile. "In the first place, I wouldn't miss this home-coming for the world. I haven't had this much excitement since—well, never mind."

"You can follow me in the carriage," Victoria specified, "but I'll ride—a horse will be faster."

"You will come in the carriage with me," her grace replied imperiously. "It has not yet occurred to you, I gather, that after your husband recovers from his joy, he is likely to react exactly as his shockingly ill-mannered emissary has just done." She cast a quelling eye upon poor Captain Farrell before continuing. "Only with considerably more violence. In short, my dear child, after he kisses you, which I have every faith he will do, he is likely to want to murder you for what he will surely perceive as being a monstrous trick on your part. Therefore, I shall be at hand to rush to your aid and support your explanation. And that," she said, banging her cane on the floor in an imperious summons to her butler, "is that. Norton," she called. "Have my horses put to at once!"

She turned to Captain Farrell and, in an apparent reversal of her earlier condemnation, regally proclaimed, "You may ride in the carriage with us—" Then she promptly ruined the illusion of having graciously forgiven his earlier rudeness by adding, "—so that I may keep my eye on you. I won't risk having Wakefield forewarned of our arrival and awaiting us on his doorstep with murder in his eye."

Victoria's heart was pounding like a maddened thing by the time the carriage drew up before Wakefield, shortly after dusk. No footmen appeared from the house to let down the steps of the carriage and help the new arrivals alight, and only a few lights were burning in the myriad windows that looked out upon the park. The whole place seemed eerily deserted, Victoria thought—and then, to her horror, she saw that the lower windows were hung with black and a black wreath was upon the door. "Jason hates anything to do with mourning—" she burst out, frantically shoving on the carriage door, trying to open it. "Tell Northrup to get those things off the windows!"

Breaking his resentful silence for the first time, Captain Farrell laid a restraining hand on her arm and said gently, "Jason ordered it done, Victoria. He's half-insane with grief. Your great-grandmother is partially right—I have no idea how he'll react when he first sees you."

Victoria didn't care what Jason did, so long as he knew she was alive. She jumped down from the carriage, leaving Captain Farrell to look after her great-grandmother, and raced to the front door. Finding it locked, she lifted the knocker and used it with a vengeance. It seemed to take forever before the door slowly opened.

"Northrup!" Victoria burst out. "Where is Jason?"

The butler blinked at her in the dim light, then blinked again.

"Please don't stare at me as if I'm a ghost. This has all been a misunderstanding! Northrup," she said desperately, laying her warm hand upon his cold cheek. "I am not dead!"

"He's—he's—" A broad grin suddenly burst across Northrup's taut features. "He's in his study, my lady, and may I say how very happy I—"

Too frantic to listen, Victoria ran down the hall toward Jason's study, combing her fingers through her hair on the way.

"Victoria?" Charles burst out from the balcony above. "Victoria!"

"Grandmama will explain everything, Uncle Charles," Victoria called, and kept running.

At Jason's study, she put her shaking hand on the door handle, momentarily paralyzed by the enormity of the disaster she had caused; then she drew a shivering breath and stepped inside, closing the door behind her.

Jason was sitting in a chair near the window, his elbows

upon his parted knees, his head in his hands. On the table beside him were two empty bottles of whiskey and the onyx panther she had given him.

Victoria swallowed past the lump of remorse in her throat and started forward. "Jason—" she said softly.

His head lifted slowly and he gazed at her, his face a ravaged mask, his haunted eyes looking right through her as if she were an apparition. "Tory," he groaned in anguish.

Victoria stopped short, watching in horror as he leaned his head against the back of his chair and squeezed his eyes closed.

"Jason," she burst out frantically. "Look at me."

"I see you, darling," he whispered without opening his eyes. His hand went to the panther on the table beside him, lovingly stroking its back. "Talk to me," he pleaded in an agonized voice. "Don't ever stop talking to me, Tory. I don't mind being insane, as long as I can hear your voice—"

"Jason!" Victoria screamed, racing forward and frantically clutching his broad shoulders. "Open your eyes. I am not dead. I did not drown! Do you hear me, I didn't!"

His glazed eyes opened, but he continued speaking to her as if she were a beloved apparition to whom he needed desperately to explain something. "I didn't know about your Andrew's letter," he whispered brokenly. "You know that now, don't you, darling? You do know it—" Suddenly he raised his tormented gaze to the ceiling and began to pray, his body arching as if he was in pain. "Oh, please!" he groaned horribly, "please tell her I didn't know about the letter. Damn you!" he raged at God, "tell her I didn't know!"

Victoria reared back in panic. "Jason," she cried feverishly. "Think! I can swim like a fish, remember? My cloak was a trick. I knew someone was chasing me, but I didn't know it was O'Malley. I thought it was a bandit, so I took off my cloak and threw it over my horse, then I walked to my grandmother's and—oh, God!" Raking her hands through her hair, she looked around the dimly lit room, trying to think how to reach him, then ran to his desk. She lit the lamp on it, then hurried to the fireplace and lit the first of the pair of lamps on the mantel. She was reaching for the second when hands like steel manacles locked onto her shoulders and brought her spinning around and crashing against his chest. She saw the return of sanity in Jason's eyes a split second before his mouth captured hers with hungry violence, his hands rushing over her back and hips, pulling her to him as if he were trying to absorb her body into his. A shudder ran through his tall frame as she arched into him, wrapping her arms tightly about his neck.

Long minutes later, Jason abruptly tore his mouth from hers, disengaged her arms from around his neck, and stared down at her. Victoria took a hasty step backward, instantly wary of the ominous wrath sparking to life in his beautiful green eyes. "Now that we've dispensed with that," he said grimly, "I'm going to beat you until you can't sit down."

A sound that was part laugh, part alarm burst from Victoria's throat as his hand shot out. She jumped back, just out of his reach. "No, you're not," she said shakily, so happy that he had returned to normal that she couldn't control her wobbly smile.

"How much would you like to bet I'm not?" he asked softly, advancing step for step as she retreated.

"Not much," Victoria quavered, scooting behind his desk.

"And when I finish, I'm going to chain you to my side."

"That you can do," she croaked, circling his desk.

"And I'm never going to let you out of my sight again."

"I—I don't blame you." Victoria shot a glance at the door, measuring the distance.

"Don't try it," he warned.

Victoria saw the dire gleam in his eyes, and ignored his warning. With a mixture of giddy happiness and a strong sense of self-preservation, she snatched open the door, lifted up her skirts, and sprinted down the hall toward the staircase. Jason followed her with long, ground-covering strides, nearly keeping up with her without running.

Laughing helplessly, she raced down the hall and through the marble foyer, past Charles, Captain Farrell, and her great-grandmother, who all rushed out of the salon for a better view.

Victoria ran partway up the staircase, then turned and began walking backward, watching Jason as he came purposefully up each step. "Now, Jason," she said, unable to control her smile as she held out an imploring hand and tried to look contrite. "Please be reasonable—"

"Keep right on going, my darling—you're heading in the right direction," he said, stalking her step for step. "You have the choice of your bedroom or mine—"

Victoria turned and fled up the rest of the staircase and down the hall to her rooms. She was halfway across her suite when Jason flung open the door, closed it behind him, and locked it.

Victoria whirled to face him, her heart hammering with love and apprehension.

"Now then, my sweet—" he said in a low, meaningful voice, watching to see which direction she meant to bolt.

Victoria gazed adoringly at his handsome, pale face, and then she ran—straight toward him, flinging herself against him and wrapping her arms tightly around him. "Don't!" she cried brokenly.

For a moment Jason was perfectly still, struggling with his rampaging emotions, and then the tension drained out of his rigid body. His hands lifted to Victoria's waist, slowly encircling her, then tightening with crushing force and hauling her against his full length. "I love you," he whispered hoarsely, burying his face in her hair. "Oh, God! I love you so!"

At the bottom of the staircase, Captain Farrell, the duchess, and Charles smiled with relief when there was only silence upstairs.

The duchess was the first to speak. "Well, Atherton," she said sternly, "I daresay you now know how it feels to meddle in young people's lives and then to bear the consequences of failure, as I have had to bear them all these years."

"I must go up and talk to Victoria," he said, his eyes on the empty balcony. "I have to explain that I did what I did because I thought she would be *happier* with Jason." He took one step forward, but the duchess's cane came up in front of him, barring his path.

"Do not even *consider* barging in on them," her grace ordered arrogantly. "I am wishful of a great-great-grandson, and unless I mistake the matter, they are even now attempting to provide me with one." Grandly, she added, "You may, however, offer me a glass of sherry."

Charles dragged his gaze from the balcony and looked intently at the old woman he had hated for more than two decades. He had suffered for his meddling for only two days; she had been doing so for twenty-two years. Hesitantly, he offered his arm to her. For a long moment the duchess looked at it, knowing it was a peace offering, and then she slowly laid her thin hand upon his sleeve. "Atherton," she declared as he escorted her toward the drawing room. "Dorothy has taken some maggot in her head about remaining a maiden and becoming a musician. I have decided she shall marry Winston instead, and I have a plan . . ."

Breathtaking romance from

JUDITH McNAUGHT

A Gift of Love
(A collection of romances from Judith McNaught,
Jude Deveraux, Andrea Kane,
Kimberly Cates, and Judith O'Brien)

A Holiday of Love
(A collection of romances from Judith McNaught,
Jude Deveraux, Arnette Lamb, and Jill Barnett)

Almost Heaven

Double Standards

A Kingdom of Dreams

Night Whispers

Once and Always

Paradise

Perfect

Remember When

Something Wonderful

Tender Triumph

Until You

Whitney, My Love

POCKET BOOKS

3010-01

**POCKET BOOKS
PROUDLY PRESENTS**

NIGHT WHISPERS

JUDITH McNAUGHT

**Available from
Pocket Books**

Turn the page for a preview of
Night Whispers. . . .

1

He'd been following her for three days, watching. Waiting.

By now, he knew her habits and her schedule. He knew what time she got up in the morning, whom she saw during the day, and what time she went to sleep. He knew she read in bed at night, propped up on pillows. He knew the title of the book she was reading, and that she laid it facedown on the nightstand to keep her place before she finally turned off the lamp.

He knew her thick blond hair was natural and that the startling blue-violet color of her eyes was not the result of the contact lenses she wore. He knew she bought her makeup at the drugstore and that she spent exactly twenty-five minutes getting ready to go to work in the morning. Obviously, she was more interested in being clean and neat than in enhancing her physical assets. He, however, was very interested in her considerable physical assets. But not urgently and not for the "usual" reasons.

At first, he'd taken great care to keep her in sight while ensuring that she didn't notice him, but his precautions were more from habit than necessity. With a population of

150,000 people, 15,000 of them college students, the little city of Bell Harbor on Florida's eastern seaboard was large enough that a stranger could move unnoticed among the population, but not so large that he would lose sight of his prey in a jumble of metropolitan expressways and interchanges.

Today he'd tracked her to the city park, where he'd spent a balmy but irksome February afternoon surrounded by cheerful, beer-drinking adults and shrieking children who'd come there to enjoy the Presidents' Day picnic and festivities. He didn't like children around him, particularly children with sticky hands and smudged faces who tripped over his feet while they chased each other. They called him, "Hey, mister!" and asked him to throw their errant baseballs back to them. Their antics called attention to him so often that he'd abandoned several comfortable park benches and was now forced to seek shelter and anonymity beneath a tree with a rough trunk that was uncomfortable to lean against and thick gnarled roots that made sitting on the ground beneath it impossible. Everything was beginning to annoy him, and he realized his patience was coming to an end. So was the watching and waiting.

To curb his temper, he went over his plans for her while he turned his full attention on his prey. At the moment, Sloan was descending from the branches of a big tree from which she was attempting to retrieve a kite that looked like a black falcon with outstretched wings tipped in bright yellow. At the base of the tree, a group of five- and six-year-olds cheered her on. Behind them stood a group of older adolescents, all of them boys. The young children were interested in getting their kite back; the adolescent boys were interested in Sloan Reynolds's shapely suntanned legs as they slowly emerged from the thick upper branches of the tree. The boys elbowed each other and ogled her, and he understood the cause of the minor male commotion: if she were a twenty-year-old coed, those legs of hers would have been remarkable, but on a thirty-year-old cop, they were a phenomenon.

Normally, he was attracted to tall, voluptuous women, but this one was only five feet four with compact breasts and a slender body that was appealingly graceful and trim although far from voluptuous. She was no centerfold candidate, but in her crisp khaki shorts and pristine white knit shirt, with her blond hair pulled up in a ponytail, she had a fresh wholesomeness and prim neatness that appealed to him—for the time being.

A shout from the baseball diamond made two of the older boys turn and look his way, and he lifted the paper cup of orange soda toward his mouth to hide his face, but the gesture was more automatic than necessary. She hadn't noticed him in the past three days as he watched her from doorways and alleys, so she wasn't going to find anything sinister about a lone man in a park crowded with law-abiding citizens who were enjoying the free food and exhibits, even if she did notice him. In fact, he thought with an inner smirk, she was incredibly and stupidly heedless whenever she was off duty. She didn't look over her shoulder when she heard his footsteps one night; she didn't even lock her car when she parked it. Like most small-town cops, she felt a false sense of safety in her own town, an invulnerability that went with the badge she wore and the gun she carried, and the citizens' sleazy secrets that she knew.

She had no secrets from him, however. In less than seventy-two hours, he had all her vital statistics—her age, height, driver's license number, bank account balances, annual income, home address—the sort of information that was readily available on the Internet to anyone who knew where to look. In his pocket was a photograph of her, but all of that combined information was minuscule in comparison to what he now knew.

He took another swallow of lukewarm orange soda, fighting down another surge of impatience. At times, she was so straight, so prim and predictable, that it amused him; at other times, she was unexpectedly impulsive, which made her unpredictable, and unpredictable made things risky, dangerous, for him. And so he continued to wait and watch. In the past three days he'd collected all the mysterious bits and pieces that normally make up the whole of a woman, but in Sloan Reynolds's case, the picture was still blurry, complex, confusing.

Clutching the kite in her left fist, Sloan worked her way cautiously to the lowest branch; then she dropped to the ground and presented the kite to its owner amid shouts of "Yea!" and the sound of small hands clapping excitedly. "Gee, thanks, Sloan!" Kenny Landry said, blushing with pleasure and admiration as he took his kite. Kenny's two front teeth were missing, which gave him a lisp, both of which made him seem utterly endearing to Sloan, who had gone to high school with his mother. "My mom was scared you'd get hurt, but I'll bet you never get scared."

Actually, Sloan had been extremely afraid during her downward trek through the sprawling branches that her shorts were snagging on the limbs, hiking up, and showing way too much of her legs.

"Everyone is afraid of something," Sloan told him, suppressing the urge to hug him and risk embarrassing him with such a show of public affection. She settled for rumpling his sandy brown hair instead.

"I fell out of a tree once!" a little girl in pink shorts and a pink-and-white T-shirt confessed, eyeing Sloan with awed wonder. "I got hurted, too, on my elbow," Emma added shyly. She had short, curly red hair, freckles on her small nose, and a rag doll in her arms.

Butch Ingersoll was the only child who didn't want to be impressed. "Girls are *supposed* to play with dolls," he informed Emma. "*Boys* climb trees."

"My teacher said Sloan is an honest-to-goodness hero," she declared, hugging the rag doll even tighter, as if it gave her courage to speak up. She raised her eyes to Sloan and blurted, "My teacher said you risked your life so you could save that little boy who fell down the well."

"Your teacher was being very kind," Sloan said as she picked up the kite string lying on the grass and began winding it into a spool on her fingers. Emma's mother had been another classmate of Sloan's, and as she glanced from Kenny to Emma, Sloan couldn't decide which child was more adorable. She'd gone to school with most of these children's parents, and as she smiled at the circle of small faces, she saw poignant reminders of former classmates in the fascinated faces looking back at her.

Surrounded by the offspring of her classmates and friends, Sloan felt a sharp pang of longing for a child of her own. In the last year, this desire for a little boy or little girl of her own to hold and love and take to school had grown from a wish to a need, and it was gaining strength with alarming speed and force. She wanted a little Emma or a little Kenny of her own to cuddle and love and teach. Unfortunately her desire to surrender her life to a husband had not increased at all. Just the opposite, in fact.

The other children were eyeing Sloan with open awe, but Butch Ingersoll was determined not to be impressed. His father and his grandfather had been high school football stars. At six years old, Butch not only had their stocky build, but had also inherited their square chin and macho swagger. His grandfather was the chief of police and Sloan's boss. He stuck out his chin in a way that forcibly reminded Sloan of Chief Ingersoll. "My grandpa said any cop could have rescued that little kid, just like you did, but the TV guys made a big deal out of it 'cause you're a girl cop."

A week before, Sloan had gone out on a call about a missing toddler and had ended up going down a well to rescue it. The local television stations had picked up the story of the missing child, and then the Florida media had picked up the story of the rescue. Three hours after she climbed down into the well and spent the most terror-filled time of her life, Sloan had emerged a "heroine." Filthy and exhausted, Sloan had been greeted with deafening cheers from Bell Harbor's citizens who'd gathered to pray for the child's safety and with shouts from the reporters who'd gathered to pray for something newsworthy enough to raise their ratings.

After a week, the furor and notoriety was finally beginning to cool down, but not fast enough to suit Sloan. She found the role of media star and local hero not only comically unsuitable but thoroughly disconcerting. On one side of the spectrum, she had to contend with the citizens of Bell Harbor who now regarded her as a heroine, an icon, a role model for women. On the other side, she had to deal with Captain Ingersoll, Butch's fifty-five-year-old male-chauvinist grandfather, who regarded Sloan's unwitting heroics as "deliberate grandstanding" and her presence on his police force as an affront to his dignity, a challenge to his authority, and a burden he was forced to bear until he could find a way to get rid of her.

Sloan's best friend, Sara Gibbon, arrived on the scene just as Sloan finished winding the last bit of kite string into a makeshift spool, which she presented to Kenny with a smile.

"I heard cheering and clapping," Sara said, looking at Sloan and then at the little group of children and then at the kite-falcon with the broken yellow-tipped wing. "What happened to your kite, Kenny?" Sara asked. She smiled at him and he lit up. Sara had that effect on males of all ages. With her shiny, short-cropped auburn hair, sparkling green eyes, and exquisite features, Sara could stop men in their tracks with a single, beckoning glance.

"It got stuck in the tree."

"Yes, but Sloan got it down," Emma interrupted excitedly, pointing a chubby little forefinger toward the top of the tree.

"She climbed right up to the top," Kenny inserted, "and she wasn't scared, 'cause she's *brave*."

Sloan felt—as a mother-to-be someday—that she needed to correct that impression for the children. "Being brave doesn't mean you're never afraid. Being brave means that, even though you're scared, you still do what you should do. For example," she said, directing a smile to the little group, "*you're* being brave when you tell the truth even though you're afraid you might get into trouble. That's being really, really brave."

The arrival on the scene of Clarence the Clown with a fistful of giant balloons caused all of the children to turn in unison, and several of them scampered off at once, leaving only Kenny, Emma, and Butch behind. "Thanks for getting my kite down," Kenny said with another of his endearing, gap-toothed smiles.

"You're welcome," Sloan said, fighting down an impossible impulse to snatch him into her arms and hug him close—stained shirt, sticky face, and all. The youthful trio turned and headed away, arguing loudly over the actual degree of Sloan's courage.

"Miss McMullin was right. Sloan is a real-life, honest-to-goodness hero," Emma declared.

"She's really, truly brave," Kenny announced.

Butch Ingersoll felt compelled to qualify and limit the compliment. "She's brave for a *girl*," he declared dismissively, reminding an amused Sloan even more forcibly of Chief Ingersoll.

Oddly, it was shy little Emma who sensed the insult. "Girls are just as *brave* as boys."

"They are not! She shouldn't even be a policeman. That's a man's job. That's why they call it police*man*."

Emma took fierce umbrage at this final insult to her heroine. "My mommy," she announced shrilly, "says Sloan Reynolds should be chief of police!"

"Oh, yeah?" countered Butch Ingersoll. "Well, my grandpa *is* chief of police, and he says she's a pain in the ass! My grandpa says she should get married and make babies. *That's* what girls are for!"

Emma opened her mouth to protest but couldn't think how. "I hate you, Butch Ingersoll," she cried instead, and raced off, clutching her doll—a fledgling feminist with tears in her eyes.

"You shouldn't have said that," Kenny warned. "You made her cry."

"Who cares?" Butch said—a fledgling bigot with an attitude, like his grandfather.

"If you're real nice to her tomorrow, she'll prob'ly forget what you said," Kenny decided—a fledgling politician, like his father.

2

When the children were out of hearing, Sloan turned to Sara with a wry smile. "Until just now, I've never been able to decide whether I want to have a little girl or a little boy. Now I'm certain. I definitely want a little girl."

"As if you'll have a choice," Sara joked, familiar with this topic of conversation, which had become increasingly frequent. "And while you're trying to decide the sex of your as-yet-unconceived infant, may I suggest you spend a little more time finding a prospective father and husband?"

Sara dated constantly, and whenever she went out with a new man—which was regularly—she systematically looked over his friends with the specific intention of finding someone suitable for Sloan. As soon as she selected a likely prospect, she began a campaign to introduce him to Sloan. And no matter how many times her matchmaking efforts failed, she never stopped trying because she simply could not understand how Sloan could prefer an evening alone at home to the company of some reasonably attractive man, no matter how little they might have in common.

"Who do you have in mind this time?" Sloan said warily as they started across the park toward the tents and booths set up by local businesses.

"There's a new face, right there," Sara said, nodding toward a tall male in tan slacks and a pale yellow jacket who was leaning against a tree, watching the children gathered around Clarence the Clown, who was swiftly turning two red balloons into a red moose with antlers. The man's shadowed face was in profile and he was drinking from a large paper cup. Sloan had noticed him a little earlier, watching her when she was talking to the children after the kite rescue, and since he was now watching the same group of children, she assumed he was a father who'd been assigned to keep his eye on his offspring. "He's already someone's father," she said.

"Why do you say that?"

"Because he's been watching that same group of children for the last half hour."

Sara wasn't willing to give up. "Just because he's watching the children doesn't mean one of them belongs to him."

"Then why do you suppose he's watching them?"

"Well, he could be—"

"A child molester?" Sloan suggested dryly.

As if he sensed he was being discussed, the man tossed his paper cup into the trash container beneath the tree and strolled off in the direction of the fire department's newest fire engine, which had been drawing a sizable crowd.

Sara glanced at her watch. "You're in luck. I don't have time for matchmaking today anyway. I'm on duty in our tent for three more hours." Sara was staffing her interior design firm's booth, where brochures were being dispensed along with free advice. "Not one reasonably attractive, eligible male has stopped to pick up a brochure or ask a question all day."

"Bummer," Sloan teased.

"You're right," Sara solemnly agreed as they strolled along the sidewalk. "Anyway, I decided to close the tent down for twenty minutes in case you wanted to get some lunch."

Sloan glanced at her watch. "In five minutes, I'm scheduled to take over our tent for another hour. I'll have to wait until I'm off duty to get something to eat."

"Okay, but stay away from the chili, no matter what! Last night, there was some sort of contest to see who could make the hottest chili and Pete Salinas won the contest. There are signs all over his chili stand stating that it's the hottest chili in Florida, but grown men are standing around trying to eat the stuff, even though it's half jalapeño peppers and half beans. It's a guy thing," Sara explained with the breezy confidence of a woman who has thoroughly and enjoyably researched her subject, and therefore qualifies as an expert on men. "Proving they can eat hot chili is definitely a guy thing."

Despite Sara's qualifications, Sloan was dubious about the conclusion she'd drawn. "The chili probably isn't nearly as hot as you think it is."

"Oh, yes, it is. In fact, it's not just hot, it's lethal. Shirley Morrison is staffing the first aid station and she told me that victims of Pete's chili have been coming to her for the last hour, complaining of everything from bellyaches to cramps and diarrhea."

*   *   *

The police department's tent was set up on the north side of the park, right next to the parking lot, while Sara's tent was also on the north side, about thirty yards away. Sloan was about to comment on their proximity when Captain Ingersoll's squad car came to a quick stop up ahead, beside the tent. While she watched, he heaved his heavy bulk from the front seat and slammed the door, then strolled over to their tent, carried on a brief conversation with Lieutenant Caruso, and began looking around the area with a dark frown. "If I'm any judge of facial expressions, I'd say he's looking for me," she said with a sigh.

"You said you still have five more minutes before you're supposed to take over."

"I do, but that won't matter to—" She broke off suddenly, grabbing Sara's wrist in her excitement. "Sara, look who's waiting over there by your tent! It's Mrs. Peale with a cat in each arm." Mrs. Clifford Harrison Peale III was the widow of one of Bell Harbor's founding citizens, and one of its richest. "There's a fantastic potential client, just waiting for your excellent advice. She's cranky, though. And very demanding."

"Fortunately, I am very patient and very flexible," Sara said, and Sloan smothered a laugh as Sara broke into a run, angling to the left toward her tent. Sloan smoothed her hair into its ponytail, checked to make certain her white knit shirt was tucked neatly into the waistband of her khaki shorts, and angled to the right, toward the police department's tent.

Look for
Night Whispers
Available from Pocket Books